1992
SAN FRANCISCO

D1604075

ONE-THIRTY IN THE MORNING
AND THE PHONE RINGS

"**R**on—fuck, man. It all went wrong. He—"*the caller lets out a spine-tingling whine like a wild animal caught in a trap.*"You just gotta get here. PLEASE."

Hearing the panic in his ex-partner's voice, newly made San Francisco Sergeant Ronnie Gilbert drops the receiver and in a flash is dressed, out the door of his Sausalito houseboat, and in his car racing toward San Francisco. Dead of night and the freeway is empty. Ten minutes and ninety miles an hour later he's crossing the Golden Gate Bridge, and fifteen minutes after that he's in the heart of the Tenderloin, screeching to a halt in front of the Midori Hotel. He cuts the engine and scans the area. A pair of junkies are nodding in a nearby doorway, but otherwise the block is quiet. On full alert, Ronnie gets out of his car and approaches the door of the residence hotel. The lobby is lit, and through the large glass frontage he can see no one inside. He tries the door and finds it unlocked. The sergeant draws his revolver and steps cautiously inside. Holding the gun with two hands, pointed slightly toward the ground, he swivels his head, checking every blind spot. His eyes lock onto the telephone on the reception desk to see reddish-black smears across the buttons. Made, he assumes, by the bloody fingers that dialed his number.

He darts around the high desk and swings his revolver. No one is in the chair or hiding under the desk. The lobby cleared, he moves silently up the stairs. The building is under renovation and all the residents have been moved out. All except the owner, Joe Chadwick, real estate developer and nouveau-riche philanthropist who—according to rumor—keeps a functioning penthouse suite to bring young girls.

The sergeant's training tells him to clear every room on every floor. But his training also told him to call for backup the moment he got the frantic call—which he didn't do.

So as he rounds each landing he ignores the rows of closed doors and continues moving upward toward Joe's suite.

His breathing heavy, heart thumping in his ears, Ronnie Gilbert reaches the top floor to find two doors opposite each other. One is closed, the other ajar. On the knob of the latter, once again, bloody fingerprints. His body is taut as he moves toward it. Putting his weight on his rear leg, both hands on his weapon, Ronnie kicks the door open, then jumps back, flattening himself against the wall. He waits two long seconds, then, after no response, lunges in, pointing his revolver as he swings his arms to cover the room. He sees no one, only an explosion of blood and brains on the far wall. Then the smell hits him——iron and shit. He moves forward, continuing to scan the room, and as he rounds the bed he sees the feet. A few steps more, then, crumpled between the bed and the wall, in a puddle of blood, the full, naked body of who he can only assume is Joe Chadwick. The man's face is shredded meat. His entire jaw has been blown off, and the back of his head is a gaping, glistening black hole.

A noise, and Ronnie spins. At the end of the hallway, through the open door of the bathroom, a teenage girl. She's sitting on the floor against the tub, shoulders hunched, bare knees pressed together. He recognizes her immediately. Her name is Crystal Lake, and she's only fourteen. He knows her from the street. A runaway with long, platinum white hair. Angelic——if not for the splatters of blood and chunks of Joe Chadwick's brains.

Crystal's eyes meet Ronnie's, then they shift to the side, as, from behind the door——

MAY 2019
(CURRENT DAY)
AMSTERDAM

A MAN WALKS INTO A SHOP

0

THE DOOR OPENS
AND THE LITTLE BELL RINGS

"Have a look around," I say, pausing from typing but not looking up from my laptop. "And if you have any questions, just let me know."

A burst of icy air wafts over me as the door closes. I hit SAVE on the computer in case I need to tend to the customer, or in case my machine randomly turns every letter of the document into X's—which has already happened twice over the last month, causing me to lose hours of work. Not that any of it was any good. Which was why, each time, after the initial bursts of panic, I felt relief. Seeing those pages disappear meant I no longer had to pretend they'd been worth typing let alone being read. But this—what I'm working on now, the story of Ronnie Gilbert—I definitely don't want to lose. In the ten months I've lived in Amsterdam—most of which have been cold and dreary—I've been trying, and failing, to write a new book. But now I think I have it—or, rather, I know I do. It's a story I should have told twenty years ago, but always found some excuse not to. Until earlier this week when the verdict in the murder trial of my old friend Ronnie was finally announced, prompting me to—

"You actually make a living selling this stuff?" a voice says. It's a male voice, but all I hear is its tone. Which says: Seriously? People actually *pay* for these?

I turn to look. Outwardly, the man is a figure from a forgotten era: tan trench coat, gray fedora, sandy-blond mustache. He's in profile, bending down, holding his tie against his chest, squinting through a thick pair of glasses at one of my framed drawings.

Taking a breath, I turn back to my computer and say, "Yeah, people tend to not like those loose sketches so much. I've got some more finished drawings on the wall behind you."

"I never did understand how you had the patience to put in so much detail," he says. "Not a surprise that after all these years you'd get tired of making the effort." And this time, not only do I hear his voice, but I realize I know it: Martin Zorn.

I immediately hit SAVE again and close my laptop. I watch the figure as he strides toward me. If it weren't for his voice, and my thoughts already being tuned to the days of Ronnie, I might second-guess my identification. The Martin Zorn I knew twenty years ago—and assumed was dead—was energetic and fit, whereas the man before me looks anything but. He is gaunt and frail. His eyes though. They make me certain. If I were walking down the street and saw those bright blue orbs emanating from the face of a stray cat, I would instantly become a believer in reincarnation.

Martin drops himself onto the small couch beside me. His trench coat flops open, as do his arms, sprawling across the cushions like useless accessories he's tired of carrying around. As if his outfit isn't dated enough, he's wearing a rust-colored paisley shirt with a blood-red tie. He eyes me through thick glasses. "Nice shingle," he says, throwing his thumb indiscriminately toward the door. "'Emit Hopper Studio.'" He's talking about the sign hanging outside my shop. "I like the 'studio' part. Seems appropriate now that you're living in the land of old Flemish masters. I'm guessing you heard the news?" He doesn't wait for me to answer. "Of course you have. You testified at the trial. Quite passionately, too, if I'm to believe what passes for journalism these days."

He's talking about the trial of Randall Fenton, the billionaire tech mogul accused of murdering Ronnie Gilbert, the legendary San Francisco private detective who, two years ago, was found dead inside a giant Australian crocodile. The case had been heard in Brisbane. I'd been a witness for the prosecution, but, for budgetary reasons, had given my testimony by a video conferencing call. Brisbane is nine hours ahead of Amsterdam, which meant my appearance put me at my computer from midnight till three in the morning. At one point the defense asked me if I might be confused about my recollections, seeing that it was the middle of the night. They had nothing else to throw at me.

"So what do you think?" Martin asks. "No question, Fenton killed him, right?"

"Absolutely," I say. "Ronnie went to Queensland with the sole purpose of questioning Fenton. A few days later, his torso was found half-digested inside a seventeen-foot croc nicknamed Tasmania—after an eight-year-old girl heard a phone ringing in the river. I find it impossible to believe the two are a coincidence."

"And yet a jury didn't convict."

"And you and I both know there's a difference between being acquitted for lack of evidence and actually being innocent." I say it as pointedly as I can. But Martin Zorn is unfazed. He just looks curiously around the shop.

"At the same time," I say, "as you surely know, Fenton is already serving a thirty-year sentence in the States for his part in the deaths in Yosemite. So there's at least some justice in that."

"Right," Martin says, chuckling. "Justice. You think Ron would agree?"

"You knew Ronnie. He was a puzzle junkie. All he cared about was finding the solution."

"Finding the truth."

I wobble my head. "Let's leave it at 'solution.'"

Martin smirks, then reaches up to his face and, as if trying to pull the thing straight, tugs at one of the corners of his mustache. "So you're not surprised to see me then?"

I shrug. "It's been almost twenty years. And, frankly, consensus was that you'd jumped off the Golden Gate Bridge. So yeah, I'm surprised to see you. Except . . ."

"Except you're not."

"I don't know. I met you and Ronnie at the same time. You're part of the same story. And with Fenton having just been acquitted . . ." I open my hands. "If there was ever a time for old ghosts to be rattled out of the wood-work, I suppose it would be now."

"Old ghosts," Martin says, bobbing his head. "I am certainly one of those." He sniffles, pulls a handkerchief from his coat pocket, wipes his nose. I notice he's wearing a wedding band. I'm surprised—and doubtful—wondering if he is in fact married. With Martin Zorn I learned not to trust appearances.

"You look like shit," I say.

Martin snorts, then, making great pains to push himself up from the couch, stands and says, "You're right." He walks past me, to the high work-bench against the rear wall, where, after the trial inspired me to begin writing this book, I'd pulled out a box of drawings I'd been carrying around for twenty years. Martin leans down and picks up one of the drawings. It's warped and badly marred by brown water-stains. "The Lyon Street Steps," he says, turning to me, appearing genuinely surprised. "When did you make this?"

"You know precisely when."

"But how——"

"I was free to keep it—along with all my other drawings. It's not like they were evidence."

"That's not what I meant."

I stand up from my chair and lean against my desk to face him. "I know what you meant." I watch as he sets down the drawing—with more care than I would expect. "You meant, 'how did it survive the fire?'"

"Yeah."

"Why are you here, Martin?"

He picks up another drawing. This one of the Whittier Mansion in San Francisco. "Because I thought we might want the same thing."

"To have a wealthy patron walk in and buy every drawing in the place?"

Again he snorts. He picks up another drawing. The Midori Hotel. I watch for a reaction. None. He just sets it down and reaches for another. "I suppose I'd like to know if you feel guilty."

"Me?" I scoff. "Seriously? After what you——" I can't even finish. I take a moment to shake off my disbelief. "If either of us is responsible for that fire," I say, "it was you."

"I'm not talking about the fire," Martin says. He reaches up and straightens one of the framed drawings hanging on the wall. "I'm talking about our old friend Ronnie J. I'm asking if you feel guilty about him." He turns and fixes his cool blue eyes on me. "Seeing that you're the reason he's dead."

THE COMMISSIONS

an

EMIT HOPPER
MYSTERY

introducing

RONNIE GILBERT

WEST
MARGIN
PRESS

PART 1

NOVEMBER 1999
SAN FRANCISCO

THE SETUP

1

THE STATION

"Name?"

"Emit Hopper."

"Occupation?"

"Laundromat owner—well, artist."

The cop looked up from typing. "So, which is it?"

I tilted my head. "Technically, both."

"We'll put laundromat owner."

"Can you put artist?"

The cop ignored me.

"Seriously," I said.

"Do you know what you're being charged with?"

"Being outside?"

"Don't be a smart-ass."

"Fine. Drawing outside."

"You're being charged with lewd behavior."

"I was standing in the courtyard of a museum, drawing a picture. How is that lewd?"

"You were taking pictures of women."

"I was taking pictures of a sculpture—of Rodin's *The Thinker*, to be precise."

The cop leaned back. "So which is it then? Were you drawing? Or taking photos?"

"Both."

"I see. So you're a photographer now too?" He leaned forward. "Should I list that under occupation as well?" He shot me a look. "You know, as long as we're being precise."

I wanted to say: "Now who's being a smart-ass?" But even I knew better. So instead I said, "I was starting the drawing from life, but was taking reference photos of the light and shadow so I could finish back in my studio."

"Uh-huh."

"It's called plein air drawing."

"It's called being a perv."

*　*　*

A different cop led me out of the bullpen and through a heavy steel door dotted with rivets so large they looked like they should be holding a bridge together.

"You're kidding." I said. "You're seriously going to put me in a cell?"

The cop didn't reply. She directed me down a pale yellow hallway lined with green bars, then slid open the door of a holding cell. Inside was one other man, standing in the corner, holding up a pair of over-sized pants with a thumb hooked through a belt loop. I turned to look at the cop as she held the door.

"And what about a phone call? Isn't that how this is supposed to go?"

"Sir, please," she said, gesturing for me to go inside.

Please, I thought. Funny how people with power over you find it necessary to be polite.

I stared at her for a few seconds, then, shaking my head, complied.

As she slid the door closed behind me, I looked at my cellmate. He was wild-eyed and grinning. I wondered if his belt had been taken from him, but then saw that his pants were brand-new and several sizes too large, and that he was also shoeless, so figured he probably came in that way—if he'd come in dressed at all. I shrugged and gave him a look that said, "Oh well, what are you gonna do?" and he gave me a thumbs-up—with the thumb *not* holding his pants. Then I lay on the metal bench farthest from him, folded my arms over my chest, and stared at the ceiling.

A short time later I heard footsteps approaching, then a voice bark, "Hopper!"

I looked through the bars to see a woman, short, late thirties, dressed in black nylon pants and a starched white button-down blouse with wide, pointy lapels.

The metal door slid open.

"Follow me," she said.

I left the cell and followed her back down the barred hallway, out the steel door, and into another hallway where the woman opened another door and gestured for me to go in.

I'd expected an interrogation room, but instead found an office, though it may as well have been a storage closet. Strewn haphazardly around the room were boxes of papers, stacks of folders, and piles of phones. There was a desk and two plastic chairs, also loaded.

"I'm Lieutenant Ocampo," the woman said, following me in and closing the door. She went to the far side of the desk, cleared off a chair, then gestured to the other. "Have a seat."

I stayed standing.

"This is totally ridiculous," I said. "I've done nothing wrong."

Her eyes told me she'd heard those words more times than she could count.

"I don't even know what I'm being accused of."

"We received a complaint of lewd behavior."

"Yeah, but from who? And lewd in what way?"

Once again the lieutenant motioned toward the chair opposite her. "Please," she said. "Sit."

Again with the *Please*.

Seeing no other choice, I moved a stack of binders from the chair to the floor, then sat.

The desk was a mess, but amid the clutter I saw my camera: Pentax K1000. A classic SLR—single-lens reflex—fully manual, 35-millimeter film. What today would be called old-school. To a camera buff it probably wasn't anything special, but seeing that I'd had it since I was twelve years old, it was special to me.

The lieutenant held up the camera. "Can't afford a peep show?" she said, jerking a thumb over her shoulder. "North Beach, twenty bucks, you'll see all the tits and ass you want."

"Except I wasn't taking pictures of women—or men. Or anyone."

"That's not what one woman says."

I raised my arms, let them drop. "I was at the Legion of Honor taking pictures of the courtyard and sculpture. Maybe a woman got in one of my shots. I don't know. I wasn't looking at the people. I was looking at the light and shadow."

"Because you're an artist?"

"Exactly."

"So why did you tell the booking officer you run a laundromat?"

"Because I do—or, rather, I own one. It's on the ground floor of my building, but I don't run the day-to-day. It's a nice neighborhood business with a steady income that offers me the freedom to make whatever kind of art I want. But that doesn't matter. What matters is this stupid charge. It's completely—"

"Technically, you haven't been charged," she said.

"Fine. Being brought in, held for questioning, whatever you want to call it. It's completely absurd. And frankly, I can't believe the cops bothered to respond to the call let alone haul me in. I'm no expert on procedure, but I've met enough cops to know the paperwork alone wouldn't be worth their time."

"Hopper . . ." she said, her brow knotting as she set my camera down. "Weren't you on that TV show in the eighties? You played the character who—"

I sighed. "You're thinking of my brother, Brian. We're identical twins."

"Right," she said, smiling as she remembered. "But weren't you some sort of a celebrity too?"

"I wrote a book a few years back—*Glass Houses* . . . ?" I let the title dangle in the air, but it didn't jog her memory. "It was full of drawings of cityscapes, which are what most people remember." Still didn't ring a bell. Again I sighed. "Also, Brian and I were in a band together in the eighties. FurTrading? You may remember our one song—"

"'The Beginning is the End'!" she said, laughing. "Oh my god. I remember you guys."

"Right. Well, now I write books, draw pictures, and generally make weird art."

"Which is what you were doing at the museum? Making weird art?"

"Exactly," I said. "Or, kind of. I was drawing—which I don't consider to be weird art—I just mean—" I stopped, took a breath. "I take commissions. People pay me to draw their houses, their neighborhoods, the church where they got married, the view from their office—the museum—you name it. Lately I do a lot of drawings of the bridge. It's not the kind of art the MOMA thinks highly of, but it makes people happy, and, more importantly, I enjoy it. I told all of this to the cops who brought me in. They had a thousand questions too, and—"

"But if you were drawing, then why do you need a camera?"

"Because I can't finish the drawings on site—or, I can, only not to the extent I would like. When it comes to light and shadow, it takes time to render the nuances, which change quickly because the sun is constantly moving.

Ten minutes and a scene can look totally different. So I take reference photos to capture the moment I want. Then, when I'm back in my studio, I use the photos to finish the drawing."

She picked up my block of watercolor paper. On the top sheet was an unfinished line drawing of the famous statue at the entrance to the Legion of Honor, Rodin's *The Thinker.*

"And this drawing, it's a commission?"

I nodded.

"Are you having an exhibition there? Or . . . ?"

"The museum isn't involved. It's a private commission."

She studied the drawing. "Not bad." Even though it was no more than a few lines, and, honestly, a poor first attempt. If the cops hadn't shown up and escorted me away, I probably would have started it over. But I couldn't see how telling her that was going to help me.

"Thanks," I said. "So do you believe me? Can I go?"

She picked up my camera again. "If I were to develop the film in here, what would I find?"

"Two dozen tedious reference photos of the Legion's courtyard."

She eyed me while trying to decide how much of an ass I was being.

"Please," I said. "Develop the film. Print it, even. You'll be doing me a favor. The one-hour joints are unreliable and disappearing every day. And the only other way to get prints made is to either send out the rolls—which takes forever—or go to the upscale art developers, which cost an arm and a leg. When all I want are fast, basic prints to finish my drawings."

The lieutenant set my camera on her desk. "Tell me. The people who 'accidentally' end up in your photos, do they tend to know you're taking pictures of them?"

"Well, I'm not actually taking pictures of *people,* so . . ."

She rolled her eyes. "You know what I mean. When you're outside drawing, do people tend to notice you?"

"And how is this relevant to what supposedly happened at the museum?"

She stared at me.

I looked at the ceiling and thought about it. "Actually," I said, "yeah. People do tend to notice me. Because I'm doing something out of the ordinary. I mean, it doesn't seem like a big deal to me, but people aren't used to coming upon someone drawing. And even more so when I'm in the busier parts of the city. Drawing at a museum, that's almost expected, but standing on a random street corner downtown with a bag of art supplies at your feet—"

"And how do people react to you?"

"Depends. Most with little more than a passing glance, but a fair amount are curious. Like I said, it's because I'm doing something unusual. Imagine you're walking along a busy sidewalk and you pass someone who's standing still, a hand cupped over their eyes, staring up at the sky. You can't help but look and see what has their attention. It's like that. Common curiosity. But most people, once they see what I'm doing, they tend to move on—though there is always the random gabber. Someone who realizes you're a stationary target and just walks up and starts talking. Also, for some reason the homeless seem to like me. Last week a guy living out of a shopping cart went into a bodega and bought me a soda—which I hadn't asked for."

"But no one finds you suspicious?"

I shrugged. "Certainly no one has ever called the police on me before—until now, that is."

"What about people inside the buildings? Do they ever wonder why you're drawing their house? Maybe think you're casing the place?"

"Not that I know of—why? Has someone accused me of that too?"

She ignored the jab. "Which means you could sit on a corner for hours drawing, taking all kinds of photos, and no one would give you any trouble? Would you say that's right?"

I opened my hands. "I suppose. Barring the occasional woman who calls the police because she thinks I'm peeking down her shirt—or whatever I'm being accused of. You still haven't told me."

The lieutenant licked her lips and began nodding. "Good," she said. "Because there's somewhere I want you to draw."

2

SPRUNG

Two cops drove me back to the Legion. Not the same pair who'd hauled me in—though I wished they had been. On the drive to the station I'd been grilled the entire way: *Why was I at the museum? Did I make a habit of lurking around public sites with my camera? Did I have any unusual proclivities that had been getting out of hand?* They were the kind of questions you'd expect, along with some odd ones as well: *How much money did I make? What were my politics? Did I have any children?* At the time I assumed they were pushing for information about the supposed incident at the museum, but after what the lieutenant had just pulled, I was starting to think something else might be going on. What that might possibly be, I had no idea. And I was wishing I'd asked a few more odd questions of my own. I decided better late than never.

"So is this because of the election?" I asked the cops in the front seat. There was a highly charged mayoral run-off election coming up, after the incumbent Willie Brown had shocked the entire city by failing to be re-elected two weeks earlier. "Is Willie so worried about losing his crown that he's suddenly trying to look tough on crime? Ordering you guys to respond to every petty call, no matter how crackpot or thin?"

But unlike my previous escorts, these two weren't saying a word.

It was dusk when we pulled up to the Legion. The museum was closed, and mine was the only car left in the lot. The cop riding shotgun got out and opened the back door for me, and it was only after she'd gotten back in that I saw the ticket under my windshield wiper. I turned to complain, but the cruiser was already driving off.

Gusts of icy wind were whipping off the ocean, and the fog was so heavy it was practically rain. I quickly got into the car, turned on the ignition, and cranked up the heater. I owned a 1990 Mazda Miata, a yellow, stripped-down

Portals of the Past, Golden Gate Park, San Francisco — Patron asked to be unnamed

two-seater with a black canvas convertible roof which a month earlier some delightful citizen had sliced so they could reach in, unlock the door, and find there wasn't even a radio. I'd paid my insurance deductible and gotten the soft top replaced, but when two weeks later it happened again, I just laid a strip of duct tape over the gash and wrote in Sharpie: PEEL HERE. The parking ticket was insult to injury, but given how wet the evening was, I was just happy the duct tape was holding.

I was frustrated and hungry, so on the drive home stopped at a Thai place along Clement Street for takeout. Waiting for my Tom Kha soup and pad Thai, I thought about how wrong the day had gone. Getting tossed in a jail cell for a lewd behavior complaint? It was absurd. And the more I thought about it, the more absurd it became. In the sixteen years I'd lived in San Francisco I'd seen more outrageous behavior than I could even remember—junkies shooting up at bus stops, hookers giving blowjobs between parked cars, homeless shitting on doorsteps—all in plain view of cops who didn't bat an eye. Which isn't to say that I thought lewd behavior should be ignored, only that I felt pretty confident nothing would come of the complaint—especially because I'd done nothing criminal. Despite my mystery accuser's claims, I had not been taking surreptitious photos. And even if there had been some sort of scenario that had caused a woman to misinterpret my motives for pointing a camera her way, I was sure that given an opportunity to present my case—meaning not in a back room with a shady cop—I would be able to offer a reasonable explanation. Problem was, I didn't even know what sort of circumstance I needed to defend myself against. Not only had no one told me the specifics of the complaint, when Ocampo gave my camera back, she'd kept the film.

A petite woman in a long, traditional Thai silk dress handed me a bag with my food, placed her hands together, and bowed. I returned the gesture, then, with dinner in hand, returned to my car. The sweet, warm smell of coconut soup filled the little two-seater. It helped take the edge off the day, but only a little. So to try and shake off my frustration I decided to take the long route home through the park.

* * *

Golden Gate Park at that hour was serene. The sunken hollows and rolling meadows were dissolving into foggy nothingness as the haunting groves of eucalyptus trees shed their bark like oversized party streamers. Weaving along John F. Kennedy Drive, I spied two stray buffalo grazing placidly in their reserve, a family of raccoons exploring a trash can, and a lone hobbyist piloting his model sailboat across Spreckels Lake. I passed the Portals of the Past portico, which I had drawn only a few weeks before, followed by the five-story cascade of Rainbow Falls, and a bit further came upon the Conservatory of Flowers, where I spontaneously pulled over, put the car in neutral, and set the parking brake.

Of the stack of commissions I currently had on my plate, the most recent was to draw the historic greenhouse. The hour was too late to do any work on site, but it didn't matter. The structure was a ruin. Four years earlier, an exceptionally violent windstorm had blown out half the glass windows in the majestic conservatory and destroyed its unique collection of rare plants. The building had since been left to rot, and now locals were banding together to raise funds for restoration. The drawing I'd been tasked to make would be auctioned off as one small part of the effort to raise money for repairs.

I considered my eventual approach. One sunny afternoon I would return to scout the light, but even then I would make only a simple sketch to capture the composition and perspective. To make the finished drawing I would have to reference historic photographs, which was not how I liked to work. I preferred to do as much drawing as possible on site and take my own reference photos. But this was a unique situation. The building was in terrible shape. The once-pristine white structure was now marred by sooty-gray water stains, and what should have been bright and manicured gardens were muddy and overgrown. I'll admit, I would have loved to draw it that way. Cracks stains—any sort of imperfection—these were what gave a subject character. But as much as I enjoyed drawing broken things, I was certain that a portrayal of the greenhouse in its current state wasn't what the organizers of the fundraiser were looking for. They wanted a majestic vision of the Conservatory, of how it had been and how it would be again, glorious and full of life. Not broken, splintered, and gone to seed. Which was one of the pitfalls of drawing for anyone other than myself. While I was at liberty to render a reasonable amount of imperfections—was expected to, actually, since, whether a patron was aware of it or not, imperfections were partly what made my work mine—no one wanted a drawing of their favorite site on its worst day. Which made me happy that I was only accepting commissions for architecture. They were far more forgiving than portraiture.

I drove off.

As I left the park and drove Oak Street along the panhandle, my thoughts returned to the ridiculous complaint at the Legion. Aside from the nonsense of having been led from the museum in cuffs, there was the gall of the lieutenant using the accusation as leverage to get me to agree to her plan, which was to meet her the next morning and—I didn't even know what. Draw some building, I assumed. She'd been as clear about that as she'd been about what I'd supposedly done wrong. For a cop—and a blackmailer—she'd been exceptionally vague. And the only reason I'd gone along with her was so I wouldn't be put back into a cell. But now that I was free to think the situation through, I was getting annoyed. And the more I thought about it, the more annoyed I grew. By the time I made it to my neighborhood I was full-on angry—and not just at Ocampo, but at myself for going along.

Then, to top things off, parking in the Mission was a nightmare. My building had a one-car garage, but with all the new tech money surging into the neighborhood and the ridiculous prices people were willing to pay—and my being in debt—I'd rented it out. A choice I regretted every time I drove, and was doubly cursing now as I circled the block. As I passed my building for a third time, I won the added bonus of getting stuck behind a bus, and found I was gripping the steering wheel so tightly that my knuckles were turning white. So rather than take out my frustrations on my already-abused car, I decided I'd focus on an outlet far more deserving: Ocampo. Whatever her plan, I would make one of my own. By the time I saw her the next morning, I intended on having hired a lawyer and a publicist—*and* called the *Chronicle*. Whatever it took, I was going to nail that crooked lieutenant's ass to the wall.

* * *

After squeezing the Miata into a questionable spot between a fire hydrant and garage, I went through my routine of opening the glove box to prove to would-be thieves that there was nothing inside to steal, then I ran my hand over the duct tape on the canvas roof to keep it from losing its tack in the wet air. The Miata's interior barely stayed dry as it was; I didn't need a gaping hole in the top to make it worse. Of course, if someone followed the handwritten instructions to PEEL HERE, there wasn't much I could do. I just hoped they would have the courtesy to smooth it back down when they were done.

The night was chilly. Rivers of fog were rushing down Guerrero Street. But that didn't stop the party. On the corner of 17th a pack of revelers was spilling out of the 500 Club. The bar was typically a dive for salty renegades, but more and more the crowd was turning bland and cliquish. These were the next generation of San Franciscans, lured to the city by the booming tech industry and, apparently, a promise that they could wear flip-flops no matter the weather. Which I supposed I didn't have a right to complain about, seeing that what they were willing to pay to rent a garage almost covered what I paid for the mortgage on my flat—and the taxes. Still, I had to step into the street to get around.

Across the street was my building, a three-story Edwardian where I lived on the top floor and owned the laundromat on the ground. The sky was dark and the shop was well-lit, and as I crossed I could see in through the large window to where a handful of customers were folding their clothes.

All looked calm and in order, but still I stepped inside to check. Two weeks earlier, for no apparent reason, the pressure regulator on the water main had burst. The sound had been so loud I'd heard it from upstairs. Luckily it had been two in the morning, when the shop was closed. My first thought had been an earthquake. I ran downstairs to find the equivalent of a fire hydrant erupting. I'd had to shut down for two days to bail the place out. My plumber said it must have been a random surge in the city's lines, but when I asked him how we could prevent it from happening again, he just shrugged and re-installed the same regulator, which was far from reassuring. I called the PUC to report the incident and ask if they were having any issues, only to be given the standard bureaucratic runaround, put on hold, then transferred again and again until eventually my call was disconnected. Everything about the situation was a pain—and expensive. Which was why I was checking on the pressure every chance I got.

Five customers were inside the shop when I walked in. The last of the early-evening crowd. Each was finishing up in relative step, either pulling their clothes from the dryer or folding the last of a load. After they left there would be a lull, followed by a trickle of loners or speed freaks who had nothing better to do on a Monday night—although with the neighborhood changing, I was noticing fewer tweakers and more tech kids. Which I supposed wasn't necessarily a bad thing. Though certainly not as entertaining. Of the faces in the shop I recognized all, and exchanged a few smiles and nods.

I went into the back office to see if there were any notes from Betty, my shop manager. When I'd first opened, I'd hired her to open a few days a week so that I wouldn't have to drag myself out of bed at six a.m. every day for the rest of my life, but after the first week she told me I had no business running a laundromat and that she would be working full-time, managing the day-to-day operations. I might have been offended had I not agreed with her, so I told her we could try it out for a month. That was eight years ago, and now I couldn't imagine what I'd do without her.

Guerrero & 17th Streets, San Francisco — 500 Club (L) and my building (R)

There were no messages, but there was a medium-sized cardboard box with my name handwritten in marker. I picked it up and found it heavy, so left it in the office while I checked on the regulator. The pressure was fine. Though if it wasn't, and the line was on the verge of surging again, I had no way of knowing. And anyway, it was almost eight. Betty would return in an hour for the routine of shutting the place down and would do her own check. Still, looking made me feel better.

*   *   *

With my drawing bag slung across my shoulder, the mysterious heavy box cradled under one arm, and the bag of Thai food dangling from the crook of my other, I left the shop, went to the front gate, and managed to open it and get through my door. I climbed the two flights to my flat, rounded the landing, and set my load onto the old church pew that I used as a shoe-tying bench. I plopped myself down, took off my shoes, then laid my head back

and let out a long sigh. I was still annoyed at the events of the day, but now that I was at home with warm food, my car parked, and having confirmed the shop wasn't flooding, I was feeling more reasonable. There was no way I was going to stand for whatever shit Ocampo was trying to pull, but I no longer felt the raging need to hire a publicist or call the newspaper. I would still find a lawyer though. I stood up from the pew and went into the studio.

My work space was the entire front of the flat, one double-wide room spanning the full width of the building. Through the window of the round corner bay, light from the 500 Club's neon sign cast long, angled shadows across the ceiling and lit the space dimly with a red glow. Without turning on any other lights, I sat at my desk, picked up the phone, and dialed my friend Adam.

Aside from being my oldest friend in San Francisco, Adam Levy was also my publisher. He'd have a good laugh at hearing the story of my day, but after that, I had no doubt he would help. More than a purveyor of books,

Adam was a born networker. If anyone knew who to call in a situation like this, it would be him.

As the line rang, my eye caught movement in the room. It seemed impossible, and I did a double-take to be certain, but, sure enough, someone had been sleeping on my couch and was now sitting up looking at me. While backlit by the streetlight outside, there was enough ambient glow for me to make out that this person was a young woman, likely a teenager—which was weird, since I didn't know any teenagers. And even weirder because I lived alone.

She was staring directly at me, and for a moment we both held perfectly still. Adam's line was still ringing, and before he could answer I hung up.

"Can I help you?" I said to the stranger in my studio, lowering the receiver.

"That's a pretty great name for a laundromat," the young woman said. "Is that how you feel about yourself?"

"Yes. Now how the hell did you get in here?"

"Betty let me in."

"And why would she do that?"

"Because I told her you might be my father."

Mid-Century Monster, Lake Merritt, Oakland, CA, sculpture by Robert Winston, 1952.
1 of 2 drawings — Commissioned by Rita Lowe. Rita grew up close to Jack London
Square. As a child, she and her two younger sisters, Leanna and Trisha, played on the
beach of Lake Merritt, home to the "Green Monster." Leanna was killed in a car accident
when she was sixteen, and for what would have been her thirtieth birthday, Rita com-
missioned two drawings of the sculpture, one for Trisha and one for herself.

3

ROCK OF THE BEAST

ran a glass of water for the young woman, then poured myself a hefty dose of bourbon. After hearing her bold pronouncement, I'd told her not to say another word until I got myself a drink. Now we were in the back of my flat, standing at the large center kitchen island of my recently remodeled great room.

"I know it's a surprise," the stranger claiming to be my daughter said as I lifted the whiskey to my lips. "I imagine there's no good way to do this."

I wanted to say there were surely better ways than sneaking into a stranger's home and lying in wait to ambush him, but mostly I was thinking about the hell I was going to give Betty for letting her in.

I downed the whiskey, allowed a few seconds for the booze to take effect, then finally gave the young woman a good look. Tall, just under six feet, she was wearing an oversized black hoodie, black jeans, and black-and-white Converse shoes. Her hair was sandy blond, and her features had that ambiguous Germanic-Scandinavian blend that, as much as I wanted to find a reason to dismiss her, could easily have been the Hopper bloodline.

"And how old are you exactly?"

She didn't answer. She was looking around. The renovations had finished less than two weeks before, and everything was still reading very new. The building was a standard early-1900s Victorian, which meant a lot of small rooms separated by a maze of walls that looked charming but were impractical for modern life. I had already opened up the front of the flat to make the studio when I'd bought the place, and this round had every non-load-bearing wall in the back removed to combine the kitchen, living room, pantry, and odd in-between closet-like hallway into one main space. The only fixed object in the new great room was the island, a six-by-fifteen-foot thing of beauty with four-inch-thick butcher-block top, double-bowl sink, and shiny new inset appliances. The work had taken eight months—and ultimately cost me three times what I'd budgeted—but the final result was incredible, like being able to breathe when you hadn't even realized you'd been holding your breath. So much that at the last minute I spontaneously decided to add a deck onto the back of the building, plunging me even further into debt, which was why I was doing things like renting out my garage and taking on commissions.

The young woman in my home turned back and stared at me expressionless, then, as if only just registering my question, said, "I'm eighteen. Two weeks ago. Which was why I figured—"

I cut her off. "And why do you think you might be my daughter?"

"My mother was on tour with your band in 1981."

"So she was a groupie?"

"Girlfriend of a roadie."

I poured another whiskey, swirled the caramel-colored liquid, and looked inside the glass. I shook my head. "No. I don't remember sleeping with any crew—or their girlfriends."

"And you remember every woman you had sex with back then? From what I gather, you guys epitomized the rock and roll lifestyle."

Despite the situation, I smiled.

"Fair enough," I said. I looked at her again. She was staring straight at me, her presence unnerving, but also impressive. For someone who had infiltrated a stranger's home, she was perfectly composed. Which was more than I could say for myself. "And your mom, she's certain I'm your father?"

"She has no idea. However, the story is, she dropped out of high school to tour with a hair band, and by the end had a parasite implanted inside of her."

"And you're sure it was my band?"

"No. But if I have my facts straight—which I'm sure I do—FurTrading was one of the opening acts of the *Rock of the Beast* tour, which opened in October 1980 and closed in July 1981."

It had been a long time ago—eighteen years and nine months, apparently—and another life. But it was starting to come back to me.

"Yeah," I said. "That was a terrible name for a tour—though they all were. But I remember. We hadn't been on the original bill, but they booked us to play the New Year's show after the headliner dropped out. It was our first stadium gig, and from there we stayed on."

"The band you replaced was called Dental Damn," the eighteen-year-old stranger sitting in my kitchen said. "Who ironically had to cancel because the lead singer broke his jaw when he dove off the stage the night before and the crowd chose not to catch him." I snickered. She continued. "Your band didn't finish the tour either. After three months your album went platinum and you struck out on your own. I'm guessing you thought you were too big for the *Beast*."

"We had a good manager," I said. "He was ruthless. And your mother, she's certain she was on tour at the same time as us?"

"Like I said, she doesn't remember you specifically, but she knows for a fact that she joined at the end of December. It was her senior year of high school. The term had just ended for winter break and, to celebrate, she and a girlfriend went to a show at the Meadowlands in New Jersey. They hooked up with some roadies to get backstage, and after partying all night, her friend went home and she stuck along for the ride."

"A senior in high school? How old was she?"

"Seventeen."

I winced at the thought of having potentially impregnated a seventeen-year-old. I would have only been nineteen myself, but still, legally, she'd been underage, which meant that after today's accusation at the museum, I could now be accused of *two* sex offenses in my life—which was a lot to learn about myself in a single day.

"And when is your birthday?"

"October twenty-seventh."

I started doing the math.

"The timing works," she said, impatient with my inability to automatically calculate the dates. "I told you, I did my research. I wouldn't be here if I hadn't. Mom joined the tour December twentieth. You joined December twenty-ninth, and your last show was April third. Given my birthdate, I estimate I was conceived between mid-January and early February. So while there was a parade of bands mom could have hooked up with, the timing of you being on scene during the window of conception lines up perfectly." She said it all as if reading a math problem from a textbook.

"Okay. And you're sure she's telling the truth? I mean, I'm not trying to disparage your mother or anything, but she did wait eighteen years to tell you this, and—"

"I never said she just told me."

"But you just turned eighteen, right? So I thought—"

"Why would you assume I only just learned about you?"

"I don't know. I guess because you're only just now looking me up, and—how long have you thought I might be your father?"

"Mom did keep a few souvenirs from the tour, though," she said, ignoring my question. "Mostly backstage passes which she laminated and tied to the end of the drawstrings on the blinds. So I guess she didn't forget the experience entirely. Anyway, I researched as many of the bands as I could, and the moment I saw your album cover—"

"You mean the one that's a giant photo of my face?"

"—I got this feeling in my gut. I just knew."

"I see, so now we're going on gut?" Her matter-of-fact manner had been putting me at ease, but at the same time, I couldn't help but be defensive. "You know I have an identical twin," I said. "Right? Brian? Who was also in the band?"

My attitude didn't faze her though. "I do," she said flatly. "So, yeah, there's him to consider as well. But if I'm to believe what I read in the tabloids, he's moved to China to play the token Westerner on a daytime soap opera. And since San Francisco was closer, I decided to start with you."

She was smiling at what I assumed she thought was a joke, but I wasn't finding any of this funny. I just stood there, my arms braced against the kitchen island, letting silence hang over the scene like a wet towel over a silk suit. I drank my second glass of whiskey.

"By the way," she said, as I began pouring a third, "in case you're wondering, my name is Larissa."

*　*　*

"Shit," I said. "Sorry. I—" But before I could attempt what would surely have been a lackluster apology, she stood, grabbed a tumbler from one of the new exposed rosewood shelves on the far wall, then reached for the bourbon.

"No," I said, grabbing hold of the bottle. "No way. I've contributed to the delinquency of enough minors already."

She dismissed me with a grunt, grabbed the bottle out of my hand, then poured herself a finger of whiskey. She threw it back, then instantly began coughing. In her defense, this wasn't just any old whiskey. I'd pulled out the strong stuff, E. H. Taylor, barrel strength, 136 proof. For a moment, she couldn't breathe. Her eyes were watering and she looked like she'd been punched in the chest.

I handed her the glass of water.

She drank half, then, the moment she recovered, began pouring herself another shot.

"What the hell are you doing?" I said.

"Getting drunk with my ex-rock-star potential-father."

I dropped my head into my hands and wondered what had happened to this day.

SLAC, Menlo Park, CA, entrance to the Far Experimental Hall of the LCLS,
National Accelerator Laboratory's x-ray laser — Patron asked to be unnamed

4

ONION TV

"That's one of the buildings at SLAC," Larissa said. "I saw it earlier, before you got home. How did you get access?"

We were in my studio, looking at finished commission drawings I hadn't yet delivered. I was showing her one from the Stanford Linear Accelerator in Menlo Park, home to the two-mile-long particle accelerator where physicists from around the world performed experiments by smashing atoms together at just shy the speed of light.

"My client," I said, finishing my fourth glass of whiskey—or it may have been my fifth. I couldn't remember. Having learned that I might have a daughter had been one sucker punch too many in a day of unexpected punches, and once I'd started pouring, I kept going. "She commissioned a drawing and got me access. How do you even know what this place is, anyway?"

"I thought I read somewhere you weren't doing this kind of drawing anymore?" she said, once again ignoring my question—something I was learning she was quite good at. "But doing more conceptual stuff? I saw a piece of yours in a museum in Los Angeles last month where you had to walk through a narrow glass hallway as rows of batting machines fired thousands of Super Balls at you from each side. The sound of all those balls hitting the glass and ricocheting around was crazy. Like a deafening rainstorm."

"Yeah," I said. "That piece was fun. Problem is, museum exhibitions take forever to arrange. You spend more time writing proposals and meeting with committees than you do making the work. And they're inconsistent. Drawing, though, I can do here, every day, and the interactions are more straight-forward. Most of the people who commission me have a personal connection to the site they want me to draw. Like this one of SLAC. The client's father was the founder of one of the labs. He's retired, and she wants to give him a one-of-a-kind memento. That's really special for me, knowing that a scientist who helped build a renowned research center will look at my drawing every day and be reminded of his accomplishment. Here's another one." I put aside the image of what felt like a futuristic portal leading into the bowels of the earth—which, in a way, it was—and took out a drawing of an interior of a house in the Sunset District. "This is for a couple who've been commissioning me for years. They move around a lot and have me make a drawing from every place they live. This is the first house they were able to buy, and now they're selling it and moving to Marin. I'm sure at some point they'll be calling me to draw that place too." I put it aside and showed her another. "And this one, a dozen friends chipped in for me to draw their friend's building as a birthday gift. I snuck their names onto the tree as if they'd all signed a card. It's not the same as making esoteric modern art for museums, but drawings like this mean a lot to the people who commission them. And you just don't get that kind of personal connection with museum work—or much else, really."

"I don't know," Larissa said. She was swaying awkwardly, also having had a lot to drink. "That installation with all those Super Balls being shot at the glass walls definitely evoked a personal experience for me. I mean, I wouldn't have thought I'd have any trouble walking through a fifty-foot hallway, but it was really intense. At one point I got vertigo and started stumbling into the walls—which was weird because they were totally vibrating with all those balls hitting them. Other people were having trouble too. One woman couldn't even go two steps in before having to turn back. Another guy had to get on his hands and knees to make it through."

I wanted to say something like: That was the point of the installation, to create an all-consuming moment, and was why I didn't confine myself to only drawing, since different mediums had different powers of conveying thoughts and emotions—or some other artsy bullshit that always sounded smart when you were drunk. But I'd already done enough of that. So I said, "I just hate doing the same thing over and over."

"Plus you get to shoot thousands of Super Balls at countless strangers."

"Yeah," I said, grinning. "There's that too."

*   *   *

"I think it surprised him as much as anyone," I said. "But it's official—Brian now lives in Shanghai. He moved this summer."

We'd returned to the back of the flat and were now sitting on the couch.

Noriega Street, San Francisco — Commissioned by Brian and Kelley Johnson

After the studio show-and-tell I said I needed a refill, and Larissa said she did too—although we were no longer drinking the barrel strength. I'd swapped out the E. H. Taylor for a spirit less like liquid fire, my regular go-to, Basil Hayden's, which was only about half the alcohol. If I couldn't keep Larissa from drinking, I could at least slow down the effects—which was probably a good plan for me too.

I kept trying to get her to tell me more about her mother and her childhood, but she kept dodging my questions. At first she'd asked about my drawings—which I was always a sucker to get talking about—and now she was asking about Brian—which I couldn't deny her, seeing that my twin brother was as much a candidate for her father as I was.

"You seem to know a lot about the band and my career," I said. "How much do you know about Brian? And what happened with *Brandice Falls*?"

Haight Street at Divisadero, San Francisco — Commissioned by James Schalkwyk. A dozen friends chipped in to buy this as a birthday gift. I snuck their names onto the tree as if they'd all signed a card.

I was talking about the TV show that had made my twin brother a full-fledged star—at least for a while.

"I know it proves how truly screwed-up America is," Larissa said. She picked up her glass of whiskey and contemplated the caramel-colored liquid as if it were a bed of hot coals she was preparing to rush over, then she took a deep breath and drank. It went down easier than the previous shots, and she looked relieved. What she didn't know was, aside from my having switched the booze to one less potent, I'd cut her most recent pour half with water.

"Yeah," I said. "Some of it was the era. *Brandice Falls* was one of the biggest prime-time network dramas of the eighties. When it premiered, Brian was a nobody actor. Sure, he'd been the guitarist in a one-hit-wonder rock band, but that wasn't the same as being on TV. The show was a large ensemble cast, and at first he had only a minor role, but the audience quickly fell in love with him, so for the second season the producers made him a main character. For almost a decade he was one of TV's biggest stars, and, as *Brandice* was wrapping up, everyone assumed he would make the jump to movies. Not many actors can do that you know, but Brian seemed perfectly poised. Then in the final episode, Brian's character, Billy, came out as gay. The writers were trying to be edgy, and Brian was all for it, but the choice essentially ruined his career. There had already been an openly gay character on the series *Soap*, which had aired in the late seventies, even before *Brandice Falls*, so the subject wasn't completely taboo. But this was different, because it was a surprise. For almost ten years Brian's character had been the tough, all-American cowboy type, and mainstream America wasn't ready for that kind of character not to be straight. Brian won an Emmy for his performance, but from then on, no one would hire him. All the movie offers dried up, and his agent said viewers needed to forget about him for a while before they'd be able to see him as someone else."

"That is so pathetic," Larissa said, grunting in disgust. "That an actor has to literally move to the other side of the world to escape the stigma of having played a closeted gay character."

"I agree. It's wrong for so many reasons. And for Brian, it completely destroyed his TV career, as well as all his hopes of working in film. But at least he was still able to act. For most of the nineties he worked solely in the theater. He got lots of leading roles on and off Broadway, and received great reviews. Only the stage wasn't where he wanted to be. Then a few years ago he started getting offers for commercial work in Singapore. *Brandice* had gotten syndicated across Asia, and for whatever reason, the cultural stain that had unnerved American audiences hadn't translated—if anything, it seemed to work in his favor. He started doing ads for high-end watches, clothes, and cologne, and in short time was flying to places like Kuala Lumpur and Hong Kong every month for appearances. His popularity grew so large that, after eight years of being denied even a supporting role in any major studio films, he finally accepted that Hollywood was never going to see him as anyone other than Billy, and signed on with an agent in Asia. Now he's starring in the hottest daytime soap opera in China, *Glory Days*. It's not the movies, but he's back on TV, so he's happy."

"Does he speak Chinese?"

"No. And honestly, I'm not sure how the whole thing works. I'm guessing his parts are subtitled, but I don't really know. I haven't seen the show, and we haven't been in much contact since he left."

Without my realizing, Larissa had refilled her glass—a double shot—and before I could stop her, was throwing back the entire thing. Basil was sweeter and smoother than the E. H. Taylor, but it was still strong whiskey—and her pour hadn't been cut with water—and for a moment she looked like she'd been stabbed in the chest with a red-hot poker.

"You okay?" I asked, trying not to laugh. I took the glass from her hand. "How about you take it a little slower from here on out?"

She nodded vigorously, her eyes looking as if she'd witnessed something horrifying.

I pushed myself up off the couch and ran her a glass of water.

She drank, and after a few seconds was able to breathe again.

I was standing, looking down at her. She looked up and squinted. Her eyes had grown a little more glazed, and she began swaying back and forth like a buoy in the ocean. "Do you have any food?"

*　*　*

Feeling pretty drunk myself, I said eating sounded like a good plan, and that yes, I did indeed have food.

I retrieved the bag of Thai takeout from where I'd left it on the pew. As I emptied the soup and noodles into a pot and pan, Larissa shuffled from the couch to the island and slid onto a stool.

"So," I said, turning on the burners and seizing the chance to steer the conversation back to her. "Just to be clear, you say you've known for some time that either Brian or I might be your father?"

She leaned forward, spread her elbows across the butcher-block top, and rested her chin atop her folded arms. "No. I don't know. Like I said, Mom never mentioned you. Only that she'd gotten knocked up by some guy in a hair band."

"And she was never interested in tracking down who your father might be?"

Larissa shrugged. "At one point she might have been. But shortly after realizing she'd turned parasitic, she also learned she had breast cancer, so I think chasing down a random rock-star sperm daddy wasn't much of a priority."

"Shit."

"Yeah. Isn't as bad as it sounds, though—or I don't know. Probably was. I just mean she always said getting pregnant was the best thing that ever happened to her since it brought me into her life—but, you know, she was my mother, so you'd kinda expect her to say stuff like that. Although there are a lot of shitty moms out there. Anyway. Getting knocked up really was a good thing since, if not for having to go to the obstetrician, she probably wouldn't have found out she had cancer until it was too late."

"So you saved her life?"

"That's what she liked to say. But let's be honest, getting pregnant was what saved her life. Whoever popped out was irrelevant." Seeming to wake up a little, Larissa pushed herself up from her slump and arched her back. "Don't get me wrong, I don't have issues about it or anything. I just don't have any illusions either. She was seventeen. Last thing she wanted was to be pregnant. I mean, if it were me, I know there's no way I would want to have a kid right now. But she was a good mom. She loved me. So it's okay."

"What does she think of you coming to find me?"

"Nothing. She died when I was ten."

"Oh—wow. I'm sorry."

Larissa inhaled a deep breath through her nose, then let it out, her shoulders rising and falling as she frowned and tilted her head. "Yeah, it's tragic. But, like I said, if she hadn't gotten pregnant she probably wouldn't have lived to see twenty. So really, she got probably a decade of life she wouldn't have had otherwise. Or at least that's how she liked to think of it. She was actually a really positive person. Even though she never really got herself together. I'm just sad she's gone."

The food started bubbling. I turned off the burners.

"So who raised you after your mother passed?" I asked. I took down two bowls and two plates from the new exposed shelves, then pulled the ladle from the ceramic pitcher of spatulas and wooden utensils on the island and began serving the coconut soup.

"My mom's brother," Larissa said. "My Uncle Phil."

I scooped up a hunk of chicken and glanced at Larissa. "Do you eat meat?"

"Savagely."

I finished dividing the soup, set a bowl in front of her, and turned to the pad Thai.

"And where did you grow up?"

"New Haven," she said, picking up the bowl. "Connecticut." She slurped some soup. "Same place my mother was born."

I pulled out a pair of scissors from the silverware drawer and set to cutting the noodles in the pan. I slid a perfect half circle onto each plate, then set a plate in front of Larissa. "It's a trick I learned when I lived in Northern Thailand," I said, pointing to the cut noodles. "In the roadside kitchens, they use scissors for everything. It's incredibly convenient."

Larissa was unimpressed. She drank her soup as I got us utensils.

"And what does your uncle think about you coming to find me?"

"I read *Glass Houses,* by the way," she said, using the back of her hand to catch soup that was dribbling down her chin—and once more ignoring my question. She was referring to my first—and only successful—novel. "The story was a bit cartoonish, but it was cool how you wove in all the drawings of houses. It's supposed to be about you and Brian, right?"

"Yeah," I said, handing her both a set of chopsticks and a fork, then sliding onto a stool. "It was based off an inside joke we'd had since we were kids. Most people had no idea, so they thought the book was some deep and mysterious metaphor. But it made Brian crack up, which was really why I wrote it. And it ended up being a hit, so I can't really complain. It made me enough money to buy this building."

"Too bad you guys can't make a movie out of it," Larissa said, looking half asleep. "Then Brian could star in it and not have to live in China."

* * *

From then on, Larissa ate in a silent, almost unconscious state. Twice, a forkful of food went awry on its route from her plate to her mouth. The first time the napkin on her lap prevented an unfortunate landing. The second time I don't even know what happened. Noodles ended up on both sides of her plate, on her hand, and two feet across the island. It didn't faze her, though.

She scooped up the food and wiped the surface without a word, then went back to eating. When she finished, she looked at me and said, "I think I need to go to sleep." Then she slid off the stool and tottered to the couch. She crawled up onto the cushions, nestled into the corner against the armrest, then closed her eyes. "Is it okay if I sleep here?"

I laughed. For someone who had essentially broken into my house and already slept on the couch in my studio—and was already curled up again—she was being exceedingly considerate. A rare trait for a drunk person.

"Of course you can sleep here," I said. I began clearing our dishes and setting them in the sink.

"I mean right here," she said. "As in, right, *right* here. On your couch."

I laughed again, then went to turn off the light.

"No," she said, and I stopped.

Her eyes were open and she was looking at me, but without moving from her tightly curled position. "Don't go yet. Stay out here and watch some TV with me."

Her voice was so sweet, there was no way I could refuse. I refilled my glass with ice and poured some more Basil, then I sat next to her on the couch and turned on the television.

I kept the sound muted as I flipped past infomercials for knives that could cut through cans, overly quaffed televangelists hustling for money, phone-sex ads, and a Seinfeld rerun, until I came to the Public Access channel and stopped. I loved the Public Access station. Everything on it was so offbeat you couldn't even call it opposite of mainstream. The shows were all produced by local amateurs, and were usually raw and confusing, if not straight-up weird. The city provided a studio on Folsom Street where anyone could book the sound stage and editing suites, or check out a hand-held camcorder to shoot offsite, all for free. There were no restrictions on content—as in literally none—other than adult subject matter had to air after 8 p.m. I'd seen a show with a hippie John-Lennon type chain-smoking joints while reading from the books of Carlos Castaneda; another with a scabby, emaciated junkie smoking crack and ranting nonsensically about UFOs, the Masons, and secret government sex cults; and of course no short-age of amateur porn. It wasn't all debauchery, though. There were programs on spirituality, race, and queer culture. Topics that network TV barely acknowledged existed, let alone addressed—Brian's career arc being proof of that. The program I'd landed on was a talk show called *Onion TV*. On the sparse studio stage were one fake potted palm, two director's chairs, and an

45

easel with a large painting of an onion sliced in half and the words "Peeling Back the Layers of Truth." The interviewer was a black drag queen named Oprah Lovefree, and her guest was Tom Ammiano, the gay former stand-up comedian turned local supervisor who was now in the running to unseat the current mayor Willie Brown. Ammiano had appeared on the political scene seemingly out of nowhere, and, until the general election two weeks earlier, no one had thought of him as anything more than another one of the countless local wackos who liked to see their name on the ballot. But the smiley supervisor had taken everyone by surprise—especially Willie, the career politician who had assumed his mayoral crown would be shined, polished, and dutifully returned to him—coming in so close that a runoff election had to be scheduled for early December. Now both candidates were campaigning day and night. Including, apparently, going on Public Access TV.

I unmuted the sound. Lovefree was asking Ammiano about the new development in Mission Bay, the area off of Third Street that for years had been a bit of no-man's-land and was now currently being developed as a new mini-city-like campus for UCSF's Medical Research center. The project was to be a legacy for Willie Brown, who was being lambasted for cronyism and back-room deals. Construction was currently in limbo, its fate in the hands of the EPA as they investigated allegations that the Brown administration was colluding with developers to skirt environmental restrictions in order to build over protected wetlands.

At the sound being unmuted, Larissa stirred. But barely. She unfurled herself from her huddled position, stretched her legs over my lap, then fell back asleep. It was all a little weird. And yet, not.

*   *   *

I woke to static on the television and Larissa sound asleep. I was sitting up, drink still in my hand, having miraculously not spilled while I dozed. I turned off the TV, then gently extricated myself from under Larissa's legs.

I cleared the whiskey bottle and glasses from the coffee table, then ran a fresh glass of water for Larissa. I set it on the table, then pulled a blanket from the basket beside the couch. As I was laying it over her, Larissa's eyes popped open and for a moment she looked unsure where she was.

"It's okay," I said. "You're fine. Just go back to sleep."

"So, will you do it?" she asked.

I tilted my head, unsure what she meant. "Do what?"

"Take a blood test?"

Had I taken even a moment to think about it, I could have easily anticipated the question. Only I hadn't, and this was the first I'd considered the idea. She was looking up at me with sedated, yet earnest, eyes, and while I'd been blindsided by her brazenness, I now saw her vulnerability. When I was her age, I was prancing around on stadium stages like an idiot, with my brother by my side. But here she was, confronting some heavy questions, on her own. I had to give her credit. Going in search of your potential father couldn't have been easy—not to mention learning that the Hopper brothers were your prime candidates.

"Sure," I said. "Why not." Then I told her to get some rest, turned off the light, and shuffled off to brush my teeth.

Once in bed, I couldn't fall asleep. I lay there in the dark, trying to wrap my head around the possibility of having potentially fathered a child, as well as the idea that whoever had impregnated Larissa's mother—be it me or Brian or whoever—had inadvertently contributed to the woman discovering she had cancer, which had given her ten years of life she might not have had otherwise. I wasn't looking to start a campaign promoting reckless anonymous sex, I was just thinking about how the consequences of our actions can ripple out far wider than we may ever know.

* * *

When I woke, it was morning and my head was cement. After stumbling to the bathroom, the smell of coffee led me to the kitchen where I found Larissa awake on the couch, an oversized set of headphones covering her ears, and a hefty portable computer on her lap.

I went to the sink and began filling a glass of water. Seeing me, she tugged down her headphones and said, "I made coffee. And there's a breakfast bagel for you." Then she resumed typing.

As I drank the water, I studied her laptop computer: two thick black slabs of plastic casing held together by a large cylindrical hinge. Over the past year, I'd been seeing objects like this more and more in cafes and even in the laundromat. Though I wasn't exactly sure what anyone did with them.

She had indeed made coffee, an entire pot. I poured a cup, took a sip, and instantly recoiled. It was beyond strong. "Mud" was a better word. I dumped three quarters of the cup back into the pot, then diluted the rest with tap water.

On the butcher-block counter was a brown paper bag.

"Ah, you went to Katz," I said, opening the bag and pulling out a bagel that I could tell was from the shop just down the street on 16th. "What did you get?" I unwrapped the familiar yellow paper to find an everything bagel with scrambled eggs, cheddar cheese, avocado, and bacon. I took a bite and closed my eyes in bliss. "Food of the gods," I said as I chewed.

Larissa glanced up from her screen as she continued to type. "If gods have hangovers like this," she said, "then I understand why they're so vengeful."

"You feel bad?" I asked, turning to her. "You look fine to me."

"Yeah, well, I feel like dog shit," she said. "After another dog has eaten it and shat it out again. I could barely make my way down the block to get food."

"How long you been up?"

"A couple hours. The phone woke me."

The bagel was good, but the cheese had solidified and the eggs were cold, so I took another bite and put the rest in the toaster oven.

"You got two calls this morning," Larissa said as I pressed the ON button. "One was from a woman with the Conservatory of Flowers who said she's very excited about your drawing, and the other was from a police lieutenant who demanded to know where you were. I told her you were asleep and she was pretty pissed."

I was still not fully awake. I was staring at the bagel warming in the electric stove, mesmerized by the red glow of the heating elements, and it took a moment for what she said to sink in. I looked at the digital clock on the stove: just after eleven. "Shit," I said, remembering the whole debacle with Ocampo—and that I was supposed to have met her at nine.

"I think it's okay, though," Larissa said. She set her computer down and came over to the island. She was wearing her black hoodie from the night before, but now she was barefoot and had changed into gray sweatpants. Her toenails were painted black, and her sweats had a logo of a howling ghost with X's for eyes. She poured herself a full cup of sludge. "I told her I was your long-lost illegitimate daughter, I'd surprised you, and that we'd gotten drunk together."

"Seriously?"

"Totally. And I think it chilled her out. She said for you to meet her at noon, same place."

I nodded. Drank some coffee. Tried to get my clarity. Then—"Wait," I said. "You didn't tell Ocampo how old you are, did you?"

Suddenly I smelled smoke and saw the top of my bagel burning in the toaster oven. I hit the OFF button, flung open the door, and yanked it out. The top was black, the seeds and garlic charred and smoking.

"No," Larissa said. "I didn't tell her."

"Good," I said, staring at my burnt breakfast. "I don't need to add drinking with a minor to my list of offenses."

"I mean, not until she asked."

The William Westerfeld House, Fulton Street, San Francisco — Commissioned by Gabbi Ferrera. Said this was the kind of place she could grow to be an old cat lady in, then quickly added, "Which is a good thing!"

5

THE ASSIGNMENT

Noon was only forty minutes away, so I ate my burnt bagel sandwich and took a quick shower. I had no idea what the meeting with Lieutenant Ocampo might look like, but I took pleasure in having inadvertently blown her off. Larissa's unexpected appearance the night before had derailed me—and not just from making the meeting, but also from finding a lawyer, which I was less pleased about. Then a darker thought occurred to me: Was it possible that the mysterious lewd behavior complaint and appearance of Larissa might be linked? A connection seemed improbable—but so was the idea that, even unconnected, the two events might occur in the same day. And yet, that's what had happened. Whatever the case, the only way to know was to keep going, so I put the thought aside and returned to the more entertaining image of Ocampo pacing outside some building all morning, waiting on me for who knows how long before finally realizing she'd been stood up.

* * *

If I'd kept moving steadily toward getting out the door I would have been right on time, or at least close enough to not being too late, but I didn't like the idea that I'd be walking into this meeting without someone having my back. Larissa hardly seemed my best choice, so I decided to take a minute to call Adam.

In the studio, I sat at my desk and dialed the office of Levied Publishing.

"Emit Hopper," I told the receptionist, whose voice I didn't recognize.

"He's currently out of the office, sir. Can I take a message?"

Sir. It had been a while since I'd published a book with Levied, but not so long that even the newest of receptionists shouldn't know who I was. I told her no, then hung up.

As I was gathering my things, I noticed a rucksack on the floor. Larissa's.

I peeked down the hallway to make sure she wasn't just then walking toward me, then I opened her bag.

*   *   *

My drawing supplies were still on the pew from where I'd left them the night before—next to the cardboard box I still hadn't opened. I wound a fresh roll of film into my camera, slung my bag over my shoulder, then found Larissa in the back of the flat, once again on the couch with her computer on her lap and headphones over her ears. Seeing me, she pulled one side of the large set away from her head.

"I have no idea how long this is going to take," I said. "But we can go for the blood test when I'm back, cool?"

She gave me a thumbs-up.

I turned to go, then hesitated. "Listen. If I'm not here by five, I want you to call Adam Levy at Levied Publishing and tell him to bail me out."

She squinted, trying to determine if I was kidding. She knew that a police lieutenant had called, but I'd told her nothing of what had happened at the museum. After a few seconds, she decided it either didn't matter or she simply didn't care. She shrugged and said, "Cool." Then she snapped the headphones back against her ears and turned back to her computer.

*   *   *

Out on the sidewalk, I reflexively peered into the shop. Betty was there, on her tiptoes, half inside a dryer, I assumed cleaning a filter assembly. Clearly the regulator on the water main hadn't burst, so there was nothing immediate to tend to, though I very much wanted to ask her why she'd thought it was okay to let a strange young woman into my home. At the same time, I knew Betty. She wouldn't reply so much as fire back a sarcastic comment about how she's always cleaning up after me, which wouldn't make any sense but would somehow sound justified enough to deflect the conversation and only make me later for my rendezvous with the lieutenant than I already was. So I kept walking.

Only, I couldn't find my car. The first of my usual go-to spots on Guerrero had a motorcycle, and the second had a pickup truck hanging so far over a driveway I wondered how the owner could rest without worrying about being towed. I tried to think back to the night before, but for some reason couldn't remember where I'd parked. It was disconcerting, and I was starting to wonder if maybe having written PEEL HERE on the tape covering the slice in the roof had been too tempting an advertisement, prompting someone to do not only that, but to also hot-wire my little yellow ride and drive away. But when I got to the corner of 18th and saw an electric bus blocking traffic because of one of its trolley arms having come disconnected from the overhead power lines, it all came back to me—including that I'd parked in a questionable spot, a bit too close to a fire hydrant.

Halfway up the block I was relieved to see the Miata—and no ticket under the wiper. But the relief was short-lived. As I got close I saw a flap of canvas sticking off the roof. It wasn't the slice on the driver's side, but a new slice, on the passenger's side. Which was annoying not just because someone had completely ignored the silver duct tape with handwritten instructions, but because I'd been naïve enough to think that people who broke into cars might actually oblige. For a moment I just stood there, staring at my doubly vandalized vehicle, once again cursing my decision for having rented out my garage. Finally I opened the door and checked the interior to confirm that my seats hadn't been slashed or that no one had taken a dump on the floor. Then, seeing that it was a surprisingly nice day for the end of November, I decided that if I already had a new air vent, I might as well put the top down.

* * *

A nice day for San Francisco was a relative statement. While the sun was out and the sky was clear, it was sixty degrees and windy, which meant it felt like fifty. A bit chilly to be driving around in a convertible. Still, I wound a scarf around my neck and did my best to enjoy the ride.

Luckily it wasn't very far. The address Ocampo had given me was on Steiner Street, close to Alamo Square Park, on what turned out to be the same block as the famous row of Victorian houses known as the Painted Ladies. As I slowed to check addresses I discovered the number I was looking for was one of those picturesque houses. I passed the address and drove along until I found parking just around the corner on Fulton Street. I tugged up the roof and was locking it in place when the lieutenant appeared.

"Do you really have an illegitimate daughter?"

"Probably," I said, getting a roll of duct tape from the trunk.

Ocampo looked at my car. "This is a pretty small ride for such a big guy."

She was right. I was six-foot-three, two-twenty pounds. And the Miata was small. But I liked my car. I could park it almost anywhere.

I held up the roll of silver tape. "Care to help me fix the newest accessory?"

I tore off a strip and set to laying it over the fresh slice in the canvas roof. I glanced at Ocampo, and she stepped over to support the flaps from underneath.

"So," I said, smoothing the tape flat. "The Painted Ladies. Can't get more iconic than that. Are you really so desperate for a souvenir you need to blackmail me?"

"I'm not interested in your drawings," she said.

I tore off another strip of tape and waited for her to say more. When she didn't, I sat sidesaddle on the passenger seat, my feet on the sidewalk, and fixed the second strip of tape to the underside of the roof. "Could you—?" I said. And Ocampo pressed down on the top of the canvas so I could press the tape flat. I stood, then sandwiched my hands above and below the pieces of tape and rubbed my hands back and forth to ensure they were firmly stuck. Then I stepped back. Standing side by side, Ocampo and I looked at the black canvas roof with its two, almost symmetrical silver strips of repairs, as if it were some grand project we'd completed together.

"I think I'll forgo labeling this one with instructions," I said. "Maybe then the next thief will think to use it."

The lieutenant squinted at me again. "You're very disarming, you know that?"

I wasn't sure how to respond.

"Come," she said. "Let's walk."

I tossed the roll of tape onto the passenger seat, grabbed my bag, closed the car door, and made to go. But Ocampo didn't move.

"Aren't you going to lock it?" she asked.

"Seriously?"

We didn't go into the park but took the sidewalk along Fulton up toward the corner of Scott Street, away from the Painted Ladies.

"Your drawings," Ocampo said. "How long does one normally take you on site?"

"Depends. If it's a sketch, could be as short as five minutes. But if I'm working on what will be the final drawing, could be as long as a couple hours."

"And that's start to finish?"

"No, just the linework. The light and shadow I apply in the studio."

"Which is what you use photos for?"

"Exactly."

She nodded. "Can you do multiple drawings in one day?"

"I guess. But I only have so much stamina. That kind of intense focus I can only do for an hour or two before needing a break. Maybe three, depending on the situation."

She nodded slightly. At the corner of Scott Street she stopped to take in the view. Catty-corner from the park was another stunning Victorian, possibly my favorite in the city, the William Westerfeld House. The owner, Jimmy, ran a head shop on the upper Haight and let his stoner employees live in the multitude of rooms. He also took in rescue dogs, mostly pit bulls. All of whom confused the tourist groups who paid to be guided through the historical site. And which I knew because I'd done a commission drawing of the crow's nest a few months back and used the opportunity to take a tour. Ocampo wasn't actually looking at the house, though. Her brow was furrowed, and she was thinking. After a few seconds she turned back to me, threw her chin toward my bag. "That your drawing kit?"

"Yep."

"And you have your camera with you?"

"I do."

"Do you know the Lyon Street Steps?"

"Of course."

"You're going to set up somewhere along the steps and draw. I'm thinking up top is probably best, where people tend to congregate. You can draw whatever you want—as long as you actually draw. You'll also take photos of people coming and going. Mainly crowd shots, and don't worry about getting everyone—there'll be too much traffic. However, anyone who looks suspicious, get a close-up—but do it without them noticing." She looked at her watch. "It's twelve-twenty. We'll meet for lunch at three. Minus commute, you'll have a solid two hours."

"Wait," I said. "You want me to do this right now?"

"Why do you think you're here?"

"Actually, I don't know why I'm here. You gave me the address of one of the Painted Ladies, but now you're telling me to go out to the Lyon Street Steps to spy on potentially suspicious people—which, I have to say, is a bit vague. As well as extremely discomforting."

"You'll figure it out."

"Okay . . . But why me? Why not get one of your cops to do it? Have them dress up like a PG&E guy and pretend they're working on the telephone pole? Or better yet, have one of *them* pretend to be an artist?"

"Because you're proving to me that you were in fact no more than an inno-cent bystander at the museum, and not some creepy dude with a sketchpad."

"Or, because photographing the public without their consent isn't legal, right? Which is why you're strong-arming me, and not your cops?"

She shrugged. "It's your choice. If you don't want to do it, then no skin off my back. I'll book you for lewd conduct and you can take your chances with the D.A."

I was sure she was bluffing. But at the same time, I wasn't sure I wanted to take the risk. And anyway, what she was asking wasn't so outrageous—except for the photographing strangers part. Which I was already thinking how I could skirt.

"You know this is full-on extortion?" I said, trying one last tack.

She stared at me. Her face emotionless.

I took a deep breath and turned toward downtown, searching the skyline as if the mass of rectangular shapes might offer an answer. When it didn't, I turned back and said, "Okay. I'll do it—but on one condition."

"Don't worry. I'll return your film from the museum."

"Not just that," I said. I took out my notebook, tore out a page, and handed it to her. "I want you to run a background check on someone for me."

"For real?" She said it incredulously, but she also took the small piece of paper. "Larissa Huxley," she said, reading. "Is this—"

"It is. I snuck into her backpack this morning and copied down her driver's-license information."

"You think she's trying to scam you?"

"No," I said, shaking my head. "Or—I don't know. I just—"

"You just realized you were on your way to meet a police lieutenant who has access to confidential files, and you figured you might as well try and learn as much about this strange young woman claiming to be your daughter as you could."

"Exactly."

"You know it's illegal for me to give you this kind of information?"

I opened my arms and laughed. "And what exactly would you call what we're doing here?"

Ocampo snorted. But she was also smirking. She looked away, possibly searching the landscape for the same answer that hadn't appeared for me either, then looked back. She narrowed her eyes. "This kid really showed up on your doorstep out of the blue, claiming to be your long-lost illegitimate love child?"

"She didn't use the word love, but yes."

Ocampo put the slip of paper into her pocket. "At the steps," she said, turning and beginning to walk back toward where I'd parked, "go about drawing the same way you would any other day, only snap a few extra photos."

Right, I thought. As if my snapping photos hadn't been what landed me in this mess to begin with.

"And so to be clear," I said, falling in step with her. "If I do this, if I act as your one-man illegal surveillance unit, then you'll forget the ridiculous lewd behavior complaint—and do the background check?"

She glanced at me in exasperation. I was definitely testing her patience. Which was fine with me.

"How about you just focus on getting the job done," she said. "Then maybe we won't need to discuss your getting drunk with eighteen-year-olds."

I wanted to say: Larissa was the one who got drunk with *me*. Or: One might argue that her drinking was done with parental consent. But instead I just said: "Fine."

6

THE LYON STREET STEPS

Reaching my car, Ocampo looked at her watch again, then told me to meet her at Tu Lan, the Vietnamese restaurant at Sixth and Market, at three o'clock.

She waited for me to get into the Miata and watched me drive off, I guessed because she didn't want me to see the car she got into—or to follow her. The whole situation was just weird. But I was going along with it, and hopefully getting something out of it as well, so weird it was going to have to be.

*   *   *

From Alamo Square Park the route was fairly direct to the Lyon Street Steps. At Divisadero I turned right, then drove through the Western Addition, across Geary and California, and up into Pacific Heights. At Green Street I turned left and was delivered a block from the top of the steps. Several vehicles were cruising slowly, looking for parking, but with my little car I easily found a spot. The time was twenty to one.

With three hundred stairs and a stunning view, the Lyon Street Steps was a popular local exercise destination. It was also in one of the most expensive neighborhoods in the city. Former mayor of San Francisco, and now California Senator, Dianne Feinstein, lived a stone's throw away, alongside countless other prominent members of San Francisco society. I always wondered how she and all her wealthy neighbors felt about living next to what thousands of people thought of as a free public gym.

To point, arriving at the top of the stairs I found an exercise class: *Gary's Grind*, as advertised on the hand-painted cardboard sign sticking out of a gym bag—Gary's, I assumed. The man himself was compact, intensely muscular, and extremely tanned, with a wide smile and dyed-black beard. Dancing along to a boom box playing Madonna's *Lucky Star*, he enthusiastically cheered his students to "bend those hips and clench those buns!" Dozens of other people were around too—runners, walkers, tourists—ascending and descending the stairs at various speeds or pacing around up top, stretching, or catching their breath. These latter folks didn't worry me. Gary's Grinders, however—five plump, middle-aged women in skin-tight spandex shaking their booties to Madonna—were not going to bode well. No matter how convincing I was as a plein air artist, there was no way I was going to be able to get away with snapping photos next to them—innocent or otherwise. Already half of them were eyeing every male running by. There was no way they weren't going to notice a sore thumb like me lurking on the side with a drawing pad and camera. I could see the headlines already: Local Artist Peeps on Grinders.

So instead of setting up at the top as Ocampo suggested, I walked down the steps a bit. This was truly a beautiful part of the city. While the air was chilly, the sky was clear and the view was striking. I could see the Marina, the Palace of Fine Arts, and all the way across the Bay to the Headlands. Despite Ocampo's questionable reason for sending me, I was certain I would be able to make a sellable drawing—not that I was feeling in any way grateful, or at ease with the situation. Only that I was doing my best to make the most of it.

A center railing divided the staircase into two lanes, which people were intuitively using as up and down. Traffic was light and the steps wide enough that if I kept close to the railing I could be out of the way. I moved down a few stairs, then back up, adjusting until I found the composition I wanted to draw. Only then did I think twice. Ocampo had sent me to be a spy. If I was aiming to be inconspicuous, standing literally in the middle of the staircase may not have been the best plan. But then I thought, the best place to hide was often in plain sight. And anyway, Ocampo wasn't here. And I wanted to draw.

I slid my bag from my shoulder, tucked it between my legs, and set about my routine.

* * *

My first act was not to sketch or to photograph, but to take a moment to look around—to really *look*. I was almost forty years old and had been drawing for pretty much my entire life, and yet almost every time I began a drawing I heard the voice of Mr. Hawbaker, my first real art teacher from eighth grade, who would always say, "Drawing is about seeing. Until you can truly see what you're looking at, you will never be able to draw it." And every time, that's how I began; by studying the scene, not just as a whole, but its parts. I observed how the angle of the shadow of the railing fell over the steps, and how the circular geometry of the hedges complemented the angular design of the staircase. I looked at the Headlands in the distance and saw not just mounds of far-off land, but the tops of an undulating surface that began at the hilltop where I was standing, dove beneath the water, then rose again to form those peaks. And how between, hidden by the waters of the Pacific flowing into the Bay, was the valley we called the Golden Gate. I held all these pieces in my mind, visualizing how I would translate them onto the page. And only then did I take out my camera.

As a rule, I avoided scouting in the middle of the day. Having the sun directly overhead was usually the worst time for light and shadow, creating the least contrast. I preferred early morning or late afternoon, when the sun was low and the shadows were long. But this was late November. Even when high, the sun hung heavily in the south, so the balance was good. Not that it mattered, seeing that my task wasn't actually to draw, but to photograph unsuspecting strangers.

Which definitely had me feeling uneasy. I didn't like spying on people. Morally, legally, and as a person who generally valued his privacy, on a do-unto-others level. I decided right then that I wouldn't do it. I wouldn't spy. Whatever had happened out at the Legion had been bullshit. And I wasn't about to break my own principles just to save myself from being punished for having *not* committed a crime. So there it was. The only photos I would take would be those I normally took, and any people who happened to be in the shots would simply be those who would have ended up in my shots anyway. And Ocampo was just going to have to deal with it—which of course meant I would too.

I set to shooting as I normally would. Beginning with wide shots of the entire scene, followed by detail shots of the foreground, middleground, then background, moving methodically left to right, top to bottom. But as I snapped away, I noticed something curious, which was that each time someone passed by—which was frequently, considering I was on a runner's highway—I lowered my camera and waited. Of course I did. The whole point of having reference photos was to be able to, literally, reference them later. Which meant I needed unobstructed shots. And people—at least when it came to documenting a landscape—were obstructions. The practice was

61

glaringly obvious when I thought about it, but one I'd been unconscious of until catching myself in the moment. What that meant for whatever may have happened at the Legion of Honor, I couldn't say.

I shot an entire roll of the view—and no people, which was sure to annoy Ocampo, but would be everything I needed to finish a drawing—then put my camera away and pulled out my pen and block of watercolor paper.

I uncapped my pen but hesitated. I was feeling self-conscious and exposed. It made no sense why Ocampo would have sent me here. Surely she didn't actually think I might get photos of any investigative use? Which made me wonder if I was being set up. But if so, then for what? To substantiate what had happened at the Legion? But why? As far as I knew, I hadn't done anything to anyone that might warrant retaliation, nor was I so important that the police would set out to entrap me. With the amount of real, horrific crime going on at any given moment, the idea felt narcissistic to even consider. And yet, naïve to dismiss.

I studied the faces of the people running by. No one bothered with even a glance. I turned and looked behind. One of Gary's Grinders caught my eye. But she was clearly hungry for anyone's gaze. I turned back and took a breath. Behaving as if everything was normal was the only way to look normal. So I resigned myself to whatever might happen, and set to drawing.

* * *

As I worked, I thought more about how I unconsciously avoided capturing people in my reference photos, and was reminded of Ocampo's asking if people tended to notice me as I worked. It was a good question, but more interesting to me was the opposite question: How much did I notice the people? Aside from making sure they didn't end up in my shots, how aware, really, was I of what went on around me?

If you had asked me even ten minutes before, I would have said that I was so used to working in chaotic environments, so accustomed to tuning out pounding jackhammers, honking car horns—even exhibitionist exercisers grinding to pop music—that, for all I knew, a completely naked woman could have been dancing around the Legion's courtyard and the only thing I would have seen undulating would have been the light across the Greco-Roman columns. That's a bit of an exaggeration, of course, but that's how focused I believed my attention was when drawing—and also why I couldn't rule out the possibility of a genuine misunderstanding at the Legion. But what if that belief was inaccurate?

I decided to put it to a test.

While I continued to draw, I quizzed myself on who was around.

Without looking at anyone directly, glancing only up and down between my paper and the view, I could tell you that on the landing down to my left, a trio of Chinese women had stopped an elderly white man and were asking him to take their photo. I knew that behind me, two or three steps up, a tourist couple—German, I guessed, with their pragmatic shorts, high wool socks, and well-worn Birkenstocks—were pausing to photograph Alcatraz in the distance. And I also knew that the middle-aged white guy who had just jogged past me was soaked in sweat not because he was out of shape, but because he was on at least his second or third lap, which I deduced because of his music. He was wearing an eighties yellow Walkman with the wire-band headphones and puffy orange pads, listening to Jethro Tull's *Aqualung*. An odd album to run to, I thought, but I'd caught a snippet of the song *Locomotive Breath* as he'd passed, which I happened to know was the second-to-last track on the album, and which told me he'd been running for at least half an hour.

I have to say, I was taken aback by how much I was aware of—or seemed to be. I of course couldn't know what all I was unaware of since, well, I wasn't aware. But I was certainly perceiving more than I would have thought myself capable of, which made me think once again of Mr. Hawbaker's dictum, and of how true it continued to be. To draw was to see. And apparently I saw much more than I even knew. Again, what that meant for what had happened at the Legion, I had no idea.

* * *

I had been working for around forty-five minutes when I sensed some-one watching me. A moment later, a tall woman, mid-sixties, dressed in three-quarter tan pants and safari hat, appeared at my side, confirming that I had been right.

"Hej!" she said with a sing-song lilt. Danish. "Are you drawing the view?"

It was a question that, after having been asked more than a few times over the years, I'd trained myself to *not* be an ass about. I mean, what did people think I was doing? The woman could clearly see the pad of paper in my hand. And more than enough lines were drawn to convey the scene. Could she not see that the image was the same as the view right in front of our faces? But of course she was just being friendly. And not everyone knew about drawing. So I did my best to be nice. As hard as it could sometimes be.

I said I was indeed drawing the view, then watched as she glanced back and forth between my drawing and the vista.

"Good, good," the woman said. Then she smiled and moved on. Par for the course of drawing in public.

After an hour, I had a solid linework drawing down. It wasn't completely finished, but it was far enough along that had this been any other day of site work I would have left. But there was still an hour before I was to meet Ocampo, so I figured I might as well use the time to my advantage. I set to fleshing out the dozens of rooftops on the houses in the Marina.

Over the next half-hour, two more people approached me. The first, a man, maybe thirty, stopped to jog in place as he looked at my drawing. He didn't say anything, just bounced up and down beside me breathing heavily as he glanced once at my drawing, then at the view. I said hello, and he just winked and clucked, then continued jogging down the stairs.

The second was the plein air artist's nightmare. The Chatty Kathy—or rather, a Chatty Karl. Late sixties, too well dressed for a noontime walk on the steps, and trailing a tiny white fluffy dog that was also too well dressed—the tartan vest cinched around its waist and purple bow tie under its neck matching his owner's outfit perfectly.

Like the Danish woman, I sensed him coming before he appeared. I heard him talking in a high-pitched, patronizing voice that could only have been to a creature leashed and unable to escape, and like seeing an accident about to happen but being powerless to stop it, my shoulders tensed with our impending crash.

"You are standing on quite a significant spot in San Francisco history," the man said, sidling up to me and launching into his monologue without any greeting—and blocking the path for everyone passing by as his tiny alter-ego stretched its leash across the lane. "In 1833, a soldier at the Presidio named Apolinario Miranda was granted land half a mile to the east of here, on a spring called El Ojo de Agua Figueroa. The grant included a small portion of the Presidio, which, as you likely know, ends right close to here."

I'd instinctually glanced at the man when he'd started talking—it's surprisingly difficult not to engage with someone who is talking to you—and instantly regretted it.

"Miranda, however, was a mean one," my self-appointed lecturer continued, seizing onto my reflexive acknowledgment as an invitation. "And when his young bride Briones grew tired of his abuse, she left him to build an adobe in what we now know as North Beach. A spirited soul in her own

right, she opened a dairy ranch in what became Washington Square, adopted a Native American girl, and in time purchased a sizable cattle ranch in the Santa Clara Valley, which, as acknowledged by many in her day, she ran impeccably. Quite extraordinary feats for an illiterate woman alone in the world. Briones died in 1889 at the age of 87, having lived under three flags and witnessed the hamlet she helped found grow into one of the largest cities in these United States."

As rich as his historical knowledge was, I really wanted him to leave. It wasn't that I didn't like talking to strangers—not that I was doing any talking. Random interactions with people I might never otherwise meet made life interesting. Aside from learning new facts about the city, chance conversations had landed me more than a few commissions, and even a couple of dates. But this guy, he was a type. He didn't care about me—or the joggers whose way he was in. I was just a fixed object to talk to, his captive audience until I either packed up and left, or told him off. It wasn't my first time dealing with this kind of character, though. I usually began with my standard joke: "I don't mean to be rude, but this is actually my office right now. So if you don't mind, I need to focus on my work." To which people tended to respond one of three ways: laugh and leave; tell me I was rude and leave; or just keep talking. I preferred the first and was fine with the second, but if this was the third then I would have to improvise. After several minutes of his historical monologue, I was just about to deliver my line when he bent down and started cooing to his bow-tied dog in a baby voice, then wandered off without even a goodbye. Even better.

* * *

At two-twenty-five I'd had enough. The linework wasn't completely finished, but it was much farther along than I would have done had I not been on Ocampo's clock.

I put the cap on my pen and slid the watercolor block into my bag. Then I took out my camera, pressed the small release button on the underside of the body, and wound the film into its spool. I popped open the back panel of the Pentax, removed the canister, then installed a fresh roll. I set the perforations of the exposed tab onto the teeth of the gears, advanced the shutter lever while pressing my finger on the film to be sure it caught, then closed the panel, clicked the shutter, and advanced the film again.

It was common for me to shoot a site multiple times, be it over hours, days, even months. By capturing even subtle changes in the sun's position,

I could later choose the hour, day, or even season I preferred to render. And while the sun had moved a bit further west in the two hours since shooting the first roll, instinct told me the earlier shots were more desirable to work from. But reference wasn't why I was shooting a second round. Ocampo was expecting a roll of film. And I couldn't count on her returning it to me.

I methodically shot another round of complete reference photos—again making sure to not capture even a single person—then wound that film into its canister and popped it out.

After sliding my camera into my bag, I took out a Sharpie. On the first roll of film I wrote, 11/23/99—12:45 p.m. And on the second, 11/23/99. But no time.

The first roll was what I would keep, print, and use to draw from. The second I would give to Ocampo.

* * *

"What do you mean, you didn't do it?"

Ocampo and I were pressed in tight, standing at the counter of the legendary Vietnamese joint Tu Lan. We were at Sixth and Market, one of the seedier blocks of San Francisco. I'd lived two years in Southeast Asia and seen cleaner back alleys in downtown Bangkok. Tu Lan was a gem, though. Hands-down the best vermicelli in town. At some point, the legendary TV chef Julia Child had visited and given them her seal of wacky approval, and they made sure you knew it. A blurred reproduction of the newspaper article with Child's face took up half the page of their oversized laminated menu.

"I went to the steps and drew," I said. "But I didn't take photos of any people, suspicious or otherwise. Not that there were any—suspicious, I mean. There were definitely lots of people."

Ocampo held up the roll of film I'd given her—the second roll, which I didn't care if I got back. "And so what's on this?"

"A bunch of reference shots for the drawing I made. To prove I was there."

Her expression told me she had so many things to say that she couldn't decide where to start. I didn't give her time to choose.

"Because this whole thing," I said. "Was just a test, right?"

A woman emerged from the crowd and asked what we wanted. She was holding a small receipt pad and pen, poised to write, while also scanning the room.

"I already ordered," Ocampo said to me. "To go."

I only had to glance at the menu to know what I wanted. "Number seventeen," I said. "Grilled pork vermicelli with an extra fried spring roll." Then I added, "Actually, make that two orders—both to go." I figured I'd bring one home for Larissa.

The woman sped off. A burst of flames shot up from the grill as one of the line cooks threw a pot of water into a giant wok. The place filled with smoke, which was another feature of Tu Lan. Five minutes inside and your clothes would be saturated with greasy smoke. It was worse than being at a campfire. If you didn't immediately change when you got home, everything you owned would smell like a Vietnamese grill for a week.

I leaned toward Ocampo. "I'm right," I said. "Aren't I?"

"About what?"

"That sending me to Lyon Street was a test. At the Legion, a woman had accused me of spying, but I proclaimed my innocence, so you tested me by seeing if I'd do it again, at your behest."

"I see," Ocampo said. "And by *not* photographing the public as I'd asked, this was your way of proving your innocence?"

"Yes."

"And for this you expect me to forget the complaint?"

I nodded.

Ocampo closed her eyes, heaved a big sigh, and shook her head. However she had anticipated her day to have gone, this was clearly not it. I understood how she felt.

From across the counter a hand thrust out a bag. Ocampo took the food, then started to move away.

"Wait," I said. "So where does this leave us?"

"I'll look at the photos, then get back to you."

"And what about the background check?"

She jerked back. "Seriously? You're telling me you *didn't* take photos at the steps because you didn't want to cross a moral line, but you're still asking me to give you—a civilian who was brought into my station on a public-nuisance complaint—access to sensitive legal documents about an eighteen-year-old? A girl that you've already admitted to getting drunk and letting spend the night? Are you trying to get me to arrest you?"

"Well, when you put it that way it sounds bad, but . . . I mean, she's the one who broke into my house and—"

Ocampo's brows shot up. "Wait—she broke into your house?"

"Well, okay, not broke in exactly. She sweet-talked my shop manager into letting her into my flat, so that——"

Ocampo flashed her hand for me to stop. "Hold on a second. A teenage girl who you'd never met gained unlawful access to your home, and—where is she now? Is she still there? Alone?"

"Yeah, but I'm sure it's fine. I mean, if she'd wanted to loot the place she could have done that yesterday before I even got home."

Ocampo looked exhausted. She started to say something, then stopped herself. Instead, she just shook her head and turned to leave. But before pushing into the crowd she stopped again. She turned and looked at me sideways. "Tell me," she said, with a curious smirk. "Of all the things you could have asked me for just now, why didn't you also ask for your roll of film from the Legion?"

"Because I don't need it to work from," I said. "The light that day was terrible. Even with that roll I'd have to go back and reshoot." Which was true. But what was also true—and what I wasn't going to share—was that I was more convinced than ever that the accusation at the museum had been a hoax. And—in what I was secretly enjoying as a delightful twist—it had been Ocampo who had helped convince me. Her sending me out to the steps had made me aware of my unconscious habit of lowering my camera whenever someone walked by. And now that I'd realized it, I was even more confident that I hadn't accidentally photographed anyone that day in the courtyard.

"Interesting," Ocampo said, bobbing her head. Whatever frustration I'd caused her was now replaced by amusement. "Given the situation, I would have thought, more than anything, you would have wanted that film back." She stepped in close, a devious grin blooming on her face. "Considering that I've seen the prints."

Corner of Clay and Spruce Streets, San Francisco — Patron asked to be unnamed. He didn't live here, nor did he have any relationship to the house or with its occupants. His request was simply that I draw "A stately mansion from Pacific Heights, preferably on the corner," with no more explanation or additional guidance. When he picked up the drawing, he finally told me his reason. "I need some aspirational art to hang above my writing desk." Which he went on to explain wasn't a desk but a sleeping bag on the floor of a dark one-room basement apartment. I don't know where he's living now, but I often see his name in the masthead of some of the world's most prestigious publications.

7

TODAY WE BLEED

couldn't decide if Ocampo was messing with me or not—I mean, absolutely she was messing with me. But in regard to having found something incriminating on my roll of film from the Legion, I couldn't be sure—especially after I'd just been feeling so confident. I watched her weave through the crowd toward the door, unclear as to whether this afternoon was ending better or worse than it had begun. I supposed it wasn't over yet.

I had to wait only a few minutes before my food was ready. I was hungry and could have easily stayed and eaten at the counter, but every minute inside Tu Lan meant that much more smoke in my clothes. Also, I'd been gone for longer than I'd anticipated, and while I wasn't exactly looking forward to taking a paternity test, I didn't want Larissa calling Adam. Explaining all of this was going to give him enough of a laugh as it was. I didn't need him hearing the story from Larissa, then calling every precinct in town.

I'd parked the Miata between a pawn shop and video porn arcade. When I got to the car I found a shirtless man leaning over my roof. He was peeling up the strip of tape on the driver's side, smoothing it back down, then peeling it up again, each time calling out, "Ziiiiip!" As I stepped up to the car he grinned, bobbed his head, then wandered off. Between the second slice in the roof and now this, I felt I now had confirmation that my directive to PEEL HERE wasn't connecting with my fellow citizens in the way I'd intended.

*   *   *

I drove back to the Mission singing *Locomotive Breath* to myself the whole way, the song having been planted in my brain by the runner at the steps. It was still before after-work time and I easily found parking, snagging the cheater spot just a few doors down from my building. As I was passing the shop, I decided I would once more hold off on asking Betty about why she'd let an unknown teenager into my home. I'd had enough confrontations for the day. Anyway, she didn't appear to be in, and the place didn't appear to be flooded. So I took both as a win.

If there hadn't been a teenage girl in my place, I would have stripped off my clothes just inside the front door and gone up the stairs naked to immediately shower and wash the smell of Tu Lan out of my hair. Instead, I went up dressed and smelling as I did. To my surprise though, Larissa wasn't there. My first thought was to look around to see if anything had been stolen. I hadn't once worried she might rob me, but Ocampo had poisoned my mind. Everything seemed to be in place.

Still, I wondered where she might be. Then, setting the bag of food on the kitchen island, I saw the handwritten note:

Parnassus Bloodwork. Meet there at 5:00—unless you're in the slammer. Today we bleed!

* * *

I took off my clothes, put them in a plastic bag so my entire place wouldn't smell like a Vietnamese grill, then got in the shower for the second time that day.

When I stepped out, the flat was still empty. Which didn't surprise me. Larissa's note had said to meet her at the lab. Which made her absence only more curious. The lab was halfway across town. I wondered not only how she'd chosen it, but how she would get there.

It was just before four. Soon there would be traffic, so I needed to leave by four-thirty at the latest. That gave me half an hour to rest and prepare— though I wasn't sure how one prepared to take a paternity test.

I put one of the orders of pork vermicelli in the fridge, then opened the other to mix up. As I was reaching for a bowl, it dawned on me what was in the cardboard box I'd hefted up the stairs the night before. I scampered down the hallway, carried the box into the studio, and sliced it open with a utility knife.

I'd been right. Inside was a set of handmade ceramic dishware. Four large plates, four mugs, and four large soup bowls. An exquisite, one-of-a-kind set, made by a woman named Claire, a retired nurse who was having a second career as a ceramicist. For years she came into the shop twice a week, Mondays to do her household wash, and Fridays her studio wash. In June she'd told me that after twenty years of living in a rent-controlled apartment she was being evicted through the Ellis Act—a legal loophole for property owners to get rid of long-term tenants by taking buildings off the rental market—and was moving to Reno to live with her daughter. I'd just received a bill for the renovations I'd started a few months before—which were only halfway finished and already twice what I'd budgeted—and I was still recovering from the shock, so the last thing I had in that moment was money. But I'd always loved Claire's work, and with her leaving town, I knew it might be my last chance to get some. I'd already started taking on commissions as fast as I could get them and, despite needing every dollar I could earn, felt it only right to place a commission of my own. I told her about the new open-floor-plan kitchen I had coming, and to make me whatever she thought appropriate. To justify the purchase, I told myself I would dedicate the sale of one of my future drawings to pay for the order.

After that I'd forgotten about it. But now, as I carried the new set to the kitchen, I considered which of my recent drawings might be the most fitting to represent Claire's ceramics. As I washed one of the bowls, I decided it would be my drawing of the Roxie Theater on 16th Street. A couple years back, Claire and I had run into each other there at the annual animation festival, *Spike & Mike's*, where we discovered we both had an appreciation for truly wrong yet utterly hilarious cartoons. After, we'd gone out for drinks and formed a friendship beyond the cursory laundromat proprietor and local patron, which was how I'd learned about her passion for ceramics. The Roxie was maybe a tenuous connection, but the whole exercise was symbolic anyway. While each person who commissioned me had their own private reason for wanting a drawing, aside from the pride I took in the work, I rarely had any emotional attachment to what I made—or at least not to the extent that they did. The Roxie, for example, had been commissioned by a woman who had worked in the box office while attending school for film editing. She was now a successful videographer in New York, and while for her the drawing would always be a reminder of her hand-to-mouth days in San Francisco, and how far she'd come, for me it was just my neighborhood theater—a place I loved and was more than happy to draw—but without the deep attachment she had. Now, though, whenever I saw a film there I would think of my friendship with Claire.

*   *   *

I mixed the vermicelli in one of her lovely functional works of art, shoved a chopstick-full into my mouth, then, bowl in hand, headed toward the front of the flat.

Roxie Theater, 16th Street, San Francisco — Patron asked to be unnamed

At my desk I saw the light on my answering machine blinking. I pressed PLAY and settled into my chair to eat my Vietnamese food as I listened.

The message was from Alma, the personal assistant of one of my new patrons, Steven Thorn. Steven owned a vacation house at Stinson Beach that he wanted me to draw. Depending on traffic, Stinson was an hour-and-a-half drive across the bridge, much of it a snaking, stomach-churning route through the Marin Headlands. It was easily a day trip, but to adequately scout the light I needed to see the site at all times of day, so part of the deal was that I get to stay at the house for two or three nights. I loved those kinds of commissions. Not only would I get paid, but I'd also get a free vacation.

Alma's message informed me that Steven's house had just come available for a long weekend, four nights, starting tomorrow, Wednesday. With Larissa here and Ocampo on my back, the timing wasn't ideal, but I seemed to recall that four consecutive nights at Steven's place were hard to come by.

I stuffed half a fried spring roll into my mouth and took out my commissions folder. At the moment I had fifteen active jobs on my plate, which was more than I preferred. I generally liked having no more than five to ten at any given time, so that when I finished one, I could feel a sense of accomplishment, then accept another. But I had renovations to pay for, so was piling them on. In the six months since resuming commissions, I'd already completed around thirty drawings. Many of them interesting sites. I'd done two versions of the "Green Monster" sculpture on Lake Merritt, as well as two of the Oakland Tribune tower. I'd drawn the Pulgas Water Temple in Redwood City, and Filoli Gardens, the historic country estate just down the road in Woodside. To my delight I was hired to draw the Lukas Glass Studio, a Mondrian-like building which for years I'd seen from the freeway but hadn't known was the workshop of a renowned stained-glass artist until being contacted by one of his former students, and I'd just started a drawing of the gorgeous Vedanta Society building in Cow Hollow, the Victorian Hindu temple where in 1914 a teenager famously set off a bomb killing his Swami teacher. All great places to have had reason to draw. Still, the quantity of work on my plate was overwhelming. Of the fifteen jobs, most were for one drawing, but two were for suites. There was the Legion set for ten drawings, and another from a commercial developer for what had initially been five drawings but was probably going to end up being more. That meant I had at least thirty new drawings I'd agreed to make, which meant I was already booked well into the next year. It was nice to know I would have an income, but it didn't leave much room for experimental art-making.

I hadn't done any work on Steven's house yet, so I flipped through the invoices until I found my notes. Reading through, the details came back to me. Steven wanted a drawing as a gift for his wife's birthday, which was just after New Year's, six weeks away. Most commissions had no deadline, but at the same time, to have one wasn't entirely unusual; so in the case of Steven, I offered my usual deal: to make his date for an additional charge. I could easily deliver in time, but only if I got access to the house soon. I picked up the phone and dialed Steven's office. Two rings, then Alma answered.

"I'm not sure about this weekend," I told her. "Are there any other times I can use the house?"

"Hi, Emit. Let me see . . ."

I ate more vermicelli as she checked her calendar.

"There are a few available dates here and there," she said. "But nothing consecutive. With the holidays approaching, Mr. Thorn has a lot of family coming and going, so nothing more than one free night until mid-January—which I know is past your deadline."

I thought about it. If I didn't take the next four days, having only one night here and there would make the timing extremely tight. The drawing itself I could do in a week, but I had no idea how long I might need for scouting. When it came to plein air work, the biggest unknown was weather. I'd had commissions where the light was perfect at the moment I happened to arrive, and others that took months to find even a passable moment worth rendering. And a place like Steven's was the ultimate in wild cards. Stinson Beach was classic northern California coast. I could go up there for four days and easily see nothing but fog. So if I waited until the last minute, gambling on good weather, I might blow the deadline. All of which meant I had no choice but to take the nights being offered. I didn't know how this would affect whatever I had going with Ocampo, or the blood test with Larissa, but if I wanted to keep the gig, this was what I needed to do.

"That's fine," I said. "Put me down for all four nights starting tomorrow. And if you don't mind, put me down for all the other open single nights as well. After this trip, I can let you know whether or not I need them, but for now I'd rather claim them before they get booked." My excuse was that I was only being prudent. If this trip didn't offer me the light I needed, then I would absolutely need the extra dates. But I was also giving myself a potential gift. People who commissioned drawings of their vacation properties rarely owned shacks, and it would hardly be terrible to have access to a free place on the ocean for a few extra days.

Tribune Tower, Oakland, CA — Patron asked to be unnamed

"You got it," Alma said, adding that she'd messenger over a packet with security codes and house instructions.

I confirmed the address of the shop, then ended the call.

After hanging up, I thought to call Adam, then changed my mind. Ocampo had implied that she'd found incriminating evidence on my roll of film. Whether her innuendo was true was to be determined. But whatever situation was at play, right now she was keeping it between herself and me. And something told me to wait for the next shoe to drop before involving anyone else.

* * *

Lukas Glass Studio, San Francisco — Patron asked to be unnamed

The blood lab Larissa had chosen was on Mount Parnassus, next to UCSF, which was known for excellent medical facilities. From the Mission I cut through the lower Haight to avoid the exiting freeway traffic on Fell Street, and as I drove, the reality of what I was about to do started to sink in: I was about to take a blood test to determine whether or not I'd fathered a child eighteen years ago. You heard stories like this all the time in the music world. Some were scams and others were real. And I took solace in knowing I wasn't the first—and surely wouldn't be the last—rock and roller, ex or otherwise, to find himself in this situation.

Curiously, though, more than how the test might turn out, I found my- self thinking about Larissa's mother. After all, she had been the one I would have had sex with. But she was a complete mystery to me. She'd been dead for eight years, and it bothered me that, if Larissa was in fact my daughter, I would never get to re-meet the mother of my child.

Larissa had been right, I didn't remember any of the women from that brief and outlandish period of my life. But I also rarely thought about that time. I had gone on to do so many random things that being in the band felt like another life—and was. Here and there I'd hear my music out in the world—mostly in convenience stores or on the classic-rock radio station, or sometimes as pirated "soft" versions in an elevator—and whenever some- one recognized me, it was usually to mistake me for my brother the actor. On rare occasion I'd get called out as the author of *Glass Houses*, but almost never as the singer from FurTrading. So there wasn't much in my day-to-day to remind me of that carnival-like life. But ever since Larissa dropped her bombshell, I'd been thinking back to those days, specifically to that first major tour, and bits of memories had been returning. Flashes of scenes, faces, even conversations. A lot of them really good. Those were fun years. Brian and I had still been a team. And we were young—damn we were young. And fearless. And of course utterly ridiculous.

Larissa had referenced the New Year's show we'd played, the one that launched us on the *Rock of the Beast* tour, and the memory had brought to mind one woman who I'd been sweet on. I still couldn't conjure her name, but I remembered that she'd started out the same as most of the girls I'd slept with, with a flirtatious look that ended as a sweaty, drunken romp on a dirty couch in a greenroom. Normally that would have been the end of it, and I would have forgotten her twenty minutes later. But she and I had actually hit it off. I remembered how she had this sweet way of looking at the ceiling and moving her head when she talked, and how her stories made me feel as if, even though I was supposed to be the star, she lived a far more interesting life. I couldn't remember if we'd met on New Year's or shortly after. All I remembered was that I'd asked her to stick around, and that she stayed with me on the bus for at least three or four more shows. The weird thing was that I also couldn't recall how or why it ended, but that when it did I was sad. I think I maybe even wrote a song about her. One that Brian would have surely mocked me for, a sappy ballad that now made me grateful we hadn't recorded a second album. Then I had a flash that not only had I written some lyrics, but that Brian and I had actually played around with an arrangement. One night in a hotel room, me trying to find a melody while Brian fooled around with some chords. Brian hadn't mocked me about it all—in fact, he'd thought it might be our next hit single, our version of the Stones' *Angie*. And that's when I remembered her name: Simone.

*   *   *

I was now at the end of Haight Street, turning on to Stanyan. I passed Kezar Stadium, wiggled my way through Cole Valley over to Mount Sutro, then parked in the indoor lot of a medical building at the address on Larissa's note. Larissa was in the waiting room when I arrived. She was wearing a light blue pullover hoodie, which I immediately took note of, considering that everything I'd seen her wear thus far had been either black or gray.

As I filled out my intake form, she wrinkled her nose, then leaned in close to me and gave a sniff. I'd changed my clothes and showered, but the Miata had still reeked of Tu Lan. Some must have rubbed off on the drive.

"What did that cop do to you?" she asked. "Literally hold you over a fire?"

"Yes."

We were shown into separate rooms. The nurse was friendly yet efficient, and the procedure the same as every other time I'd given blood: tourniquet, hand squeeze, needle prick, small vial filling with black-red fluid, followed by cotton, bandage, "Bend your arm, please," then the small paper cup of apple juice.

Back out in reception, I had just finished paying the bill when Larissa came out.

"Forty-eight to seventy-two hours," the receptionist told us. "Good luck."

Larissa and I walked down the hallway in silence. As we boarded the elevator, she turned to me.

"What do you think 'good luck' means?"

*   *   *

We walked together through the parking garage.

"You're kidding?" Larissa said as we approached the Miata. "This is your car?"

"Yeah."

"What are you, a twelve-year-old girl?"

"Twelve-year-olds don't drive."

"Precisely."

She went to the passenger door and I to the driver's. Looking at her across the roof, I said, "What do you suppose people do after testing to see if they're related?"

"If you say go out for ice cream, I'm going to barf."

"You don't like ice cream?"

"I love ice cream. I just don't want you getting all mushy dad-figure on me."

"Me either. Come on. I have an idea." I got in the car.

She got in too, looking extremely suspicious. "Where are we going?"

I turned the ignition, looked at her, and smiled. "We're returning to the scene of the crime."

8

FOR THE LOVE OF EDITH

"Your car smells like a Vietnamese barbecue," Larissa said.

I laughed, then drove us across the inner Sunset, through Golden Gate Park, then into the Outer Richmond. Most of the drive we were silent. An easy silence; Larissa watching the scenery as I contemplated Larissa. While earlier I'd toyed with having doubts about her intentions—and had Ocampo fueling my suspicions—really, that's all it had been. Toying. Truth was, I trusted her. And not just because she could have robbed my flat and didn't, or even because I thought she might be my daughter. She may not have been what most people considered warm or open, but she was very much what-you-see-is-what-you-get, and I liked her. Weird thing was, I kind of liked Ocampo too. So it was more than possible that after all this was over, I would need to reevaluate my intuition.

At Lincoln Golf Course I cut up to our destination: the Palace of the Legion of Honor; the replica of the eighteenth-century Parisian building of the same name that sits atop a cypress-lined cliff overlooking the Golden Gate, and home to a collection of classical art.

We parked in the lot beside the newly installed—and oddly contrasting—bright red steel modernist sculpture *Pax Jerusalem* by sculptor Mark di Suvero, and only after we got out of the car did Larissa realize where we were going.

"You're taking me to a freaking art museum? I would have preferred ice cream."

We climbed the stairs and walked the path into the grand courtyard where we came upon Rodin's most iconic statue, and my old friend, *The Thinker*. I stopped and looked around. The space was open and airy, surrounded by stone columns. I positioned myself exactly where I'd been

Legion of Honor, San Francisco, 1 of 10 drawings — Patron asked to be unnamed

standing the day before, in what was essentially the middle of the courtyard, and did my best to replay the afternoon, from drawing to being arrested—or whatever I'd been; detained, brought in for questioning, abducted. Drawing at the Lyon Street Steps had shown me that my ability to tune out the chaos of my surroundings wasn't the same as my being unaware. And yet, for the life of me, I was still unable to come up with any scenario where I might have been mistaken for a peeping tom. If there had been even one questionable interaction, one peculiar, awkward, or even ordinary event, such as a child dropping a bottle from a stroller and the mother bending over to pick it up, then I could have at least seen where there might have been cause for misunderstanding. But there'd been nothing. Yes, there had been a few people around, but no one had stopped to see what I was drawing, no one had stood beside me to take their own picture of *The Thinker*, and no one had even said hello. As far as I could remember, not one person had even come within ten feet of me out there——and if they had, I now knew I would have lowered my camera.

Larissa was standing beside me, watching with a curious, yet also confused, expression.

"Is this, like, your version of church or something?"

I looked at her and smiled. She had no idea what was going on. And for the moment I was fine with that.

Out of habit, I had my drawing bag and camera with me. You never knew when a fleeting beam of sunlight would pass across a building in a way that made you feel like it was the perfect drawing you hadn't yet made. And I'd learned the hard way that it's almost impossible to recreate those moments. The light just then wasn't anything to celebrate though. The sun had set and the sky was foggy, making the courtyard a flat gray. To get good contrast I would need to come back another day. But since I was there, I decided to snap a few photos, just to have them. Larissa photo-bombed every one.

*   *   *

I was a member, so I got us tickets. The attendant informed us that the museum would be closing shortly.

Inside, just past the guard, was another well-known Rodin sculpture, *Saint John the Baptist.*

"Wow," Larissa said. "This guy's great. Doesn't it totally look like he's going, 'Yo, wassup?'"

"There's a story behind this piece," I said. "Rodin had made an earlier work, *The Age of Bronze,* for which his peers accused him of surmoulage, which is essentially being called a cheater. So for this sculpture he used an amateur model, and made the piece rougher and larger than life to prove them wrong."

Larissa scoffed. "Peers."

After the sculpture rooms we entered the painting galleries. Walls of trompe l'oeil still lifes depicted hyper-realistic dead game birds, rabbits, and fish. The next room had an excessive number of chubby cherubic babies in the arms of holy suffering peasants.

"I know this place is supposed to be full of masterpieces and all," Larissa said. "But a lot of this stuff creeps me out."

"Yeah, it isn't what I'd choose to live with."

"You think the artists actually liked painting these?"

"I don't know. We think about making art differently these days. More

85

as expression than as a trade. I imagine it's like the difference between when people married to join houses versus people now marrying for love."

Next came the portrait rooms; generals with swords, duchesses with excessively frilly gowns, and wistful young women with eerily white skin.

"A lot of the pieces in this museum," I said, "and a lot of art in general—at least up until the Industrial Revolution—were commissions. Before cameras, art was the only way people could own a likeness of themselves, or whatever it was they wanted an image of. Which is why you see so many portraits of royalty and merchants. Those were the people who could afford to hire artists. And obviously a lot of religious works too. The church commissioned some of what we now consider some of the greatest—"

"Propaganda."

I laughed. "Which it all was, really. Kings didn't have their portraits painted so they could marvel at an artist's creative interpretation. They did it so the people would know who was king—and because they were vain. And the church, they were all about promotion. So, yeah, we're looking at historic advertising. But it's also why we know a lot of the artists we do. Da Vinci, Michelangelo, they were court painters. We know their work because they had wealthy patrons, and the wealthy were who also subsidized museums, which is how those artists' images survived over others. All those Rodin sculptures we were just looking at? They're here because Alma Spreckels, a wealthy San Francisco socialite, went to Paris in the early 1900s and was charmed by an up-and-coming genius sculptor she'd met through one of her rich friends."

Larissa grunted. I looked at her and she rolled her eyes. "That word," she said. "*Genius*. It annoys me."

"Nevertheless. 'Big Alma,' as they called her, brought Rodin's work to America for the Pan American Exposition in 1915. She's also responsible for this museum being here. She persuaded her rich sugar-magnate husband Adolph to donate it to the city. If not for her wealth and influence—and interest in the arts—Americans might never have heard of Rodin. That said, patronage isn't the only reason we know the art we do. I think most work continues on because it's simply damn good—which is what inspired the patronage in the first place. Because it's not like every work of art ever commissioned ends up in a museum. I'm sure there have been countless pieces commissioned by wealthy patrons that we don't see because they don't have the staying power."

"Or because whatever rich person funding the next museum doesn't deem them worthy."

We moved into the next gallery.

"Things started changing after the Renaissance, though," I said. "Art became more accessible, so much so that everyday working people began to regularly commission paintings. As decoration, but also, oddly enough, as a form of courtship. If a man was interested in a woman, he'd pay an artist to paint her portrait, then give it to her as a gift. Some women would have dozens of portraits of themselves from all the suitors they turned down."

"Can you imagine being that artist?" Larissa said. "'Here we go again, *another* portrait of Edith.'"

"And what about poor Edith? Every week, having to sit for yet another damn portrait paid for by some slob at the market who wanted to sleep with her. At a certain point she probably just asked the artist if he could paint her from memory."

"And what about you?" Larissa asked. "Ever consider drawing the Ediths of the world instead of buildings?"

"I used to do portraiture," I said. "Figure work too. But it's been years. And these days I prefer the autonomy of cityscapes."

"You mean scenes that look like the aftermath of a nuclear apocalypse?"

I smiled. "Most people say they're peaceful. But yeah, I guess same thing."

"Hey, I'm not being critical. I assumed drawing pictures devoid of humans was your idealized version of the world. Which is fine by me. I know most places I go I'd like to erase people from the scene. I was just thinking about how much you enjoy the—" she pantomimed a dreamy-eyed, heartfelt pose "—'personal connections of commissions.'"

"I do. But I also appreciate that buildings don't worry I'm going to make them look fat."

As we continued through the museum, Larissa kept asking me about different pieces, which made me think I'd maybe set the bar too high talking about Rodin and patronage. I had to keep reading the wall placards to answer, and by the time we reached the Baroque gallery she deemed my knowledge of art history 'far inferior to what an allegedly successful artist should have,' and gave up asking.

We were only about a third of the way through the museum when a guard informed us that the building would be closing in fifteen minutes. We sped our way through the rest of the galleries, Larissa randomly pointing and saying, "Crap. Rip-off. Uninspired. Belongs in the bathroom." Until eventually a guard who had been following us got uncomfortably close.

"I think he wants us to leave," I said.

"Or hire me as a docent."

* * *

Outside, night had full-on descended. As we navigated the path back toward the parking lot, Larissa stopped beside one of the two stone lions guarding the entrance and asked for my camera.

I handed it to her.

Behind us, the museum was looking especially stately. Stark beams from spotlights hidden in the grass cast majestic lighting up onto the façade.

Larissa studied the camera for a moment, assessing how it worked. Then she raised it up to her eye and focused the lens. Not on the lions, or on the building, but to the side, on a bronze sculpture on the lawn, *El Cid*. In the spotlights and fog, the heroic depiction of the Spanish knight atop a horse looked as if a fearless warrior were charging into a blazing nighttime battle. Holding steady, she pressed the shutter release. Then she lowered the camera and studied it again. "Why do you keep using this old thing?"

"It's an elegant device. It does everything a camera should, simple and precise, without any bells and whistles."

"Yeah, but there's simple, then there's efficient. You have heard of a thing called technology, right?"

"At one time, this was."

"And at one time people's idea of a sexy pickup line was to commission a portrait."

"Poor Edith. She should have just married the artist, then she could have shared in the profits." I decided to take a play out of Larissa's book and changed the subject. "So when I got home this afternoon, you were out. Where did you go?"

Larissa advanced the film again, lifted the camera to her eye, and this time pointed it at me. I relaxed my stance and smiled.

She pressed the shutter and lowered the camera. "I was at The Arcade."

"Playing video games?"

She laughed and handed me the Pentax. "Oh my god. For a guy who lives in one of the hottest neighborhoods in the city, you know nothing about what's going on."

"I know that up until recently the Mission was not the hottest part of the city. Not until the tech swarm descended."

I advanced the film, raised the camera, and focused the lens on Larissa.

She raised her hand and turned away just as I snapped a picture.

"The Arcade is a nonprofit computer center in the Tenderloin," she said, sitting on the stone stairs. "Started by Faith Chadwick."

"I know that name," I said, trying to remember where I'd recently heard her mentioned. Then it came to me. "It was last night. On that Public Access show. They were talking about shady real estate deals. She's the developer catching flak over the Mission Bay project for trying to build on protected wetlands." I sat down beside Larissa and put my camera back into my bag. We were both facing the parking lot, and I could see the Miata. It was one of only three cars left and reminded me of the ticket I'd gotten the night before. I reflexively looked around to make sure there weren't any DPT vehicles.

"Yeah," Larissa said. "I've heard the rumors, but I enjoy politics about as much as I do paintings of musket rifles and dead pheasants. I know of Faith because she also started The Nest."

"Right," I said, my memory jogged again. "There's a story with that place. It had been big news a few years back. Her husband got shot by a homeless person, and so she donated a building to be a rehab center—is that right? I have to say, I don't think I would have had it in me to have been so kind."

"Actually," Larissa said, "the story is even more tragic. The Nest is a nonprofit for runaway kids. Faith and her husband opened it a few years before he died. It's this really progressive model, a sort of cross between a shelter, halfway house, and commune where teens can live if they take on roles to run the place. One night, Faith sent one of the kids from The Nest over to another one of their buildings. She didn't know her husband was going to be there, or he didn't know the girl was coming, or something like that. She let herself in with a key, and he thought she was an intruder and got a gun. I don't know how it happened exactly, but her husband ended up getting shot. The whole thing is just sad." Larissa leaned forward and fussed with the laces on her Converse shoes. "The amazing thing is, Faith didn't blame the girl. She actually took responsibility for the mistake and made sure the girl wasn't prosecuted. And after, she put even more time and money into The Nest. She started programs to help kids get their GEDs, and even offered scholarships for college. And now she's opened The Arcade, which is a computer education center."

"And why were you there?"

"Volunteering. It's a really cool place. It's in this old Deco building full of murals of retro dot-matrix-y eighties video games—hence the name. It just opened. Faith got some bigwig at Apple to donate like, thirty computers, and the place is run by older kids from The Nest and volunteers from the community who donate their time to tutoring." She cinched a fresh bow on one of her shoelaces. "I figured since I was up here, I might as well check it out. I taught HTML to like twelve kids today."

"Up here? I thought you lived in Connecticut."

For a moment she looked called out. Then she said, "No. I'm going to school at Stanford."

"Oh . . ." Now it made sense why she'd been able to identify my drawing of the Linear Accelerator. "How long have you been there?"

She turned to me. "Are you going to get pissed that I waited to come find you?"

I shrugged. "Depends. How long have you thought I might be your father?"

"A while."

"As in, the whole time you've only been forty miles away?"

"As in, I wanted to wait until I was eighteen." She turned so she was full-on facing me. "Don't be angry. Being a legal adult was important to me. I wanted to be my own person when we met—at least in the eyes of the law."

"Okay . . ."

"Think about it from my perspective," she said. "My mom is dead, and I didn't know what kind of person you might be. You could have been a burned-out rock and roller who would have refused to take a blood test for fear he'd have to sign on as my official guardian. With my being a legal adult, it was one less complication to deal with—for both of us."

I thought about it, and agreed. "Fair enough," I said. "And smart."

"Thanks. I'm glad you understand."

"I do. And really, me being a burned-out rock and roller could have been the least of your worries." And that's when I told her about how the last time I was here at the museum, I'd been arrested for lewd behavior.

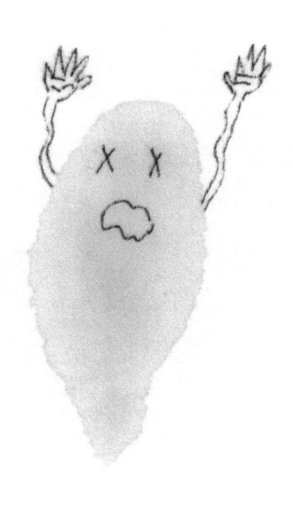

9

HOWLING GHOSTS

"That is totally messed-up," Larissa said.

"I know—wait. Do you mean the woman at the museum or Ocampo?"

"The cop," Larissa said. "She's like, totally dirty. Screw her for abusing her authority. But also you—" Larissa winced. "I mean, it is pretty pervy to take pictures of women without them knowing."

"I was *not* taking pictures of women," I said sharply. "But yes, I agree, *had* I been, it would be pervy. And I also agree that it's messed-up for Ocampo to be extorting me." Though I left out the part where she'd insinuated that there was actual proof against me—and that I'd asked her to do a background check after going through Larissa's bag.

Larissa looked back at the Legion, as if she were worried someone might be coming. "So how are you, like, not banned from the museum now?"

"Because I wasn't officially arrested—and because I didn't actually do anything. You seem to keep forgetting that very critical fact."

Larissa was confused. "So why are you even bothering with this cop then? And why haven't you called a lawyer?"

"Um, because maybe I got derailed by a strange young woman breaking into my house to inform me she might be my offspring?"

"I didn't break in," Larissa said. "And anyway, I prefer the word 'spawn.'"

* * *

We were both getting cold and so I suggested we do something more exciting, like go to the Top of the Mark, downtown. "It's a posh spot where we can have a bite and get a three-sixty view of the city."

"I don't need exciting," Larissa said. "Or fancy. But I would like to go somewhere that doesn't make me feel like I need to join the AARP."

I said I knew exactly the place.

I drove us back to the Mission and surprisingly snagged one of my cheater spots on the first pass. Then I walked us to 16th Street.

"If this is the hottest neighborhood in the city right now as you claim," I said, "you're about to see why. Which means it's also going to be ruined soon after all the uncool people who are flocking here drive out what makes it cool—or hot. I can't remember, which is it?"

She squinted at me. "I'm both confused and entertained by how simultaneously insightful and obtuse you can be."

"You're welcome."

I took her to Adobe Books, a hole-in-the-wall bookshop that hadn't seen sunlight in years and felt like the only hoarder's home you were happy to visit. The shelves were crammed with used books of all shapes and sizes, as were the floors, with stacks crowding the aisles to the point of obscuring passage. There were old couches, sunken and without feet, covered in threadbare blankets, and a love seat that had long given all its love but still wanted to try. There was no overhead lighting—or, if there was, the switches had been covered over with garage-sale art and tattered Deco prints. Lamps draped with sheer scarves lit the maze. Piles of books were used as stands for tabletops on which more books were stacked. The cave-like antiquarium was enchanting in its chaos, and most days you'd find at least one random person asleep on a couch with an open book on their chest. In the back was a small gallery space. Twelve by twelve feet, if that. I'd thought I remembered there being an opening that night, and I was right. A handful of art-goers were milling about, and the gallery was selling cups of Two-Buck-Chuck—the bargain-bin wine from Trader Joe's grocery store that had been made famous after a snobby wine critic had supposedly been fooled into thinking it was high-end. Charles Shaw wines actually sold for three dollars a bottle, but Two-Buck clearly had a better ring. Cups were a dollar a pop and Larissa bought two, but I refused mine.

"I'll give you a twenty if you give those to a panhandler and spare us the inevitable headaches."

She drank both herself.

The exhibit was definitely *not* classical art, as was Larissa's request, and very much late-twentieth-century San Francisco. The walls of the small room were covered with black-and-white photographs of men's penises. A didactic explained that the photographer was a prostitute, and that these were all photos of her clients' genitalia after the act of paid sex.

"Again," Larissa said, "I'm thinking I might have preferred ice cream."

"You said you didn't want any gushy dad-figure stuff."

"True. And you did say you were going to take me to do something more exciting."

I'd been going for contrast. Though, in retrospect, taking my eighteen-year-old potential daughter who I just met to an exhibit of male genitalia right after telling her I'd been arrested for being a pervert might not have been the smartest move. I thought to explain that, while I knew there was an opening, I hadn't known the content of the show. But standing in front of dozens of semi-erect, moist penises for any longer than we had to seemed to only exacerbate the irony, so I suggested we get tacos.

16th Street was hopping. Bar Elixir, the Kilowatt, Dalva, the music was pumping and you could smell the stale beer from the street. The sidewalks were packed. Techies, Townies, Marina girls, transvestites, I can't say they were all getting along, but they were all hanging out. There was no short-age of panhandlers, and with the 16th Street BART station being a hive for hookers and black-tar heroin dealers, you had your share of junkies and neon-pink vinyl miniskirts roaming the streets as well. Yeah, I supposed the neighborhood was hot. But to me it was just the Mission. Where everyone in the city came to get lit, then stumbled home to wherever they might be lucky enough to have a bed.

Taqueria Pancho Villa was a large cafeteria-style Mexican joint with easily fifteen employees working behind the counter making assembly-line burritos and cooking buckets of meat on long, flat grills. There was always a line out the door, and sometimes it even moved fast. When you got to the counter, bits of beef and chicken would fly at you as mounds of charred meat were being cleaved two feet away.

"I know you were married once," Larissa said to me while we were standing in line. "To your former editor. And that you guys didn't have any children. Have you ever wanted kids?"

The line had moved us from the sidewalk to the doorway. Pancho Villa was one big open space with high ceilings in a building that may have once been a bank. In front of us was a large room and behind was the open street, both with ample opportunities for someone to dart away and pretend they hadn't heard a question. I, however, was trapped in its doorway with nowhere to run, face-to-face with a young woman who might very well be my daughter, being asked my thoughts on children.

I made a pained expression as if I'd just watched a very wide strip of tape being ripped from the chest of a very hairy man.

Larissa laughed.

Seating was two dozen tables with acrylic tops so thick you could sink your fingernails in—and a lot of people had. The chairs were low, uncomfortable box-like things covered with thick bands of stretched leather, most of which were over-stretched and left that way; I assumed so no one would stay very long. Larissa and I ordered, took our number, then sat crammed amid a hundred other people. In a stroke of luck, before she could press me any more on the subject of whether I'd ever wanted kids, one of the many Mariachi bands that roamed the neighborhood stepped inside and began to play. Between the large guitarrón bass guitar, trumpet, and accordion, we would have had to have known sign language if we'd wanted to communicate. The trio played three songs, the only one I recognized being the classic love song, *La Llorona*; and as they finished performing, we were also finishing eating. We stood, and that's when the only non-Latin employee appeared at our table. A young white man with Down syndrome who bused tables and could instantly tell you the day of the week you were born. If you'd eaten at Pancho Villa, you'd been asked and answered by him more than once. Larissa told him October 27, 1981, and he immediately said "Tuesday," then swept our small plastic food baskets into his bin and moved to the next table. It wasn't world-class dining, but it was definitely San Francisco. And the grin on Larissa's face as we exited the loud and sticky-floored taqueria told me she was plenty happy.

* * *

Back outside, we dodged drunks, beggars, and more than one person sprawled unconscious on the sidewalk.

"I've been meaning to ask," I said, "what was your mother's name?"

"Why? You think you might actually remember her?"

"Maybe. I was thinking back to that tour, and I remembered a woman I was sweet on for a while. It's a long shot. I just thought it would be nice if she had been your mother. Her name was Simone."

Just then we were once again interrupted by a roving band, this one a group of thirty men in suits and fedoras who began singing *Bird on the Wire* by Leonard Cohen, a cappella. They were a local men's choir called

the Conspiracy of Beards, who sang only Cohen songs. In the midst of the urban cacophony they were harmony incarnate. If Leonard couldn't make your heart weep, these guys could. We stayed for *Bird on the Wire* and the classic *So Long Marianne* before they moved on. I couldn't have dialed up a better night if I'd tried.

*　　*　　*

It was after eleven when we got home. Larissa said she was tired. I had two couches in the flat, one in the studio and one in the living area, and in her short time at Hotel Emit, she had already slept on both. The studio was far more private, so I offered to get her officially settled there.

I pulled a clean set of linens, an extra pillow, and a blanket from the hall closet, and told her she could use one of my work benches for her things. She didn't have much, only her laptop and rucksack, which held her toiletries and a few changes of clothes. As she was laying them out, I noticed her clothes were essentially all the same: three identical plain black T-shirts, one black hoodie, one pair of black jeans, one pair of gray sweatpants, and several pairs of underwear and bras, all also black, and of identical style. Pretty much an entire wardrobe of black—which made the light-blue pullover she was wearing that much more curious. That's when I saw it had a fresh stain on one of the pockets.

"Salsa," she said, tugging out the front and looking down. "Oh well."

"Come," I said, "let's get that out before it sets permanently."

"Don't worry about it," she said. "I'm a clumsy eater. You saw me last night with the Thai food. You probably thought it was because I was drunk, but I'm telling you, I'm like that all the time. I have stains on pretty much every piece of clothing I own. That's why I draw faces on them." She went to the bench and held up the gray sweatpants she'd been wearing that morning. What I'd taken for a logo was actually a stain, a splash of food or drink having flown off course during its path from utensil to mouth. Only she'd transformed it. Around the edge she'd traced an outline with a thin black marker, and inside she'd drawn eyes and a mouth to turn the shape into a howling ghost.

"I love it," I said. "Only how about we try to save this one from becoming art?" I got my keys. "Come on. It'll be easy—and anyway, I've got a load to do as well. It's one of the benefits of owning a laundromat."

I gathered my bag of Tu Lan clothes from the shower-room floor, then we went back downstairs.

"So why a laundromat?" Larissa asked.

"Why not?" We'd left the exterior gate and were walking to the front door of the shop. "It's an honest neighborhood business."

"Are you implying that art isn't an honest business?"

I inserted my key and undid the lock. "No. Only that with art you're never done."

"Right."

"Interesting," I said, letting us in and turning on the lights.

"What?"

"You didn't ask what I meant."

She shrugged. "I took it to mean that art isn't a regular job where you get to clock out and go home. That just because you finish a drawing or a book or an installation of hundreds of Super Balls being shot at strangers, doesn't mean you ever feel done." A thought crossed her mind and she wobbled her head. "So, then, okay. I get it. This place, it's like your normal life—or what you keep to try and make yourself feel you have a normal life. One that's routine and consistent."

"Actually," I said, locking the door behind us, "I couldn't care less about normalcy. And the only routines I like are the ones I can pick up and put down at will. Consistency, though—" I switched on the power for the machines "—when it comes to having a regular income, now that I'm all for."

"And how's that working out?"

"Well, half of what I earn I pay Betty, and the other half I spend on insurance and replacing blown water regulators—and of course paying off my renovations. Then there's the part where Betty lets strangers into my house to ambush me—which is definitely a strike against normalcy."

"To be fair," Larissa said, "I told Betty I was your cousin's daughter here to visit colleges, and that you'd promised to pick me up from the airport but didn't show."

"Not bad. But I thought you said you told her I might be your father."

"Did I say that?"

I laughed and moved toward the machines. "Come on, let's get this stuff in the wash."

Larissa stopped at a washer as I went into the back room. "I don't know why I even bother buying light-colored clothing," she said. "I should just give in and commit to head-to-toe black."

On the shelf in the office I found a bottle of stain remover and another of detergent. As I was turning to go I saw there was a large envelope on the desk. It was addressed to me with a sticker of the bicycle messenger service, Aero Delivery. Then I remembered. Alma, Steven Thorn's assistant, had sent over the information for the Stinson house.

Stepping into the main room, I saw Larissa pulling her stained blue hoodie over her head. Underneath she had on a T-shirt—black, of course—which was being tugged up and exposing the skin of her midriff. Her shirt continued higher to reveal her bra—also black. It wasn't exactly indecent, but the problem was, right then, someone had stepped up to the window, cupped their hands against the glass, and was peering in.

*Pulgas Temple, Redwood City, CA — Commissioned by Mari Grayle. This monument to the
Hetch Hetchy water reservoir is a favorite spot for bridal photography. Mari was to go one
step further and get married on the grounds. Day of the wedding, she drove herself, and as she
approached the entrance she kept going. She commissioned this drawing for what would have
been her five-year wedding anniversary, but was now what she called her five-year "Ditching-
Her-Man-at-the-Altar Anniversary." When she told me the story, she was as happy as could be.*

10

AN IRREGULAR CALL

t was nighttime, so for someone outside, the lights inside the shop illuminated the scene like a stage. I was in the rear, Larissa was in the center, and a man was at the front window. My eyes met his as between us Larissa was appearing to undress.

Larissa got her pullover off, tugged down her shirt, saw that I was staring past her, then turned toward the window to see what had my attention. The man was smiling and waving.

"Friend of yours?" Larissa asked me.

"Not that I know of," I said.

She flipped the guy off.

The face at the window laughed, then the man knocked on the glass, pointed at me, and wiggled his finger to come near.

I waved my hand and called out, "We're closed."

The guy just kept wiggling his finger.

I sighed, handed Larissa the stain remover and detergent. "And this is also the Mission."

"We're closed," I said again to the guy, going to the door. I was glad I'd locked it after coming in.

"I'm not here to do my laundry," the man said through the glass. He was a white guy, younger and better dressed than I would have expected for someone accosting a laundromat proprietor at that hour. And he didn't look drunk. "I'm here to talk about you photographing strangers in public places."

That had my attention. Now I definitely wasn't going to unlock the door.

"You're going to let me in eventually," the man said. "So you may as well do it now."

We stared at each other for a few seconds, then I went back to Larissa. I tossed my dirty clothes into a washing machine, then unlocked the coin box with my master key. I scooped up a handful of quarters and gave them to her. "Use these to run the wash," I said, then I went back to the door.

"If you have something to say," I said, "then say it. But I'm not letting you in. And I can easily camp out here all night."

Again the man laughed.

Behind me, I heard the clunk of the coin slot being pushed into the washing machine and the beep of the electronic buttons being pressed.

The man's brows rose crookedly in a way that said, "You sure?" Then he shrugged, stepped back, and spread his arms wide as if to say, "Okay. Have it your way." Then he sauntered off.

I watched him move slowly and aimlessly down the sidewalk, then returned to Larissa. "You good here?"

"Yeah. What about you? Did he have something to do with what happened at the museum?"

The washing machine clicked into its first cycle and we both looked. Sudsy water splashed against the porthole window as the clothes began to churn.

Someone rapped on the window again. I turned, ready to give the guy an ultimatum to either go away or I would call the police, only to see that, yes, it was the man, but he wasn't alone. Someone else was at the door with him. And not just any someone. Lieutenant Ocampo.

*   *   *

"I told you you'd let me in eventually," the man said after I'd unlocked the door. I'd opened it for Ocampo, and he had followed her inside.
"Somebody want to tell me what's going on?" I asked, closing and locking the door behind them.

Ocampo ignored me and walked up to Larissa. "I'm guessing you're the potential daughter?"

"Maybe," Larissa said. "Though if you're here to haul him off and torture him, you should know he hasn't had a chance to write me into his will yet."

Ocampo chuckled and turned to me. "I like her."

"So what is this?" I said, waving my finger between the lieutenant and the man. "I take it you two know each other?"

"Emit Hopper," Ocampo said, "meet Inspector Sergeant Martin Zorn."

*   *   *

"Scared the bejeezus out of you, didn't I?" the inspector said, patting me on the arm. He offered his hand. "Martin Zorn." He was five-foot-eight, fit, and had a wide, friendly smile. His eyes were exceptionally bright blue, and he seemed affable enough. "It's a pleasure to meet you. You're very talented. Music, books, art—a contemporary Renaissance man. Sorry to hear about the snafu out at the museum."

"Thanks," I said, suspiciously, shaking his hand.

"You don't remember me," he said. He was still smiling—and holding my hand. "On the steps today. The guy jogging in place beside you? I gave you a little nod before moving on."

"Right," I said, remembering.

"Don't feel bad," he said, once again patting my arm. "There was a lot going on." Only then did he let go of my hand.

As if moving in a prearranged choreography, the four of us took up different positions around the shop. Larissa fell back by the office door, while the lieutenant and the inspector and I formed a triangle in the front. Ocampo stood in the center, leaning against a folding station table, Zorn sat in one of the plastic bucket seats, and I stood on the far side, arms folded, back against the wall.

Ocampo said, "Inspector Zorn was also at the steps today to observe the crowd."

"And you," Zorn added. His legs were spread, and his arms were draped across the back of the seats next to him. He was grinning and looked as if he were chewing gum, even though he wasn't.

"More specifically," Ocampo said, sliding a large, sackish purse from her shoulder onto the high folding table, "how other officers in the crowd responded to you."

"Other officers?" I said. "Let me guess. Gary's Grinders? No, wait. The chatty guy and his dog? With the matching tartan vests and purple bow ties?"

Again Martin laughed. It was almost midnight and we were in a laundromat, yet he looked as pleased as if he were sitting on a beach in Mexico. He looked to Ocampo. "I think we've played with him enough."

Ocampo tilted her head to give permission.

"It was a training exercise," the inspector said to me. "Newly made sergeants up for plainclothes duty get tested for their observational skills. We place them in a series of increasingly complex public settings, then test them on what they observed. Today was easy stuff, day one."

"We usually plant trained undercover officers in the crowd to perform a range of roles and situations," Ocampo said. "But the *players,* as we call them, can be a challenge to staff because we have to pull from outside the district to ensure they're not recognized. Even still, no matter how skilled they are, cops always have a way of looking like cops—"

"Ever go to a music festival and play 'spot the narc'?" the inspector said. He held a hand out flat and wobbled it. "There's always that guy who just kinda, sorta has the right clothes, but at the same time, doesn't look quite right?"

"Which is why Inspector Zorn proposed hiring civilian extras. I have to admit, at first I was skeptical. We'd never tapped the public before. So I said no. Then the day before the annual training sessions were to begin, you landed in my holding tank and I figured why not give you a try."

"Yeah," I said. "Lucky timing. I hope I failed miserably."

"On the contrary," she said. "You did great. Which is why, if you want, you can do it again. Only now you can be official. We'll even put you on payroll. I'm sure the money isn't nearly what you get making drawings, but for a city gig, it's a hefty day rate. And for only a few hours' work."

"And we pick great locations," Inspector Zorn said. "Popular areas that I'm guessing a guy like you would want to draw, even if you weren't being paid."

"That is true," Ocampo said. "Popular sites make for good testing grounds. Though, as the inspector said, today was only the beginning. Over time, the settings get more complex. Larger spaces and denser crowds."

"Okay . . ." I said. I wanted to be annoyed—and was—but I was also relieved. And slightly amused. "And if I say no?"

"Then you don't get paid by the city to draw pretty pictures," Zorn said.

"And that's it?" I looked at Ocampo. "We'll be done? What about the lewd behavior complaint?"

Ocampo smirked. "Truth is, I couldn't follow through even if I wanted to. The woman who called it in left the scene and didn't leave a name. Unless she comes forward, there's nothing I can do to you."

I pursed my lips. I still had my arms crossed. "And so, all that today? With the subterfuge and making me think I was spying for you? It was all just a game? That's a pretty twisted thing to do to someone, don't you think?"

"Maybe," Ocampo said. "But keep in mind, you weren't brought in without reason. There was still a complaint call made on you. But I'm willing to let that go and move forward if you are. Which is why we've come in person.

To explain, and to give you this." From her large purse Ocampo took out a nine-by-twelve-inch manila folder and handed it to me. "A peace offering."

I stepped forward and took the folder. It was about an inch thick and heavy.

"Your photos from the Legion," Ocampo said as I undid the clasp. "As well as from the steps today. I had the lab print you 8x10s of both rolls. Negatives are in there as well."

I looked inside. There were fifty sheets of thick photographic paper and a glassine envelope of negatives. Suddenly I wished I'd given her the roll from Lyon Street that I'd *wanted* to work from.

"I also fixed your parking ticket," Ocampo said. "And there's this too—" she handed me another envelope, only much thinner. "The other thing you asked for."

At the mention of the "other thing," I glanced at Larissa.

I looked back to Ocampo. "Thanks." I was shocked by how accommodating she was suddenly being. And yet, at the same time, found myself equally as distrustful as when she'd been extorting me, only in a different way.

"Like I said, if you're interested in being an official Irregular Player, we've got plenty more training exercises over the next two weeks."

"An Irregular?" Larissa chimed in. "As in Sherlock Holmes?"

I'd caught the reference too. Irregulars were everyday people Holmes used to help him with his investigations, who weren't detectives but had special skills or knowledge. "That's right," Ocampo said. "Nice catch. I guess that's why you're early admission at Stanford."

Larissa squinted. "How could you—" Then a smile grew on her face as the answer came to her. "Emit asked you to do a background check on me, didn't he?" Her eyes lit up. "That's the 'other thing' in the second envelope?"

"He did," Ocampo said. "And it is."

"Nicely played," Larissa said, nodding at me with approval.

Ocampo was smiling. Which was annoying. Everybody in the room— everybody but me—was way too satisfied. Including Inspector Zorn, who continued to sit there flashing his blue eyes and smiling his wide, cocky grin.

Ocampo pushed herself away from the folding table and threw her chin toward me. "Read that report—you'll be happy you asked for it." Then she slung her bag over her shoulder and moved toward the door.

Inspector Martin Zorn stood and again offered his hand. "Thanks for letting us barge in so late," he said. Again we shook hands. "And we mean it. If you want to be an official player in our little war game, you'll be a welcome addition." His voice was as friendly as if we were members of the same elite club. "We're running exercises every day, but for obvious reasons we can't use you in every one. Sprinkled here and there, though, you'll be a great spice to add to the mix. We've got a scenario in a few days I think you'll be good for. I'll hit you up with details." He was still holding my hand. My inclination was to tell him to fuck off and take his pal Ocampo with him. I was still feeling used, and also distrustful that we were all now best buddies doing each other favors. But at the same time, if I could double-dip by getting paid to make drawings I'd be able to sell, then I might be able to overlook the last two days. Besides, I'd already lived them. And I had renovations to pay for. As if reading my mind, the inspector added, "It's easy money. Cold hard city cash." Then he clucked, slapped my arm, and let me go.

"I'll think about it," I said. Then I stepped ahead of them and unlocked and opened the door. The lieutenant walked out and the inspector followed.

"We'll be in touch," Zorn said as he passed by.

"One question," I said, and they both turned. I looked at Ocampo. "In Tu Lan, when you said you'd seen my photos from the Legion. Was that just you keeping up the game?"

Ocampo grinned. Then she and the inspector walked off.

11

EXPOSURE

"That's cool," Larissa said as we walked up the stairs to my flat. By the time my two new best friends had left the shop the wash cycle had finished, so we'd put the clothes in the dryer and locked up. "Not only are you off the hook for being a pervert, now you get to work undercover for the police."

"'Cool' isn't the word I would use," I said. "And I'm also not thrilled with the phrase 'being off the hook for being a pervert.' Sounds like I *am* a pervert, only I'm not being charged."

"Yeah, yeah, yeah," she said as we got to the top of the stairs. "Bitch, bitch, bitch. Why can't you just be happy you're not being blackmailed?"

I sat on the church pew and set down the three folders—the packet of info for Steven's house, the photos Ocampo had given me, and the background check on Larissa—then began untying my laces. "Because," I said, "I still don't trust them."

Larissa kicked off her Converse shoes, each with the other foot. "Then maybe you should have someone run a background check on *them* too," she said, snatching the folder of photos from the pew and sticking her tongue out at me as she walked toward the great room.

Shoes off, I followed her down the hall—report in hand.

Larissa sat at the island and slid out the stack of photos. She put the Lyon Street set aside and began flipping through the prints from the Legion. "Go ahead," she said without looking at me. "Read my *dossier*. You know you're dying to."

I really was.

I opened the folder and pulled out several thin, waxy sheets of fax paper with poorly legible type and CONFIDENTIAL stamped across each page. I read through the basic information: date of birth, height, eye color, et cetera.

Then a list of immediate family: Mother, Nicole—damn. Not Simone. Oh well. Would have been nice to have remembered her. Deceased. Father Unknown. Yep. List of other living relatives: Maternal grandparents, also deceased. One uncle—oh. Apparently Uncle Phil had a drinking problem. Three DUIs. On the next page was a list of achievements. "Holy crap," I said out loud, without meaning to. Impressive was an inadequate word. High school graduation at fourteen; MIT undergraduate degree at sixteen; entrance to graduate studies at Stanford at seventeen, and winner of more awards than I knew existed.

"Criminy," I said. "Why didn't you tell me you were a genius?"

Larissa groaned. "Ugh," she said, dropping her head back and sticking out her tongue. "I told you, I HATE that word. Everybody and their dog gets called that these days." She went back to looking at the photos. "It's meaningless."

"Sure," I said. "For someone who's been called it countless times."

She rolled her eyes, then looked at me in exasperation. "And how much difference would it have made? Would you have been more inclined to want me to be your daughter if you knew I was somehow—" she used air quotes "—'special'?"

"No—or at least I don't think so. But I take your point."

"Anyway," she said, picking up the photos again. "It's not the kind of thing one says about themself. In my experience, people who like to brag about how amazing they are at something usually aren't."

It was hard to argue with that.

I went back to reading. As she'd told me at the Legion, Larissa was currently at Stanford. What she hadn't told me was she was in the Computer Science Department with a focus on—I read it aloud: "Integrated Ethics and Information Technology." I looked up. "What does that even mean?"

"Asks the guy who defines art as making people walk through a narrow glass hallway through a barrage of Super Balls."

"Yeah, but at least it had a decipherable title."

"Right," she said, chuckling. "*Getting Through the Day.* That was actually pretty good."

"So you're studying, what then? The Internet?"

She looked at me with what I now understood was the look an eighteen-year-old genius gives to—well, probably everyone—when, despite all her intelligence, she fails to grasp the fact that what to her are rudimentary ideas are for most people incomprehensible.

"I'm not studying the Internet," she said, looking back to the photos. "I'm influencing the future of global information sharing." Suddenly I felt less bad for my drunken art babble the night before. "You might not see it," she said, "but the Web is where the world is going. Soon everything we do will be online. The public thinks the Internet is new, but the first iteration was invented in the 1960s, and now it's—well, it's kinda like San Francisco. Was inhabited by native peoples for centuries, then some Europeans showed up and 'discovered' it, then some renegade Puritans found gold, and suddenly the population began doubling every day. Well, that's the Internet right now. The Wild West times infinity. And if we don't do what we can to shape it . . ." She shook her head and laughed bitterly. "Imagine every dystopian sci-fi film you've ever seen, and that will be a good day."

"Okay . . . And so, your field is what? Ethics of world domination?"

"I have a degree in Computer Engineering, and yes, now I'm doing a doctoral in Ethics, with a focus on Machine and Meta Ethics."

I just stood there, letting it all sink in.

After a few seconds she glanced up at me. "These photographs are terrible, by the way."

"As in uninteresting, or unusable?"

"I don't know—both?"

I set the confidential document aside and for once was happy that Larissa had changed the subject. I went to the fridge, opened the door, and assessed the assortment of leftovers. "You want to split this Vietnamese food?"

"How can you be hungry?" she asked. "I'm still digesting that giant space capsule of a burrito."

I took out the container of extra spring rolls and bit into one cold. I was still mulling over the prospect of Larissa—or any teen—leading the charge to save humanity from a dystopian nightmare. "I think I've read enough science fiction to understand the basic premise behind Machine Ethics," I said. "But what does Meta Ethics mean?"

"You tell me. What's the difference between a partial truth and a lie?"

I was about to remind her that answering a question with a question was annoying, when I understood. "I see. So you're studying the nature of morality?"

She looked at me. Our eyes met for a second; then she frowned and said, "Yeah. Close enough."

"So how do you apply that to the Internet?"

"Well, that's the job," she said. "Isn't it?" She shook her head at the prints. "Seriously, these photos really are terrible."

"Says the girl who's questioning the presumptions of right and wrong."

"Who better to say then?"

I laughed. "You know they're not supposed to be art, right? They're not even supposed to be pleasing to look at. They're just for reference."

"If you say so." She motioned toward the spring roll in my hand. "I want one of those."

I stepped over and held out the container. "Don't get grease all over those prints," I said. "I need them to work from."

She took a spring roll, bit off a chunk, and set the remaining portion on the island counter. "Whatever," she said, wiping her fingers on her pants. "So what's the big reveal supposed to be in these photos, anyway?"

"I don't know. Amateur pornography?" I set down the food container and picked up the report again. "How old were you when you first knew you were interested in technology? Did your mother get a chance to see how brilliant you were before she died?"

Larissa picked up the half roll she'd set on the island-top, popped it in her mouth, and once again wiped her fingers on her pants. "I don't know how you can even draw from these photos," she said, sounding only half audible from chewing. "Like this one—" She held up a detail shot of *The Thinker*'s hand on his chin.

"That's so I can compare the size of the hand to the head," I said, setting the report down and picking up my spring roll. "Oftentimes artists draw hands and feet too small. Whereas Rodin, if anything, made them overly large. I mean, look at those things. They're enormous, meaty paws." I burped and tasted burrito and realized I was in fact more full than I'd thought. I held up the third and last fried roll. "You want this?"

Larissa shook her head, and I put my remaining bite along with the last roll back into the fridge.

"So I take it there's no surreptitious photos down any blouses or up any skirts in there?" I said, going to the sink and washing the grease off my fingers. I put a little soap on the sponge and wiped the butcher block counter where Larissa had laid the fried food and left a shiny spot of Tu Lan grease.

"You're not going to turn into one of those anal clean freaks now that everything in your house is new, are you?"

"Give me your fingers," I said.

"For real?"

"Yes, for real. I'm telling you, my drawing paper is very sensitive. Any hint of oil and it will stain the page. If you have Tu Lan all over your fingers and I touch these photos when I'm drawing, my commissions are going to look like I made them in a first-grade art class."

Larissa shook her head, but she held out her hand for me to wipe her fingers with the sponge. "You really are a weirdo," she said. "And not in a good way." Then suddenly she stopped. "Holy crap." Her eyes went wide and her mouth fell open.

"What?"

She had gone through the entire stack of photos and was holding the last one.

"Seriously," I said. "Enough with the jokes."

Larissa held up the photo.

I leaned in and looked. The photo was a wide shot of the Legion's courtyard with *The Thinker* in the center. At first I didn't see it. Then, at the far right edge of the picture, between two columns, the image was as clear as day. A woman. Straight on facing the camera, pulling up her shirt, flashing her breasts.

Warming Hut, Crissy Field, San Francisco — Commissioned by Katarina Palova. Katarina walked her golden lab, Izzy, along the path from the Marina to Fort Point every morning

at dawn for eleven years—every day of the dog's life—always stopping at the cafe for
water and a snack. When Izzy passed, she commissioned this in memoriam.

Palo Alto, CA — Commissioned by Korri Rolla. Gift to her grandparents, who purchased the house as newlyweds in 1950 and were coming up on half a century of being happily married in their beloved home.

Shotwell Street, San Francisco — Commissioned by Dana Howe. The two square bay windows of the middle building were initially those of two separate subdivided apartments. Dana lived in the unit on the left. A woman named Jackie lived on the right. As Dana told it, "Forgetting to close your curtains can be the best thing to ever happen to you." The rest she left to my imagination, which wasn't difficult seeing that she and Jackie had just purchased the building together and were combining those two separate units into one.

PART 2

MAY 2019
AMSTERDAM

ONE LAST DRINK

12

WANTED MAN

"I did not kill Ronnie Gilbert," I say, scoffing at the accusation.

Martin Zorn shakes his head. "Didn't say you did. I'm asking if you feel guilty for his having died. Seeing that he was in Queensland working for you."

The former police inspector and I are in my storefront in Amsterdam, twenty years after being officially introduced by Lieutenant Ocampo in my laundromat in San Francisco. Back then I had no idea what was to come, of how much my life would be thrown into the shit. But of course, no one ever does. And while the gaunt and pale shell before me no longer resembles the brazen, overeager cop who wanted nothing more than to save the world, it's hard to forget the damage his twisted version of justice caused.

"It's true," I say. "Ronnie was in Australia working on my case. But that hardly makes me responsible for his death."

Martin smirks, nods his head, and moves past me toward the front of the shop.

We both know what he's trying to do, and I'm not going to let him get away with it. I met Martin Zorn all of three times in the week before he disappeared—presumably having either jumped off the Golden Gate Bridge or fled to Mexico—but it had been plenty enough to work out that he had a way of making you feel as if he alone were on the side of the angels. He is right, though, the legendary San Francisco private detective Ronnie Gilbert had been working for me when he died, looking into the disappearance of my wife, Julia Bowman. In the fall of 2011, Julia and two other women, Rachel Adams and Darlene Fenton, had gone missing while hiking in California's Yosemite Valley. Six years later, in the spring of 2017, torrential rains had unearthed two partial human skeletons. One was identified as Rachel Adams, while the other was too damaged to test. Having known Ronnie since 1999, I'd hired him to investigate. He'd gone to Queensland to question Darlene's husband, the billionaire tech mogul Randall Fenton, and two days later Ronnie was dead, found half-digested inside a seventeen-foot crocodile nicknamed Tasmania because of its gargantuan size and unusual orange and white markings, a fate which I found impossible to be an accident. That had been in May 2017. This was now May 2019, exactly two years later, and Randall had just been acquitted in Ronnie's murder—despite my testimony. Which I'm angry about, but feel no guilt.

"And what about you?" I say to Martin. "For someone who is so willing to cast blame, you seem to be forgetting that the only reason I knew Ronnie was because you'd been playing the hero protector. If not for your twisted version of altruism, he and I may have never met—not to mention my building would have never been set on fire, and a young woman would still be alive. And then of course there's that pesky little detail of your having killed two people—and not as the unintentional consequence of a series of unpredictable actions, but by your intentionally aiming your gun, with your own hand, and firing. And yet you come here, after twenty years, and—"

"Post arrived," Danielle says, stepping through the curtained doorway of the adjoining space. Danielle is my part-time studio assistant. She has her earbuds in and is looking down at the mail in her hands as she emerges, not realizing Martin is here. "Finally," she's saying—a bit loud since she's also listening to music—"that prig from Glasgow sent the check for—" Then she sees Zorn and stops. It's not unusual for someone to be here; it is a public shop, after all. But something about the former police inspector, whether it's how he's standing, his mustache and odd clothing, or the all-around weird air he's exuding, causes her to pause. Which is surprising, seeing as Danielle is not one who is easily put off. Of Caribbean descent, raised in Wales, she's what I would call a bad-ass woman who gives no fucks. She's twenty-four, dark-skinned, with long black dreadlocks, the tips of which—at least this week—are dyed green, and is in Amsterdam studying painting at the University of the Arts. She works for me three days a week and in return gets internship credit toward graduation, plus, because I'm able to, I also pay her. In the beginning I taught her the pragmatics of my practice: mixing inks, stretching paper, caring for pens and brushes. Then we moved on to the nuances of working with ink washes. She took to it all quickly enough, and was only going to work with me for a semester, but apparently I offer more than the average part-time job and, in her words, am "not completely intolerable," so asked if she could stay. My business isn't exactly what you would call thriving, but I like having her around, so I said yes. These days she mainly takes care of my social media—meaning she does it all. Seeing that I neither use it nor care to learn.

Martin flashes his wide and still-charming smile at Danielle, then drops his gaze down to her chest. She's wearing her usual uniform of baggy green cargo pants with the cuffs rolled half up her calves, but it's the tight brown tank top that has his attention. It clings to her breasts so snugly that she appears almost topless, the outline of her nipples and barbell piercings perfectly visible.

"Sorry," Danielle says, pulling out her earbuds. "Didn't know we had a customer." She says it in her most haughty British accent, which, because I know her, I understand to be disdain. Which is also not unsurprising, considering that Danielle is generally not what I would call friendly. But again, her extreme reaction is odd, since it's not like Martin is the first customer—man or woman—to stare at her tits, and she's never shown any reaction to being visually molested before—or at least not negative. I can't say for certain, since it's not something we've ever discussed, but it seems to me that she comes in to work dressed this way on purpose, thinking it will help me make sales—which, frankly, it does. I would never ask her to exploit herself in such a way, but I can say with absolute certainty that I've sold more than a few drawings because of how alluringly Danielle's tops fit. She squints at Martin. "So are you buying? Or are you here to start him drinking in the middle of the day?"

Martin snorts, an amused smile appearing under his dirty mustache. "I like her," he says, looking at me. "Got your number. Reminds me of someone else we used to know."

"Brilliant," Danielle says. Then she drops the mail on top of my computer and disappears through the curtain, back into the studio.

I watch her go, impressed by how finely tuned her judgment of character is, then I turn back to Martin. "Listen," I say. "I wish I could tell you I'm happy to see you. But I'm not. If anything, it's just weird. Ronnie died and I'm sad, and I'm also sad and angry and frustrated that Randall got off. But seriously, what is this, Martin? It's been twenty years. What the hell do you want?"

Martin Zorn frowns and shakes his head. "Nothing sinister." He steps over to the table by the door and picks up one of my business cards, glances at it, then puts it in the pocket of his trench coat. "A friend of ours died. His murderer was found not-guilty. I thought maybe we could have a drink, toast to the legend that was Ronnie J. Gilbert."

A laugh catches in my throat. This is beyond strange. It's one thing to have an international fugitive who almost got me killed walk into my shop out of the blue, but another for him to claim it's only to toast to an old friend.

And yet, looking at the frail figure that is Martin Zorn, I can clearly see he is not well—more than unwell. He's sick. And suddenly it dawns on me that, maybe after all this time on the run, he's had enough. Maybe he's ready to come clean. I think of everything that happened back in San Francisco twenty years ago—and of the book I'm writing. And if he's ready to talk, I certainly have more than a few questions.

So I say, "Yeah. Okay. Let's have a drink. I've got an excellent bottle of—"

"Can't right now," Martin says. He wraps his trench coat around his thin waist and cinches the belt. "I have an errand to run first." He pulls a phone from his pocket and looks. "Shouldn't take long. It's just before six. How about we say seven? I'm staying at the Canal House. Over by—"

"I know it," I say. "There's a whiskey bar not far from there. JD William's, on Herenstraat. It's the only place in Amsterdam with a good selection of bourbon and rye. We can go there and catch up." I say this last part sarcastically, but he ignores it.

"In an hour, then," Martin says. Then he leaves.

I wait several seconds after he's pulled the door shut, then I pick up my phone and press STOP on the voice recording I'd started the moment I realized who'd walked into my shop.

13

GOD DAMN MARTIN ZORN

My shop consists of two adjoining spaces: the storefront, which is public, and a large studio apartment, which is private. Separating the two is a doorway with a heavy curtain, which—for the same reason there's a heavy curtain over the front door—is less for privacy than to keep the spaces warm. Winters are damn cold in Amsterdam, and even though it's May, spring isn't quite here yet. Every time the shop door opens, ice-cold air rushes in, eviscerating in seconds all the warmth my way-too-small heater takes hours to generate.

The storefront is narrow but deep. The private space—which serves as both my live area and studio—is larger, about twice the width, making it more square. For Amsterdam, that private area is quite spacious, though it's still just one large room. On one side there's a kitchenette, a dining table for two, a small sofa, a coffee table, and a decent-sized bed—by European standards. On the other side is a drawing table, a computer desk, a work trolley on wheels, and a set of floor-to-ceiling shelves loaded with supplies. It's not ideal, having every part of my life in one room, but it's cozy. If I were living with someone else it would be a different story. But of course, so would everything.

I step through the curtain to see Danielle at my main computer. It's a large-screen desktop iMac, which I use for organizing reference photos, documenting drawings, and laying out books—but not for writing. For that I use the small Mac laptop. Mainly because I like to go out to write. I enjoy the studio, but only for work I can't do anywhere else. Whenever possible, I'd rather be out in the world, in a café or bar or—when it's not freezing cold—on a bench alongside a canal. There's a lovely park on the west side of Amsterdam, and also the botanical garden, which is renowned for its collection of rare plants from around the world. The Rijksmuseum is a beautiful building with a large collection of art, but the Van Gogh Museum, while significantly smaller, is one of my favorite places to go and work. I can sit for hours in the drawing galleries, contemplating the elegance of Vincent's marks. The downside is the inevitable comparison I start to make to the tragic artist, wondering where I rank on the social scale of creative-crazy. Which, best as I can tell, is currently not so far in the crazy direction as to be unsung, destitute, and destined to become legendary in death, but also not so far functional as to receive national awards and multi-million-dollar commissions while alive. Basically, the middle. Which I have mixed feelings about. Point is, I like getting out of my workspace. Being surrounded by art, beauty, and activity helps me focus. I think it's because the nature of my work is so solitary; it's just nice to not have to sit alone in a room all the time.

Danielle doesn't look at me as I come in, but says, "I'll be off in just a sec."

"That's fine," I say. "What are you working on?"

"Your Instagram feed. I'm attempting to make you wildly popular again."

"If you say so." I go to the sink and run a glass of water. "I'm actually heading out. I'll probably be gone a few hours, so you're welcome to stick around and work on any school projects you might have." My computer is much nicer than hers, and my studio more private than the computer labs at the university, so I often let her use it for her artwork.

"Nope," she says, punching a key and pushing back her chair. "I'm done." She puts on her coat, grabs her backpack, then leaves, all in one swift motion. Not even a goodbye. So fast I don't even have time to swallow a drink of water and make a sarcastic comment. Danielle has never been one for pleasantries—which is a trait I like about her—but even for her this was a gruff exit. Or, I don't know. Could just be me. It's definitely been a weird day.

* * *

I hear the little bell clang as Danielle leaves. I take another drink of water. God damn Martin Zorn. I want to say his appearance is unbelievable, but then I remind myself, if ever there was a time he might resurface, it should be no surprise that it's now. For the same reason I'd been inspired to start writing this book, then pull out the suite of drawings I hadn't looked at in almost twenty years, I'm guessing Martin was induced to slither out of whatever dark hole he'd been hiding in: the memory of Ronnie Gilbert. So yes, it is believable. I think what has me more surprised is that after months of wintry boredom, something is actually happening.

I go to my computer and do a search for Martin Zorn. Unsurprisingly, there are dozens of websites, posts, and blog entries, even a few memes. I find several articles and a couple of websites dedicated to The Nest Murders and The Cult of The Nest, along with more than a few mentions of Zorntown. None of them are of any use. What next? Call the San Francisco Police Department? No. Ocampo is long gone. Maybe call Interpol? The FBI? No. I'm not looking to get the ex-inspector arrested. If anyone is going to interview the outlaw Martin Zorn, it's going to be me.

*　*　*

I use the toilet, then pack up my supplies: laptop, sketchbook, wallet, and phone. I don a hat, scarf, and coat, then head to JD William's, the whiskey bar where Martin and I are to meet.

It's a short walk, about ten minutes, which I set off on quickly and without pleasure. The tall, crooked buildings of Amsterdam are some of the most picturesque I've ever seen. But the backdrop of formless gray sky, the stick-bare trees, and the icy wind off the canals makes them hard to appreciate. Plus, I know the way too well. Old town is a system of concentric U-shaped canals. Unlike a gridded city where you can take lefts and rights in varying order, allowing you to alternate blocks for no other reason than to break the monotony and still arrive at your destination without going out of your way, if you take one deviation in old Amsterdam you can find yourself in a completely different part of town from where you intended. During the warmer months, and assuming you're in no hurry, such circuitous wanderings can be a pleasure. But if you need to be somewhere at a specific time, or simply want to run a quick errand—or if it's winter and you don't want to be stuck in a maze of icy, uneven cobblestone—then, to get anywhere, you're forced to take the exact same route every time. This was my first major disappointment after having excitedly moved here. That, in barely two weeks, the thought of leaving my home brought on a heavy tiredness, as if someone had dropped a sopping-wet cloak over my shoulders. A frustration which quickly grew into annoyance as my second disappointment soon followed: the throngs of oblivious—and often drunk—tourists.

Which is why, like many Dutch people, I eventually got a bicycle. So that I might more quickly traverse the annoyingly familiar ant trails one needs to take every day. I love riding a bike, and am a confident cyclist—and, truth be told, will be forever grateful to Amsterdam for reintroducing me to an activity that is not only practical, but also healthful—but, like all my pleasures here, was short-lived. For one, Amsterdam is plagued with bicycle thieves, which is why you never see a bike even close to being lightweight or desirable. And two, there's winter—which, as far as complaints go, I realize is becoming a bit of a tired refrain for me. But when it comes to bicycling, the song is real. Cobblestone is a nightmare when covered in ice. And the last thing I need is to go down and break an arm or wrist. The long, dark hours of winter are challenging enough to fill as it is. I wouldn't dare try to pass them without being able to draw or write. All of which is to explain why I am currently hoofing it along the all-too-familiar path to Prinsenstraat, quickly, and on foot.

It's only as I'm arriving at the bar that I wonder why Martin would surprise me at the shop, only to immediately rush off. Was it because of Danielle? Was he hoping to find me alone? And she spooked him? Then another thought occurs to me: that maybe his plan was never to meet for a drink, but to lure me outside, into some sort of trap.

*   *   *

JD's is crowded, and even though I'm half an hour early, I scan the dimly lit room to see if Martin is already here. I don't see him. All the tables are full, but I spot a couple of empty stools at the end of the bar and head toward those. Settling onto one and putting my bag on the other, the thought that Martin might have it in for me makes me happy I've arrived early—though, admittedly, the idea that he's orchestrated some elaborate scheme doesn't make any sense. For one, I picked the place. And two, if this were a trap, for what reason would I need to be captured?

The bartender saunters over and I order a double Basil Hayden's and a side glass of ice water. I know better than to ask for ice *in* the drink. The owner is a pretentious connoisseur who insists there is only one correct way to consume American whiskey—straight. Personally, I think the correct way to drink anything is to pour whatever you like into your mouth however you like it. But I can appreciate his being a purist. It's hard to find bourbon or rye outside of America. Most whiskey in Europe is scotch, which I detest, or Irish, which will do, and seeing that JD's has the largest selection of American whiskey in Amsterdam, if not all of Europe, I'm fine to order it to his approval, then, as soon as he walks away, mix it how I want.

I glance toward the door and once more question Martin's motives. Even if he was telling the truth, and his only aim is to reminisce about Ronnie Gilbert, why risk coming out of hiding? Again I think of his condition. And the prospect that maybe he really is here to confess. But again, why not just tell me what he needed to in the shop? If he was worried about Danielle overhearing, how is a public bar any better? Also, an errand? What does Martin Zorn have to do in Amsterdam? Of course, could be anything. I have no idea the life he's been living since he slipped out of San Francisco and fell off the grid. Hell, he could live here for all I know—have been living here for the past twenty years—and have only said he was staying at the Canal House so I wouldn't think he'd come to Amsterdam just to see me. But if that were true, what would be the point of lying? What's the point of any of what he's doing?

The bartender brings me my Basil Hayden's and side glass of ice water. After he walks away I drink half the water then pour in the double shot. I give it a minute to let the ice chill the booze, then I drink most of it. I glance to the door again. No Martin. I am early, though.

While I wait, I take out my laptop. I read through what I'd been writing, and once again find it uncanny that Martin walked through my door when he did. I'd been writing a story told to me by Ronnie, of the night in 1992 when he'd received the call that sent him racing across the bridge to the Midori Hotel. He'd arrived to find the lifeless, disfigured body of Joe Chadwick, and the fourteen-year-old Crystal Lake, a runaway teen who had been taken in by the Chadwicks' charitable center, The Nest, sitting with her arms around her knees in the bathroom, a mess of blood and brains streaked in her platinum-white hair. It had been a story etched deeply onto my mind, and the crux of everything that would follow. From there I had skipped ahead, to 1999, when I'd been accused of lewd behavior at the Legion of Honor, then returned home to find Larissa waiting to ambush me in my flat. So, yes, uncanny timing for Martin Zorn to walk into my shop. Another few days of writing and he would have appeared on the page. I reject the thought that I might have conjured him.

Picking up where I'd left off, I begin typing, and next thing I know I'm on my third drink and Martin is half an hour late. Now I'm angry—not at him, but myself. I was so worried about whatever scheme he might have concocted that it never occurred to me he wouldn't show. And now I'm cursing myself for having let him leave the shop. Twenty years ago he managed to disappear into thin air, and when suddenly he reappeared, what did I do? I just let him walk out the door again. When I should have run over, slammed the door shut, and not let him out of my sight until he told me every god damn thing I wanted to know.

I down the last drops of Basil and shake my head. Part of me still wants to believe he just got lost on the ant trail and will walk in the door any minute, but I know he won't. I know he's not coming. And as much as it pains me to admit, I'm not surprised. Which only makes me more angry. That I let him go, yes, but also that I was stupid enough to have believed he would come back.

I pay my tab and head to the Canal House.

*   *   *

I walk quickly, as if that will somehow better my chances of his actually being there. But when I arrive, the desk manager confirms what I'd already assumed, which is that no Martin Zorn is registered at the hotel.

Stands to reason. For two decades, Martin Zorn has been on the run. Surely he would have used an alias.

Of course, I have no idea what name he might use, but, in an attempt to think like Martin, I ask, "How about Ronnie Gilbert?"

The manager searches the register. "Sorry, sir."

Then, because it's Zorn, I try, "Emit Hopper?"

Again, no one by that name.

The manager is starting to get suspicious, so I try one last tack. "Medium height, fedora, trench coat, dirty mustache? Looks like maybe he's ill?"

The manager shakes his head. "No, sir. No one by that description is staying here."

I thank him, then leave.

Outside, night has fallen, and despite it being May, it's damn cold. But I'm still fuming with myself. After twenty years, the outlaw inspector chose to step back into my life, and I was too slow to realize I needed to do whatever it took to make sure he didn't disappear again.

God damn Martin Zorn.

14

TULIP

wake to Danielle making coffee. My head is thick and my vision blurry. I want to blame the less-than-adequate wall heater—the damn thing could suck the moisture from a cactus. But it's surely because of the booze. In my frustration of having let Martin Zorn slip away—and in the desperate hope that he might eventually show—I'd returned to JD's for another round. This time I decided I no longer cared about winning the proprietor's approval, and ordered it exactly how I wanted it, with water and ice.

"If you want to drink from a toilet of stale piss," the bartender said, "then who am I to stop you?"

I agreed with him so much that when I finished that one, I ordered another—the same way.

I have only a vague memory of stumbling home.

"You're in early," I say to Danielle as I slide my feet to the floor, even though I have no idea what time it is. I've given up thinking it's weird that my twenty-four-year-old female employee who comes to work dressed in revealing outfits lets herself into my home while I'm sleeping. There has never been anything sexual between us. Yes, I do find her attractive. Physically, but more so personally. I like her confidence, and her fuck-you-ness. And I'll admit, on occasion I have wondered how things might be if she had a daddy complex or a thing for mentors. Which, despite the tired cliché of older-artist-younger-protégé, isn't to say I would have automatically accepted. Or who knows. If I'm a man of morals, it's probably by accident. The sad fact is, even if she was interested, I don't know if I'd be up for it. Lately I just feel spit out. Of life, love, of everything. It could be the winter, the loneliness, or age—or the fact that I'm technically still married but haven't seen my wife in almost a year. But that's another story. Whatever the cause, to drag some poor soul into my tiny, self-indulgent existence—not to mention subject them to my clearly over-middle-aged body—feels downright cruel. But luckily—luckily?—I haven't had to confront any of that with Danielle. In the eight months she's worked with me, not once has she exhibited the slightest flirtation, jokingly or otherwise. Nor have I felt any inclination to make a pass at her. Which, I think, more than the small wage and access to my computer, might be why she stays—because I *haven't* tried to sleep with her.

"I'm not here for work," Danielle says.

I look up from rubbing my eyes with my palms. My vision is still a little blurry, but I don't need to see her clearly to know something is on her mind. Her voice is uncharacteristically soft, absent of the icy razor of sarcasm that usually accompanies even her most banal of responses. And to top it off, she's bringing me coffee. Which definitely means something is awry. I take it, and, as she wheels my studio chair close, I wrap my hands around the warm mug and say, "Okay. What's up?"

She sits, looks me square in the face, but doesn't respond. So I drink some coffee. It's brewed exactly how I like: half a cup of regular black, half room-temperature water. Essentially warm coffee-flavored tea. I drink one sip, then another. "Come on, Danielle," I say. "Talk to me. Silently staring at me while I'm in my underwear is weird."

"Your mate is dead."

My heart explodes in my chest. "Adam?"

"No," Danielle says. "The bloke who was here yesterday."

"The—you mean Martin?"

"If that's his name."

It takes a moment for this to sink in. Mostly I'm getting over the thought that Adam, a real friend—maybe my only real friend—and someone I actually care about, might have died.

"He was found this morning," Danielle says, "floating in Prinsengracht, close to Westerkerk."

"Drowned?"

"Don't know."

"How long?"

"Don't know."

"How do you know it's him?"

"Watched the tug lift his body."

"Shit."

Westerkerk is close to JD William's bar, and Prinsengracht canal is only a stone's throw away. Had Martin gone into the water on his way to meet me? And not been found until morning? And if so, was it an accident? Or something else?

"So how——"

"I told you what I know," Danielle spits, her familiar bite returned, which I find oddly comforting. "The question is, what do *you* know?"

I shake my head, confused.

"Yesterday, right out there——" she throws her head toward the curtained door dividing the spaces "——I step in to find you and this dodgy bloke arguing about arson and murder. Now he's dead. Obviously you two have a past."

"And what about you?" I ask, staring defiantly back at her as I take another drink of coffee—a long drink, letting the confrontation linger. "Why do you care? I saw the way you reacted when you saw him here. And don't tell me it's because he was staring at your tits. I've seen lots of people ogle you, and all you've ever done is use it to upsell them a drawing—which, by the way——" I tilt my head and give her a smile "——I appreciate. I'm just saying it seems to me that yesterday might not have been the first time you'd seen that dodgy bloke, as you call him. Because we both know the mail hadn't just arrived when you walked in. It had been sitting on my desk back here all day. Which tells me you were eavesdropping and chose that moment to 'innocently' interrupt. Which means if anyone's got information to spill, it's you."

Danielle tries to hide a smirk, but can't. For a moment she turns her head toward my drawing table, contemplating a retort. Then she turns back, motions with her chin toward the mug of coffee in my hand, and says, "Drink up. There's someone we need to talk to."

*　*　*

I down the coffee and tell Danielle I need to have a bite before I can go anywhere, to which she responds by tossing me a small white pastry bag. "Croissant. Now put some clothes on."

As we walk, I realize I haven't once been outside the shop with Danielle. The entire time we've known each other we haven't gone out for a meal, had a drink, or done any sort of socializing. Granted, the outdoors have been cold and uninviting. But still. It brings to mind something I've been thinking about, which is: what the hell happened to me? I've always been a bit of a loner, but I've also always had friends. For the almost year I've been in Amsterdam, though, life hasn't been my regular "I prefer my own company because I'm an artist" kind of alone, but more of a "this totally sucks I can't connect to anyone" kind of alone. Which, in this moment, is amplified by the fact that the person I feel closest to in Amsterdam is someone I've not only never been outside with, but with whom I've barely had any personal conversation.

It's late morning, and there's a nip to the air. But, amazingly, as Danielle and I walk, a hint of blue appears to be trying to overtake the all-consuming gray that calls itself the sky. We move quickly, and in silence, Danielle keeping half a pace ahead of me, so that no matter how fast I go, we're never side by side. Which is fine. I'm still processing Martin's having suddenly appeared after twenty years only to turn up dead. But I do take note of—and appreciate—the way Danielle navigates; the decisive turns she takes, and the way she cuts diagonally across the bridges, purposefully choosing which side of the canals to keep to. It's the movements of one who knows the ant trails of Amsterdam all too well. And once again makes me wonder if, or how well, Martin knew his way around.

Danielle leads us over the bridge across Singel, then onto a side alley, Oude Nieuwstraat, in what's known as Singelgebied. Prostitution is legal in Amsterdam, and Old Town has three red-light districts. Singelgebied is one of the two smaller areas, where the women are generally older and heavier than those selling themselves in the larger, more touristy district of De Wallen. I follow Danielle past half a dozen windows of working women lazily displaying themselves in lingerie and stockings, watching as she scrutinizes each one. Then, mid-block, she stops. Behind a large square window, a sixty-ish white woman in a silk kimono looks up from where she's sitting on a stool, absentmindedly scrolling on her phone.

As Danielle steps up to the window, the woman sets down her phone and opens her door.

"Hey Kitty," Danielle says.

Without moving her head, the woman's eyes glance over to me, then back to Danielle. Her face is a mask of garish makeup.

"He's okay," Danielle says. "He's the artist I work with."

Interesting choice of words, I think: *with* instead of *for*.

The woman looks back at me, then raises her arm to lean against the doorframe. Her kimono, which I now see is stained and threadbare, spills open, exposing a fraying pair of red lace panties, sagging belly, and two large, veiny, pendulous breasts.

"Tell him what you told me," Danielle says.

Kitty gestures with her chin across the street. I look to see another large square window, this one with heavy black drapes drawn and the telltale red light lantern—unlit. "Last week Saturday," she says.

"Eight days ago, you mean?" Danielle cuts in.

Kitty nods. "Mmm-hmm. Client cruised the windows and picked out Tulip. She let him in, then five minutes later they leave together. She closed shop and ain't been back since."

"What'd he look like?"

"Like one of those old detective sorts. Trench coat, hat, mustache. Thin."

Danielle looks at me, raises her brows.

I say to Kitty, "You think they knew each other?"

Kitty wobbles her head.

"Like old friends, or . . . ?"

"Couldn't say."

"And are you and Tulip close?"

Kitty closes her eyes, two swaths of thick blue makeup falling on her face like curtains. "She brings the girls on the street tomatoes from her garden. I invited her out for a pint once, but she refused. Is okay, she has a life of her own. But she is a good person, I think, so I worry."

"And the guy she went off with, could he have been a regular?"

"Never seen him before."

"And you two work these same windows all the time? Meaning you would know her regulars?"

Kitty looks at Danielle. "You know something about Tulip?"

"The bloke you saw her with was fished out of Prinsengracht this morning."

Kitty's partially tattooed brows go up.

"When was the last time you tried to call Tulip?" I ask.

"Yesterday," Kitty says. She picks up her phone. From the complexity of her movements, Tulip doesn't appear to be in her Favorites. She puts the phone on speaker and, rather than ring, we hear the line automatically connect to an automated voice, then disconnect. The message is in Italian, which I speak enough of to understand that the line is no longer in service. "Same as all week," Kitty says. "Same for SMS. Undeliverable."

"And you've asked around?" I say. "Talked to her other friends? What about where she lives? Have you gone to look for her?"

"The girls on the street here, ain't no one seen her. I don't know where she lives."

"And when she left with the man, did she look frightened?"

133

Kitty shakes her head. "No. But they were in a hurry."

"As in, the man had told her something that made her want to leave? Or, the man was forcing her to leave?"

Kitty shrugs.

"And has she ever taken off before? Suddenly, with or without someone, and left her window vacant?"

"I can't say what Tulip does or doesn't do. But her window has been empty now one week." She looks at Danielle. "You know how it is, no reason to let a room sit dark if you can sublet the rent."

"What about the other girls?" Danielle says. "This bloke in the trench coat bothering any of them as well?"

"Not that I heard," Kitty says. Again she closes her eyes, and once more the curtains of blue makeup fall. "But . . ."

"What?"

Kitty opens her eyes and raises her brows worryingly. "Tulip owed money."

"Russians?" Danielle asks.

Kitty nods.

15

CHRIST ON A BIKE

"Explain to me about the Russians," I say.

Danielle and I are at a table in the window of Café van Zuylen, with a view across the Torensluis bridge and Singel canal. It's one of my favorite places to write. Back before the never-ending purgatory that is winter, I passed many a day on the arched overpass, sitting at either one of the outdoor café tables or on the benches surrounding the statue of Multatuli, writing, drawing, reading, or simply watching life go by. For as much as I complain about the maze of streets—and the weather—for a few months out of the year, there is no better outdoor urban living than Amsterdam.

"Some girls are run by the Russian mafia," Danielle says. "Even though that's not how it's supposed to be. Dutch law allows for sex workers to be independent, but sometimes girls need money—or drugs—and the Russians are happy to help. Problem is, even after you pay back what you owe, they think they own you."

In a loud but friendly Irish brogue, the woman behind the bar asks what we fancy. I call back a slice of apple pie and espresso. "Twee," Danielle says. The Dutch word for two.

"So," I ask Danielle. "Who is Tulip to you?"

"No one. I've never met her."

"Okay . . . And so how—"

"I know Kitty from school. She models for my drawing class."

"And that's why you're worried about her friend? No offense, Danielle, but you've never struck me as one to give a shit about anyone, let alone a friend of a model from one of your drawing classes."

"True. But the girls, they keep an eye out for each other."

I raise my brows. "Okay. I was pretty sure I'd caught the previous hints, but—are you a sex worker?"

Danielle laughs. "Why would I need to do sex work with the fortune you pay me?"

"I'm not judging. I'm just—"

"No," Danielle says. "I'm not a sex worker." She continues laughing. Something I haven't seen her do much of, and would like to see her do more. She has a lovely smile.

The barmaid sets two plates of apple pie on the table. The slices are enormous, as thick as they are wide, each topped with a fluffy mound of real whipped cream.

"And here we are my lovelies," she says, in a singsong Irish accent. Then she scrunches up her nose. "You two hear 'bout the body they pulled outta the canal this morning?" We look at her. She glances back and forth between the two of us. "Shot in the head, I heard. As if the junkies and pickpockets aren't bad enough. Christ on a bike, now we gotta worry 'bout guns too?" She shakes her head and sighs. Then suddenly her eyes pop, "Oh!" she exclaims, and she darts to the counter. "Wouldn't want to forget these now, would we?" And she returns with the espressos. She sets them on the table, puts her hands on her hips, and smiles a big happy grin. "You two enjoy, now." Then she walks off.

Danielle breaks off a corner of pie crust and pops it into her mouth.

"Shit," I say, looking out the window. I'm not feeling bad, just confused. I turn back to Danielle. "You didn't mention Martin had been shot."

"Didn't know."

I aim my thumb toward the bar. "She just said he was shot in the head. If you were close enough to identify the body, how did you not see that?"

Danielle shrugs. Slides a forkful of apple pie into her mouth.

"But you're sure it was him?" I ask. "I mean, if you couldn't see that he was shot in the head, how can you be sure it was the same man who'd been in the shop yesterday?"

She answers while chewing. "Because I was standing close enough that when the crane pulled his corpse from the canal, water was practically splashing onto my feet. And after they lowered him onto the street, I could see his mustache and stupid paisley shirt. The peelers had their barricades up to keep back gawkers, but I was barely three meters away."

"Peelers?"

"Coppers. Police."

I nod, thinking.

"And three meters is ten feet American."

"I know how far three meters is," I say. I want to ask her again how, if she'd been close enough to see his mustache, she didn't see a bullet hole in his head. But then I think: what do I know about bodies in the water? Or gunshot wounds, for that matter? Maybe it was *because* he'd been in the canal that the wound wasn't as easily noticeable. So I ask, "What do you think happened?"

Danielle shrugs, scoops up a dollop of whipped cream with a finger. "How the fuck should I know?"

"But yesterday, when Martin came into the shop, you recognized him?"

Danielle shakes her head.

"But you came out to see him—and you reacted. I saw it. Normally you're not fazed by anyone. Then after seeing Martin, you darted off without saying goodbye."

"I never say goodbye."

"Fine," I say, finally pulling my plate toward me and picking up my fork. "But you'd known Tulip had gone off with him. Because Kitty told you. And she'd given you a description. Why would she do that?"

Danielle cuts another forkful of pie but doesn't eat it. "Few days back," she says, "Kitty's modeling for my figure-drawing class. During the break, she pulls me aside and says she's worried about her friend, that she's disappeared off with a dodgy-looking john, so she's spreading the word to working girls to watch their backs."

"But why tell you? I mean, if you aren't a sex worker . . ."

Danielle contemplates me as she eats the bite of pie. She chews, swallows, then heaves a big sigh.

"I'm not a sex worker," she says. "However, my grandmother was. Though she didn't get the honor of such a respectable title." Danielle picks up her cup of espresso, sets it down. "Great Britain in all its greatness had colonized what they'd deemed the West Indies, and helped themselves to everything and anything they wanted. Including village girls."

"Your grandmother being one."

"After being taken to England and kept for years as forced labor, she arranged it so she became pregnant by a high-ranking naval commander, then used the baby as leverage to gain her freedom. She barely escaped with her life. Twice the man attempted to have her killed. Wasn't until she got the ear of the great commander's wife that she had any protection."

"Which is why you have sympathy for sex workers?"

"That, and an upcoming exhibition at the next Biennale."

My brows shoot up. "You're doing an art piece based on your grand-mother's experience?"

"An installation of oral histories of contemporary sex workers." She gestures broadly to the city beyond the window. "Every one of these women, they have a story of how they came to be where they are."

"That's incredible, Danielle. Congratulations. And for the Biennale—wow. Good for you. Why didn't you tell me?"

Danielle slides a forkful of pie into her mouth and screws up her face. "Do you tell me about every project you're working on? Ever since you testified in that trial, you've been writing day and night. Haven't said a word what about."

"Fair enough. But I am glad to know. I look forward to seeing how you present it. Congratulations."

"You said that. But it isn't about me, or even about my art. It's about the women. About their voices not having a place to be heard."

I raise up my espresso and drink to her.

As I'm setting my cup down, I ask, "What was her name? Your grandmother?"

In a flash, Danielle's face hardens. Then, seeing what I assume she understands is only me with the best intentions, she relaxes.

"Vea," she says.

I nod. Eat some pie. Let some silence pass.

I'm not really sure what else to say, and Danielle doesn't seem very open to telling me any more, so I go back to our original subject.

"So Kitty," I say. "When she took you aside at the drawing class to say Tulip had gone off with a strange man, was it because she knew you interviewed sex workers for your project?"

Danielle nods.

"Because you'd interviewed her?"

Again she nods.

"And had you interviewed Tulip?"

"No. Was supposed to, though."

"Too bad. And so when you saw Martin come into the shop—"

"I heard his voice and peeked around the curtain like I always do—you know, to see if maybe he was a buyer I could help close, since that's something you're not very good at. I saw how he was dressed, and remembered Kitty's description of the bloke Tulip had gone off with. Which is why I stepped out, to get a read. I'm pretty good at that, you know, first impressions and all."

"You do know how to close a sale, I'll give you that. The earbuds were a nice touch, by the way."

She smirks.

"As for your read, what did you think of Martin?"

"He was putting on a show."

"For who? Me?"

She shrugs. "I can tell you he didn't give a shit about my tits."

"Meaning what?"

Again she shrugs.

"Okay . . . And so after you bolted—"

"I didn't bolt."

"Fine. After you left the shop in your normal brusque and hurried manner, where did you go?"

"None of your business."

I shoot her an annoyed look. She rolls her eyes.

"I went out with some mates. What's it matter?"

"You didn't go to see Kitty? Or spread the word about Martin?"

"Why would I do that?"

"Because after what Kitty had told you, maybe you were concerned that Martin was dangerous—especially after you overheard us talking about arson and murder."

"Or maybe I understood that whatever the deal is between you two, it's your private business. Just like I don't really care why Tulip went off with your dodgy mate. Don't mistake me wanting to give voice to these women for me having a savior complex." She picks up her espresso cup. "Thinking I can rescue these woman with my art would be as patronizing as believing I'm saving the savages by bringing them Jesus." She finally drinks her espresso. Sets the cup down. "So, no. I told no one that I'd seen your mustached mate with the bad taste in clothes. I went about my own private business, then early this morning I'm walking home and come upon a bloated corpse being fished out of the canal and realize who I'm looking at. And here we are."

"Okay . . ." I say. "But if you truly have so little interest in meddling in anyone's affairs, why are we here, then? Why wake me up to tell me Martin is dead? Then take me to see Kitty?"

Danielle scoops another dollop of whipped cream from the top of her pie, puts her finger in her mouth, and sucks it clean. "Because," she says, the mischievous glint I know to be Danielle returning to her eye, "maybe I enjoy having a cushy day job and an all-access pass to your flatbed scanner and fancy computer. And if you're caught up in some dodgy bullshit with blokes getting murdered, then maybe you're next on the list to be offed and dumped into the Singel. Which means I gotta find another pathetic sod who's willing to overpay me to use his studio."

She wipes her finger around the edge of her plate, gathering up the last of her whipped cream, and once again slides her finger into her mouth, this time managing to grin as she does. And suddenly it occurs to me how right Martin was. When it comes to sarcasm, Danielle really does remind me of someone.

16

THE ANT TRAIL

pay for the pies and espressos, then Danielle and I part ways, both of us agreeing that she doesn't need to come into work today, and that she'll let me know if she hears any news of Tulip or Martin. One good thing about Danielle not really caring about me—or anyone, seemingly—is that I don't have to beg off telling her the story of how I knew Martin Zorn. More than her not even wanting to ask, she was probably happy I didn't offer. It's an ironic silver lining, but I'll take it.

Despite the chill in the air, I'm not ready to go home. Walking has always been my best engine for thinking—or not thinking, depending on the problem—so I set off to wander. It helps that above the high, jigsaw-like gabled rooftops there is what appears to be an actual sky, and that falling across the crooked, cobblestone roadways are the faint hints of what promises to be shadows in the shapes of those ever-leaning brick façades, cast by the curious and ever-brightening object I dare call the sun. It's the first real promise I've seen that there may be a future other than gray and bitter cold, and the joy it stirs in me is offset only by the knowledge that a man I once knew was found shot in the head this morning. Not that I'm mourning him. For the past twenty years, if you'd said the name Martin Zorn to me, without question I would have said that he deserved to be punished—though I wouldn't have said executed and dumped in the polluted stew of the Singel canal.

Of course, I don't know for certain that he was executed. Though if he was, it would make an interesting ending for this story. Sounds insensitive, I know. Maybe even cruel. But this is where almost forty years in the entertainment industry and being just successful enough to keep working but not successful enough to never have to work again leaves you. Ronnie has been dead two years, the Nest Scandal was twenty years ago. Both are interesting premises. However, the murder of a well-intentioned but idealistic—and ultimately broken—cop who'd killed three people, then spent twenty years on the lam—now, that equals book sales.

*   *   *

As I walk, I ask myself a series of questions: Who was Martin in Amsterdam to see? Me or Tulip? Or both? Did Martin know I was living here? Or had he simply found himself walking through Old Town when he saw the *Emit Hopper Studio* sign hanging outside my shop, and, given that Randall had just been acquitted in the death of our mutual friend Ronnie, been spurred by an uncontrollable urge to kick sleeping dogs? The latter feels a bit coincidental for my taste, but it is a possibility, as are, of course, a dozen other potential scenarios. Which is the problem of being a novelist, and makes me think again of my intended subject of this book, Ronnie, and something he liked to say: "You have to look at a thing straight on before you can look at it sideways." And so, in honor of my old friend, I put aside my flights of fancy and ask, simply: What do I know?

I come up with these statements:

• Eight days ago, Martin Zorn went to see a prostitute named Tulip, who hurried off with him and has not returned.

• Yesterday, Martin came to see me, ostensibly to reminisce about Ronnie, then left, claiming to have an errand to run.

• That evening, he failed to show for drinks.

• This morning, he was found dead in a canal, shot in the head.

• Also, he lied to me about staying at the Canal House.

Seems succinct enough. However, which of these do I *actually* know? Only that Martin came to see me, that he didn't show for drinks, and that he wasn't staying at the Canal House. The rest are either conjecture or assumptions. That Martin was the man Tulip left with seems likely given Kitty's description, as does his being the body fished from the canal this morning as reported by Danielle. However, I have firsthand proof of neither. And the body especially has me unsure. While I trust that Danielle is certain of what she saw, I'm not convinced that someone can be close enough to a corpse to recognize the face and *not* see that they've been shot in the head. As for the gunshot, I have only the hearsay of a gossipy waitress. So, before I can even begin to speculate on Martin's motives, I'd like to confirm for myself that, one, the man is in fact dead, and two, by what means. After all, it wouldn't be the first time people assumed Martin Zorn was no longer of the living. Including most of the San Francisco Police Department twenty years ago.

* * *

Approaching Westerkerk, the four-hundred-year-old Renaissance church near where Martin's—or somebody's—body had been found in the canal, I look around to see where he may have met his demise. I walk to the apex of the bridge spanning Prinsengracht, lean on the railing, and look over. There is no sign of a crime scene. Whatever investigation was being conducted by the authorities has been packed up. Nor are there any clues as to why this spot, in all of Amsterdam, is where his body would have been dumped— assuming, of course, that this is where he went over. He could have gone in further upstream and floated down, or been dumped from a boat, which, now that I'm here, I'm thinking is a likely scenario. Of all places in Amsterdam, this is a terrible spot to commit a murder. This stretch of the Jordaan is a popular tourist destination, bustling with people seven days a week. In the late hours it's of course a different story, since Amsterdam is a sleepy city, especially in the winter, but still. With Westerkerk, the Anne Frank House, and the area chock-full of restaurants, boutiques, and hotels, it's generally swarming with tourists. As this afternoon proves. The only visible hints of crime I see are the thousands of selfies being taken outside a building where a young Jewish girl famously managed to hide from the Nazis for nearly two years before being tragically captured and murdered. Which makes me think that the only reason to leave a body here is to guarantee that it *would* be found. Which I suppose is interesting, and begs the question: Who would want to make a statement by dumping Martin Zorn in so public a place? Seeing that he'd been living off the grid for twenty years, that list could have dozens of people on it, if not more. Including Russian gangsters.

The bells of Westerkerk begin to ring. With nothing more to be gleaned here, I move toward home.

Turning onto Prinsengracht, I keep to the road to avoid the crowded sidewalk outside the Anne Frank House. It's a common move since far fewer cars use the streets than bicycles, and bicyclists are accustomed to tourists mindlessly stepping into their path. Still, I look to make sure the way is clear. In Old Town, the division between roads and sidewalks is often indistinguishable. Both are paved with the same red brick, the only separation being short vertical bollards spaced too far apart. Which is why every bicycle is equipped with a robust bell. As a pedestrian, it only takes being scared half out of your shoes once by the sudden jolting ring as you feel the wind of a bicycle passing inches from your elbow to remember to look before you step in any direction other than forward.

As I get closer to home, I consider my next moves. Aside from confirming that the body found in the canal was Martin, and that he had in fact been shot, I decide I also want to know more about Tulip. I'm hoping the nature of her relationship to former police inspector Zorn will fill in some blanks. But how to do that? Surely Tulip isn't her real name—does anyone in the sex industry use their real name? I suppose I could go back to Kitty, see if she'll introduce me to their mutual friends. Hopefully one who knows where Tulip's house is. Also, I can talk to Danielle. See if she'll make more introductions as well. It's at least a place to start. But first I need to confirm the identity of the body pulled from the canal this morning. Because Martin, I swear, if this is the second time you're not for-real dead, I might actually kill you myself.

*　　*　　*

My shop, the Canal House, and Westerkerk are each points along one big ant-trail circle I know all too well. Which, in moments such as these, of wanting to switch to autopilot, serve me well. With little effort I've been able to lose myself in thought, and next thing I know I'm home.

I step down the three steep stairs to my door. As I take out my keys I hear a voice behind me say, "Man zonder titel Hopper?"

I turn to see two uniformed police officers. Young, broad-chested, with close-cropped hair, they're dressed in black uniforms with two bright yellow bumblebee stripes across their chest and arms.

"I'm Emit Hopper," I say, stepping back up to the street.

"Korps Nationale Politie," one of the pair says, as if it weren't obvious. "Do you know a man by name of Martin Zorn?"

"I do," I say. "I believe he was found dead in the Prinsengracht canal this morning, is that right?"

For a moment this throws them. It's one of the lessons I learned from working around cops, that only guilty people pretend to not know things.

"He came into my shop yesterday," I tell them. "I hadn't seen him in twenty years and, as far as I know, there's still an international warrant out for his arrest. My assistant was there when he came in, and this morning she witnessed a body being pulled from the canal, which she believed was his, and she informed me. Which is how I know. Am I correct? Was the body Martin Zorn?"

144

The cops are just staring at me. I'm talking very plainly and calmly, looking them each in the eye, but in a friendly way, as if I have nothing to hide—because I don't.

"I didn't kill him," I add. "If that's what you're wondering."

Both officers smile at this. Good-natured smiles. One even chuckles a little.

"Man zonder titel Zorn," the first cop says, "he was your friend?"

Now it's my turn to smile. "Twenty years ago he was intimately involved with an organization that set my building on fire, which killed a young woman and almost killed me. Then he murdered two people and disappeared. So, no, I would not call him a friend."

The cop who'd been speaking nods several times. He glances quickly at his partner, then, seeming to make a decision, says, "Man zonder titel Zorn was not murdered. He committed suicide."

17

REVELATION

'm shocked, and the officers just stand there watching as I let the information sink in. Martin Zorn, suicide. After a few seconds I ask if they're sure,
and they say yes. Comparing timelines, we determine that after leaving
me, Martin had gone to the Brouwer—another popular hotel close by—
where earlier that day he had checked in, without a reservation, and without
luggage. He retired to his room and remained there until approximately
two-fifteen in the morning, when, as reported by the proprietor, he went
out again. Half an hour later, just before three, several calls were made to
112 by citizens residing close to Westerkerk reporting what sounded like a
gunshot. Police responded; however, not until daybreak did they locate the
body, as it had drifted under the deck of a houseboat. Speculation was that
Martin had stood at the edge of the canal so that, after firing a bullet into his
head, his body would fall into the water.

"Could it have been an execution?" I asked.

Unlikely, was the answer, seeing that a note was found this morning by
a Brouwer employee who'd entered Martin's room to clean. It was taped to
the mirror and read:

*To authorities, friends, and all I have disappointed. I have gone to the canal for
one last drink.*

——*Martin Zorn*

"And so how did you know to visit me?" I ask.

"Your business card," the officer says. "It was placed on the bureau. The
only item in the room appearing to have belonged to Man zonder titel Zorn.
Other than the note."

Again I let this sink in. And again the cops watch me as I do.

"We understand that Man zonder titel Zorn was a controversial figure," the officer says. "And a full investigation will be conducted. At your earliest convenience the Korps Nationale Politie requests you submit a formal statement." Then he touches his cap and bids me a pleasant day, and he and the other cop walk off.

I watch them go, then let myself inside the shop. My mind is spinning. But before I have even a moment to sort out what I might think, I realize I'm not alone. Someone is in the studio, rummaging through my things.

*　*　*

For a moment I stand perfectly still and listen. I have no element of surprise, though. The little bell on the door has alerted whoever is behind the curtain that I'm here. The sound in the studio stops. Seems we've both halted in our tracks, waiting for the other to make a move. A few tense seconds pass, then the curtain is tugged aside.

"What are you doing?" Danielle says.

"I could ask you the same thing."

"I'm scanning my sketchbooks."

I just stare at her.

She closes her eyes. "It's a weird day," she says. "I wanted to keep busy."

"And to check in on me?" I want to say. But I know she'll never admit it. So instead I say, "Martin committed suicide."

"For real?"

"Appears so." I tell her of my encounter with the police.

"You should check this out," she says.

We go into the studio. Danielle sits at my computer and I stand behind her, watching over her shoulder as she pulls up a YouTube video. It was shot by someone in the crowd who'd gathered to watch the police preparing to lift Martin's body out of the canal. Given the situation, I probably shouldn't feel impressed, but I can't help but marvel at the rig, a large crane mounted on the wide, flat boat. Dangling from a hook on the end of a cable is a stretcher, which is lowered into the water. Several uniformed police are standing on the edges of houseboats, and two divers in wet suits are in the canal. Together they slide the corpse—along with the trench coat I instantly recognize—onto the stretcher, and secure it with straps. The crane then hoists the body out of the water, swings the stretcher over the roofs of the houseboats, and lowers it onto the cobblestone street where several more uniformed officers are waiting with outstretched arms to receive it. As Danielle had noted in her recollection, water is dripping from the body the whole time. Then, as the camera follows the movement of the stretcher—bobbing and jostling from being a phone held by an amateur—I catch a flash of the back of someone's head—who appears to be Danielle.

"See," Danielle says. "There I am." And I wonder if that's the reason she's showing me the video, to prove she was there.

As the stretcher is unhooked from the cable, the camera zooms in on the face of the body, and I see that, without question, it is Martin. Which, given my conversation with the police, is no longer a surprise. What I find interesting, is that I can see no sign of a gunshot.

"That one's good for seeing his body being taken out," Danielle says. "But this one's better for seeing his face." She closes the video and opens another. This next video starts off shaky and distorted, then quickly stabilizes and zooms in on Martin's face. It's from a different angle. And here, clearly, a wound can be seen on his temple. It's circular and black, and looks as if it's been cleaned. Which I suspect is a result of hours in the water.

"There's more if you want to see," Danielle says.

I shake my head, then sit down on the couch.

"Do you believe it's true?" Danielle says, spinning around to face me.

"You mean that Martin committed suicide? I don't see why not."

"Is that why you didn't tell the police about Tulip?"

I look at her.

"I wasn't eavesdropping. You just didn't mention her when you recounted the story to me. Am I wrong?"

I shake my head. "No. I didn't tell them. I guess with it being a suicide, she didn't seem relevant."

"Or maybe because you want to find her before they do."

I can't help but smile.

"So what was the deal between you and this bloke, anyway?" she asks—to my surprise. "Because it looks to me as if he came here to say goodbye. Which you don't do unless someone is important to you."

And for the first time, I actually feel bad. I've spent so many years focused on my own feelings of self-righteousness that I'd pushed aside all empathy for Martin. Which doesn't mean I've changed my mind about him. Only that it may be time to admit that, in the grand assessment of Martin Zorn, there is a great deal of gray area.

"Can you help me find her?" I ask.

"Tulip?" Danielle says. "Depends. What do you want me to do?"

"I'm thinking maybe go back to see Kitty, find out who Tulip's friends are, see what any of them know. I'm guessing they're more likely to open up to you than me. At the very least try to learn where she lives, or maybe her real name, since I'm guessing Tulip is just a sex-worker alias."

Danielle looks uncertain. "You could ask the rental agency leasing her window," she says. "Her name would probably be on the agreement."

"Maybe," I say, "but I don't know that anyone is going to give out that kind of information to a stranger of no relation. You know the Dutch. They tend to be sticklers for the rules." I see she's still looking uncomfortable. "What?" I ask. "Are you concerned I'm trying to take advantage of your trust with the sex-worker community?"

"A little, yeah. I may not be a crusader looking to save the downtrodden sex worker, but I also have no desire to exploit them in any way."

And with that word, *crusader*, it hits me.

"What?" Danielle says, seeing the revelation cross my face.

"I can't believe it."

"Tell me," Danielle says, looking thoroughly annoyed. "I hate guessing games."

"It seems impossible, but . . ." Like the little bell on my front door ringing each time someone walks in, a little bell has rung in my mind. I look at her and laugh. "God damn," I say. "I think I know who Tulip is."

Golden Gate Bridge, view from Fort Baker — Patrons asked to be unnamed. A couple who came to the studio looking for an anniversary gift for themselves. "Something definitively San Francisco," they said, then joked, "But not the bridge." They both had ideas, but were unable to agree. After

an hour of arguing in the studio they left, frustrated. I assumed I wouldn't hear from them again. A week later the husband called and said, "We'd like something of the bridge."

ICB Art Center, Sausalito, CA — Commissioned by Peter Sullivan. During the Second World War, the ICB was one of twenty buildings constructed as a wartime shipyard, enlisted to produce what was known as Liberty ships. When the war ended, production stopped and the site was abandoned. In the late 1950s, the ICB was taken over by artists who used the vast industrial space as studios, and over the years grew it into a thriving community. In the late nineties, Peter bought the building and vowed to keep the tradition of artists' studios alive.

110 Sutter Street, San Francisco — Commissioned by Jim Winter. Jim had been Head Groundsman for a midwestern college football field. In anticipation of the big annual rivalry game, he'd tried a new fertilizer, which resulted in the dirt drying out and becoming loose. Players from both teams were slipping and sliding on every play. Jim was immediately fired and run out of town. Adam, my friend and publisher, turned down his autobiography, but introduced us at a party. I'm not a college football guy, so didn't know the story, which apparently is infamous—so much so that for years Jim continued to get death threats. I asked him why he'd come to San Francisco and he said because of Cable Car Clothiers, the downtown haberdashery famous for its mail-order catalogue of British clothing, where he bought all his clothes. I said that sounded like a funny reason to move somewhere, to which he said, "Not as funny as watching those kids flailing around like a bunch a drunken roller-skaters on an ice rink!" Then he burst out laughing and asked how much I charged for commissions.

North Beach, San Francisco — Gift to Larissa

PART 3

1999
SAN FRANCISCO

THE BUTCHER'S WITNESS

Marshall Beach, San Francisco — Not a commission. Is included here because Larissa and I hiked the Battery to Bluffs trail one afternoon during her winter break from Stanford, and because I can usually sell a drawing of the bridge.

18

ICE CREAM FOR DINNER

Stinson Beach was only twenty miles as the crow flies from where I lived in the Mission, but once out of the city, as you passed under the towering industrial-orange uprights, with the city behind you and the open horizon of the Pacific at your side, you felt as if you'd gone traveling the world. It was enough to make you forget that you were steeped in debt, might have a teenage daughter, and that your most recent career opportunity was an offer to play an extra in a police training exercise. Well, almost. I was just hoping the house I was tasked to draw had a hot tub.

After crossing the bridge, I followed the winding freeway through the rainbow tunnel and down to Sausalito, past the harbor of houseboats and seaplanes, then turned west toward Muir Woods. As I climbed into the hills, the terrain grew lush and the roads turned windy, and I really started to enjoy myself. The Miata may not have been the highest-end of sports cars, but it handled the tight switchback roads beautifully.

By then it was almost four. Much later than I had wanted to be on the road, but that morning one of the heating units had blown in the shop, and I'd had to spend the day calling around for a replacement. After finally finding one, I arranged for Betty to meet the installer. It was the first time I'd seen her since Larissa had arrived, and I decided I wasn't going to give her a hard time for letting a strange young woman into my flat. Betty had been fed a good story, and in the end Larissa turned out not to be a thief, so all was well, as they say. But Betty had other thoughts.

"What's wrong with you not picking up your niece from the airport?" Betty roared the moment I stepped inside the shop. Four-foot-ten, mid-fifties, and barely a hundred pounds after bingeing at an all-you-can-eat buffet, she was half my size but immensely formidable.

"She's not my niece," I said. "Or—I suppose she could be . . ."

Betty slapped me on the arm. "Your problem is you do not live in the real world." She waved her hand. "Drawing pictures, telling stories, you are lost in the clouds when the rest of us have to live on the ground."

"That is most certainly my problem."

"But she is good? You take her to see college campuses? She looks like a smart girl."

"She's going to Stanford."

Betty's eyes lit up. You'd think Larissa was her kid. "You see," Betty said, wagging a finger at me. "Is good to help family."

I said it was, and that I would be away for a few nights for work, then gave her the number for the Stinson house in case she needed to reach me. To which she replied in standard Betty fashion: "Drawing pictures is not work."

With that interaction out of the way I was finally able to hit the road. I'd lost half a day of scouting and gained another bill to pay, but I was just relieved the water regulator hadn't blown.

As for Larissa, I chose not to invite her to Stinson, and she seemed perfectly fine. She said she was going back to Stanford and we could talk again after the lab results came in, which wouldn't be for at least another day, or possibly not until Monday. But as she was packing I found myself feeling sad to see her go, and impulsively said, "Or, if you wanted, you could camp out here. I know you liked volunteering at The Arcade, so . . ."

She looked at me with wide, surprised eyes. "For real? You don't mind me staying at your place while you're gone?"

"You were already here alone and didn't run off with anything, so I think it'll be fine. And this way, if the test comes back positive, we can celebrate together. And if not, then we can have a concession dinner."

She smiled and put her bag down. "Cool," she said. "Thanks." And when she didn't add a sarcastic comment, I knew my offer had made her happy.

I might have said that at this point all the chaos in my life was in relative order, if not for the surprise photograph from the Legion—of the woman flashing her breasts.

The night before, after Lieutenant Ocampo and Inspector Zorn had shown up unannounced at the laundromat to inform me that Ocampo's extortion had been nothing more than an audition, Larissa had spotted the woman in the photograph. Clearly Ocampo had seen her too, which is what she'd been taunting me with. Why she hadn't made a big deal of it seemed obvious. If the photograph was proof of any sort of lewd behavior, it was on the part of the woman, not me. Which got me off the hook for being a peeping tom, but left me with more than a few questions.

To start, who was the woman? I didn't recognize her, and after I'd gotten over my initial shock, I'd gone into the studio and come back with a magnifying glass—which Larissa found hilarious. "If you really need to study a pair of tits," she said, "there are about a zillion websites out there." But even as I scrutinized the photo, I found the woman's face was conveniently, if not intentionally, masked in shadow. I did find one identifying element to her, though: what looked like tattoos covering both of her hands and fingers. She was too far away and the photo too grainy to make out what they were, but I was sure it wasn't just a trick of the light; both her hands were heavily tattooed. It was definitely a clue. Though what good it might do me, I couldn't say.

Next question was, who had made the complaint? I saw two possible scenarios: One, that a museum visitor had witnessed the scene, been offended, and called the police. Or two, that the woman who flashed me had made the complaint. The former had a ring of logic; the latter was more disconcerting. Either way, I had no recollection of the woman whatsoever—and certainly none of her exposing herself. Which made me think she must have been skulking in the shadows, waiting for the perfect moment when I raised my camera so that I would catch her on film but not actually see her between the columns. I'll admit, the prospect of someone doing such a thing intrigued me. Was it an impulsive act? Or had it been planned? And if planned, was she flashing anyone and everyone who happened to be in the courtyard? Or was I, Emit Hopper, specifically, the intended target?

*   *   *

Traffic along Highway 1 was surprisingly not too heavy, and it was just before five when I arrived at the small beach town. I drove past a surf shop, a seafood bar, and a taco stand, then turned up the hill. The road was immediately steep, and as I wound up through the neighborhood, I studied the houses. Most were older, modest structures, little more than gussied-up beach houses, while others were modern, lavish homes. I'd already assumed that my patron Steven's house would not be a shack, and I was not disappointed. His was the last property at the top of the hill, the equivalent of a small estate. I pulled up to the entrance, consulted the packet of instructions Alma had messengered to the shop, punched in the code, and waited as a large iron gate slid open. I drove in, parked, then entered another gate on foot. The grounds were beautifully manicured. There was a small yard with beds of flowers and lemon trees lining the walkway. Inside the main house the design was minimal and airy. The entire wall facing west was a floor-to-ceiling accordion glass door. On the other side was a deck which spanned twice the width of the house with a panoramic view of the Headlands and Pacific Ocean.

I went out and leaned on the deck railing. The sun was setting, and a cold wind was blowing in. It was too late in the day to get any reference photos, but I was unconcerned. I had the house for four nights, which meant I would have three full days where I could watch the light and start a drawing. Tonight I could rest.

A tour of the grounds revealed a fire pit, barbecue, and hot tub, all of which I intended to use that night. There was also a pool, though covered for the winter. Aside from the main house, there were two smaller buildings, a utility shed and a yoga studio, the latter being what Steven wanted me to draw. The keys to the studio were somewhere in the main house—the packet of info would tell me where—so for the moment I peeked through the window. The small building looked to be one room, mostly empty save for some lightweight exercise equipment and a yoga ball. This was Steven's wife's workout area, which was why he was giving her a drawing as a gift. I hoped she was as dedicated to her exercise practice as her husband thought, otherwise the drawing would only be a reminder of her procrastination. It wouldn't be the first time a well-intended art commission had backfired. I once had a woman commission a drawing from Joshua Tree for her girlfriend. They'd fallen in love there while on a camping trip, and the drawing was to be a gift for their anniversary. When she came to pick it up she broke down crying because the girlfriend had left her, then she asked if she could have her deposit back. I had to tell her no. I'd already spent the money to fly to Palm Springs, rent a car, and stay; plus, there had been my time to make the drawing. I didn't have the heart to make her pony up the rest of what she owed for a drawing she didn't want, though, so I told her I'd try to sell it, and if I did, I'd return her deposit. A few months later, I put the piece in a group show and it sold, so I was able to give her money back. Which made me feel better, and her too. So that story ended well. But it was one of the pitfalls of this sort of work. As much as I had been touting to Larissa the warm and mushy side of people buying not just a drawing, but a symbol of something very personal, that same intimate connection also left the door open for a multitude of ways for situations to go awry.

Joshua Tree National Park, California — Patron asked to be unnamed

The yoga studio faced west, which meant late-afternoon or early-evening light—and also that I could sleep in. My first round of scouting done, it was time to eat. The kitchen of the main house was loaded with pots and pans and cookware as if outfitted by a professional chef, but the fridge and pantry were curiously sparse—especially for a place that supposedly had people staying almost every night. A few spices and a bottle of olive oil and that was it. Not even a spare bag of pasta. I decided to drive back into town for supplies, then settle in for the evening.

I wound the Miata down the hill and found the aptly named Stinson Beach Market. For dinner I bought a fat cut of New York strip steak, one potato, a bunch of scallions, and a bottle of Russian River Pinot. For the next two days I bought a loaf of bread, eggs, butter, and a small bunch of bananas. I was sure I'd also come back down for fish tacos and oysters.

As I was backing out of the parking area I noticed people gathered across the street, at the edge of the beach, at an ice cream stand. I drove across and parked in the lot between two Vanagons of surfers peeling off their wetsuits and loading boards onto roof racks. The wind was calmer than up on the hill, and the sound of crashing waves filled the air.

I ordered a single scoop of chocolate ice cream in a sugar cone and sat on a picnic table at the edge of the sand. The majority of beachgoers had long packed up, but there was still a fair number of people milling about, mostly couples and families, some walking their dogs, all enjoying the sunset. The view wasn't very picturesque, mostly a heavy layer of fog lying low on the horizon, but it was the end of a day at the beach, and that was good enough for me. I ate my ice cream and mindlessly stared out at the darkening sky over the water. After savoring the last bite of cone filled with melted ice cream, I was ready for dinner. I loved being an adult.

In the parking lot a police cruiser and a National Parks jeep had pulled in and stopped in the middle of the lot. I determined I could just barely get around them, and was opening the door to the Miata when two uniformed cops approached. One asked if this was my vehicle and, when I replied that it was, asked for my license and registration. As I handed over the cards I wanted to say, "You can tell Ocampo and Zorn the joke's gone far enough. I'll be back in a couple of days and will tell them then if I want to play in their little game." But of course I didn't.

One of the cops stood watching me with his hand on his gun while the other walked to the front of the Miata, then the rear, while looking at my license and registration.

"Can you tell me why your vehicle is reported as stolen?" he asked.

"I have no idea," I said.

"And you're certain this is your car?"

"Yeah. I mean, my keys work. And you have my license and registration. I've got my insurance card somewhere too if you want it."

The cop with my cards looked to the other cop and made a slight movement with his head. The other cop moved forward.

"Sir, if you could step to the rear of the vehicle, please."

"What's the problem?" I asked. "This is obviously my car, and I haven't reported it—" But before I could finish, the second cop had my arm in his hand and was turning me around and deftly slipping cuffs around both my wrists. I was being arrested—for the second time in three days.

Mission District, San Francisco — Commissioned by Amy Holiday. Amy had moved to Portland and requested a drawing of the block she'd lived on in the eighties. Only after I'd shipped her the piece did she realize she'd given me the wrong address, resulting in my drawing the wrong row of houses. She called me, laughing. "Totally my fault," she said. I offered to draw the right block for her, but she laughed again and said, "Whatever. I barely remember living there anyway."

19

HONEY

Seeing that I was being driven up along the coastal highway, away from the beach, I figured Stinson didn't have its own police station. My guess was they were taking me to Mill Valley. For half an hour I sat in the back seat of a police car that handled the winding road far less gracefully than the Miata—handcuffed. Which, frankly, I didn't see the need for. The entire drive, the cops didn't say a word. Who knows why. I didn't care. I was fine to forgo conversation and focus on other things—mainly keeping a belly full of ice cream in my stomach along those snaking roads.

By the time we arrived in Mill Valley it was all I could do not to throw up. As I was being led into the station, the booking officer took one look at me and my pale complexion and said, "Good work, Mitchell. I love it when they're scared." Then she gave me the largest smile of contempt I've ever seen. I couldn't help but wonder what it was with me and cops lately.

Given the storm in my stomach, I was actually hoping they'd put me in a cool, dark cell so I could sleep it off, but instead I was sat in a wooden chair next to a desk where the arresting officer started asking me questions. Deja vu had never been so tedious.

"You live in San Francisco—on Guerrero Street?"

"I do."

"Why were you in Stinson?"

"Staying at a friend's house."

"And what's the address?"

I told him, and he paused.

"The Jerry Garcia house?"

"Excuse me?"

"You don't know where you were staying?"

"I told you where I was staying."

He shook his head as if I'd rambled off a string of nonsensical words. "And who is your friend?"

I had the impulse not to tell him. Seemed to me it was none of his business, and had nothing to do with my car being incorrectly reported stolen. But of course anything less than complete cooperation was not going to bode well for me.

"Steven Thorn."

The cop nodded. He appeared to know the name. "And Mister Thorn gave you permission to use his home?"

"He did. My things are there in the entryway. I arrived just before sunset and was only popping into town to buy groceries. Why did you say it was the Jerry Garcia house?"

He looked suspicious. "You really don't know? I thought you said you're friends with Mister Thorn?"

"I am—or, rather, we're business friends. I'm an artist and he hired me to draw the place—specifically the yoga studio, as a gift for his wife." I gave him these last details in the hope of sounding more legitimate, but he only looked at me like I was trying to prove the lie by over-embellishing. Seemed I couldn't win either way. So I doubled down by adding, "I'm staying for four nights."

The cop narrowed his brow and leaned back in his seat. It was becoming clear to me that, whether in the city or across the bridge, trying to explain my life as an artist to a booking officer was never going to be a good tack for earning trust. And at this point I almost didn't care. All I wanted was to either be put in a cell so I could rest my churning stomach, or be driven back to my car with an apology. And since the latter didn't seem to be high on the list of options, the sooner I was in a room where I could lie down, the better. But the interview wouldn't end. It was as if the cop was certain I was a high-level criminal, and the only thing preventing my full-blown confession was that he hadn't asked the right questions. And so round and round we went.

"Can you explain to me," the cop said, after pursing his lips and thinking really hard, "why the car you were driving had two slices in the roof?"

"Because I live in the city," I said. "Where there's an inordinate amount of senseless crime."

"So it wasn't because you'd sliced the roof to get inside?"

"Twice? Then repaired it with tape? And how do you explain the fact that the registration with my name was in the glove box? *And* that I had keys? Why would someone who has keys slice the roof to get in, *then* repair it?"

"Then how do you explain the vehicle being reported stolen?"

"I have no idea. It's obviously a mistake. I'm the owner. I've given you proof. What more explanation am I supposed to give?"

The cop rubbed his chin and considered me. If I hadn't been so nauseous, I would have been livid. Still, I was close.

"You said you were in Stinson to draw Mister Thorn's house," the cop said. "What does that even mean?"

That was it. I couldn't take any more. I leaned forward and pressed my chest to his desk—seeing that my hands were still cuffed behind my back. "You're going to make a call," I said. "To Lieutenant Ocampo of the San Francisco Police Department. I'm a private contractor for the sfpd, and she's my contact. If you really want to find out what it means for me to draw houses, then you should go ahead and keep asking me stupid questions." I wasn't exactly sure what that meant, but I was pissed off. And cooperating clearly wasn't getting me anywhere. Besides, what was the worst that could happen? They put me in a cell? I *wanted* that!

The cop was unimpressed by my having dropped Ocampo's name. But I was insistent enough that he couldn't ignore me—even though he'd been doing a damn fine job thus far. So he said okay, he'd make the call. Unfortunately I didn't get to hear it, as I was moved to another wooden chair in the hallway—*not* a cell. I could only imagine the shit it was going to put me in with Ocampo. But that was a mess for Tomorrow-Emit. Today-Emit needed to be released, grill a steak, and soak in a god damn hot tub.

* * *

Several long, boring, and physically uncomfortable hours passed. Somehow I'd managed to doze off—and not fall off the chair—and by the time the cop kicked my foot to rouse me, my stomach was at least settled.

My cuffs were finally removed, and I was led out to the reception area. As I rubbed my wrists, I saw a man, early forties, white, around five-foot-six, with broad shoulders and a bit of a paunch, leaning on the intake-window ledge, yakking it up with the desk sergeant. He was wearing light-blue denim jeans and a pink polo shirt under a tan windbreaker, looking like he'd just come from golfing with retired comedians. He'd had the sergeant in stitches, but when she saw me she went instantly deadpan. The man kept his smile, though. He straightened up and put out his hand. "You're Hopper, yeah?"

I nodded, shook his hand.

"Ronnie Gilbert," he said. "Your buddy Ocampo sent me to spring you. She also told me to drop you over the side of Highway One and make sure your body hit a few rocks on the way down, but I figured I'd give you a chance to talk me out of it." He laughed and slapped my arm. "Come on. You can buy me dinner."

The desk sergeant was already sliding my wallet and keys across the window ledge. She was scowling.

I took my things, signed the release form, and asked about my car.

"You'll have to follow up with the arresting officer about that, sir," the woman said. She might as well have spit in my face. I wanted to think she just didn't like suspected criminals, but it was feeling personal.

"They'll have it in impound," Ronnie said. "Which is closed for the night. You can get it tomorrow. Now let's eat. It's already past my bedtime."

*   *   *

"How could you not know you were staying at Jerry Garcia's house?" my new friend and rescuer Ronnie said.

We'd pulled into the Buckeye Roadhouse, a lodge-style building five minutes from the Mill Valley Police Station, perched just off the freeway as you headed toward the city. Ronnie had driven us in his black Ford Mustang. Not the classic sixties muscle car with long hood, side vents, and hunched rear fender, but a newer, more refined version. Still, while I'm not much of a car guy, I knew enough to know it was a serious car. I also knew that Ronnie loved it. The exterior shone as if it had just been triple-waxed, and the interior—full red leather, from seats to steering wheel to stick-shift cover—also looked as if it had been oiled only hours earlier. Plus, the sound system was incredible. I don't know how many speakers were in that car, but it seemed to me if there had been a place to put one, Ronnie had. From the moment we'd left the station he'd cranked Tom Petty's *Full Moon Fever*—which was why we hadn't had any conversation on the short drive—and it sounded as if we were there in the studio while it was being recorded. Then there was what I can only call the personal touch: a miniature Matchbox version of the exact same model of car, also black, mounted on the dash.

"For one," I said, after we got out of the Mustang and I stood watching Ronnie open the trunk, "I've never met any of the guys in the Grateful Dead. And two, Jerry's been dead for a few years now, so . . ."

Inside Ronnie's trunk was a cardboard flat of mason jars and two brown paper bags full with what looked like freshly harvested pot but I had to assume wasn't. He grabbed one of the mason jars. "You like honey?" he asked. "I keep bees." But he wasn't offering me the jar.

I followed him up the wooden ramp into the Buckeye. The dining area was closed, so we went to the bar. The room was small and looked like a cross between a ski lodge and a hunting cabin. It was a fine enough place, but it wasn't the fifty-foot deck of what I now knew was a house owned by one of the most famous musicians to ever come out of San Francisco. Of course, it also wasn't a stiff wooden chair in the Mill Valley Police Station, so I decided not to complain.

The time was just after eleven, and as we entered, the bartender called out, "Kitchen's closed," only to realize who had walked in, then his tone immediately became friendly, as did his tune. "Señor Gilberto!" he said, trilling the words with glee. "We're always open for you. You want the usual?"

"You like steak?" Ronnie said to me.

"I do."

"Duo the usuo," Ronnie said to the bartender, leading me to one of the booths.

I slid in, but Ronnie stepped to the bar. The place was tight, and everything was pressed close, with barely enough room to squeeze past the bar to get into a booth, so he was only a couple feet away.

"How's doin' Rhett?" Ronnie said to the bartender, setting the jar of honey onto the bar and pushing it forward.

"Can't complain, but I will." He pointed to the honey. "For moi?"

"For the missus. Cause we both know ain't nothing going to make you sweet."

Rhett laughed, picked up the jar, and kissed it. "Much obliged," he said. "What you drinking?" He'd said it not just to Ronnie but to me, looking my way and jerking up his chin.

"He's buying," Ronnie said, "so tonight it's the good stuff. Blanton's, on ice."

I was liking this guy. And not just because he'd gotten me out of handcuffs.

"Same," I called out. "Double."

Rhett clicked his cheek. "Wouldn't respect you if it wasn't."

As Rhett poured the whiskey, I glanced around. There were only five other patrons. Two were in the far booth, an older white guy, early sixties, and a Filipina woman, forty at best. They were laughing, having a good time.

And at the bar were three men, one heavyset white guy with a goatee, and two thin dark-skinned men, Indian, I guessed. The trio looked like they shopped from the same rack: tan khakis, button-down shirts patterned with boring variations of picnic-table plaid, and sleeveless North Face vests.

Ronnie joined me in the booth with the drinks. "It ain't Jerry's house," he said, raising up his whiskey. "But they do a damn fine ribeye." He drank, then shook his head. "Still can't believe you didn't know where you were. Garcia sold the place back in the seventies, but everybody knows it was his. It's famous."

After downing most of my double, I opened my hands and let them drop. What the hell did I know from Jerry Garcia's house? Steven sure as hell hadn't told me.

"So you're back to drawing buildings?" Ronnie asked, reaching for two coasters and setting his drink atop one.

I finished the rest of my whiskey. "Wouldn't you rather ask if I'm a car thief?"

Ronnie shook his head. "Of course you're no thief. Curious mix-up, though. Cars generally don't go calling themselves in stolen. You piss anyone off lately? Maybe a lady friend you played selfish with and didn't give a happy ending to one too many nights in a row? Dissatisfied and getting a little revenge?"

"No lady friends at the moment. And no recent exes who may have gotten drunk and thought to punish me—or at least no recent ones." Though when it came to "recent," I realized I might have to broaden my definition. I'd potentially had sex with Larissa's mother eighteen years ago, and that was only coming back to me now. But I left that part out.

"Is definitely a brain-teaser," Ronnie said. "Not run-of-the-mill, I'll give you that. Had your plates been switched, I woulda said a couple of jackals made a swap with whatever ride they boosted. Classic way to cruise the town without getting pulled over. Usually middle-school kids. But this one's weird. Even more so because they brought you in."

"Yeah," I said. "Why would they do that? What more does a person need to do to prove he actually owns his property?"

Ronnie shrugged. "They didn't book you, did they? So you got nothing to worry about. Maybe their c.o.'s been bustin' their balls and so they've been playin' it extra close to the books. They're just doin' their job."

"Yeah, well, I'm getting pretty sick of cops doing their job. Seeing that it keeps winding me in handcuffs for shit I didn't do."

Ronnie grinned, leaned back in the booth, and opened his hands as if to say, "Please, tell me more."

So I told him about the scene at the Legion, Ocampo's fake extortion, and Inspector Zorn showing up at the laundromat to offer me a job.

"What a ride," he said, laughing. "And you got no clue who the chick is who waggled her hooters at you?"

"I have the photo. But you can't recognize her. For all I know she could be the same person who's been slicing the roof of my car and calling it in stolen."

"You still get groupie stalkers?"

"Not since the band broke up, which was over a decade and a half ago."

Ronnie tilted his head. "Then I wouldn't go full conspiracy nut just yet."

A waitress appeared at our table, a fiftyish woman wearing a Harley Davidson T-shirt. "Hiya, Ron," she said, setting a set of napkins and silverware in front of each of us.

"Hiya, kid," Ronnie said, even though she was clearly a decade older. He pointed to my empty glass. "Another?" And when I nodded he said, "Another for my friend."

"You got it," she said with a smile, then she walked off.

"So, this flasher," Ronnie said to me. "You say you got the photo? Can I get a gander?"

"It's back at the house."

"And seeing this is the second curious incident to befall you in almost as many days, I once more need to ask: Any enemies? Anyone you piss off lately?"

"Honestly," I said, "the only person I can think of who might pull any kind of prank on me is my brother—and he's not an enemy. He's just my twin. He and I have a thing for playing practical jokes on each other. Only none of this feels like him. He would never involve the police. And there's no punchline. I mean, where's the payoff in getting me arrested? Plus, he's in China, and the last thing he wants is bad press. So yeah—or rather, no. I don't know who it could be."

The waitress set a fresh drink for me and two waters on the table and walked off.

"Your brother," Ronnie said. "Brian Hopper? The actor?"

"Yeah."

"Shit deal he got after that *Brandice Falls* thing."

I took a sip of my fresh bourbon and arched my brows. "Impressive," I said. "You keep up on the careers of many TV stars?"

"I'm a news sponge. What about patrons? Any unhappy art buyers? Someone who didn't like how you drew their house?"

I put my drink down and smirked. "How do you know about my commissions? Ocampo tell you?"

Ronnie shrugged. "Told you. I'm an information junkie. I'm one of those guys, I see a newspaper on a bus seat with an unfinished crossword puzzle, I gotta do it. Can't help it. It's an affliction."

"And so what about you?" I asked. "How is it that you're who the lieutenant called to scoop me up from the station? Are you a cop? Or . . ."

"Private," Ronnie said. "I was on the force years back. Most guys, they put in a solid thirty. Me, I was in and out in four. I play it solid, but I'm not one for the mundane. And most department cases, they're run-of-the-mill—husband kills wife, gangbanger shoots gangbanger, junkie robs liquor store. Not the sort of intricate plot-weaving stuff like you write—or that tickles my machine. What turns me on is when a thing doesn't fit into a tidy box—" he tilted his head and put out his hand "—when you gotta come at it from a new angle and look at the thing sideways." He picked up his water. "And by working private, I get to pick and choose my gigs, you know what I mean?"

I nod. "It's why I like being an artist. Freedom and autonomy. So you've read my books?"

Ronnie shook his head—a little too vigorously. "Don't take it personal. I might read somebody's poetry to try and get a sense of how their noodle bends, but all my eruditing is strictly nonfiction." He coughed a little into his fist to clear his throat. "No, you I know from your rock and roll days—heck, we might have even stood in the same room together a time or two." He drank some water. "Back in the day, before I signed up for a uniform, I worked insurance fraud, and moonlit as security. Did a lot of nights at the Fillmore and Warfield. A lot of cops did the same, which is where I made a few friends and got the idea to join up. After the job went down the pisser and I first went private, I did a ton of work for you rocker types. Mostly paternity cases. Some stalker stuff. And divorce too." He shook his head. "Man, you guys had it good—too good. No other line of work do teenage girlies throw their panties at your feet. Of course most of you were a bunch of morons who didn't know your dicks from your guitars. I can't tell you how many rock and roll fortunes went to settling sex cases. But that's another story."

I decided not to tell him about Larissa.

"And you know," Ronnie said, "once I got listening, I got to like a lot of the music. You know who I really liked? Def Leppard. You ever meet those guys?"

"Once. We opened for them at a festival in Berlin."

"Brits, you know. And the drummer—you remember what happened to that poor kid? Lost an arm after wrapping his car around a tree. Damn fine car too. Stingray Corvette. I gotta say, I was impressed as hell how he could still wail on the drums after that."

Our waitress appeared with our food. Two juicy, sizzling steaks with a mound of mashed potatoes and pile of steamed spinach. She asked if there was anything else she could get us, and Ronnie told her hot sauce. Only, before he got the words out, she'd produced a bottle of Tabasco from her back pocket and was setting it on the table.

"What?" she said. "You think I fell off the bimbo-bus yesterday?"

"I think you're an angel in the choir," Ronnie said.

She smiled, then turned to me. "You good?"

"I'm great," I said. "Thanks." Then she was off again.

I picked up my fork and knife. "Actually," I said, as I cut into my steak and watched Ronnie douse everything on his plate with Tabasco, "now that I think about it, I did have one suspicious incident with a commission. This was in July, when I first started up again. They weren't unhappy exactly, but it did get weird."

"Talk to me," Ronnie said, taking a bite of potatoes and spinach.

"Brotherhood Way, out by Lake Merced, you know it?"

Ronnie nodded.

"Along that stretch there's a handful of churches. I got a call from a pastor of one inviting me to do a commission. I went to the church and, after giving me a tour, the pastor brought me into his study. He served me tea and scones and paraded out at least a dozen pieces of art he'd had commissioned—drawings, paintings, photographs—all of the church. He was proud of his budding collection and talked about how for centuries the church had been commissioning artists, and that he felt it was his mission to continue the practice. We agreed on a price and I made him a drawing. When I delivered, he was pleased. He paid me and that was that. All easy enough. Then about a month ago, I get a call from a woman saying she's a member of the congregation and that the pastor had been let go. She was reluctant to share details, but, seeing that she was the one calling, felt she had no choice. It seems the good pastor had been caught misusing church funds for all sorts of personal activities, one of which was for art commissions. She said it was a shame, but now the pastor was gone, so it was over. Only he'd taken all the artworks with him. The congregation was working on getting them back, but for whatever reason they were having trouble. Something about proving ownership—I didn't ask for details. Point is, she was calling all the artists he'd commissioned in hopes they would produce another piece of art to replenish those the pastor had taken with him."

"Was she offering to pay you?"

"No. She was hoping I would do it out of generosity, seeing that the church had been victimized."

"And I'm wagering you're not that generous."

"I am not."

Ronnie snorted. He wiped a blob of Tabasco-soaked mashed potato from his cheek and said, "And so you're thinking one of those angry parishioners is taking revenge?"

I slid a piece of fatty beef into my mouth. "I'm not thinking anything," I said, covering my mouth as I chewed. "I'm only relaying the story."

Ronnie shook his head. "God freaks have been known to pull some seriously batshit shenanigans, for sure. But I don't see the payoff. How does discrediting you get them new art? Or do anything but devalue your art if and when they get their collection back?"

"Unless by tying me to a sex scandal they in turn tie the thieving reverend to one too."

"There you go again, with the over-wrought plots." He ate a bite of steak.

"You're the one who said he liked the stuff that doesn't fit into a tidy box," I said. "Looking at things from a different angle."

"What I said was most crimes fit into a tidy box. Not that I go out of my way to pull them out. I only look at a thing sideways after I've given it a good long look, straight on. Whereas you, you wanna lie on your back and look at everything upside down and backwards before you give yourself a chance to see it straight."

I smiled. "Makes me think of one of my earliest lessons in drawing," I said. "Before you can make a mark, you have to really see what you're looking at. You have to take it apart and understand how it's put together before you can know how to draw it."

"Exactamundo. And for your little conundrum, the question you need to ask is: Who benefits?"

"Right . . . Well, as far as the church goes, there's no one I can see who benefits from messing with me."

"Nor I. Also, our not-so-good pastor hired not just you, but a slew of artists, yeah? Are these vindictive God-jobs discrediting all of them too?"

I had my mouth full of steak, but the question was rhetorical, so I answered by tilting my head.

"What about other patrons?" Ronnie asked, moving on. "Any other unhappy situations? Direct or indirect?"

"Most of the time people are happy," I said. "Though there's always the occasional misunderstanding." I told him about the Joshua Tree incident, then another, where a guy wanted a drawing of the house he grew up in, only he lived in Miami and hadn't been back to the Bay Area in decades. A huge tree was now on the block, which apparently hadn't been there when he was a kid, but, because it was there when I went to draw, I'd put it into the piece. Most of his building was still visible, but the tree was covering the one window that had been his bedroom, and he was disappointed. "Stuff like that," I said. "Which isn't my fault and causes some awkward conversations, but not enough for retaliation. Certainly not enough to provoke someone to try and smear my reputation—or at least that I'm aware of."

"Assuming ruining your good name was the goal."

"If not that, then what?"

Ronnie shrugged. "Who called it in?"

"You mean the complaint at the museum?"

"Yeah. Was it the supposed victim?"

"I don't know. She didn't stick around."

"And where'd she make the call from? If my memory serves, the Legion doesn't have pay phones. Did she go inside? If so, the staff would surely remember."

"She could have used a cell phone."

"Or maybe she didn't make the call. Could have been one of the biddies who likes to take tea at her favorite hall of antiquities, getting her Depends in a bind thinking you were out there playin' perv."

"I was thinking the same thing. Problem with that theory is, if the call was made by an angry museum-goer who was so offended as to call the police, then why not stick around?"

"Who knows. Maybe she thought she'd already done her civic duty. Maybe all you've got yourself here is loyal devotee, flashin' you her love, and a jealous nobody as a witness," Ronnie wiped his mouth with his napkin. "It's not as sexy as having a bitter enemy who lives and breathes your demise, I know. But like I said, more times than not, most things fit into a box."

"Yeah," I said, still thinking about it. I'd been plowing through my food and was mopping up the last smears of mashed potato with my last bite of steak. "But it's not just the flasher that's bothering me. You were a cop. Don't you think it's weird that officers even responded? I mean, I don't care how slow of a day it is, would a cruiser really have bothered to head out for a lewd behavior complaint? Not to mention haul me in?"

Ronnie picked up his drink and thought about it. "Normally I'd say no. But it's the museum we're talking about. Not the highest tourist traffic, but high enough. And you gotta remember, we're in the middle of all this election nonsense. Best my knowledge, the Richmond is voting Willie's way, but who knows, maybe there's some stuffy interest group using this Ammiano threat as leverage in City Hall. So to pacify the plebes, King Willie sends down a directive to be tough on crime. You know how the mudslinging of politics can go. One rogue story about a wacko artist waggin' his winkie out at the museum could become the poster child as to why the mayor ain't doin' his job, and tank an election." Ronnie threw back his whiskey and smacked his lips. "Listen. I ain't saying you're teeing off the course here. I'm just saying maybe it's a possibility that random girlies are still throwing their panties at your feet."

20

A ROOM WITH A VIEW

t was late, and Ronnie offered to put me up for the night. From the Buckeye we drove ten minutes to the Sausalito Marina. He parked in a spot that I assumed was reserved as his, then we walked through a wooden entryway and along a raised dock past a dozen houseboats of wildly different styles and sizes. At a large, boxy, two-story structure atop a cement hull, we took a gangplank across. Hung above the door was a hand-carved wooden sign, Knot Guilty.

"I didn't name her," Ronnie said as we passed through the door. "I bought the place on auction after a defense lawyer got snagged by tax evasion and his assets seized by the IRS."

"So I take it the sign was wishful thinking on his part?"

"Serves him right for punning."

I caught only a dark glimpse of the interior as Ronnie took me directly up to the roof deck. The house had three decks, and the top was the full footprint of the house with a railing all around. There were potted plants and trees, a trellis with jasmine, a set of teak wooden chairs and table, a covered bar, and, at the far edge, three stacks of rectangular boxes that I realized were bee hives. I went to the railing and looked at the view. Ronnie's was one of the taller residences on his pier, and from the roof you could see the silhouette of Mount Tamalpais to the north and the twinkling lights of Belvedere Island to the east. Ronnie went to the bar, then joined me at the railing and handed me a drink. I assumed bourbon and was correct.

"Careful with your confessions up here," he said.

"What do you mean?"

"I mean don't say anything you wouldn't say on a crowded bus full of reporters. There's no privacy on a houseboat, and it's a gossipy community.

Which is funny, since half the folks who end up out here think of themselves as outsiders."

"Seems an odd place to live for a private investigator. I'd think you'd want the opposite."

"True, true. But it works in my favor. Problem with being private is you ain't got no one watching your back. And as lovable a guy as I am, in this line of work, you make enemies. If anyone comes sniffin' around looking for whatever sniffers look for, I've got eyes and ears without tryin'. And anyway, I keep another place up north. A cabin off the grid for when I really need to hide."

There were several rows—streets?—of houseboats between us and Mount Tam. Ronnie pointed in that direction. "You can't see it so good from here," he said. "But a few docks over are The Gates. Old floating renegade village. Back in the fifties, the beatniks piled themselves on old WW-two landing craft like penniless sea lions. In the sixties, the hippies moved in and built compounds to escape the 'hill people' of dry land. Your buddy Jerry Garcia probably lost more than a few nights there. These days it's on its last sea legs, sinking into the water, but the hippies still won't let it go. It leans way tribal—and feral. A load of artists and musicians still nesting in its midst. I'm surprised you don't know it."

"I was out of the music business by the time I moved here."

"Even so," Ronnie said. He finished his drink. "Okay, history hour over. Bedtime for this bucko."

He led me down to the second level, to what he called his guest bedroom. While there was a single bare mattress on the floor, the room was full of metal shelves loaded with boxes of magazines, notebooks, and case files. I wasn't surprised, seeing that Ronnie was a self-proclaimed information junkie, but it did make me want to suggest to him that instead of telling people he had a guest bedroom, he should say he had a place for them to crash in his storage area. In any case, it was somewhere to sleep. So after spreading a sheet over the mattress, I said thank you and passed out the moment I lay down.

* * *

I woke to a phone ringing and the muffled sound of Ronnie answering. There was no clock, but there was a window and I could see it was morning—or at least daytime. The sky was such a flat gray that there was no way to know what hour it might be. The air was rich with the briny smell of the sea—and coffee. The latter got me up.

I went downstairs to see Ronnie in the kitchen, a cordless phone to his

180

ear. His eyes met mine, then he slid open the glass door to the deck and motioned for me to go out. It was his domain, so I obliged. As I passed the counter, I saw a carafe of French press coffee and pointed. He gave me a thumbs-up and slid the door shut behind me.

The deck off the kitchen stretched the length of the houseboat. The area was long and narrow, crowded with potted plants and trees. An eight-foot-high trellis of bougainvillea spanned most of the length, forming a wall between his deck and the dock. At first it seemed like a solid barrier against nosy neighbors, then, after I sat in one of the two rusting iron chairs and began inspecting the small yellow lemons on a potted tree, I noticed through a small opening in the trellis a neighbor peering through their window, trying to get a glimpse of me. I knew then that Ronnie hadn't been exaggerating when he'd said the houseboat community didn't have much privacy.

A few minutes later, the door slid open and Ronnie stepped out with a mug of coffee.

"Here ya go, sport. And sorry for the exile. Business to tend to."

"It's fine," I said, taking the mug. I sipped trepidatiously. After my previous morning with Larissa I didn't know what to expect, but found an excellent cup of coffee.

"And not to give you the bum's rush, but I need to go into the city. I can give you a ride as far as the Gulch."

"I've got a house in Stinson I need to get back to," I said. "Which I need to draw. Plus, all my stuff is there. Any idea when I can get my car back?"

Ronnie laughed. "Yeah, that's a sticky one. I called my buddy at impound. Sorry to tell ya, but that toy hamster-mobile you call a car will be stuck in red tape for at least another day—if not longer. I tried to pull some strings, but the cop who scooped you up has a noodle up his ass about you. The desk sergeant? You remember her?"

"The one who hates suspected criminals?"

"The one who hates you."

"Me? What did I do to her?"

"You as proxy. Your brother—the twin. Seems a few years back, he and she had a little thing. Which didn't end so good."

I wasn't surprised. Brian didn't have the best track record with leaving hearts—or tempers—in one piece. I drank some coffee. "And so because I'm Brian's brother, she's taking it out on me?"

"Would appear so."

"And so what about the other cop? The one who arrested me? What's his

181

problem? Tormenting me out of sympathy for his fellow officer? That seems a bit sadistic—not to mention unprofessional."

"It would be," Ronnie said. "If he weren't her fiancé."

"Shit."

Ronnie laughed. "But you're right. It is unprofessional. And he knows it. Which means he'll yank your chain for as long as he can, then he'll hand over your toy ride and you can figure out a good practical joke to play on your brother as payback. In the meantime, you can take a taxi back to Stinson, but it'll cost you an arm and probably both your legs. Or there's always the bus."

I took a deep breath and thought about it. "Any car rentals around here?"

"There's one just down the road. I can drop you, but it has to be now. I got something urgent in the city."

We went back inside and Ronnie looked up the number of the car rental. I called, only to learn they were out of cars.

"Guess I'll take that ride," I said.

*　*　*

While Ronnie gathered his things, I looked around. The first floor—or water level, as I supposed it was called—was one large open space with two wooden support beams to keep the ceiling from crashing down. By the plaster remnants on the timber, it looked as if at one point in time there had been walls and separate rooms, but they'd been taken out, making the kitchen, dining, and living area all one. A move I could appreciate. The place was packed, though. Everywhere you looked there was something, like a well-curated curio shop. Lining the kitchen shelves were jars of nuts, grains, and pastas. On the counter sat a large, round five-gallon clay pot. Across its tapered opening was a rubber lid with a burping nipple. By the sour smell, I guessed he was brewing kimchi. Newspapers and magazines covered every surface, open, and several layers deep. The bookshelves were crammed with books, and every available crook or corner had some knickknack or odd object. A large dining table was covered in newspaper, and on it was a pile of what looked like freshly cut weeds, and strung between the two wooden beams was a laundry line with stalks of a different plant hung up to dry. I smelled them, but couldn't determine what they were.

I hadn't even finished my coffee when Ronnie came bounding down the stairs, saying, "Time to roll."

Minutes later, we were on the road, heading to San Francisco—and away from the house I was supposed to be drawing, my clothes, my supplies, and my Miata. I decided I would rent a car in the city and drive back. How that might work for swapping it out with the Miata I still hadn't sorted. Ronnie told me he didn't have time to drop me before his errand, but that it shouldn't take long, so he could take me to a rental shop after. I tried to find out what was so urgent, but extracting information out of Ronnie was harder than getting a straight answer out of Larissa—plus, he was more adept at turning the tables. I asked him what he was working on, and instead of getting his story, found myself talking about coming home from the snafu at the museum to find a strange young woman asleep on my studio couch.

Ronnie roared. "And there goes another rock and roll fortune!"

We glided over the headlands and crossed the bridge. Ronnie took Lombard Street across the Marina to Van Ness, then turned left onto California Street. Three blocks down he hung a right onto Hyde, then took the next right onto Pine. We were spiraling into somewhere. Such was driving in a city that liked its one-way streets. We crossed Larkin, and as we approached Polk Ronnie turned off the music and slowed and looked around. This wasn't the heart of the Polk Gulch, but it was close. We were on a nondescript block. On one side was a brick elementary school, on the other a large post office. The rest of the block was condos. Ronnie passed two open meter spots, then pulled up alongside a police cruiser which was blocking the driveway to one of the condo buildings.

Ronnie rolled down his window, and the cop in the passenger seat of the cruiser rolled down his.

"I owe you guys some hipster avocado toast," Ronnie said.

The cop snorted. "I still like donuts."

Ronnie put the Mustang in park, turned on his hazards, and killed the engine.

"Hang tight," he said to me. Then he got out, leaving the car to block one of the three lanes of the one-way street.

I tried to see what was going on, but my view was obstructed. Ronnie had gone to the driver's side of the cop car and, best I could tell, was talking through the window to someone in the rear seat. I couldn't hear, though. Ronnie had left his window down, but the cop had rolled his back up.

A few minutes later, Ronnie was back. He opened the driver's door and pulled his seat forward. A teenage girl, her face caked in makeup, climbed into the rear seat. She had long, dirty-blond hair, and wore a sleeveless black leather vest and plaid miniskirt. The pungently sweet smell of her cheap perfume filled the Mustang.

Ronnie pushed the seat back and got in. "This is Taylor," he said, glancing in the rearview mirror and starting the engine. "Taylor, this is nobody whose name you need to know." He looked at me. "You got time for another stop?"

I didn't see how I could argue.

*   *   *

Ronnie turned off his blinkers, drove to the corner, then hung a right on Polk. We drove a dozen or so blocks, and had just crossed Greenwich when Ronnie asked, "What's the address?"

The girl in the back seat waited until just before the end of the block, then said, "Here," pointing to a six-story apartment building, one in from the corner.

Ronnie hung a fast left onto Lombard, downshifted, then pulled in front of another large apartment building with a row of five garage doors. He stopped perpendicular in front of one and put the car in park, turned off the ignition, and put on his hazards.

"You got keys?" he asked, turning around to look at Taylor. I looked as well. She was already holding up a set in front of her face.

"You need me to stay here and watch the car?" I asked.

"Actually," Ronnie said, narrowing his eyes and seeming to consider the scenarios. "The LT have you sign any sort of NDA?"

"You mean about the training—"

He cut me off. "I mean about not hanging around any water coolers."

"Right," I said. He didn't care about Ocampo or my pathetic job offer to be a live-action police silhouette. He was asking if I knew how to keep my mouth shut. "I was never here," I said.

"Good. Then you should come in."

The three of us got out of the car and walked around the corner to the front door of the building Taylor had pointed out. She opened the front door with her key and we went inside. It was one of those buildings that made me think of thirties gangster movies, with high ceilings, elaborate plasterwork, and no doorman. Taylor led us to an elevator with an iron accordion door, and the three of us—four if you counted her perfume—crammed inside the small carriage and rode up to the fifth floor. We were silent, but the elevator sounded as if it were giving a deathbed confession.

Apartment 504 was at the end of the hall. Taylor let us in, and Ronnie closed the door behind us. Heavy drapes covered the window, and the room was dark. Ronnie went to the corner and turned on a lamp, revealing

184

a large studio apartment. Taylor and I stood in the center while Ronnie looked around. I didn't know what he was looking for, but even I could tell something was off. Minimally furnished with a bed, loveseat, and floor lamp, the place had just enough effects to make it look like someone lived there, but only on the surface. The one plant was plastic, the one photo on the wall was of the stock models that had come with the frame, and the kitchen counter had nothing on it. It was like an Ikea decorator had staged the place, only with an even cheaper budget. There wasn't even a table to eat at. The prominent feature of the room was the bed, with a plush duvet and half a dozen puffy pillows with frilly cases. Directly across from the foot of the bed was a double-wide floor to ceiling mirror. Ronnie went right up to it, cupped his hands, and peered in as if it were a window. He stepped away, looked at Taylor, then went into the bathroom, to the right of the mirror.

Taylor and I followed him.

"You know about this?" Ronnie said, feeling around the edge of the inset cabinet above the sink.

The bathroom was small and tiled pink. There was barely room for the toilet, sink, and claw-foot tub, let alone for the three of us. Ronnie leaned over and began feeling around behind the toilet tank.

"The shitter?" Taylor said. "Yeah, I mighta used one once or twice in my life." She seemed just as perplexed as I was.

Then we heard a click, and a panel popped open above the tub. It was a door, about three feet off the ground, three feet high, and two feet wide. Hinged on the interior, the seams followed the lines of the tile, so that once it was revealed you knew it was there, but if you hadn't thought to look for it—because who would?—you'd never notice there was a secret panel.

"What the fuck?" Taylor said.

Ronnie stepped into the tub, opened the secret door all the way, then disappeared through the opening.

I looked to Taylor, who seemed genuinely surprised. Then I stepped into the tub and peered into where Ronnie had gone. It was a small room, the length of the double-wide mirror, and as deep as the bathroom. There was a chair, a mini-fridge, and a tripod with a large and expensive-looking camera. The mirror was one-way, and through it you could easily see into the main room. The camera was pointed directly at the bed.

Ronnie pulled his sleeve over his hand and opened the mini-fridge. I could see it was packed with plastic bottles of soda. Then I noticed a bag of potato chips on the floor beside the chair. It had been opened, and from how far down it had been rolled, looked to have been mostly eaten. Scattered on the floor were crumbs. Ronnie closed the fridge and nodded. "Hell of a seat to catch a show."

* * *

"I had no fucking idea that was there," Taylor said after we were all back in the main room. "You're telling me some shitbag has been sitting in there jerking off and making movies every time I'm here?"

"How many times have you been here?"

"Only a couple, but——" She scoffed. "Fucking hell. I knew there had to be something messed up about this shit."

"Why?"

"The whole thing is like, ultra-secret, you know? I get, like, two hours' warning. Just an address and time."

"Who gives you the information?"

"I don't know. I get a page."

Ronnie glared at her.

"What?" Taylor said. She reached into the small faux-leather backpack on her shoulder, pulled out a pager, and offered it to Ronnie. "Check it out for yourself."

Ronnie took the pager and scrolled through. "There's three other addresses in here."

"Fuck," Taylor said, adding a bitter laugh. "You know, now that I think about it, all those other places had the same big mirror across from the bed. I thought it was just your classic johns-liking-to-see-themselves-fuck setup, not this gonzo-voyeur videotaping shit."

Ronnie took out a small notebook from the inside of his windbreaker, along with one of those old-school four-color ballpoint pens. He clicked a color and began copying down the addresses, dates, and times of all of Taylor's messages. Then he turned the pager over and copied down the model and serial number.

"And who gave this to you?" he asked.

"Girl from The Nest."

That I recognized. The Nest was the youth shelter in the Tenderloin, run by Faith Chadwick, who'd recently opened The Arcade—where Larissa was volunteering.

"You crash there?" Ronnie asked.

"Sometimes," Taylor said. "But they totally make you do chores and shit to earn your keep. Washing sheets and cleaning dishes and all kinds of cooking and servant shit. Mostly I go there when it's raining. But they check all your stuff at the door."

"You got a habit?"

Taylor folded her arms. "I can take it or leave it."

"And what about the keys? You keep them or drop them somewhere?"

"I keep 'em. Same set opens all the apartments, which—fuck. I knew was weird. I just didn't think this weird."

"You get them from the same girl who gave you the pager?"

Taylor nodded.

"And what's her name?"

"Ashley. But I ain't seen her in a while. I think she OD'd."

"You know her last name?"

Taylor laughed. "That probably ain't even her first name."

"How do you get paid?"

"Credit in my name at the check-cashing joint on O'Farrell. Morning after the trick, I show ID and tell 'em Western Union sent me, and they hand over the cash. So we good? You'll get those cops to forget the bust? If that undercover who took me to The Nest finds out I was hooking again, he'll for sure send me to Juvie."

This made Ronnie stop. "When was this?" Of all we'd just seen and learned, this was what grabbed Ronnie's attention.

Taylor didn't seem to notice, though. "Couple months ago," she said. "He picked me up giving a BJ in the toilet of the Nite Cap. I had a couple balloons of tar on me. He said he had me on hooking, possession, and underage drinking. But—"

"But if you went to The Nest and got your shit straight, he'd let it slide."

"Yeah. He said he'd be checking in on me, make sure I was staying clean and not turning tricks."

"And did he?"

"Yeah, I don't know. I saw him a couple a' times when I was there, yucking it up with old lady Chadwick. He must bring in a ton of kids 'cause he was going around asking how we were all doing. I split after like the second week though. Chadwick is just way too eager to be the mom I never had, you know? Always telling us how much potential we have and trying to get us to play games and keep journals and shit. Some of the kids are into it I guess, but I don't know. Was pretty cheesy for me."

"And this cop, the undercover. You remember his name?"

"Yeah, it was some weird pirate shit. Like Zoro or something."

I looked to Ronnie, and his eyes darted over at me, but only for a second.

"What?" Taylor said, catching the exchange. "You know him?" She sounded hopeful. "Can you fix it with those unies so he doesn't find out?"

"I can," Ronnie said. "But you gotta do something for me."

Taylor looked offended. She waved her arm at the room. "What the fuck do you think this is?"

"I think this is you knowing that I can have your tar-smoking, dick-sucking, fifteen-year-old hooker ass thrown into the shithole of the system faster than you can piss in a john's mouth unless you keep helping me, that's what."

Taylor actually looked hurt. "Damn, dude. You don't have to be so harsh about it."

Ronnie reached into the side pocket of his windbreaker, took out his wallet, and handed her a business card. "Next time you get a page, you call me," he said. She took hold of the card, but Ronnie didn't let go. That was the only time I saw her flinch. She looked up at him. He was staring at her, hard. "And I don't mean two hours after your little cinematic fuckfest," he said. "I mean the minute you get the page. Your beeper goes off, you don't buy a pack of smokes, you don't get a fix, you don't scratch your ass. You find a phone and you call me. And if you don't, and I find out you burned me—because trust me, kiddo, I will—then Zoro is the least of your worries, you hear me?"

He let go of the card, and Taylor shoved it inside her bag. She closed her eyes and nodded. "I hear ya."

"Now go," Ronnie said. "And don't get busted again."

Taylor left, and Ronnie looked at me. "Let's wait a few, so we don't follow her straight out."

"It's none of my business," I said. "But don't you think you were a little rough on her?"

He snorted. "Teenager who lives on the street turning tricks for speed and heroin?" He laughed. "That kid's already tougher than you and I will ever be. Playing rough is the only game she knows."

"And Zoro? Am I making a leap to think she was talking about Inspector Zorn?"

Ronnie turned toward the mirror, looked at me in the reflection. "That's a baby goat of a hop compared to the leaps I'm making."

21

HOT BOX

"I don't need to remind you to not go writing any books about this stuff, do I?"

Ronnie and I had left the apartment building and were back in his Mustang. He was driving me to a car-rental shop on the edge of the Theater District downtown.

"And no gabbing around the water cooler, either," I said. "You don't need to worry about me. I just want to get back to Jerry's house and soak in the hot tub—and hopefully get my car back before it reeks permanently of rotten steak. How the hell do I do that, anyway?"

Ronnie took out another one of his business cards. "I'll rattle some more cages," he said, handing me the card. "Call me tonight and we'll see what we can do." He pulled into a bus lane on Mason Street, across the street from the rental shop.

"Thanks," I said. "Much appreciated."

"Anything for a guy who shared a stage with Def Leppard."

I got out, closed the door, and watched as the Mustang sped off with a deep, powerful rumble that the Miata could only dream to make.

* * *

I rented a car easily enough and by noon was on my way back to Stinson. I was hungry, but wanted to get back to the house as soon as possible to catch the light. A lot had happened over the past eighteen hours—and twenty-four, and forty-eight, and . . . I still hadn't begun to process having been led to a secret spy room by a teenage prostitute. And I wasn't sure I wanted to.

It was just after one when I arrived back in Stinson. I went to the grocery store again. This time I continued straight up the hill after shopping.

No amount of ice cream or beach views was worth tempting fate. Back at the house I held my breath as I punched in what I thought were the gate and door codes. Luckily I remembered right. Once inside I wanted to eat, but also needed to work. I knew I needed afternoon or evening light, so I had to at least look before fixing food. I downed a tall glass of water to fool my stomach, then went out to check the light on the yoga house.

Fortunately the day was clear. The sun was just creeping to my side of the mountain and was starting to hit the front of the studio. It would continue more as the day progressed, but the stark angle was looking great. I took an entire roll of reference photos and felt enormous relief. Getting good light reference was often the most time-consuming part of a commission. The act of drawing—not to pun—was linear. Assuming I didn't screw up the perspective, overwork the shadows, or spill ink all over the damn page, once I started I could easily predict how long the piece would take. Time to pinpoint good light, however, was not nearly as easy to predict. I'd gotten lucky, though, which, after the night before, I felt was deserved—not that life really worked that way. In any case, having gotten good reference photos meant I was home free. I could start the drawing whenever I wanted. Now it was time to eat.

Buying another steak had felt indulgent—especially having eaten one with Ronnie the night before—but I'd done it anyway. And it was damn good, too. As was the half-bottle of wine I drank in the middle of the afternoon.

After lunch, I assessed the light on the guest house again. The sun had moved farther to the west and was shining more directly onto the front of the small building. The shadows were less dramatic, and, in my opinion, less interesting. I knew then that the shots I'd gotten had been at the perfect time.

*   *   *

When I woke from my nap the sun was setting. I'd slept much longer than I'd intended. Not that it mattered. Despite having been delayed by a malfunctioning dryer at the shop, detained for a second time by rogue police, and taken on a weird adventure with a colorful private investigator, I'd still managed to tackle the hardest part of my job on day two—and without having even slept one night in the house. Now I could truly enjoy the perks of my profession. I was going to settle in and enjoy what had once been Jerry Garcia's house. The house was cold though. Outside was thick with fog. The marine layer that had been hovering just past the coastline had moved in and

190

engulfed the mountainside. I crumpled up some newspaper and started a fire in the wood-burning stove.

There was a turntable and a bookshelf lined with records. I flipped through and found—fittingly—a slew of Grateful Dead LPs. I'd never been much of a fan one way or the other, but if ever there was a time to give the band an honest listen, it seemed to be now. I put on the first of a three-album set called *Europe '72*, and decided it was time for a drink.

The house may not have come with groceries, but it was plenty stocked with booze. And staying in a patron's house to draw was the adult version of being a teenager with a babysitting job at the neighbor's; the stocked bar being the equivalent of a freezer full of ice cream. Mostly Steven Thorn liked scotch. I, however, did not. To me, the smokiness tasted like a drunken hillbilly had fallen asleep at the still and scorched what should have been a perfectly good batch of bourbon. Steven also liked tequila, though—real tequila, made from agave, not that sugarcane crap everybody drank as teenagers that left them shuddering as adults. So with the fog creeping in off the ocean, a fire crackling in the stove, and the Dead playing on the turntable, I poured myself some Siete Leguas Reposado and settled in front of the wall of glass to watch the last of what should have been a sunset, but was really just light gray turning to dark gray.

I was pouring a second tequila when the phone rang. The house wasn't mine, but I'd given the number to Betty in case there were any more issues with the dryer, and to Larissa if the results came in from the blood lab. Also, the Mill Valley police knew I was here, and I supposed it could have been the desk sergeant calling to apologize for taking out her grudge against my brother on me. I highly doubted it, but a man could dream. I answered the phone.

"You get that soak you were dying to have?"

Ronnie.

"Not yet," I said. "But the hot tub most definitely awaits."

"You alone up there?"

I hesitated. "Yeah, why?"

"I've always wanted to see Jerry's House."

* * *

Ronnie offered to bring crab if I fired up the grill. I told him I'd be waiting. Forty-five minutes later he was there with two enormous live crabs, two heads of artichoke, and a fat joint.

"I haven't gotten stoned in years," I said.

"Well then, we should go burn one in Jerry's old practice studio."

That's when I learned that the small building Steven's wife was using for yoga, the structure I was to draw, had been Jerry Garcia's former practice studio. I found the keys and we let ourselves in to look around. There was no hint of the late musician, and I wondered how Jerry would have felt about the yoga ball. The small building was an A-frame with one main room and a bathroom. Ronnie pulled a cord hanging down from the high ceiling and a wooden staircase dropped gracefully to the floor, revealing a loft. We climbed up to find a space just large enough to hold a twin-sized mattress under the pitched ceiling. That's where Ronnie fired up the joint. Smoke filled the tiny space, and even though there was a window, we didn't open it, so that by the end we were practically breathing more smoke than air. At one point Ronnie started coughing. "Man," he said. "Reminds me of being a teenager. We used to roll up all the windows in my buddy's car and fire up a doobie. Called it hot-boxing."

"My brother and I did something similar," I said. "Only one of us would fart under the covers, then pull the blanket over the other's head. Not nearly as intoxicating, and definitely less enjoyable."

Ronnie laughed so hard I thought he might choke. Yeah. Getting high in the loft of a legendary rock star's former personal studio. Good times.

* * *

I don't know how long had passed or how I ended up there, but I found myself standing over the grill, staring at two crabs. "Is it weird that we're cooking these creatures alive?" I said. I was stoned out of my mind.

Ronnie came over and looked as well. Beside the crabs were the two heads of artichoke, each wrapped in foil. The scene looked like a strange planetary landscape where the crabs were having a conversation next to silver rocks.

"Everything is weird when you're baked," Ronnie said. "Now close the lid or else they'll get tough."

I did, tried to swallow, and found my mouth was as thick as paste. I had a glass of tequila somewhere but decided I needed water. I went into the house and immediately forgot what I was doing, so went back outside—only to remember, then went back in again.

* * *

"I'm not saying I've worked for the Clintons," Ronnie said. "But let's just say that if you were a sitting president who liked receiving blowjobs in the Oval Office and you needed a former intern investigated, you might hire a guy like me."

Somehow we managed to cook, crack, and eat the crabs—though we made a hell of a mess, which made it good that we'd eaten outside—and by the time we cleaned up it was full-on night and the air was cold. Ronnie had gotten a fire going in the pit. We huddled close, while trying to avoid being touched by the flames licking wildly in the wind. I'd poured us fresh drinks in clean glasses and asked him to tell me more about his work.

"You did background on Monica?" I said, handing him a glass and sitting across from him. He was leaving me to infer that he'd worked for president Bill Clinton during the sex scandal with his former intern Monica Lewinsky, which had resulted in impeachment for high crimes and misdemeanors.

"I'm saying if such a situation might arise," Ronnie said, "then that's the kind of work I might do."

"And what about that sex room today? What the hell was up with that? And why did you bring me?"

"Calculated risk," Ronnie said.

I tugged out one of the heavy wool blankets from the plastic bin and spread it over my lap. "Yeah," I said. "I don't know what that means—or, I know what a calculated risk means. Just not in regard to you inviting me to join you with a teenage prostitute in a room where I'm guessing gonzo porn movies are being made."

"I wasn't sure what we'd find. Could have been a setup."

"I see. Meaning that if you'd walked in and gotten clubbed over the head, you wanted me to get it too?"

He snickered. "I've had a lot of things done to me, but never been clubbed in the head. Though I suppose there's still time." He took a sip of tequila, then set down the glass. I'd set mine down as well. The drink had ice and the night was cold enough. "No," Ronnie said, warming his hands at the fire, "the girl could have been sent to me to make it appear as if I was the one taking her to the room." He leaned back and pulled one of the wool blankets onto his lap as well. "Think about it. A forty-something-year-old man like myself walking into an apartment alone with a fifteen-year-old dressed how she was. If someone had been waiting, snapping pictures, from the street or the hallway, the optics could look bad for me. Especially if she'd been paid to say I was being untoward."

"Why would someone do that? To discredit you?"

"Possibly."

"Then I'll ask you the same as you asked about my situation: Who benefits?"

Ronnie clicked his tongue and pointed at me. "Good man. There may be hope for you yet." Then he picked up his drink, took a sip of tequila, and set the glass down again. "I've got a client," he said. "Name unimportant. Let's just say not without money or influence. Who's being blackmailed for having sex with an underage girl."

"With a secret recording made in that room?"

"Not in that room specifically, but one with a similar setup."

"Is he a pedophile?"

Ronnie's face pinched as he cocked his head. "That's the thing. I don't think he is."

"How can you be sure? And would it matter?"

"Well, that's a bit of the rub in this business. You get a client, your job is to protect their interests. That said, law states that if I'm aware they've committed a crime, I'm legally bound to report it. So it gets sticky. To do your job you have to also investigate the hand that feeds. Question is, how far. You have to remember, the people who hire me aren't having their best moments. This guy, for example . . . Let me give you the situation."

Ronnie held up his hands as if he were showing me the size of a fish he'd caught, then he looked at me as if he were looking over the top of his glasses, only he wasn't wearing any. "Now, mind you, this is the story as he told me, which, as much as I would like to believe in the honesty and unquestionable righteousness of the unfortunate citizens who write my checks, I took with a truckload of salt. Anywho. As my guy tells it, he's at some highfalutin benefit auction—black tie, big checks for the right causes—and all night one of the sweet young things on the catering staff keeps giving him the eye, touching his elbow, stepping in a little extra close as she's offering him a puff pastry. After one too many free martinis, he starts flirting back, and at the end of the night she gives him her number. The poor slob waits weeks before calling her. When finally he does, she gives him an address of a building similar to where our girl Taylor took us today. Not a dump, but also not a place so fancy you've got a doorman or cameras watching your coming and going—and just big enough so the other tenants aren't too interested in anyone else's business. When he shows up, he's nervous. He's never done anything like this before—" Ronnie chuckles "—which is what they always say, and I never believe. What's important is how they say it. There's no steadfast rule, but you read 'em with your gut. Some you know instantly not to stick a pin in, for fear the shit they're full of will blow up all over you. Others you figure for tourists who've been playing in the shadows longer than they're admitting, and have now found themselves in over their head."

"That's a lot of metaphors," I said. "Which is this guy?"

Ronnie laughed. "The latter. He was as pale as a poster in a hairdresser's window that's been in the sun too long, and his hands were shaking when he told me. Story goes, enough time passed from when he got the number to when he calls this sweet young thing that when he gets to the apartment, he can't be sure she's even the same girl from the party. She's got all the right assets in all the right places, though, so he doesn't say no. They have their fiesta, he leaves the cash on the bedside, then they part. Three months go by, then one day a package is delivered to his office. Inside is a videotape and a note that says, 'What will you give a girl for her sweet sixteen?'"

"Shit."

"He spends a day or two losing his mind, then he calls me."

"And so what do you do? Broker the payoff? How can you be sure they won't come back for more?"

"Blackmail is a slippery game. Every situation is different. And this one is well orchestrated. They don't offer any specifics of what they want, or the consequences if he doesn't comply. So I have to consider maybe it's not money they're after. I have to ask, 'Why this guy? Where does he have power or influence? What might they want from him that only he has?'"

"Who benefits?"

"Exactamundo. My guy's in government, so I've got a few ideas how they might want to strong-arm him, but until I have more information, that's all they are. Ideas. One thing I know is, whoever the mastermind, they're playing a long game, and this was only their first move. Which tells me there's a bigger scheme at work. One I don't yet have the opera glasses to see. For now they want him to know they have something on him, and to let him stew."

"Is it maybe because what they want is time-sensitive? And they're waiting until a critical moment to tell him what they want done?"

Ronnie tilts his head. "Maybe. Though if it were me, and that were the aim, I would do it all at once. Videotape and demand, bing bang. 'Act now or else.' This way you catch him by surprise, with no time to do anything but react. But, same time, stretching it out works just as good. When it comes to existential threats, the best way to get someone to do what you want is

195

to wear them down. Day after day, night after night, let them wake up and fall asleep wondering when the next shoe is about to fall. Waiting can drive a person mad. I don't know if you've ever lived in fear, but the anticipation can be worse than the punishment." Ronnie waves his hand. "But all this is mental masturbation. Practically, letting months pass before sending the tape is just smart. Think about it. Our guy knows the location where he met the girl, and the location where he was filmed. And our blackmailers need time to cover their tracks. They have to figure he's going to make a call to a guy like me, so by the time I come sniffing around, they'll want to make sure there's not one trace of the chickadee or the hidden viewing room. Still, I gotta run it all down. I get hold of the catering only to find the staff is transient and paid in cash, and that too many gigs have come and gone for anyone to remember who worked one event four, five months ago. I dig up the lease on the apartment to find it's paid through a holding company to an agency who manages hundreds of short-term sublets. And, after bullshitting my way into the former love nest apartment, aside from new tenants, I find the secret room has been replaced with a spacious walk-in closet. I spend days running down shell companies and fake names only to end up with nothing. Which was how they planned it. Knowing I'd have to spin my wheels to confirm. 'Cause that's the job."

"What about the apartment we went to today?"

Ronnie held up a finger. "Now that's where I get a leg up. The lease trail was still a runaround—which is what I spent my afternoon sniffing out—but the unit is still active. Which means I can maybe snag one of their players."

"By using Taylor? How do you know you can trust her? That the moment she left us she didn't report back to them? They could be shutting down the apartment as we speak."

Ronnie shook his head. "That's another point in my corner. The kid may be a hustler, but she's nobody to them, just small bait they use to hook big fish. They pay one girl on the street to give another girl a pager and some keys, probably some junkie who doesn't ask questions, and like that they've created an unbridgeable gap. When it's time to hook the john, they send a page from an untraceable line with the time and info. I can chase down the pager registration—which I will, along with the source of the money that gets wired to Western Union—but dollars to lattes those will be run-arounds like all the other paper trails. Point is, street kids like Taylor are loose ends. Untrustworthy. So the people behind these kinds of operations go out of their way to make sure she can never lead back to them. But shielding themselves can work against them too, and leave them vulnerable in an entirely different way. With no direct contact, Taylor's got no one to report to, which also means they can't keep tabs on her. Which means chances are in my favor that the room we saw today will stay intact—at least until they finish filming their next round of big fish." He shook his head. "As to whether they shut it down on their own accord or use other girls there, that I don't have the manpower to watch. Even if I had eyes on the building 24-7, it's too big a location. We'd have to know everyone coming and going in order to rule them out. Not just the tenants, but every friend, associate, and casual screw. Each of their schedules and habits. It's too much to track. Short of renting the room across the hall and doing round-the-clock surveillance, our best bet is the girl."

"But why are you so sure she'll call you when she gets the next page?"

"Because she's on her own out on the street. I told you, I used to be on the force. I know the game. Which is how she came to me in the first place. I still have plenty of friends in the department, so I put word out that if anyone collars an underage hooker to give me a shout. Patrol picks her up, and rather than book her they call me. Saves them the paperwork, and now I owe them a favor. Whether she pans out is the risk I have to take. Most of the time these things go nowhere, but with Taylor I hit a bullseye. And she's hit one with me. Normally the unies collar her and she gets thrown into the system. But now she's got a chip to bargain with. She now has more allegiance to me than to the faceless pimps who she's just discovered have been secretly filming her. Faced with Social Services or keeping her freedom for telling me what she knows, it's a no-brainer."

"But how can you be sure the room Taylor took us to is connected with your client?"

"That's a fair question. And truth is, I can't. But think about it: What are the odds that two identical setups are operating at the same time in the same general locale? And there's another thing. You remember when she mentioned a cop named Zoro, and you mused whether she might have been talking about Inspector Martin Zorn?"

"I do. I also remember that of everything we saw and heard in that room, his name was the only thing that made your head whip around."

"Good catch," Ronnie said. "And you're right. Because Inspector Martin Zorn wasn't always an inspector. Back in the day, he used to be a beat cop in the Tenderloin. And my former partner."

City Hall, South San Francisco — Commissioned by Arlene Pred, who worked here as a clerk for thirty-six years

22

THE SWITCHBOARD

Agreeing that we were both cold and that the firepit was no match for the wind on the edge of a continent, Ronnie and I extinguished the pit and moved inside. The fire I'd started earlier in the wood-burning stove was now just coals, but they were still hot enough that with a little kindling and a fresh log, flames jumped quickly to life and the iron potbelly quickly began to radiate heat.

"When you're fresh out of the academy," Ronnie said, sorting the quartered hunks of wood in the bin, already preparing the next piece to feed the fire, "you get paired with a veteran, otherwise it's the blind leading the blind. Assignments change every morning, until you get the ropes. Then, after about a year, you start settling in with a steady partner. That was me and Zorn, our first assignment the Loin."

"Sounds like a rough beat to cut your teeth on," I said.

"Maybe not as bad as you'd think, but not the cushy beat of the Richmond where you were picked up. The Loin was where every runaway kid who fell through the cracks landed. Rape, hooking, and boatloads of drugs. Crack was queen. Smack, too. Every day, people OD'ing on the streets, and most of the time we were playing cleanup. You remember Taylor talking about The Nest?"

"The youth center."

"It's run by Faith Chadwick—you heard of her?"

"I have. She's a wealthy philanthropist and, according to Larissa, an all-around saint."

"Yeah, well, depends on your definition of saint. She and her late husband, Joe Chadwick, made a small fortune in downtown commercial real estate. His story—at least to start—is less interesting. White kid from a good family. Daddy gave him a fortune to play monopoly. Her story, on the other hand . . ." Ronnie snorted and drank his tequila.

"Faith Chadwick was an original hippie," Ronnie said, leaning back and settling in. "I know it's fashionable to glorify the Summer of Love, but from what I hear, it was a shit show. Can't say I think very highly of what's become the tie-dye amusement park of Haight Street these days, but I'll take Hippie Disney Land over what it used to be. Back in the late sixties, so many kids were pouring into the Haight, there wasn't anywhere for them to go. A guy named Al Rinker started what he called the Switchboard. He wrangled local residents to offer up their extra rooms or couches to the flower children— though in truth they weren't so hard to wrangle, which is a subject I'll get back to. If you were fresh in town and wanted a place to sleep, or were a kid living on the street and needed a shower, the Switchboard would connect you to these generous locals he called Crash Hosts. The service was a quick hit. In part because Al posted flyers on every telephone pole he could staple into, but also through word of mouth. Back then, all you had to say was 'three-eight-eight-seven-thousand,' and if you were more than a day off the bus, you knew it was the number for the Switchboard.

"I wasn't wearing the uniform back then, so I can't say firsthand, but I think maybe for a time it did some folks some good. Operations were run out of a storefront on Fell Street by volunteers, and rent was funded by donations. But like all good days, theirs were short-lived. By the early seventies, operations had devolved into an abandoned bus and one stoned Okie, and what had begun as an idealistic community service had degraded into what you can probably guess was the most base of human impulses. Most of the Crash Hosts turned out to be chickenhawks looking to prey on fresh young chickens—and that went for males and females, on both sides. A host would invite a kid in, give them a hot meal, a shower, fresh clothes, then offer to tuck them in for the night. Occasionally the arrangement might evolve into a twisted mutually beneficial arrangement—room and board and maybe some pocket money in exchange for sex—but after a week or maybe three, would inevitably end with the chicken absconding with an armload of the hawk's valuables.

"Which brings us to our now-notable community philanthropist Faith Chadwick, who was one such chicken. As a teenage runaway on the streets of San Francisco, she made use of the Switchboard's services—which fared as well as you might expect. Over and over, her Crash Hosts attempted to exploit her for sex, sometimes through force.

"Now, if you're to believe the Chadwick party line, these experiences are what led our dear Faith to open The Nest, hers ultimately being a storybook San Francisco tale: destitute young waif rises from the streets to meet her Prince Charming and become one of the most influential commercial real estate developers in the city. And to show how she hasn't forgotten her past, she donates one of her buildings to be a youth center."

"Only one of her kids kills her husband."

"Which is why I said Joe's story began a lot less interesting than it ended."

A log shifted in the wood-burning stove, and Ronnie reflexively reached forward, opened the door, and used the poker to stoke the glowing coals.

"The Nest opened in 1990," Ronnie said, closing the stove door and settling back onto the couch, "which was the same year Zorn and I got paired up and assigned to the Loin. We'd both been on the force about a year, but it was our first steady partnership. Like I said, the neighborhood was the bottom end for anyone on the street. And as far as services for youth, there wasn't much. The Switchboard was long gone—which was for the best, and, if it had managed any good, served as a lesson for future enterprises not to accept private donations for what had essentially amounted to 'pay-to-play' privileges for degenerates. You had Glide and Saint Anthony's, who offered daily soup kitchens, and you had Hospitality House, who offered informal counseling and arts and crafts. You had Huckleberry House, who offered beds, but they required parental consent, which, for the majority of kids on the street, was no offer at all. Then you had Larkin Street Services, which was the first to offer no-strings housing. But The Nest, that was the first all-inclusive facility. And it all came about because of Faith Chadwick's experience with the Switchboard."

Ronnie was on a roll, and I wasn't about to stop him.

"A portion of the Chadwicks' holdings were a string of former hotels and SRO's," he said, once again looking at me again over the top of glasses he wasn't wearing. "Single-room-occupancy hotels, if you don't know, all in the Tenderloin, and they'd converted one of them into a working commune for runaways. At first they took a lot of flak—'Real estate tycoons evict low-income residents' kinda reactionary rattle—but they did their best to relocate as many of the residents into their other buildings, and after buying out full-page ads in the *Chron* promoting their philanthropy, the chatter eventually died down. Such is what having money affords you. Even still, the kids were the ones who took the real convincing. Teens like Taylor, they don't end up on the street because they like it—or because they trust authority. Having been on the streets herself, Faith Chadwick understood this, which was how she knew the only way to help these kids was to meet them where they were at. Nest volunteers walked the Loin offering food packs and first-aid kits. To the young females, who they knew they couldn't stop from turning tricks, they offered condoms and pregnancy tests. They did this all with no pressure to get sober or accept made-up grandpas-in-the-sky, but always with an invitation to pop by for a meal and bed if they wanted. It's not popular with the political correctos these days to use this analogy, but kids on the street, they're like feral cats. You can't just walk up and pet them. You gotta put out a saucer of milk and walk away. Let them come to you.

"And it worked. So much so that all the cops patrolling the Loin—hell, probably the city—knew it. Walking a beat, our job was to patrol for crime. We weren't welfare workers. I can tell you firsthand, it's not like you see in the movies; there's no such thing as 'the cop with a heart of gold.' The job was, you catch someone committing a crime, whether they're eight or eighty, you arrest 'em and put 'em into the system. The Nest made us think twice though. Instead of the paperwork to ship them off to Social Services only to see the same faces land back on the streets three months later, kids we were used to seeing again and again began to disappear, and a lot of them were ending up at The Nest. Got to where, if we picked up some kid giving a hand job between parked cars, or smoking crack in a doorway, instead of throwing them in cuffs, we'd take them to Faith's. You might think that sounds like the right thing to do, but in no way was it protocol."

An ember popped inside the stove and grabbed both of our attentions. Then suddenly Ronnie looked worried. He got up, went to the glass door, and looked out. "Did we douse the fire in the pit?"

"At least twelve times," I said. "But we can check again."

Ronnie laughed. "Holy moly," he said. "I'm still baked."

"Yeah," I said. "You know it's bad when the tequila is sobering."

He sat on the sofa again. "What the hell were we talking about? Oh, right, Faith Chadwick." Ronnie shook his head. "I know I said there was no such thing as the cop with the heart of gold. But Patrol Officer Zorn, he was the exception that proved the rule. There are two kinds of cops: the guys who want to be cops, and they guys who take the job because it's a job—" he stopped himself "—okay, three kinds. There's also the ones who want to bust heads. But that's beside the point. Even the ones who want to be cops, most get tired of being on the street. If they don't want to promote, or don't want the liability of being in charge of a squad, they transfer down to the Hall of Justice or work in the record room filing reports. The others, they hustle for rank. Try to make sergeant so they can get off the street and sit behind a desk. It's the rare duck who wants to walk a foot beat their whole career."

"And that was Inspector Zorn?"

"I tell ya, back then I admired him. The job gets to people in different ways. Some get bitter, some get numb, some lose themselves in a bottle. Me, I got cynical and moved to Sausalito so I could wake up and go to sleep listening to the water. It coulda been age. I was early thirties when I signed up. I'd already done a stint in the army, then another in insurance, so was feeling old. Whereas Zorn, he was barely legal to drink when he came out of the academy. Whatever the reason, where I did everything I could to get as far away from the cesspool as possible, Martin Zorn dove in head-first. He got a place in the heart of the Loin, making home right smack in the shit. Off-duty, he volunteered at The Nest, walked the streets handin' out kits, and, no surprise, he and Faith Chadwick got close—"

"You mean like hooking-up close?"

Ronnie tilted his head. "If it were anyone else, I would say maybe. But Zorn was too much of a crusader, so I could easily see him leashing himself with the chastity restraint." Another ember popped in the fire and Ronnie leaned forward, opened the stove door, grabbed a quarter log from the wood bin and tossed it in. "But don't get me wrong," he said, stoking the glowing coals until the log caught fire, "Zorn had ambition too—we both did. In those early days I was set on at least making my bars as captain, maybe a star as commander, maybe higher. But Zorn was even more lofty. Where I was set on climbing the ladder, Zorn was hell-bent on changing the world. He believed if he got off the beat and made rank, then he could change the world. Three years in, he and I were being partnered enough regularly that we'd formed a bond, and after another year we both took the sergeant's exam and both passed." He closed the stove door and picked up his glass.

"From there we were assigned to different stations. Didn't take long after getting the bump, though, for me to realize the disillusionment I'd felt on the patrol wasn't limited to the street. And the same musta been true for Zorn. We'd been off the beat barely six months when he comes to me with a proposition." Ronnie finished his drink and smacked his lips. "You ever hear of Operation Midnight Climax?"

I shook my head.

He laughed, motioning for me to hand him my glass. "Oh, buddy, you're going to love this one."

23

OPERATION MIDNIGHT CLIMAX

Ronnie scooped up my glass of warm tequila and walked into the kitchen. I heard the rattle of the ice dispenser and the clank of cubes tumbling into glasses, then the pop of the fat cork on the bottle of Siete Leguas. Then he was back, handing me a fresh drink.

"Salud," Ronnie said, raising up his glass and drinking. I returned the gesture, then drank some of my refreshed tequila. Ronnie sat on the sofa, but not all the way back, on the edge, facing me.

"Operation Midnight Climax," he said, "was a top-secret CIA experiment in mind control. Back in the fifties, everybody and their comrade was scrambling for a leg up in the Cold War spy game, so the CIA began experimenting with brainwashing through sex and drugs. In San Francisco, and across the Golden Gate in Mill Valley, a guy named Sidney Gottlieb cooked up apartments like the one we saw today—and I mean whole shebang the same: mirror, camera, easy chair, even snacks. Gottlieb and another angelic soul, a narcotics agent named George Hunter White, paid prostitutes to seduce men, dose them with LSD, then bring them back to the apartments to have sex—all while White was in the secret room, settled into his easy chair, watching behind a one-way mirror. The setup was heavily scripted, and the girls were given detailed prompts of what to say after the deed was done. The idea was to feed these unsuspecting men subliminal messages to determine whether, between post-coital bliss and having been dosed with acid, they could be coerced into revealing secrets or even committing crimes.

"The project went on for over a decade until the CIA shut it down. It managed to stay hush-hush until the seventies, when a reporter got hold of the story and it all came out. My point is, as cadets we learned about this delightful episode of human history in the academy as a lesson in what *not* to do as law enforcement. Well, shortly after getting promoted out of the Loin, newly-made Inspector Zorn comes to me with a story. He's been nesting with the Chadwicks for a couple years now, so he's like family. He tells me Joe Chadwick has gone off the rails, and word is he's been playing Switchboard, taking advantage of girls in their embrace. I tell him to take the kids to the D.A. and get their stories on record. But he says no, he doesn't want to endanger The Nest, and anyway, the girls won't talk. I ask Zorn if he has any actual proof, and he says no, which is why he's coming to me. He wants to pull his own version of Operation Midnight Climax to catch Joe Chadwick in the act." Ronnie's eyebrows shot up and his eyes fixed on me like lasers. "I'm telling ya," he said, "if he'd been anyone else I would have thought he was pulling my leg—or trying to entrap me. But this was Crusader Zorn, as earnest as earnest gets. So I tell him what we both know, which is that any evidence gained in such fashion would be inadmissible, not to mention cost our jobs if not prison time. But he says it doesn't have to go that way. The goal is to keep it in-house. Use the tape as leverage against Joe, to force him out of the foundation. 'Win-win,' he says. Joe stops abusing the girls, and we get to keep the shelter alive. That's when I realize, as rotten as my cynicism was for the job, Zorn's idealism was worse. I tell him, 'Marty, this is going too far. You want to save the world, I get it. But you gotta play by the rules. Otherwise you're just as bad as they are. It's Ethics 101.' He says 'Yeah, yeah, you're right.' But I know he's blowing me off. And so I tell him so. And that's when he lays into me, calling me a waste of a life, saying I give the badge a bad name, and loads of other crap, and so I let him have it right back, calling him a self-righteous SOB who's got his head so far up the ass of his high horse that he thinks the smell of shit is roses. To which he storms out, flushing whatever friendship we once had down the toilet."

Ronnie took a drink. "It's about three months later when I get the call. Middle of the night, I'm on the houseboat. It's Zorn. He can barely speak, but he doesn't need to. I can hear the fear. So I jump outta bed and shoot across the bridge, our lover's spat forgotten. He's a brother in arms and needs my help. So I go. I'd managed to get a location out of him and it's one of the Chadwicks' SROs, the Midori. At that hour I'm in the Loin in no time. I stop out front and go inside. The place is under renovation, empty of residents, so no one's around. I pull my gun, 'cause I don't know what the hell I'm gonna find. Then I see bloody fingerprints smeared across the phone.

"Zorn told me the penthouse, so I creep up to the top floor. There are two doors. One is cracked open. Freaking bait if I'd ever seen any. I kick the door open, then jump back and wait. Nothing. One, two, then I duck inside. First thing, I'm hit with the smell—iron and shit. Smacks you like a wall and grabs your stomach and yanks. I'm telling you, at this point I'm sweating. That's when I see the remnants of what looks like an exploded watermelon on the wall, which I know is some sorry sap's brains. Chunks of meat stuck to the plaster; lines of blood streaked down to the floor. I'm clearing the room when I see the feet. A little further in, I see the body on the floor, crumpled between the bed and the wall. Joe Chadwick. He's naked, steeped in a pool of blood. His face a horror show. His jaw is gone, completely blown off, nothing but a mess of shredded meat. The back of his head a gaping hole.

"I catch movement and swing around and point my weapon. Down the hall is the bathroom. The door is partially open, and through the gap I can see a girl, a teen. She's on the floor, her knees pulled to her chest, but all I see is her hair—" Ronnie shook his head "—and brother, this is an image I'll take to my grave. 'Cause I know this girl. Crystal Lake. From the street. She'd been a wild one, but still. Only fourteen. I'll never forget, she had this long, straight, almost angelic platinum-white hair. Only now it's clumped with black, dried chunks of blood and brain. I lower my gun and move toward her, but as I do, someone steps out from behind the door."

"Zorn?"

Ronnie grinned. "Faith Chadwick."

"Shit . . ."

"She's holding a towel, wiping blood from her hands. She opens the door and, like it's any other day, says, 'Hi, Ron. He's next door.' It takes me a minute to realize who she's talking about. But at the moment, he's not the one who has me worried. I take a step toward the girl, and Faith gets in my way. 'It's okay,' she says. 'I've got her.' I look at Crystal and this girl's got the most terrified eyes you've ever seen. 'I know,' Faith says. 'But you gotta get Martin. He's not right.' And so I leave the room and go into the hallway and there he is, Sergeant Martin Zorn, standing like a shellshocked soldier having wandered off the battlefield, blood all over him and white as a sheet.

"And that's when the cop in me kicks in. 'Where the fuck is the PD?' I yell at him. 'You need to call this in.' But my man isn't listening. He starts babbling. 'Something must have gone wrong,' he says. 'She must have gotten nervous, and Joe caught on that he was being recorded. He went berserk and started beating her. Then he pulled a gun and somehow it got out of his hands and into hers, and she blew his head off.' 'What the fuck are you talking about?' I ask him. Only he starts making these terrible whimpering sounds, like a wild animal caught in a trap. I'm telling you, I'd never seen him—or anyone—like that before. His hands are shaking, and he's in a real state. So I tell him it's all right. That everything's gonna be all right. I grab his face and make him look me in the eyes. 'Just take a breath,' I say. 'And tell me what happened.' And that brings him around. He gives me the story.

"Zorn says he'd learned that the top floor of the Midori was where Joe had been taking the girls he plucked from The Nest, and after I'd given him the brush-off, he'd gone ahead with his plan, installing his own version of Operation Midnight Climax, to catch Joe in the act. He says with the building under renovation, he'd been able to pull it off without Joe knowing. And ever since, he'd been waiting for the moment to make his movie. Finally Faith came to him and said one of the girls, Crystal, had confided that Joe was puttin' the moves on her. Zorn says he sat her down and explained what they were doing with the secret recording room. He knew it'd be a risk, but thought it worth the gamble. And Crystal'd agreed. She'd go with Joe to the empty SRO, and before the deed she'd turn on the recorder behind the one-way mirror."

Ronnie stopped, snorted. For a while he'd been looking at the fire, not really seeing, but immersed in reliving the moment in his head. After a few seconds of silence he looked me, knotted his brow. "I gotta tell ya, hearing this, my brain's boiling. And I'm near blowing my stack. I mean, this guy—this cop, who'd been one of the few on the force who made you believe there was still honor in this world—he'd set this whole thing up. He built a god damn recording room and arranged for this kid—because let's be clear, that's what she was, a kid—to be taken to a sex hideaway so he could record her getting fucked by Joe Chadwick—all so that he could save her! I mean, it was just fucking insane."

Ronnie took a deep breath. You could see he took no pleasure in reliving the story.

"It's taking everything I have," he said, "not to haul off and kick the shit out of him, right there. But I keep cool. All I can think is, I gotta sort this shit out. Especially because I know that on the other side of the door is Faith Chadwick, filling Crystal's head with crap knows what. So I ask him, 'What about Faith? What the fuck is she doing here?' 'I called her,' Zorn says. 'You freaking called her?' I say. 'Martin, what the fuck were you thinking?' And like that Zorn starts going to pieces again. So I grab him. 'Hey,' I say, slapping him a few times. Harsh, I know, but I gotta wake him the fuck up. 'Martin,'

I say. 'Come back to me.' And eventually I get him talking again. 'Faith and me,' he says. 'We made a plan. We knew Joe was gonna bring Crystal here. I was to take point in the room next door in case anything went wrong.' I ask him if that's what he did and he says it was, that he came early and camped out next door and waited with his ear to the wall. 'I couldn't be in there,' he says. 'I couldn't watch.' And I'm thinking I don't know if that was better or worse. He tells me he heard Joe and Crystal enter the apartment. For a bit things were quiet, then he heard a commotion, what sounded like her being smacked around, then hitting the floor, so in a flash he's up on his feet and out his door into the hallway, but before he can get inside Joe's place he hears a shot."

"Wait a minute," I said. "I'm sorry to interrupt, but can we back up? If Zorn knew this was going down, and he had the girl, Crystal, ready to talk, why didn't he just take her to the D.A. as you'd initially suggested? And put her on record?"

Ronnie pointed at me. "Now that's a damn fine question. And one I was pontificating on myself. My guess is he didn't make the call because nothing had transpired yet. According to Zorn, this was her first time with Joe, and listen, I knew as well as he did that the justice system isn't all faith and trust. A runaway teen accusing an upstanding philanthropist of propositioning her isn't cause enough for the D.A. to squeeze a fart let alone consider a charge. Especially when it came to a kid like Crystal, who had more busts than Mick Jagger has hits. But the question was moot anyway. The past had passed, and we were where we were. And like I said, my boy was having a moment, and I was letting him have it. Zorn had just admitted to being on-site when a situation involving a juvenile—which he'd orchestrated—resulted in the discharge of a firearm, killing a man. And instead of calling it in to the station, he called the wife—his co-conspirator—Faith Chadwick, then me, his former partner. Which meant now I was up to my god damn eyeballs in the shit right along with them."

"Hold on," I said. "They were recording all of this, right? Even if Zorn was in the next room, as twisted as the situation was, they got the shooting on tape?"

Ronnie shook his head. "That's the other thing Zorn tells me. That, for whatever reason, the recording never got going—even though a minute before he's telling me Joe lost his marbles because he'd caught on."

"Or maybe he caught the girl trying to start the recording? Since Zorn wasn't there to do it himself?"

"Maybe, but again, I can barely get him to answer even the simplest questions let alone explain how he knows whatever he claims to know. And with every second we're standing out there in the hall, Faith's in the room with Crystal, and I'm getting more and more nervous. So I tell him we all gotta be in the same room. He agrees, and we go in. Faith and Crystal are still in the bathroom. Faith's got Crystal sitting on the edge of the tub, and she's washing the blood off her face. I push past Faith and kneel down in front of Crystal. The girl puts her head in her hands. 'Look at me,' I tell her. And she lifts her head. Streaks of mascara are running down her cheeks, and it's then I see the bruise on the side of her head. Pistol-whipped. 'You have to call the police,' I say to Crystal. Faith starts to protest and I tell her to shut up. 'You hear me?' I say to Crystal. 'Faith, Martin, me, we can't be here. You have to call the police and tell them what happened.' But Faith's not having it. 'I'm not leaving,' she says. 'I'll call the police myself. I'll tell them she was scared and she called me and I told her not to do anything until I got here.' And that's when I've had enough. I don't know if it was the cop in me, survival, or plain just being pissed. But I spin around, lay into her. 'On what phone?' I say. 'The one downstairs? With Zorn's bloody fingerprints? I think you're not grasping the situation here. This is going to be a full-on official murder inquiry. The inspectors are going to follow up on every word you say, starting with phone logs—one of which is to me. And I can't just play it off as some call with silence on the other end, seeing that there's also a toll booth record of me crossing the bridge, which puts me right here in this shit-boat with you as one rotten conspiracy charge.' But Faith is staring at me with these cold, vacant eyes, and that's when I realize she's even more hinky than the scene. This broad's husband just had his head blown off—his god damn naked dead body is barely three feet away—and she's as cool as a popsicle in Poland. Made the hairs on my arms stand up like static electricity. And that's when I know the ship isn't just sinking, it's already sunk, and the only way to not drown is to drag us all to shore. 'Timeline is everything,' I say. 'Time of death we can wiggle, but the calls we can't.' I spin around to Zorn. 'The gun goes off and you do what? How long until you go downstairs to make a call?' It's taking everything for Zorn to answer. 'Fast,' he says. 'Five, ten minutes maybe.' 'Who first?' I ask. 'Who'd you call?' 'Faith,' he says. 'And how long until you called me?' 'Immediately after,' he says.

"Now my noodle is really spinning, running scenarios. Finally I go to Crystal and tell her: 'Okay. You go downstairs and wipe Zorn's prints off the phone—do NOT pick up the receiver. Then you press ALL the buttons.

And only then do you touch the receiver. Do it in that order. And DO NOT actually make a call. The point is to leave your prints on the phone—in the blood.' I look at Faith. 'You can stay. But we're doing it my way.' And so Faith takes the girl downstairs and Crystal does as instructed. In the meantime, I go to Zorn and tell him 'You gotta get the fuck outta here.' But he's not registering. I've seen people in shock, and he was one. I don't relish sending him out into the world on his own, but I have no other choice. 'You gotta get the fuck outta here,' I tell him, 'and come up with a story where you were. Because wherever it is, it wasn't here.' When the ladies get back, I tell Crystal: 'You're the one who called me, you hear? Not Zorn. Zorn was never here. Joe brought you to this room. It was just you and him. Joe attacked you, pulled a gun, and you accidentally shot him.' I take out one of my business cards, crumble it up a few times, hand it to Crystal. 'You've had this a long time,' I tell her. 'The cops are gonna ask why, of all people, you called me. You tell them after you shot Joe, you called Faith, and she told you to call Sergeant Zorn, but you didn't have his number. You had one of my cards in your purse, though, so you called me instead. That will explain why I'm here.'"

"Sorry to interrupt," I said again. "But I have to ask. Am I wrong, or are you now instructing a witness to lie?"

Ronnie chuffed. "I'm not just instructing her to lie, I'm inventing the whole god damn story—and not just for any old witness. An underage victim, and possible murder suspect. But what the hell am I supposed to do? It's easy to look back now to say I should have walked out the door, called the PD myself, and given a full statement, starting with three months earlier when Zorn came to me with his Operation Midnight Plan. Call it loyalty, the blue wall, or deer-in-the-headlights syndrome, but in the moment that's not what I did. And once I have Crystal wiping down prints, I'm no longer coincidentally involved, I'm full-on, actively complicit, so I have to see it through. I've worked out how Faith and I came to be on the scene, and as long as the ladies play their part, I'm betting fifty-fifty it will hold up. Zorn, on the other hand, there's no easy way to explain his being there—not to mention he'll never hold up under questioning—which is why he has to go. At that moment all I'm thinking is the barrage of protocol that's about to descend on us from my colleagues, and needing to hold up under its scrutiny. So as much as Zorn doesn't want to go, I tell him again he has to. And it's only when Faith tells him it's all right that he actually does. Which is when I double down on my willful complicity.

211

"I tell Faith: 'Wipe down the scene. But do a bad job. Make sure every trace of Zorn is out of here, but leave you, Crystal, Joe, and me. I want it to look like you got here before me, panicked, and tried to clean up, then I stopped you. You'll say you were in a state of shock at seeing Joe dead and, without thinking, instinctively tried to protect his reputation. You had no idea this recording room was here. You say nothing about Zorn playing construction worker or what you two were intending. You assume Joe built the secret room, and this was the first you'd learned of his proclivity of plucking kids from The Nest to perform in his personal cinema.'" Ronnie looked at me. "And I tell ya, brother, the scary thing is, she doesn't bat an eye. She goes right to work.

"Next I take Crystal downstairs, out of the crime scene, and make her run through the story again. 'Keep it simple,' I tell her. 'Joe brought you to the room. Joe tried to rape you. You shot him in self-defense. You called Faith, then you called me.' It's a concise, plausible story. And where it's not, I'm hoping the stink of the secret camera room will cover up whatever smells rotten. When Faith comes down after messing with the evidence, I make both ladies repeat the story back to me, two, three times. I throw them as many curveball questions as I can conjure, and they do good. And when I think they've got it down pat, I call the PD.

"The Tenderloin station is only a few blocks away on Eddy, and it feels like seconds from when I make the call to when the cavalry shows up. Which is when the real circus starts. First thing, they separate us. The ladies I'm sure they're grilling, but for me, they're pullin' out the rack. 'What was I doing there? Did I know about the secret recording room?' On and on. And I never blamed them. The scene was as hinky as it gets. And there I am, right in the middle of it. So I stay cool and say my lines, then ask for my union rep.

"Eventually I'm sent home, suspended with pay pending investigation. Which was par for the ride. My rep says to stay out of it, and so I do. I don't call Zorn, I don't call friends in the department. I don't want to raise one brow that might imply I'm either worried or nosing around for insider info. When I'm called in for a follow-up, I learn that the story we concocted held. The presumption was that Joe Chadwick had built the room himself for his own personal scrapbook of illicit trysts with young girls. Faith had made a mess of the scene, but just the right amount. Preliminary evidence substantiated the story that Joe had taken fourteen-year-old Crystal Lake to the room, pulled a gun, attacked her, and, during a struggle, was fatally shot. Prints on the gun were Joe's, as was gunshot residue on his hands, suggesting he'd been holding the weapon when the altercation turned unfortunate for him. Even the call to me seemed legit, considering that the first obvious choice of cop to call would have been Zorn, only he'd been out of town, in Mexico, taking a scheduled vacation."

"Whoa," I said. "That's interesting. How'd he swing that?"

"Seems he'd calendared time off starting three days before the incident and for another week and a half after."

"So he'd planned an alibi?"

"That he did. Which mighta pissed me off had it not served to strengthen our story. The investigators signed off, though I received an official reprimand for not following procedure. The one sticking point the boys had with me was that I hadn't phoned PD the moment I'd gotten the call from Crystal. The Loin station was a stone's throw from the Midori, whereas I was all the way across the Golden Gate. I said her call had sounded personal. Crystal had known me from when I was on the beat. She was calling me because she couldn't get Zorn and needed someone she knew. I said I had no idea the bloodbath I was about to walk into at the Midori until I walked in. And that was enough for them. Still, they couldn't just let me off with nothin'. And anyway, the reprimand would have no effect on my career. They just needed me to know that they could have done whatever they'd wanted to me, but hadn't.

"The only pesky detail they couldn't get around was the recordings. No tapes were recovered from the scene, nor were any recovered in any subsequent search of the Chadwick residence, Joe's private office, or The Nest. If Joe had gone to all this trouble to build a recording studio, where were all the recordings?"

"A legitimate question," I said. "If any tapes had actually existed, which you knew they hadn't. Not even of that night, since you said the recording of Joe's death had never gotten started."

Ronnie fluttered his brows. "I would have said the same thing—only, when I say there were no tapes recovered from the scene at the Midori, I mean no tapes at all. Not even a blank one."

"Okay . . . So then Faith destroyed it, right? Who else? And since the cops believed there were lots of tapes, they must have thought the same—I mean, her motive is obvious: prevent proof of Joe's sex with minors ending up on the nightly news. Surely they pressed her on it?"

"One can only assume."

"Right . . . Makes sense from their point of view. But from yours . . . If there was nothing on the tape from that night, then why would she take it? Which has to mean there *was* something on it."

"I did tell her to clean up the scene," Ronnie said.

"And to get rid of all traces of Zorn. Which means—wait, what are you saying? That Zorn's version of events wasn't true? That there was something different on that tape from the story they were telling you?"

Ronnie pressed his lips together and closed his eyes.

"Okay," I said. "And what about other girls from The Nest? Did the cops interview them, or did any come forward and say they'd been with Joe?"

"A few interviews were conducted, but as far as I know, no relevant information was obtained. As a whole, the kids who end up at The Nest tend to be a pretty cynical lot, at least when it comes to authority. And they also tend toward being independent and headstrong. So it seems to me that, if someone they'd trusted had been taking advantage of them, at least one would have spoken out." Ronnie shrugged. "But at the same time, so many kids come and go from there, who's to say any of the ones who had been abused were still around? The reason half of them were on the street to begin with was because their home lives had been riddled with abuse. If they'd had the gumption to be able to run from that, I don't see why they wouldn't bail from The Nest first sign of the same sort of behavior."

"Right, making it so none of the kids who had been abused were left. And what about the story released to the press? If I remember right, the official word was that Faith had sent a kid from The Nest to make a delivery, and Joe thought she was a burglar, which was why he pulled a gun and somehow got shot. There was no mention of any secret recording room. I mean, it's one thing for you to have succeeded in tampering with the crime scene and instructing witnesses to lie, but from what I heard you saying, the police conclusion wasn't so far from the truth: that Joe was a pedophile who'd been killed trying to rape an underage girl. So how do we get from that story to the completely fictionalized press release promoting Joe Chadwick as an upstanding and innocent philanthropist who mistook one of the young women from his foundation as a burglar?"

Ronnie's nostrils flared as he breathed in and bobbed his head. "Simple answer: political grease. The Chadwicks had their hands in a shit-ton of lucrative pies at the time. Multiple big construction contracts with the city. And they were in tight with a lot of heavy hitters because of their charitable foundation. Every week, the Society Page had a dozen photos of

San Francisco's elite shaking hands with Joe or kissing Faith's cheek. Word in the locker room was, Joe Chadwick may have been a pedophile, but the only evidence they had was circumstantial: the word of a fourteen-year-old ex-meth head; what appeared to be a recording room; no statements from any other underage witnesses; and no videotapes. Even if Joe had been alive, the D.A. wouldn't have been able to prosecute. And with him dead . . . Well, let's just say the powers that be saw no benefit in sullying the Chadwick name and threatening all the good they were doing."

"Meaning everyone got on board with the story that Joe had been the bad apple, and, now that he was gone, could move forward with the shiny good apple Faith, as if nothing had gone awry."

"Nail on the noggin. I also heard rumors that, with Joe's being the only prints on the gun, Faith'd been pushing for a ruling of suicide, and for all mention of Crystal to be struck from the official record. But while she had some thick juice in City Hall, she would have needed acres of fruit to squeeze that one through. Even still, the D.A.'s office held a press conference. 'A minor who shall remain unnamed fatally shot entrepreneur and philanthropist Joseph Chadwick in an act of accidental self-defense—' you like that? *Accidental self-defense.* I'm no wordsmith, but you tell me, which was it? An accident, or self-defense? '—The minor is not being charged, and has been placed in the state foster system where she'll receive counseling. We're deeply saddened by the loss of this cherished contributor to our beloved blah blah batshit upon bullshit. And that was that. Next thing I know, I'm back on the job, and the only word spoken to me about Joe Chadwick is a firm directive from my C.O. telling me the case is closed and if I keep my head down and my nose clean he's sure I'll get a bump in rank in no time."

"So they covered it up?"

Ronnie shrugged. "Them and me both."

"And what of Inspector Zorn?"

"What of him? As far as anyone knew, he had nothing to do with it. During the time of Joe's death he'd supposedly been traveling through Mexico in a jeep, unreachable, and oblivious to the news of Joe's death. When almost two weeks later he returned to town—conveniently with souvenirs for all his friends and photos of himself on the beach—whatever strange behavior he might have exhibited was chalked up to the shock of learning a man he'd trusted as a community leader was a pedophile, and now dead. There was no reason to question him. And why would anyone even think to? He was Crusader Zorn."

"But I still don't understand," I said. "Why would Zorn involve you? Why call you that night? Unless—" Then it came to me. "Because you knew he'd built the room. Because he'd told you he was going to do it, months before. That's why he called you that night. By putting you on the scene, he implicated you, and made it so you couldn't give evidence against him. It was a chess move on his part, neutralizing you as a threat." It made sense, but I couldn't believe it. "He set you up."

Ronnie shrugged.

"No? But he had to have. Why else would he involve you?"

"You didn't see him. He wasn't capable of calculating one plus one let alone concocting Shakespearean plot twists."

"So then it was Faith," I said. "It had to be. You said he called her first, right? She instructed him to call you. To cover *her* ass."

Ronnie smiled and opened his hands as if to say I'd gotten it right. But what could be done.

"As far as setting me up," Ronnie said, "the incident didn't hurt my career—if anything, it curried me favor. But after that, the job wasn't the same. I'd already been disillusioned, but this . . . During my PTO, I'd taken to spending more time up north. Found a little spot in Monte Rio, along the Russian River. Loved it so much, I eventually bought a place. I keep it simple, no phone, no cable, no nothin', so when I need to, I can escape from humanity completely. Some people, lying on a couch for an hour a week talking about daddy is the answer, but for me, nature is my way of clearing the noise from the noggin—along with as many crossword and Jumble puzzles as I can find. That's also when I started keeping bees. You can learn a lot from bees. They're practical creatures. They have roles, and, well, it got me thinking about my own. And I decided I no longer wanted to be part of the hive."

"Which is when you went private?"

Ronnie nodded. "For the next six months I was a model cop. I did everything my lieu told me. I kissed as many asses and did as many favors for as many people as I could. I'd always been able to make friends, but my number-one priority was to get in as many good graces as humanly possible. Then I took early retirement and hung out my shingle."

My hand was on my chin as I was thinking it all through. "Makes sense now," I said. "Why you were nervous about going into the building alone with Taylor today." I laughed. "I imagine you must have been pretty knocked off guard when you got a client who had been secretly recorded with a minor, only to be led to a teenage prostitute who not only took you to an apartment with a secret recording room, but then mentioned The Nest and Inspector Zorn. No wonder you were tripping out."

Ronnie laughed along with me. "Like a dosed john in a CIA brainwashing scheme."

Then the next thing I knew, Ronnie was on his feet, putting on his coat.

"Shit," I said. "You're leaving? Now? After a story like that? You sure you can drive?"

"Got an early morning," he said. "And I'm fine. That car of mine, she drives herself."

"You sure? You're welcome to sleep here."

Ronnie shook his head. "I'm good, sport. I like to sleep in my own bed. Oh, reminds me. You got that picture?"

I didn't know what he was talking about.

"The babe flashing her lovelies at you from the museum."

"Right," I said. My head was still spinning from stories of CIA spy rooms, pedophiles, and police cover-ups, not to mention the fat joint and half a bottle of tequila, but I got up and found the photo in my bag. "It's hard to see without a magnifying glass," I said, showing him the picture. "But can you make that out? Her hands are tattooed."

"I can make out she's got a nice rack."

"That too."

"Can I keep this?"

I squinted at him.

"To do some asking around," Ronnie said. "I won't defile it."

"I thought you said it was nothing to worry about. That it was probably just a museum attendee who got offended by what she thought was a photographer and his model doing a risqué photo shoot?"

"I said it could be. But of course, if you don't want me poking around . . ."

"No," I said. "That would be great. Please. Poke. And, thank you."

Ronnie slipped the photo inside his windbreaker. "When you heading back to the city?"

"I've got two more nights here," I said. "But I already got my photos, so we'll see how long I stay."

"Man, if I was you I'd dig in here for as long as I could." He walked to the door. "Hit me up tomorrow. See if I've got anything for you."

"You really think you can find the woman in the photo?" I said.

Ronnie smirked. "You really think you can draw Jerry's studio?"

Stinson Beach, CA

24

HOME

For a long while I lay awake thinking about the stories I'd heard. I almost couldn't believe they were true, and at the same time—assuming Ronnie wasn't lying, because, why would he?—I couldn't help but feel complicit. I mean, how many of us walk around with knowledge of a cover-up in the shooting death of a prominent figure? Then it occurred to me: maybe more than I realize.

I woke late and groggy. I would say I was alone, but the joint I'd smoked was still right there with me. Booze had been proving to be a significant part of my life again, but I hadn't smoked pot in years, and I couldn't say either was leaving me better off. Not that they ever had.

I put on coffee—the house was well-equipped with beans and an Italian moka pot—and opened the curtains. The day was so socked in with fog I could barely see the palm trees beyond the deck let alone the ocean. It was possible that it would burn off, but then again, it might not, which made me even more relieved that I'd gotten reference photos the day before.

I made eggs and toast then settled onto the couch with a book. But between the gray weather, being alone in a warm house on a cold cliff, and having gotten the work done I was there to do, I fell back to sleep even after two cups of coffee. I wanted to say it was because I was on vacation and relaxed, but really it was because I was hung over. My days of the rock and roll lifestyle truly were gone.

When I stirred a short time later I found myself thinking of the blood test Larissa and I had taken. I'd given her the number for the house and asked her to call if the results came in, but I could also imagine her coming up with some annoying—yet what she would argue utterly justifiable—reason not to let me know. So I dialed my flat.

The line rang until the answering machine picked up. I still had one of those old machines that recorded messages. It didn't have a tape, but it also wasn't the electronic voicemail the telephone company was pushing everyone to use. I wasn't against technology, I was just a screener; I liked being able to hear a message as it was being left. I listened to the recording of my own voice telling me to leave my name and number, then after the beep, said, "Larissa? Are you there? Pick up if you are." I waited five seconds, then said it again. Eventually the time ran out and my line hung up on me. I called back, only this time I punched in my code to listen for any messages. There was only one, from Inspector Martin Zorn, saying he was holding a training exercise at the Peace Pagoda in Japantown the next morning.

I'd already been on the fence about working with Ocampo and Zorn, and after what I'd learned from Ronnie, I was feeling even less inclined. At the same time, it was a paying gig, and I was fairly sure I'd be able to sell a drawing of the Pagoda. Still, I was unsure.

It was early afternoon and the fog was there to stay. Perfect time for my long-awaited soak. I went outside and cranked up the heater on the hot tub. The wind was howling and cold. I went back inside and gathered a towel, bottle of water, and book, then, after giving the tub some time to heat up, I stripped bare and scurried across the deck to slip gleefully into the bubbling-hot water.

The soak was everything I had hoped for: blissfully naked in a hot bowl of water on the edge of the world. Twenty minutes later, the bliss was done. Could have been my epitaph. After drying myself off I thought of fish tacos, so I drove down the hill and ate two at a picnic table in the wind and fog. By the time I'd returned to the house I knew I didn't need two more nights. My impromptu party with Ronnie had been enough of an event, and I didn't need a vacation. If I was going to sit alone inside somewhere, I wanted access to my studio. I'd also decided I would take the gig with the city. Despite his questionable role in Joe Chadwick's death, Zorn had seemed nice enough when I'd met him—cocky, sure. But he was a cop, so I took that as part of the job. And anyway, it wasn't like I'd be working side by side with him—and it was money. I called the inspector and left a message saying I would be in the plaza outside Nihonmachi Mall at ten the next morning. Then I dialed my flat again. Once more the call went to voicemail, and once more I spoke to the machine hoping Larissa was listening. This time announcing that I was coming home early. Whether or not she was there and heard me, I couldn't know. She didn't pick up.

I had just finished putting my bags into the rental car when I realized that, while I'd gotten photos of the yoga house slash Jerry's former studio, I hadn't done any drawing. Apparently I was even more hung over than I thought. Evening was approaching and the weather was too blustery to set up for a full-on linework drawing, so I took out my notebook to do a quick sketch. Just the basics, to get down the depth perception and perspective, aspects which I could only get by working on site. Later, back in the studio, I would use those rough marks as a blueprint to make a finished drawing. I did two five-minute sketches—two because the first one didn't fit on the page. Clearly my hand-to-eye coordination wasn't at its sharpest. Which was good to be aware of as I was about to navigate a treacherous coastal road in an unfamiliar car that handled with the grace of a tractor.

After giving the house one more pass to make sure I hadn't left anything behind, I dialed Ronnie. The line rang once, then I heard a click and the ring changed to an electronic buzz. After two buzzes, a woman answered.

"I'm looking for Ronnie?" I said.

"Answering service, hon. Important messages I forward immediately to his BlackBerry. Don't worry, is completely confidential. Tell me what you need."

I said my name was Emit, but before I could continue she cut me off.

"You heading home early?"

Taken aback, I hesitated, then said, "Yeah."

"Your car is still in the pound, hon," she said. "Mill Valley PD wants to hold it a while longer. Something about a suspicious smell from the trunk."

I pinched the bridge of my nose. The steak. Rotting. And eventually the eggs too.

"Ron said not to worry none. Means they'll be logging your groceries as evidence."

Sure, I thought. Right after they jimmy the lock and destroy my trunk— even though they had keys.

"He also said he'll ring you if he's got any news."

There didn't seem to be anything to say other than, "Okay." So I did, then she hung up.

*   *   *

The trip home was like driving through clouds, and the closer I got to the city the denser they grew. Exiting the tunnel, what should have revealed a majestic view of the bridge was nothing but a wash of gray. The path across town was the same, as was arriving to the Mission. At least the car was warm. The rental was new and insulated and didn't have two holes in the roof. None of which I could have said about the Miata.

Parking was another story. Most of my regular go-to spots were too small for a normal-size car. Then I remembered that I didn't have a neighborhood parking permit. The meter maids weren't strict about enforcing the two-hour limit, but they did cycle through at least once if not twice a day. Until I got the Miata back, between 8 a.m. and 8 p.m. I would have to move the rental every two hours. That wouldn't be annoying at all. By the time I found a spot three blocks away I was wishing I'd stayed at the house and curled up in front of the wood-burning stove with a book.

Lugging my things past the shop I paused at the window to see if Betty was inside. She wasn't, which was fine, and the place appeared not to be flooded, which was even better.

As I let myself in the gate I wondered if Larissa was home, and when I opened my front door I knew she was. Even from the bottom landing it sounded as if there was a party.

I carried my things up the stairs and was rounding the landing when I saw someone stepping out of the toilet room. A young Asian woman. Our eyes met as she was zipping up her pants.

"You're just in time for tacos," she said, then she went into the shower room to wash her hands.

The pew was loaded with coats and rucksacks so I dropped all my things in the studio, then headed toward the music. I met the young woman again in the hallway.

"I'm Tally," she said. "You must be Emit. Nice to meet you." She had shoulder-length black hair which was flipped to one side, revealing a shaven left side of her head and an earlobe lined with small rings.

"Nice to meet you too," I said, then I gestured for her to go ahead and followed her to the back of the flat.

Stepping into the kitchen I saw Larissa and two young men. Larissa was raising a glass to drink. Seeing me, she froze. "What are you doing here?"

"I used to live here," I said.

Tally went to the island where, surrounded by an assortment of Mexican takeout and bottles of booze—my booze—sat a boombox. She turned down the volume, then, like a model on a game show, gestured with both hands to the two young men. "This is Viraj—" a brown-skinned young man with jet-black hair and the eyes of a sleepy puppy grinned and waved "—and this is Kai—" a tall, clean-cut white guy who looked to be the oldest of the group, in his mid-twenties, raised his chin to say hey "—and this," Tally said, motioning to the island of food and drink, "is what we will happily share if you choose to not throw us out."

I'd already had tacos for lunch, but I wasn't going to be an ass by saying so. And anyway, Tally was far too charming. "Sounds good," I said. "Thanks." Then I offered my own wave. "Good to meet you guys. I'm Emit."

"Everyone here is pretty cool," Tally said. "Except—" she scrunched up her nose "—for the tacos. All that's left is vegetarian." And the group laughed in such an awkward way that I realized no matter how much I felt like a regular person, to them I was not only old, but Larissa's dad—who had come home early to catch them raiding the liquor cabinet. The day was not faring well for me holding on to my youth.

I decided to put them all out of their misery. "Actually," I said, "I'm just going into the front room to work for a bit. You guys are fine to hang out as long as you want." Then I turned and beat a quick exit to the studio.

Larissa followed.

"To be fair," she said, "you weren't supposed to be back for two more days."

"It's fine," I said. "We agreed you could use the place. I don't expect you to be a loner."

"Cool, thanks. Why are you back, anyway? Something go wrong with the house?"

We were now in my studio.

"No. A gig with the cops came up for tomorrow morning, so I decided to come back early."

"Oh wow," Larissa said. "You took it. Cool. So listen—" I looked at her "—Tally and Kai live in the city, but Viraj is from Stanford, and I told him he could crash here for the night."

"That's fine."

"And actually, I've been sleeping in your bed. I was planning to wash the sheets before you got home, but—"

"It's fine," I said. "Really." I was definitely feeling like the fifth-wheel-old-guy. "I can sleep downstairs."

"In the laundromat?"

I laughed. "No. In the second-floor unit. I'll explain later. Go back to your friends. I'll bug out of here in a bit."

And with a girlish grin she scampered away.

* * *

I no longer owned the second-floor unit, but I was still managing it. When I'd bought the building in 1986, the second floor had been a rental unit and there'd been a bodega on the ground floor. In '91, when the store owner, Mo, died, the business languished and eventually failed as his two sons fought over how to run the place, so I took it over. My second book had just bombed and I was growing tired of drawing cityscapes, so I let the brothers out of their lease and opened the laundromat to ensure I always had a steady income. To pay for it I converted the building to condos. I kept the top unit and sold the second floor to a guy named Dan, a barista I knew from one of the neighborhood cafés, Muddy Waters, who had come into an inheritance. Dan quit slinging coffee and spent some of his windfall on the down payment for the condo, and the rest at the blackjack tables in Reno. Within a year he was broke. He defaulted on his loan and skipped town. The bank took possession of the second floor and sold it to an investment firm in Hong Kong. At the closing, the company's lawyer offered me a small salary if I would continue maintaining the unit. Having sold the place to get cash to open the shop, I saw no reason to turn down more money, so said yes. After that, no one moved in or even visited, and ever since, I'd been collecting payment for doing little more than making sure a cleaning service came in once a month to run the shower, flush the toilet, and vacuum. Which was fine with me. An empty unit meant I didn't have to worry about noisy neighbors.

In the catch-all drawer of the table at the top of the stairs I found the keys, then gathered my things—which were conveniently already packed from having gone to Stinson—along with a towel and roll of toilet paper, then I went downstairs, out my front door, and unlocked the door to the second-floor flat.

This wasn't my first time sleeping there. At the height of my renovations I used the kitchen every day and sometimes slept in the bedroom to avoid the early-morning work crews. Despite having no intention of moving anyone in, the holding company had furnished the place—minimally, but stylishly, which was enough for basic living. The sitting room had a couch, coffee table, and large, overarching floor lamp; and the bedroom had a California King-size bed with a thick down comforter and way too many pillows. To this day I don't understand people's obsession with covering an entire bed with pillows. It was hardly a deterrent, though. While the kids were upstairs partying, dad was more than happy to adapt.

* * *

Gough Street, San Francisco – Commissioned by Lyam and Manon Lesueur

It was still early evening, so I went back upstairs to work in the studio for a bit.

At my drawing table I began the routine of turning on lights and pulling out my tool trolley. Looking through my unfinished drawings, there was one piece I kept meaning to get to but for some reason kept putting aside. A fairly simple one of a building on Gough Street for a French couple who had just moved from Paris to be teachers at the French American International School in Hayes Valley. I'd been drawing in the Mission one day when they rode by on their bicycles, each with a toddler strapped onto the back, and stopped to see what I was making. On the spot they asked for a commission, which I'd started that same day, then let sit for weeks, and still hadn't finished. I thought to work on it, but once again found myself distracted. I was thinking about the upcoming assignment with the police, and my supplies. My standard M.O. was to go out with one large shoulder bag, which I would tuck between my feet while I was working. It was compact and easy, but also slightly awkward. And after having stood for hours on the hard concrete of the Lyon Street Steps, I wanted to make my next outing more comfortable. From under the workbench I retrieved my French easel. I'd set it on the prep table and was unfolding the telescoping legs when the phone rang.

Larissa and her friends had turned up the music again, and so as I answered, I put a finger in my ear.

"Where the hell are you?" the voice on the other end said. It was Ronnie. "Sounds like you're hosting a telethon."

"I am," I said, closing the studio door. "It's for the Save-the-Emit Foundation. Would you care to donate?"

"No, but I'll let you buy me a beer."

"That'll do."

"Zeitgeist. Thirty minutes."

25

LOVELY

The Zeitgeist was a biker bar five blocks from my building. For a time it had been a rough-and-tumble place, but lately the definition of "biker" had been expanded to include bicyclists, and the bar had become popular with the messenger crowd. It was still surly, though. The staff was famous for going for days on nothing but whiskey and crystal meth, and a year before, the owner had been shot to death, the killer unknown. The main attraction was the beer garden, which took up the entire adjacent lot. Lined with picnic tables, at one end was a rack for bicycles, at the other, a junked old truck from the forties filled with succulents. They also had an outdoor grill where you could get a damn fine sausage or burger. It was a great place on a warm day, which this was not. But Ronnie had picked it and it was close—and it was also somewhere to go other than my flat, which had been overrun by teenagers.

I headed there on foot and was a block away when I saw Ronnie's Mustang—parking in a handicap spot.

"I'm guessing your disability is that you don't give a shit?" I said, coming up to him as he was getting out of the car.

"And my super power is having a gal at the DMV who's sweet on me."

The street in front of the bar was lined with over a dozen motorcycles, backed perpendicularly against the curb, their front wheels all tilted at the same angle like a Hell's Angels chorus line.

"Ronnnnieee!" said the six-foot, barrel-shaped bouncer with an enormous smile and forearms the size of my head. He hopped off his stool and grabbed Ronnie by the cheeks and gave him a kiss on the forehead.

"You'll have to forgive Isaac," Ronnie said. "He likes people."

"Aw, now, come on," Isaac said. "You're not just people, you're friggin' Ronnie J. Gilbert."

"Get ya a beer?" Ronnie asked. He aimed his thumb at me. "He's buying."

Isaac picked up a full pint from the floor just inside the door. "I'm good, thanks. But you can get me another time."

We went inside and got in line. There were three, one for each bartender. Zeitgeist wasn't a place where you crowded the bar and waved your arm. The bartenders were notoriously unfriendly, and if you wanted a drink, you followed their rules. And if you wanted another, you tipped extremely well.

The line beside us was moving faster, and I made to switch.

"Uh-uh," Ronnie said. "We're staying in this one."

I decided to neither argue nor ask why. Instead, I said, "I've been thinking about everything you told me out at Stinson."

"Oooh," Ronnie said, wincing. "Yeah. About all that . . . Chalk it up to Mary Jane. Gal's got a problem with diarrhea of the mouth."

"You don't need to worry," I said. "As far as I'm concerned, you brought over a video for us to watch and I was too distracted with Mary Jane's tan lines to remember much of it."

This made Ronnie smile. "Good man. But you've got a question about the plot?"

"You and Zorn," I said. "Have you two spoken much after the night of Joe Chadwick?"

Ronnie looked at me in a way that made you feel like you were going through a metal detector at the airport, only it wasn't a machine but a giant drooling creature with a thousand scrutinizing eyes. It occurred to me how lucky I was to have been able to smoke that joint with him. Without it, I doubt his tongue would have ever been as loosened.

"We've found ourselves in the same room once or twice," Ronnie said. "But we've never spoken."

"Interesting. That has to call to his guilt, then, wouldn't you say?"

Ronnie wobbled his head. "Some puzzles you don't solve by hammering away. Some you need to put down and walk away from, let yourself be distracted by something else before picking them up again."

"You mean like quitting the police force, becoming a private detective, and waiting years for a client to randomly show up with a blackmail tape that was made in an apartment identical to Joe Chadwick's sro penthouse?"

If Ronnie had been anyone else he might have been offended. But instead he just smirked. "You have a clever way of putting things. Maybe I need to give your song lyrics another listen."

"Nah," I said. "I'm much more clever in person."

It was our turn at the bar.

"Three Dickel's," Ronnie said to the bartender. "Straight."

The woman immediately turned to grab the jug-sized bottle of bourbon that was right behind her. Dickel's was the house whiskey.

I wanted to ask Ronnie who else we were meeting, but I was distracted by the bartender. She'd lined up three glasses and had begun moving quickly back and forth, filling all three at once while somehow not spilling a drop. But it wasn't her pouring skills that had my attention. It was the tattoos covering her arms—and hands, and fingers.

"You've got a hell of a nice rack on you darlin'," Ronnie said.

The woman's head popped up. "What the fuck did you just say?" She'd stopped pouring and looked like she was going to crack Ronnie upside the head with the giant bottle.

"Your tits," he said. "I said you've got a great pair."

But before she could follow through with the swing she was gearing up to take, Ronnie had taken out my photo from the Legion and was holding it in front of her face.

For a second she was confused, then she relaxed and laughed.

"Well, god damn," she said. "So you found me. What the fuck do you want?"

Ronnie slid one of the shots of bourbon in front of her and another in front of me. Then he picked up the third and raised it up. "To say you've got a damn fine rack, and—" he downed the double in one quick toss "—for you to buy my friend here a drink."

"You got some serious balls," she said to Ronnie. "And you," she said to me, "for someone who's supposedly an artist, I would have thought you'd be more observant. You had no idea I was even there, did you?" Then she picked up her drink and threw it back with even more ease than Ronnie had.

Not wanting to ruin the moment, I tossed back my whiskey as well. A shiver went through my shoulders. It wasn't the finest of spirits.

"There," she said. "You've had your free firewater. Now get the fuck out."

"Not until you tell us why you decided to grace my friend here with your lovelies. He's a stand-up guy and all, but I don't know that he deserved those—and he especially didn't deserve you calling the cops on him. Now, what's a sweet girl like you doing making a false report on a law-abiding citizen?"

"I don't have to tell you shit," she said. "Now get the fuck out of here."

Then she threw up her arm. "Isaac!" she called out. "I got a couple a' assholes over here."

The line behind us parted as the hulking but agile Isaac shot over, but the moment he saw us he stopped in his tracks. "These guys?" he said. "What's the deal, Abbs? Ronnie's good people."

"Your gal here," Ronnie said. "She's been——" But she cut him off.

"Just pullin' your chain, sweet-cheeks," she said to Isaac. "Your buddy here said you were looking a little lazy, and I bet him a round you were still lightning on your feet."

"Ah, good ol' Ronnie J.!" Isaac said, grabbing Ronnie by the shoulders and giving him a quick squeeze. If he'd wanted, he could have picked up good ol' Ronnie J. and chucked him right out the door. But instead he said, "No way, babe. Their round's on me." Then he lumbered back to his stool by the door.

"Somewhere we can talk?" Ronnie said. "Abbs?"

"Name is Abigail," she said. "And we can talk right here." She glanced toward the door. "But not a word to Isaac."

"You tell us what we need to know, and our very large friend will stay a very happy friend."

Abigail set to pouring another round of shots. "Prick's name is Anselm Keller——" she glanced up as she poured "——German tech-bro who runs a douchey startup in SOMA." She finished pouring and set the bottle down. "I don't even know what the fuck he does, some stupid online shit to sell pet food to the richie-rich. Anyway, this girlfriend of mine—you don't need to know her name—she strips over at the Century. A few weeks back she says she's got this gig at a startup. These tech dorks got a truckload of coke and they want some tits and ass to go along with it for the night, and do I want to come party with them. It was good money, so I said what the hell."

"I'm guessing Isaac was having his weekly knitting circle and going to bed early that night?"

"Isaac was losing his shirt playing poker up in Russian River, which is the only way he knows how to play."

"So what's this have to do with you making a false report on my friend here?"

Abigail picked up her shot and threw it back as easily as the first. Ronnie didn't touch his. I left mine as well.

"The techie-douche Anselm," she said. "That night he's talking all kinds of trash. Going on about how he hates San Francisco, thinks it's full of loser artists. One in particular——" she looked at me "——Emit Hopper."

Ronnie looked at me, I looked at him, then I picked up my whiskey and drank it.

"He say why?" Ronnie asked.

The tattooed bartender rolled her eyes. "Who the fuck listens? All I know is he kept going on and on until someone finally called him on his shit and said if he hated this artist prick so much, then he should put up or shut up, so he offered me a grand to tell the cops you were a perv."

"What about my car?" I asked.

"What about it?"

"Did you do anything to my car? Cut the roof? Report it stolen?"

"Why the fuck would I mess with your car?"

Ronnie picked up his whiskey. "So, Abbs, let me make sure I got this straight: A startup tech bro named Anselm Keller paid you a thousand bucks to tell the cops my friend here is a sex offender. That about the size of it?"

The tattooed bartender nodded. "Yep." She looked at me and smirked. "The tits I gave you for free."

* * *

Outside, Isaac told us to have an awesome night, and as we walked away we could hear him say, "Friggin' Ronnie J. Gilbert. Awesome."

Neither of us spoke until we were at Ronnie's car, and I was the first. "In answer to the obvious question," I said, "no. I have no idea who Anselm Keller is. And I have no affiliation with any startup companies. You think she was telling the truth?"

"I think it's a hell of a good thing she's screwing Isaac," he said. "We got lucky with that one." He opened his car door. "I got a full day tomorrow, but the day after? Pop by this Keller's office and hear what he's got to say?"

"Sure," I said. Ronnie got in and shut the door. He started the engine and powered down the window. I leaned over, laid my arms on the roof. "You have to tell me, though. How'd you find her?"

"Body like that, tattoos, willingness to bare herself in public, figured odds were good she might work the strip scene. I showed her photo around and hit a bullseye at the Lusty Lady. Manager said she used to perform there. They had some bad blood when she left—imagine that—so he was happy to point me to where she'd landed next. Still, I slipped him a hundred for his troubles and to keep his mouth shut, which you can find a way to pay me back for."

"I can draw you a picture of the Knot Guilty—or of your car." I pointed to the miniature replica of the Mustang mounted on his dash. "I'll even make sure to include that. Then you can have a drawing of the car inside your car."

He laughed. "Don't you worry. I'll hold your marker for when I need it."

"So you believe her story about Keller?"

Ronnie shrugged. "Only one way to know." Then he revved the engine and put the car in gear. "Day after tomorrow. I'll pick you up at noon." I stood back, and the Mustang sped away.

I had a full dose of cheap whiskey churning in my belly and a curious story swirling in my head. I stumbled back home to sleep in a bed with too many pillows in a flat I no longer owned.

26

DEFINITIVELY AMBIGUOUS

I slept soundly in a bed that I was probably the only one to have ever slept in. The next morning I went to the Pork Store on 16th for Eggs in a Tasty Nest—two over-easy eggs on top of a mash of hash browns, bacon, peppers, onions, and cheese—then went across the street to Café Macondo for a proper espresso. With an eclectic assortment of rugs, chairs, and huge potted plants, Macondo was one of my favorite cafés. You could get coffee during the day and wine at night. Used to be the place was constantly buzzing with artists, writers, and musicians. During the day they'd be working on their future masterpieces, and at night they'd be performing or just hanging out. But that morning, as it was more and more, the café was dead. Another sign of the changing times. I downed my espresso standing at the counter, then returned to my flat. My bedroom door was closed and Viraj was asleep on the back couch. I quietly gathered my drawing bag and French easel, then drove to Japantown.

*   *   *

I parked in the garage of the Japan Center and walked to Peace Plaza, the public square set between two of the three buildings that made up the Japanese cultural center and shopping mall.

I wasn't sure where exactly I was supposed to take position. Inspector Zorn had said only the pagoda. Figuring there wasn't anything more to know, I searched for a spot that offered an interesting composition. On the drive over I'd been thinking of Japanese woodblock prints and their often elegant geometry, so rather than set up in the middle of the square, I stepped into the shrubbery where, squeezed between a wall and a bush, I found a view framing the pagoda between the foliage. Then I began setting up my rig.

A French easel is a classic and ingenious device. You've surely seen one, without knowing it by name. When packed up, it looks like a wooden brief-case turned on its side, with a T-shaped easel attached to its face. Unpacked, three legs telescope out to form a tripod, holding the box flat at waist height. It takes all of three minutes to set up, and once together the box acts as both a tabletop and drawer. The lid and easel can be adjusted at any angle, and can hold varying sizes of canvas or pads of paper. The drawer gives easy access to tools, and a hinged side panel can be flipped out as an additional surface. Designed for painters, it was more rig than I needed for drawing, but I liked its stability.

After setting up, I took out my camera to shoot reference photos. The morning was gray, and the scene had no contrast. If I wanted to finish the drawing properly, I would have to come back another day for light and shadow. More on my mind, though, was whether I was expected to photograph the crowd. I was pretty sure Ocampo's instructions at the Lyon Street Steps to photograph "suspicious" people had just been part of her initial ruse, and now that I knew my true role, I didn't need to do it. Not that it mattered much either way, seeing that I'd ignored her then, and certainly wasn't going to do it now. I decided I wouldn't even fake it. I took a few shots of the pagoda just to have them, then put my camera away and began drawing.

I was about a half hour in when a man in a baseball cap, puffy vest, and shorts strode over.

"Looks like you're drawing?" he said. "What's that take you? About two or three hours?"

It was Inspector Zorn. He was in costume and I assumed talking in code, so I played along. "Yeah," I said. "I imagine I'll be done around noon or one."

"Awesome. Have a nice day."

Such was the extent of my instructions, and contact with the inspector. Occasionally I glanced around to see if I could identify who the cops-in-training were, and was pretty sure I spotted two who were on the force—and who would fail the exercise. One was a guy who literally stood in the middle of the square, watching people and taking notes, and the other was a woman wearing combat boots who pressed herself at the far corner of the square behind the pagoda, between the building and a retaining wall, with her arms crossed and mouth pinched the entire time I was there.

An hour later another man approached me. Japanese, late sixties. I wondered which category he belonged to: cop, curious passerby, or Chatty Karl. Turned out to be none.

"Hopper, right?" he said.

"Yes sir."

"Beautiful book, *Glass Houses*," he said. "Funny, too. I think most people didn't get it."

I laughed. A true fan—and one who knew I was me, and not Brian.

"Thanks," I said. "Which they somehow hold against me."

He waved off the idea. "You can't listen to people," he said. "I worked forty years for PacBell. I've been called more names than I knew existed. May I?" He pointed to my drawing.

"Of course." I showed him.

"Marvelous. Might this be for sale?"

"Sure." I gave him my card.

"You wouldn't take requests, would you?"

"I would, and do."

"Wonderful. You know the Pacific Telephone Building at 140 New Montgomery?"

I said maybe.

"Oh, you know it. Grand structure. Eagle statues at top. My entire life I worked in that building. If you could draw those eagles, I would hang it above my dining-room table."

I said I'd have a look, and we agreed he'd call to talk details. Then he pointed to my drawing of the Pagoda and, with a spontaneous grin, said, "and you know what? I want that too." Then we shook on the deal and he walked off.

I was feeling quite pleased. Two drawings sold and it was barely after noon. I finished the line drawing and packed up. It was a quarter till one, which I figured would give the observing trainees something to note. I took myself to sushi boat for lunch.

*   *   *

After eating, I wandered around the Japan Center. There were food stalls, fountains, tables and chairs, and a plethora of shops, including Kinokuniya, an enormous bookstore with an entire floor of manga, and Mai Do, a stationery store where I stocked up on gel pens.

It was still early in the day. If the weather had been better I would have gone out to work on another commission. Though I did have a few interiors on my list. Off the top of my head I could think of two: the Swedenborgian Church, an historic Arts and Crafts building designed in part by Bernard

Maybeck, where a couple had gotten married and wanted the memory captured as a drawing; and the Legion of Honor, where I still had six drawings to make, a combination of interior and exterior. The church was complicated in that it required scheduling, so the Legion it was.

From Japantown it was an easy drive out Geary to the museum. I parked, got my ticket, and went inside. I already knew what I wanted to draw. There were two identically mirrored marble passages, which had always been my favorite feature of the Legion. I set up the French easel at the top of one, then began by shooting an entire roll of film. I started three line drawings and was pleased to say that I passed the rest of the day there without incident—well, almost. A security guard did ask me to move a few inches to the side to ensure that other museumgoers could pass, but his heart wasn't in it. He was just bored and wanted to feel useful.

* * *

Driving home I cut through the park and took Fulton so I could stop at Falletti's, the grocery store and deli that had one of the last twenty-four-hour film processing kiosks in the city. I arrived just before closing and dropped off the roll of film I'd shot at the pagoda and museum, along with the roll from Stinson. Returning to the Mission, I circled the neighborhood for twenty minutes before finding parking. I really needed to get the Miata back, and intended to call Ronnie the moment I got home.

Opening the door, I found the flat sounding surprisingly quiet. I dropped my things in the studio then headed for the back. As I approached the bedroom I heard giggling. The door was open, and I saw Larissa and Tally on my bed. Larissa was lying down, her feet on the floor, as if she'd been sitting on the edge and fallen backwards. Tally was lying across Larissa's stomach. They were clothed, but I was glad I hadn't walked past fifteen minutes later.

"Hey," Tally said, seeing me.

"Sorry to interrupt," I said, which I was. I made to keep walking.

"Wait," Larissa said. I turned back.

Tally moved as Larissa sat up. "Check it out," Larissa said. She tugged at her T-shirt. Oddly, it was white, and not so oddly, in the center was a large stain which had been turned into one of her cartoon ghosts with arms reaching out as if it were flying. Only this one was smiling. And had female lips.

"I'm not the artist you are," Tally said, putting the cap on a fine-point Sharpie. "But it's super fun to draw ghosts."

"She thinks it's hilarious that I'm such a slob," Larissa said. "So she made

237

me put on one of her shirts and tickled me while I ate breakfast. How'd it go? I take it you didn't get arrested again?"

"Not today," I said. "Thanks for asking. You guys hungry? I was thinking of ordering pizza."

"Yes!" Tally said. "I'm in."

"Sure," Larissa said.

And I left the room.

"Oh, hey!" Larissa called out. I came back. "I totally forgot to tell you. The blood lab called with the results."

I froze. So much had been going on that I'd almost forgotten. "And?"

"It's positive."

I was stunned. "Wow. So . . . I'm your father?" I did my best to sound happy—which I was. Or, rather, I wasn't *un*happy. Mostly I was taken off guard. I guess I'd expected . . . I didn't know what I expected.

"Is it really such a surprise?"

I shook my head. "No—I mean, I guess not. But . . ." I found myself smiling. "Well, there we go. Now we know for sure. We should celebrate."

She wobbled her head. "Well, we don't know for *sure* for sure."

"What do you mean?"

"You're an identical twin."

"And?"

"*And*, a blood test can only determine family, it can't differentiate between identical twins."

"Okay . . ."

"Which means while the results confirm that I am in fact of the Hopper bloodline, they can't tell us who actually inseminated my mother."

"So you're saying that either Brian or I are most certainly your father, but finding out definitively which of us is father and which is uncle is impossible?"

"Not impossible. There are researchers who are working on DNA sequencing who could probably sort it out, but the technology is still new and not publicly available. Maybe in ten years or so it will be more accessible, but right now it would probably cost, like, fifty grand, and that's even if someone would do it."

"Wait," I said. "So you knew this would be the case?"

"Duh. How did you *not* know? It's, like, common knowledge."

I was suddenly angry. "Maybe for a genius who has a stake in knowing about these things. But for normal people like me who don't think about this stuff, DNA and blood testing is definitely *not* common knowledge."

"First off, stop freaking calling me that——" she was angry now too "——I told you I hate that word. And second, being 'normal'——" she mockingly used air quotes "——is not an excuse for ignorance."

Tally was watching us go back and forth. With the conversation suddenly heated, she got up and quietly left the room.

"You know what?" I said, stepping aside to let Tally slip past me, "you're right. I need to stop calling you a genius. Because you're definitely not one. You might be smart enough to have earned a college degree before you could drive, but when it comes to empathizing and treating people with respect, you're an absolute idiot."

Then I walked away.

*   *   *

I went into the studio and laid out the drawings I'd started that day. I wasn't thinking about the work, though. I was pissed off and just needed something to distract myself.

A minute later Larissa appeared in the doorway. She stared at me blankly.

"What?" I said. "No clever sarcasm? Like, 'How is that any way to talk to your maybe-daughter?' or, 'Guess we're not celebrating?'"

"You're right," she said, sitting on my drafting chair and tucking both legs underneath her. "I suck at these things. I'm sorry."

She did look genuinely sorry. Which only annoyed me more. I wanted to be angry with her, but it was hard to be angry with someone who's agreeing with you.

We were both quiet. I left my drawings and sat on the couch. Larissa stayed on my chair, looking contrite.

"I just think you're not fully grasping the gravity of this," I said.

"Maybe. But tell me, how does knowing definitively make a difference?"

"What do you mean how——?" I was instantly angry again. "It is *literally* the difference between having a child and not having a child. Which in my book is a pretty significant qualification."

"You see?" she said, also instantly heated. "This was why I waited until I was eighteen to come find you. So we wouldn't have any of these stupid parental expectation issues."

I was speechless.

Larissa sighed. "Listen, I don't know what childhood was like for you. From what you've told me, it sounds pretty not so bad. But for me, growing up was chaos. Mom was seventeen when she dropped out of high school and ran off with the rock and roll circus, and when she came back pregnant, my holy-roller grandparents wanted nothing to do with her. She hadn't found out she had cancer yet, and when she did she decided not to tell them since they'd already turned her away. Her brother, my uncle Phil, was only two years older, but he at least had a job and his own apartment. He took Mom in, and after I was born, helped her with her treatments. And for a while, I think they were happy. Grateful for life. The three of us our own weird little family.

"Then the years started going by, and things started to get bad. It just wasn't what either of them had thought their lives would be like, you know? And really, they were still kids themselves—*and* they were siblings. You have a brother, so you know how it is. You guys know exactly how to push each other's buttons. Mom and Phil loved each other, but they never should have been living together. Then you throw me into the mix."

She took a deep breath and shook her head. "I think at first," she said, "when neither of them knew what was going to happen with Mom's cancer, it had been easy for them to be selfless. There was the birth, then chemo, and all of that made it easy to ignore their petty differences and individual desires. But then time went on and eventually they realized Mom wasn't actually going to die, and suddenly that 'grateful for one more day' high started to crash. They realized living with your sibling sucks, raising a kid sucks, and neither of them was getting any younger—and people assumed they were a couple. They both wanted real relationships, but their situation was far from ideal for finding a partner. And let's be clear, it wasn't so great for me either. There were more than a few screaming matches between Mom and Phil, and a lot of randos who came and went through our house. There'd be nights where each of them would have someone in their bedroom. The mornings would be this awkward scene in the kitchen with no one really sure what to do. Then, when I was nine, Phil had this girlfriend, Denise, who had pretty much moved in after their second date and immediately started causing friction, so Mom took me and we left. We went to a motel for a week, then moved into a dumpy apartment by the train station. Six months later, Denise disappeared and Phil asked us to move back. Then Mom's cancer returned, and a few months later she was dead."

Larissa paused and looked out the window. She was shaking her head slightly, remembering the time.

"It's a fucking shame," she said, looking back at me. "Is what it is. No matter how much she tried, she was never able to get her shit together. It was like everything was always just out of her reach. She'd survived cancer, but she never really got to live, you know? I spent a long time feeling guilty about that. Like it was my fault. That if she hadn't had to deal with having a kid, then she might have had more of a life. But always there was the big story about how, 'if not for getting pregnant she wouldn't have found out she had cancer,' which was somehow supposed to make it all right. But who really knows, you know? I mean, she could have easily gotten an abortion and still lived. I honestly don't know why she didn't. Instead, she survived cancer only to be saddled with a kid. I mean, I know she chose to keep me and all, but . . ." She shook her head. "And Phil wasn't much better. He could never keep a job. Mostly because he preferred going to the bar and could never wake up on time. There'd be mornings I'd have to go in and turn off his alarm because it'd been going off for half an hour. With him too passed-out to hear.

"I don't mean to paint a bad picture of them. They both loved me. And even though their lives never seemed to work out, they never stopped encouraging me. I was a smart kid and Mom especially loved that, but I also think that maybe I wasn't so much smart as I was a normal kid who found refuge from an unstable home at school. It was survival for me. I looked around and saw these two people who were supposed to be taking care of me, and they could barely take care of themselves. School was the one place where I felt safe, and could count on getting at least one meal a day. That's why I hate the word *genius*. People look at me and see this young woman who is so smart and has everything under control. Whereas I look at me and I see a girl who's desperately trying to keep from being hungry, homeless, and alone."

She was getting angry, as if she were defending herself against an accusation—which I supposed she was, from herself, in her head.

"I do think that if Mom had lived longer," she said, taking a breath and calming down, "she would have eventually gotten to a place where she was proud of herself. During that time we'd moved out, she was really making headway. She'd gotten a steady job and managed to get her GED and even enrolled in city college. But then halfway through her first semester her cancer came back." She laughed a little. "It's funny, because you asked whether Mom got a chance to see how smart I was before she died. Well, I think it was me who gave her the encouragement to go back to school." She instantly started crying. "Can you imagine? Here's this adult woman, who fought every day to live, and the only reason she believes in herself is because she looks at her kid and thinks, 'If I made someone like her, then I must be good too.'" She let herself cry, then took a breath and wiped her eyes. "But by then it was too late. The cancer had come back and . . . She just got a bum deal, you know? She had, like, one blaze of glory. Running away at seventeen. And that was it. Can you imagine? Having run off to party with a bunch of hedonist musicians for a few months being the most freedom you ever got to feel? I mean, who ever thinks that the stupid shit they're doing in the moment might end up being the best time of their lives?"

I wanted to say there was more to life than teenage freedom. And that some might say having been able to see how brilliant her daughter was, and also to be inspired by her, was more than a lot of people get. But Larissa wasn't looking for me to placate her. She just needed to tell her story.

"Anyway," she said, taking a deep breath and rubbing her eyes. "After Mom died, Uncle Phil and I kept living in the same apartment, and I hated it. He always liked playing the role of the one with his shit together, having taken in his sick kid sister, but really, he was a bigger mess than Mom. And when she died, he fell apart. Out drinking every night. In the first six months he got three DUIs. The third time they threw him in jail and I had to bail him out. Freaking ten years old and I had to max out my dead mother's credit cards—which my drunk uncle had been too negligent to cancel—to get that same uncle out of jail." She laughed at the absurdity of it. "Maybe it's terrible to say, but life after that felt like drowning. Getting to leave and come to Stanford to build the life I have now, that felt like waking up from one of those dreams where you're gasping for breath thinking, 'Thank fucking God that wasn't real.'" She looked at me. "Pretty messed up, huh?"

I shook my head. "You saved yourself. I'm sure your mother hoped for nothing more."

Larissa didn't look so sure. She turned toward the window again. "Any-way," she said. "I don't know why I'm telling you all this." She looked back to me, her face tired. "I don't expect a sob story will make up for my dis-regarding your feelings. It's just . . ." She paused to find the words. "I see people doing all kinds of stupid shit they don't want because they think they have to. Out of duty or obligation or some bullshit martyr complex that worships sacrifice." Her eyes turned defiant. "But nobody owes me anything, you know? Personally, I don't give two shits whether you're my father or my uncle or some random ex-rock star who Mom just happened to be on tour with. Whatever relationship you and I have, whatever friendship and respect we develop, should be based on how we feel about each other as people. Not because some blood test says we're suddenly supposed to care. You could be my father and we could both hate each other and never want to talk again, or we could be completely unrelated and both think we're the most awesome people ever and stay best friends for life. You see what I mean?"

"And here you were," I said, "doing so good with the apology."

"I'm serious," she said. And she was. She looked like she was about to cry again.

"I know," I said. "And I understand. It's a pretty enlightened position you've taken."

"And so are your feelings still hurt?"

I shook my head.

"Good," she said. "Because I like you. I really do. And I don't know your brother, but I know that whatever you and I are, I'm glad we're family. And even more so that we're friends."

"Me too."

"Okay, then," she said, instantly relieved. She clapped her hands together and let out a final exhalation. "Good. I'm glad we worked this out. And thank you for letting me completely take over your house." She had a sudden look of embarrassment. "It's hard for me to admit this, but I'm not used to having very many friends. And Tally, she's like, really, *really*, freaking cool."

"She is really cool," I said.

"So you don't mind if I stay up here for a while so I can hang out with her?" I could see the crush in her eyes.

"Well," I said. "I'm taking my bedroom back—and I need my studio to work. But other than that, you're welcome to call this home."

She jumped up, grabbed my face, and kissed my forehead. Then she stepped back—still holding my face—and took on a serious expression. I braced myself for what was coming next.

After a few long seconds, she finally spoke. "You want a cold leftover vegetarian taco?"

"I do," I said, as gravely as I could. "I'm also wondering if you've heard of a guy named Anselm Keller?"

She let go of my face. "For real?"

I nodded.

"Yeah," she said, sneering. "I know Anselm Keller. He's a total asshole."

23rd & Shotwell Streets, San Francisco — Patron asked to be unnamed. A woman who lived six months in this apartment was moving to the outskirts of Chico, a rural area in northern California, claiming the overhead electrical wires of the city had confused her senses so badly that she'd failed to detect a gas leak in her apartment, leaving her to pass out and be found unconscious by her roommate. When she returned several months later to pick up the drawing, she had a patch over one eye, having had her cornea pecked by a chicken.

27

E-L-T

"Yay!" Tally said. "You two made up!"

Larissa said she'd tell me all about Anselm Keller, but that first we should celebrate. "To being friends who are actually happy to be family," she said. I agreed. We'd gone to the kitchen, where we found Tally washing dishes.

"Thanks for cleaning up," I told her as I assessed what bottles were left after Larissa's party.

"Of course!" Tally said to me. Then she saw Larissa open the fridge and peer in. "I hope you don't mind, but I ordered that pizza for us."

"Great."

"I'm hungry now, though," Larissa said, pulling out the tray of leftover tacos. "I still can't believe you ordered so much vegetarian."

Tally stopped with the dishes and wiped her hands on a towel. "I know. But Kai and Viraj were all up my ass making sure we had enough. Kai was like—" she closed her eyes and affected a prissy voice "—'No one takes vegetarians seriously and you need to be more sensitive about people's dietary restrictions and blah blah blah we're sensitive eaters.'" She folded the towel and set it on the island. "So I ordered like three times more than we needed so they wouldn't get their cow-loving panties in a bind."

"Vegetarians are the worst," Larissa said, taking a bite of a cold taco straight off the tray.

"What are you doing, silly?" Tally said, pulling the taco out of her hand and putting it on the metal pan from the toaster oven. "Heat these up."

"Hey, I was eating that!"

"Would you like a taco?" Tally said to me, her eyes wide. "Pizza probably won't be for at least half an hour still."

"A taco will be great," I said. I'd found a bottle of Don Julio Anejo tequila that I'd stashed away for a special occasion and was lining up three glasses. "One is good for me."

Tally loaded three tacos onto the small metal baking pan and slid it into the toaster oven. "Yeah," she said. "And whatever about vegetarians—" she pressed the power button "—and vegans are even worse. You know how can you immediately tell someone's a vegan?"

I shook my head.

"They tell you."

"Yeah," Larissa said. "Like, within four seconds of walking into a room. They're like the Jehovah's Witnesses of food."

"Totally!" Tally said. "They should call themselves the Butcher's Witnesses."

"And instead of *The Watchtower*, their literature is *The Boring Dinner*."

And the two fell on each other laughing.

The sight of two young people being smitten was sweet—so much so, that, if I hadn't been feeling touched by Larissa's having shared the story of her childhood with me, I would have forgone the glasses and just started guzzling tequila straight from the bottle.

* * *

"Cheers!" we all said together, raising up our shots of straight tequila.

"Here's to unusual family," Larissa said. "In all definitions of the word." And we all drank.

"So," I said to Larissa. "Anselm Keller."

"Okay. But why the interest?"

"Apparently he paid a stripper-slash-bartender at the Zeitgeist to tell the cops I was a pervert."

"The Zeitgeist has strippers now?" Tally asked.

"No," I said. Then I explained the situation.

"So what's this Keller guy got against you?" Tally said.

The tacos had finished warming and Tally set the metal tray atop a pot-holder on the island.

"That's the thing," I said, picking up a taco. "Nothing, as far as I can tell. I don't know him. But Larissa, you said you do. Could he maybe know that you and I are related and have some beef with you?"

"What the hell are you talking about?"

I took a bite. "You said he's an asshole."

246

"Yeah, he's an asshole, but I don't *know* know him. I know *of* him." She picked up a taco, doused it with salsa. "And anyway, how could he know we were related? You and I didn't even know until today. And when that bartender flashed you, we hadn't even met."

"Yeah, but—I don't know. I'm just trying to figure this thing out."

"So who is this guy, anyway?" Tally said, watching as Larissa attempted to take a bite of taco, only to spill half the contents onto the counter and floor.

Larissa grunted and set to cleaning up the mess with a napkin. "Ugh. He's basically the ruin of the internet. He owns Insta-Pet. One of the thousand stupid online pet food sites."

"Oh my god—is that the one with the cute sock puppet?" Tally said. "I love those commercials."

"No, that's Pets-Dot-Com. And also, no, the puppet is not cute." She shoved what was left of her taco into her mouth, managing to get most—but not all—of it in, and talked while chewing. "The whole trend is just sickening. I mean, yes, the Internet is the new capitalist frontier, blah blah, but the business models are a disaster. I've seen Keller's numbers. They are literally in the red like forty percent of their revenue per quarter."

"I think it's weird that you know that," Tally said. She turned to me. "Isn't it weird she knows that?"

"It's all weird," I said. "So, Anselm—"

"So Anselm Keller started Insta-Pet and he's an arrogant prick—" she tugged out her shirt, which was really Tally's white shirt, to see a new stain of salsa "—and if this were the real world and not the Internet, he'd have been bankrupt and run out of town years ago. He's burned through countless rounds of venture capital and still hasn't turned a profit."

"And he knows you know this?"

"What are you talking about? Everybody knows it."

"I'm confused," Tally said.

"Me too," I said.

Larissa sighed and looked back and forth between us. I was glad Tally was there—and that she was someone Larissa was sweet on—otherwise she probably would have called me a moron.

"Doesn't matter," she said. "Or it does, but—the real reason I dislike Keller is because he's a hypocrite. He's a for-profit business but half his staff are volunteers, which he poaches from his nonprofit foundation. He boasts ethically sourced ingredients in his Insta-Pet brand pet food, yet he uses factories in China which are known to use child labor and defy pretty much every quality standard of the civilized world. Not to mention that he plasters pictures of puppies and kittens on everything he does to prey on people's sympathies."

"Who doesn't like puppies and kittens?"

"That's what I'm saying. It's basically pet porn. Anyway. You guys obviously don't care about the ethics. I'm just saying that, even aside from all his shady business practices, Anselm Keller is the epitome of what people hate about tech. With his whole, 'I'm not special, I'm just trying to save the world' schtick, and, 'I'm too cool to be cool' attitude."

Tally looked at me and winced. "Yeah," she said. "I don't know anybody at all like that." And she and I started laughing.

Larissa looked back and forth between us, confused, until she finally realized we were making fun of her.

"Whatever," Larissa said. "I'm just trying to give you the lay of the land. If Keller has some beef with you, you're never going to find out from him. He's notoriously difficult to get a meeting with. Which is part of his bullshit ironic power game."

I stopped laughing and offered Larissa a big, loving smile. "So what are you saying? That if Ronnie and I walk into his office tomorrow, we're probably not going to get a meeting?"

"I heard God had to book an appointment three weeks out, and even then Keller made him wait an hour."

* * *

We'd finished eating our tacos, Larissa was cleaning up the mess of bites gone wrong that encircled her, and Tally had just returned to washing the large pile of dirty dishes in the sink when the doorbell rang.

"I'll get it," Tally said, turning off the tap.

"No, babe," Larissa said. "You do plenty. I'll get it." And she darted down the hallway, leaving Tally and me alone.

"I hope this isn't weird for you," Tally said, scrunching up her nose. "Larissa and me."

"Not at all," I said.

"Cool, thanks. I know she totally barged into your life and dropped the long-lost-kid bomb, and now she's pretty much moved in. She's got some boundary issues, but—" she scrunched her nose again, this time with a smile "—I kind of like it."

"Me too," I said. "Kind of."

She laughed. "Yeah, well, I've got plenty of issues of my own. Larissa's family life was difficult, but at least it was loving. Mine was anything but." Tally moved a stack of plates into one of the two sections of sink, which was full of soapy water. "I'm Taiwanese. First generation, and the second of two girls. My father wanted boys and would have drowned us both in the river like a sack of kittens if he could have gotten away with it. He was old-world Asian and thought girls were a waste of time and money. My sister and I had to share everything from a bedroom to clothes to meals. I don't know his excuse for thinking we could be his concubines. He started coming into our room when I was ten. I was twelve when I'd had enough. One night when he slipped into my bed, I fought back. I pushed him into the hallway and he threw me down the stairs. My mother did nothing. So I ran away. The streets weren't any better, but at least I was away from him." She wiped the counter with a sponge and rinsed it under the tap. "I ended up getting a pretty serious meth habit, but some good people took me in and were patient, even when I kept running away and screwing up over and over again."

"Was it The Nest? Is that where you found help?"

"Yeah. Faith Chadwick saved my life." She turned off the tap and dried her hands again on the towel. "Everybody there was really awesome. They never gave up on me, and eventually I realized that's what real family is. It has nothing to do with blood. But with love." She folded the towel and slid it over the handle of the stove, making sure it was perfectly aligned. "Because without love it's hard to make it in this world, you know? But Faith made it so I could start my own life. Which is what the center is all about. That's why she called it The Nest. A place kids can go to feel safe until they're ready to fly on their own. Now my previous life, with parents who hated me, then of living on the street, feels like an old horror movie I never want to see again. I've got a steady job working at a bakery and an awesome apartment on the Lower Haight with super-cool roommates, and I thank the universe every day for how lucky I am."

We could hear Larissa coming up the stairs. I looked to see her rounding the landing with a large pizza box.

"Eek," Tally said as I looked back. She'd been speaking very matter-of-factly, but now her eyes were wide and her face uncertain. "That was a lot of information!" She stepped close to me and put both her hands on my arm. "I hope not too much for you?"

"Not at all," I said. "I appreciate you sharing."

"Okay, cool. I just, I can't be ashamed of my past, you know? Because that's the path that led me here, and here is awesome. So, thank you. I really do appreciate how rad you are. Larissa is lucky."

"You can stop talking about me now," Larissa said as she walked back into the kitchen with the pizza.

"Emit was just saying how we should all play a game," Tally said. "Weren't you?"

"We're only three," I said, happy to play along. "But I've got cups and dice for Liar's dice. I also have cards—and a horribly inappropriately named dominos game called Mexican Train."

"You have dice?" Tally said. "Let's play Yahtzee!" Then she jumped up and down and said, "Yay! I love playing games!" Then she called out, "Group hug!" and squeezed the three of us together. "We're an E-L-T," she said. "An Emit, Larissa, and Tally sandwich."

The three of us stayed up till one in the morning, eating way too much pizza, polishing off the bottle of Don Julio, and playing Yahtzee. I had to agree, we were for sure an unusual family.

28

INSTA-PET

As much as I was enjoying time with Larissa and Tally, I wanted my flat back, so told them they could sleep on the second floor. By that point I'd gotten maybe a little too comfortable with treating the empty unit as my own, but considering there was a housing shortage in my neighborhood, I used the argument that I was doing a good thing by putting a vacant space to use. I thought of it as taking yet another play out of Larissa's book, one that questioned the legitimacy of right and wrong—which was another way of saying I was doing whatever the hell I wanted and using intellectual bullshit as justification.

*   *   *

The next morning I took full advantage of living alone by walking around in my underwear, making coffee the way I liked it, then going into the studio and getting straight to work. I began by paying bills and filing invoices, then I took out my folder of commissions. I sorted the sites by those I would enjoy and those that would feel more like work, then organized them in alternating A/B order so that I wouldn't do all the fun ones first. I was pleased to find that most fell into the A column—the ones I would enjoy. There was a commission for two historic sites, one of the Sanchez Adobe in Pacifica, a two-hundred-year-old structure dating back to the Mexican-American War, and the other of Mission Dolores, the oldest building in San Francisco. Mission Dolores was only a block up the street from me, and I was very much looking forward to drawing it. There was another for a building on Nob Hill, the patron's request being, "I want it to look like you can't tell whether it's the street or buildings that are crooked." He also said he'd pay more if I put in his vintage VW Beetle, since I never drew cars. So that would be fun.

Islais Creek, San Francisco — Patron asked to be unnamed

Then there was a commission for the old grain silos on Pier 90 along Islais Creek. A young woman who had never bought a piece of art before wanted a gift for her grandfather's ninetieth birthday. As she'd explained, in the early fifties he'd gone from working as a longshoreman to manning what was called a "Marine Leg," the conveyor belt that hauled buckets of grain out of a ship's hold up to the wharf tower. Like the drawing I'd done of SLAC, those were the kinds of commissions that were the most rewarding. Creating triggers to memories. The only drawing I was not looking forward to was a view of Mount Davidson and Diamond Heights. It would be an interesting piece, capturing some amazing geography, and large—which meant good money—but also meant hundreds of rooftops and windows, which could be beyond tedious to render. After being at the Legion and telling Larissa about the history of commissions, it made me think about the Renaissance, about how successful artists had studios where they employed students and other skilled artists to execute different aspects of the work. Some were really good at rendering faces, others clothing, others backgrounds, so the master artist would negotiate a price with the patron based on size, timing, and how much of the piece he would do himself. Sometimes he would do only the basic sketch and his apprentices would do all the actual work. I found myself wishing I could do that with the vista drawing, or at the very least find someone to draw all the damn windows.

Next I had two calls to make. The first was to my brother, Brian, to tell him about Larissa. I'd been waiting until we learned the results of the blood test. But now that we had confirmation of his having a fifty-percent chance of being her father, he needed to know. I didn't have a direct number for him in Shanghai, since he was still getting settled, but I did have the number for his agent in Los Angeles. I opened my address book, found the number, and dialed. A receptionist put me on hold.

While I was waiting, I heard the front door open. A minute later, Larissa appeared in the doorway.

"Come in," I said. "I'm listening to muzak."

"For fun?"

"Yes, it's what I do when I'm lonely. How was your night?"

"That bed is suuuper-comfy," Larissa said. "I love all those pillows. Smells like you made coffee, yeah?"

"You'll have to boil it down for a few hours to get it how you like it, but yeah, help yourself."

After five minutes and three "Please hold and I'll connect you's," Brian's agent Justine came on the line. The moment I heard her voice I was reminded of why I no longer lived in Southern California.

"Emit! Ah-mazing to hear from you!"

I told her I had an important family matter to discuss with Brian, and if she could get word to him to contact me I would appreciate it.

"Ouch," she said. "I hope everything is okay?"

Larissa came back with a cup of coffee and sat on the couch.

"No one has died," I said to Justine. "So nothing to worry about. But please tell him it's important."

Justine promised to get him the message ASAP, and I hung up wondering if anyone in the entertainment industry would agree that learning you'd accidentally fathered a rock and roll child was considered a family matter.

"Just one more call," I said to Larissa.

"Is it about Anselm Keller?"

I leaned back in my chair. "As a matter of fact, yes. I was going to call Ronnie and tell him not to bother picking me up. If what you said is true, then our plan to confront the online pet food king about why he'd paid Abigail to report me to the police isn't going to be as easy as we'd hoped."

Larissa frowned. "Unless you'd thought to call his board of directors and suggest that you're highly interested in organizing a new branch of volunteers."

"And by 'you,' you mean *you* you? As in, Larissa Huxley, defender of the ethical Internet?"

"I wasn't sure it would work," she said, "but he agreed to meet with me and two of my associates—unnamed of course—today at noon."

"Are you actually coming?"

She recoiled. "Hell no!" She drank some coffee, then reconsidered her response. "Though I was tempted. I would love to hear why he's sending mercenary flashers to stalk you."

I dialed Ronnie.

"Glad you rang," Ronnie said. "I looked into Keller. Fucker sounds about as easy to see as the Great Pumpkin."

"Yeah, that's why I got us an appointment."

"He agreed to meet with you?"

"I'll explain it when you pick me up—oh, and any word on my car? I'd call myself but it seems there's a wanted poster out there with my face on it."

"Sure thing. I'll make the call, then head your way."

*　*　*

"Talk to me," Ronnie said as I got into the Mustang. So I told him Larissa's opinion of Anselm Keller and that she'd gotten us a meeting.

"Yeah," he said. "I did some asking around. Guy sounds like a real—what did Abbs call him? Douche. But your girl, she sounds like the real deal. Nice going there."

"Yeah, well, I had nothing to do with that."

"Which is probably why she turned out all right. In other news, you can get your little yellow bean out of the hands of Mill Valley's finest today."

"Yeah? They're releasing my car?"

"Yep. I can drive you over after our little visit."

The offices of Insta-Pet were on Tenth and Folsom, South of Market. An area that, for years, had been a wasteland of industrial buildings and a sprinkling of SROs, but also rich in a style of building I'd always coveted. Two-story jobs that looked as if back in the early days they'd been used as stables, and, when the automobile came around, were turned into garages. Their ground floors generally had large roll-up doors and fifteen-to-twenty-foot ceilings, and the second floors were wide open spaces with

Larkin Street, Nob Hill, San Francisco — Commissioned by Shaun Supanich

checkerboard windows. I'd dreamed of buying one as a studio, but had never been able to scrape together the cash. And once the tech wave swept in, it was too late. Apparently the same style of spaces that appealed to artists also appealed to startup companies, and what used to be vacant rat-infested buildings on the cheap were now the priciest real estate per square foot in town.

Insta-Pet was in one of those style-of-stable buildings. Two stories, brick, entrance through the roll-up door. The interior had been renovated in fixer-upper chic, stripped down to its barest materials and adorned with brushed steel and repurposed wood. The young woman at the desk was trendy and petite. I told her we had an appointment with Anselm and she asked if I was sure.

"Larissa Huxley," I said.

Her eyes darted back and forth between Ronnie and me without moving her head.

"She's on her way," I said.

She told us we could wait in the lobby. Ronnie told her we would wait upstairs.

Without giving her a chance to try and assert whatever power she thought she had, we walked up a set of wide recycled two-by-twelve planks suspended by wires. The second floor was an open floor plan with a couple dozen employees at two twenty-foot-long work tables in the center. At the far end of the space, across from the top of the stairs, were two offices and a meeting room with glass walls, which offered no privacy, but allowed the light from the building-length wall of checkerboard windows to shine in and illuminate the space. Everything was out in the open, with nowhere to hide, and I wondered if the same was true for the restrooms. The defining feature, however, was the handball court running the entire width of the right side of the room, the dividing wall also made of glass. Inside of which were Anselm Keller and another man. I recognized Keller by the eight-by-ten-foot photographs that lined the wall opposite the court. Most were of dogs and cats, but two were of a smiling man wearing a baseball cap. It didn't take much to guess that this humble figure was Keller.

"Meeting room or beanbags?" Ronnie said to me.

On the left side of the room, beneath the wall of photographs, was a full kitchen, dining area, and lounge. Aside from a long table and chairs, there were a half dozen large beanbag seats.

"The lounge has an espresso machine," I said.

"Lounge it is."

Of the twenty or so employees, no one gave so much as a glance as we strolled past the work tables to the kitchen and Ronnie set to making espresso.

"Damn," Ronnie said. "This is a La Marzocco. The Ferrari of espresso machines."

"You sure you know how to work one of these?"

Ronnie looked at me the way Larissa often did—a look I was getting really tired of. "Fresh beans," he said. "Grinder. Scale. These guys know what they're doing—at least with coffee." And he set to work.

As Ronnie pulled us each an espresso, I turned and surveyed the scene. The two dozen or so kids—I say "kids" because not one of them could have

Mission Dolores, San Francisco — Patron asked to be unnamed

been over twenty-three—were working at the long tables, each at their own computer, and each wearing headphones. Anselm and his handball partner were running back and forth inside the court, the sound of the small rubber ball smacking against the wall and the squeaks of their athletic shoes echoing throughout the office. Ronnie and I could have been looting the place and I doubted anyone would have noticed.

Ronnie and I sat next to each other at the enormous dining table fashioned from a single piece of redwood, our backs toward the wall, looking out over the floor of computer workers while their leader got his daily exercise.

Ronnie motioned to the workers. "Do you think they wear headphones because it's fun, or because they need them to cancel out the sound of their dear leader smacking a ball around their work space?"

"Reminds me of an installation piece I did once."

Ronnie looked at me, confused. I chose not to elaborate. He tended to always be the one who knew more than anyone else in the room, so I took a little cheap pleasure in seeing him confused.

We'd finished our espressos and had been there for at least ten minutes before Anselm left the court and strode across the long room. He'd clearly seen us, but still he took his time, stopping to chat with one of his employees while wiping sweat from his neck with a towel.

When finally he found his way to the lounge, Anselm came up to the table, smiled a big, friendly smile, plopped himself in a chair opposite us, and said, "Hey guys, how's it going?" as casual as if we were at a frat party. He drank from a water bottle, then carelessly tossed his sweaty towel onto the table of old-growth redwood that probably cost as much as my entire kitchen remodel. "Huxley's 'associates,' I presume?" Then he stared at me for a long second, appearing to recognize me. Which, considering the disdain he supposedly had, I would expect he should.

"I'm surprised there are no animals here," Ronnie said. "I would have thought that rather than a handball court, you'd have a dog run."

"Yeah," Anselm said. "We tried that. But no one wanted to pick up the shit." He chuckled. If I hadn't been poised to dislike him, I would have said he was an easygoing-enough guy. "So, is Larissa actually coming, or is it just us boys today?"

"Explain to me how a for-profit company is also a nonprofit."

Anselm drank from his water bottle again. "Insta-Pet has two missions," he said. "One is the for-profit business of providing animal lovers with the highest-quality organic and ethically sourced food possible for their beloved pets. The second is a nonprofit foundation which supports international animal rights and aids local communities in bolstering rescue efforts."

"Which is run by volunteers?"

"And profits from the former, which fund the latter."

"And how's that working out for you?"

Anselm chuckled again. "True, we've hit a few snags. But we're carving new territory, you know?" He took up the towel, wiped his forehead, and set the sweat-soaked cloth on the chair next to him. He looked at me again and squinted. He seemed to be asking himself a question, then found the answer. He smiled that big, bright smile that I was certain closed him more than a few deals, and shook a finger at me. "It took me a minute," he said. "But . . . Yeah. I thought I recognized you. You're that actor? The one who got blacklisted out of TV for being gay? Man, seriously bum deal. You have my sympathies. I'm one hundred percent against all forms of prejudice. Race, nationality, or sexual orientation."

Ronnie butted in. "So why then are you trying to ruin him even further?"

Anselm looked genuinely confused. "I honestly have no idea what you're talking about."

"You know, when people feel the need to use words like 'honestly' and 'sincerely,' it usually implies they're being anything but."

Anselm laughed, a good-natured laugh. But also one of innocence. "Maybe, but it's still true. I assumed Larissa sent you to discuss donating to our charitable foundation, or—" he looked at me hopefully "—maybe volunteer for an ad campaign? You'd be in good company. We've got an impressive lineup of celebrity donors. That Hollywood bigotry crap doesn't scare me."

"So you don't hate San Francisco and its population of loser artists?" Ronnie said.

"No way, man. I love San Francisco. And like I said, I have no tolerance—"

"For intolerance. Yeah, you told us. Listen, we know all about your after-hours cocaine stripper parties." Ronnie threw his chin toward the glass-walled court. "And hey, you'll get no bones from me. I know if I was able to bilk millions out of celebrities using sad-eyed kittens I'd feel entitled to hire a few pairs of sweet titties to bounce around that big aquarium there too. It's when my balls got swollen enough to think I could attack the character of whoever I pleased that I'd need to check myself."

"Wow," Anselm said, shaking his head and standing up. "I don't know if this is Larissa's idea of a joke, but it's time for you guys to—"

"Sit the fuck down," Ronnie said.

Anselm recoiled, but he was also still smiling—I wondered if he ever stopped. "Excuse me?"

"I said sit, the fuck, down. We're not done talking."

He was unafraid. Still smiling, he waved a finger between the two of us. "You two don't even know Huxley, do you? I knew you looked too square. I thought it was maybe some kind of retro thing, but—you're for real?" He looked excitedly around the room. "This is hilarious. What is it? Some kind of hidden camera stunt?"

"We're not fucking around," Ronnie said. "And we're not leaving until we get answers. You can call the cops if you want. The 850 station is only five minutes away. Ask for Sergeant Neely. Or Taylor."

"You're cops?"

"Former. Which is why I'll forever be closer to their hearts than you'll ever be. So how about you sit down and tell us why you paid an amateur stripper a thousand bucks to accuse my friend here of being a pervert?"

Anselm cocked his head and smiled. Then he sat back down. "Please. Tell me more. This is interesting."

"Cocaine fiesta you threw a couple weeks back. You hired a pair of strippers and spent the night talking shit about San Francisco artists. One in particular. Someone called your bluff, and so you put out a reputation hit."

"On you?" Anselm said, pointing at me. He was enjoying what he found to be an entertaining scene.

I nodded. I saw no reason to tell him I wasn't Brian—or that we actually knew Larissa.

"I see," Anselm said, tenting his fingers. "Let me guess. This stripper—big chest? Covered in tattoos?"

"That'd be her."

He laughed. "Yeah, I remember her." He chuckled. "And there's definitely a story there—only not the one you think. A few weeks ago, we hosted a fundraiser. A delightfully civil cocktail hour for an elite set of influential donors—Mayor Brown stopped by to say hello, by the way, since we're trotting out our connections. Overall, I'd give it a four and three-quarters out of five stars evening. Delancey Street did the catering—" he raised his brows "—you guys know them?"

Ronnie nodded. "Foundation providing recovering addicts places to live and jobs to help them rebuild their lives."

"They're an excellent organization," Anselm said. "And their restaurant is world-class. I use them whenever I can. It's my way of showing our donors that their money is doing good in the community beyond what we do for animals."

"Right, because serving skewers of dog and cat meat probably wouldn't go over very well."

Anselm laughed, but with obvious discomfort. "Man, what is it with all the animosity? I honestly—" he caught himself, smiled "—yes, honestly— don't know why you're so agro, but whatever it is, you can't just walk into my place of business and insult me."

"You're right," I said. I had to admit, as much as I appreciated Ronnie's hard-boiled style, he was coming on a bit hard for the easy-going Anselm. "But we were told you have a grudge against me, and we're trying to find out why."

Anselm shrugged. "I don't know what to say. I recognize you, yeah, but I don't even know your name, let alone have it out for you."

"But you know someone who does," Ronnie said.

"You mean the chick with the tattoos?" Anselm nodded. "Right," he said. "You guys are gonna love this. Like I said, few weeks back I'm hosting a fundraiser. Delancey Street does the food, but last minute the caterer bails. I heard Yahoo was throwing a bash and poached all the good local crews. Staffing isn't my area, so I can't tell you who we used—" he waved his hand dismissively "—I think we did an Ask Jeeves and hired the first listing that was available. Anyway, next thing I know we've got a battalion of inappropriately dressed servers drinking our champagne and doing lines of coke in the bathroom—so, okay, there's your cocaine fiesta. Have to admit, they were actually pretty entertaining for a while. A gaggle of flirtatious chicks with big tits cruising around pinching asses. The money crowd in this town can be kind of stiff, to put it mildly, so it was a good laugh. But you know that stuff only goes so far. Someone said something and someone else got their feathers ruffled and next thing I know, the woman I think you're talking about is throwing a drink in someone's face—and not just any someone, but P. J. Johnston, Willie Brown's press secretary. Willie was actually busting a nut laughing, but still I had to get the woman out of here." Anselm chuckled. "I'm taking it you've met her?" We nodded. "Well, as you can imagine, she did not go willingly. She pulled the tablecloths from two drink tables at the same time on her way out. Needless to say, it made for a hell of a good laugh for the rest of the night." He looked at us. "And that's it, boys. That's all I've got. Whatever this delightful woman has done to provoke you to come barging in here with your chests all puffed, I have no idea. But sounds to me like she's playing us off of each other."

Ronnie inhaled deeply through his nose, then exhaled. He looked to me, I shrugged, then he nodded. "Okay," he said, standing. "Appreciate your help."

"Yeah?" Anselm said. "Really? That's it?"

"That's it."

Anselm also stood, and I followed.

"If you don't mind," Anselm said to me, "can I ask, how exactly did this woman attempt to frame you with the police?"

"She flashed me while I was taking photos at a museum," I said. "Then she called in a lewd behavior complaint."

Anselm made a pained expression. "That's weird."

"We thought so too," I said. "Which was why when we tracked her down and she blamed you, we came in guns blazing."

Anselm bobbed his head. "All right," he said. "I hear ya. Well, I sincerely—" Again he caught himself. He pointed to Ronnie and snickered. "I will forever be aware of my adverbs because of you." He looked back to me and offered his hand. "I sincerely hope you get to the bottom of this conflict you're experiencing. I never got your name—"

Ronnie still looked disgusted, and I knew Larissa's opinion, but I thought Anselm Keller was a decent enough guy. Maybe a little smug, but worse had surely been said about me. So I shook his hand. "Emit," I said. "Thanks. We appreciate your time."

Anselm offered his hand to Ronnie.

Ronnie shook it reluctantly. "Ron," he said. Then we left.

"'I hope you get to the bottom of this issue you're experiencing'," Ronnie sneered when we were outside. "Shit like that really crawls up my canal. When I was a cop, I saw guys who were experiencing getting their spleen carved out with a rusty nail by another guy who was experiencing being looked at wrong, and newborn babies who were experiencing starving to death because their mother was experiencing being a junkie."

We got to his car and stopped.

"Yeah," Ronnie said, looking at me and laughing at himself. "I know, I know. Funny how you can literally get bloody needles and human shit thrown at you on the beat and not let it get under your skin, but then you meet a guy like that . . ."

"You mean a techie?"

"I mean a hypocrite. It's these new hipster types. They really get under my skin. They're too cool to be cool, you know what I'm saying? It would be one thing if he thought the fame hierarchy was bullshit and was trying to create an egalitarian world. But you saw him in there, playing handball while his minions sat at their stations. Guys like that, they pretend to be the man of the people, doing their part for community, but he's still a power-hungry opportunist—which would be all roses for me, if not for his pretense. It's the playing a 'cool laid-back dude' that sticks in my craw."

"Funny, that's basically Larissa's problem with him too."

"Yeah? Well, I'm liking your girl more and more." He looked at his BlackBerry, shook off his annoyance. "So listen. I've gotta be in the North Bay by four. But there's a lead I want to check out. I have time for one more quick stop, then I can drop you at the Mill Valley station for you to pick up your ride."

I said that sounded fine and got in the car.

"So I know you don't like him," I said, buckling my seat belt. "But I believe him."

"Yeah," Ronnie said, starting the engine. "Me too. As much as I'd prefer not to."

"Which means Abigail was lying."

"Imagine that," Ronnie said, as he gunned the Mustang into traffic.

I asked where we were going, and in response, Ronnie cranked up Nirvana's *In Utero*. So loud it was like Cobain was there in the car with us, screaming in our ears.

Excelsior Water Tower, San Francisco — Gift to Ronnie

29

NAPLES AND PERU

Ronnie drove the Mustang through SOMA and onto the freeway heading south. Eventually we exited at Alemany and headed toward the Excelsior, a cozy hilltop neighborhood where all the avenues were named after countries and the streets after capitals. It might have been the only place in the world where you could say you were standing at the crossroads of Paris and Russia or, in this case, Naples and Peru.

"Wait," I said, as we drove up Naples. "I was just here."

Ronnie turned the music down and slowed. "Yeah?"

"Yeah . . ." I said, looking around. "There."

Ronnie stopped the car in the middle of the street. It was a residential area with no traffic around.

"That house," I said, pointing to a single-family home with a cathedral window. "Not the one with the palm tree, but the one to the left. I drew that as a commission a few weeks ago."

Ronnie drove up the block until he found a spot, then pulled over.

"What's the story?" he said, putting the car in PARK but leaving the engine running.

"It's an interesting one—nothing weird—or, I don't think so. The woman who commissioned me, she lives in the city, but she grew up in Utah, in a Mormon family. When she turned eighteen, the church sent her on mission to San Francisco and she had an awakening. She ditched her partner and hooked up with a poet who lived in this house. It was her first time realizing she could choose how to live, and she decided not to go back. She hid out here for I don't know how long. Apparently at one point her family had tried to kidnap her, but the poet helped her start a new life."

"That's quite a tale."

Commissioned by Beth Shultz

"Drawings are personal," I said. "Sometimes I hear a good story. I'm sure not as many as you, though. Why? Is this where we were headed?"

"Think the family could have anything to do with coming after you?"

"No. This was years ago. She has her new life, free of the church. And the poet is dead. Which is why she commissioned me. She's putting together a chapbook of his work, and wants a drawing for the cover."

Ronnie nodded, then furrowed his brow as he scanned the area. "Where were you standing when you drew the house?"

"Directly across the street."

"Which means someone in either of the houses next to the one you were drawing could have thought you were spying on them?"

"I suppose," I said. "I did draw a few of the houses to the right and left. Why?"

Ronnie pulled his notebook from the pocket of his windbreaker. I watched as he flipped through the pages. When he found what he was looking for, he showed me. Scribbled in a barely legible scrawl were three addresses. One was of the house out here in the Excelsior, to the right of the house I'd been commissioned to draw. The one with the palm tree out front.

"Are these the addresses from Taylor's pager?" I asked. "Of where she'd been sent to have sex with johns to be recorded, then blackmailed?"

NOSY NEIGHBOR

COMMISSION

?

"Yep," Ronnie said. "Only this one is looking a tad out of the way for a Midnight Climax room—but of course you never know. Which is the reason for the visit. I'd already run down backgrounds and they're all dead ends. A series of runaround dummy corporations and phony rental agreements. But you're right to think of Taylor. You remember how she said she got paid?"

"Western Union. The day after the trick, there'd be a credit waiting for her at one of the storefronts in the Tenderloin. I don't remember which store, though."

"The store location is irrelevant. What *is* relevant is the mailing address attached to the bank account that issues the payments."

"And this is the address?"

"One and the same. And also where a well-known plein air artist stood across the street with his pen and paper in hand—and camera."

******

"Shit," I said. "So you think someone involved with the blackmail scheme was inside and saw me out here drawing and—what? Thought I was on to them? But how? I thought you said this was a dummy address?"

Ronnie was looking around, brow still furrowed. "Hang tight," he said. Then he cut the engine and got out of the car.

He walked down the row of houses to the address associated with the bank account. I had to crane my head to see through the rear window. Ronnie walked past the house, subtly checking it out, then turned back, walked up the short set of steps, and rang the doorbell.

Five, ten seconds passed, then he knocked. After another few seconds he squatted down, flipped open the mail slot, and peered in. As he did, I saw curtains move in a house two doors up, to the left of the house I'd drawn. A few seconds later, the door of that house cracked open and a Filipina woman in her seventies came out. Ronnie saw her, walked past the house I'd drawn, and greeted her on the sidewalk. Ronnie pointed to the house with the palm tree, and for a few minutes the two spoke; then Ronnie backed away, offering a smile and a wave. He set off down the block, away from where we were parked. The woman went back inside and watched through her window as he went. At the end of the street, which was the bottom of the hill, he turned. I assumed he was circling the block so the woman wouldn't see him returning straight to the Mustang. These were long blocks, and we were on a hill, so I knew it would be a while.

Five minutes later, the driver's door opened and Ronnie got in. By that time the woman had stopped watching. Sweat was beading on his forehead. He wordlessly started the car and drove up the block and turned left onto Peru. Then he hung another left onto Vienna and pulled over again.

"What did you get?" I asked.

"Neighbor," Ronnie said, cutting the engine. "A Mrs. dela Cruz. Says the house with the palm tree was being used by a Bible camp. Groups of kids—male and female, and of all ages—would come for weeks at a time for group study."

"Okay . . ."

"Place is empty now. I'm guessing the minute after they saw you. The vigilant dela Cruz said she saw a large box truck being loaded in the middle of the night a few weeks back—lots of mattresses and suitcases. And no one's been here since. Which looks about right. There was a mountain of mail just inside the front door. So yeah, I'm thinking you spooked them."

"And because of that they tried to get me arrested?" I looked out the window. "I get that pimps for teenage girls would be paranoid—but a Bible group?"

"My guess, the Bible study is only a ruse. To placate a nosy septuagenarian neighbor."

"So you thinking it's a Midnight room after all?"

Ronnie clucked. "No, too out of the way . . . And the group of kids doesn't line up."

"Brothel?"

"Or film set. Could be making movies with the kids."

"To then blackmail pedophiles who buy them? Or maybe as a separate business?"

"Couldn't say."

"Still. Whoever it was that saw me standing across the street, I get that seeing me drawing and taking pictures makes them nervous, thinking I'm some kind of spy. But then—what? They get my license plate, find out who I am, and set up an elaborate flashing incident at the Legion? Then call in my car as stolen? It just seems so . . . I don't know, overly complicated. And to what end? If we ask your question of who benefits, how does any of it serve them?"

"Maybe they just wanted to see how you responded."

"What do you mean?"

Ronnie breathed in deep through his nose. "I'm just noodling out loud here, but . . . if these folks thought you weren't who you appeared to be, but maybe some P.I. or an undercover agent, then maybe they did it to call you out." Then he shook his head. "But no. That doesn't play. 'Cause if they knew to track you to the museum, then they'd have already found out who you were and would have known you were an artist legit. Damn." He looked at me and grinned with genuine pleasure. "Gotta give it to ya, sport, you really got quite a brain-twister here. And after me trying to file you away into a regular old box."

"You look way too pleased about this," I said.

"What can I say? I haven't had my daily dose of Jumble."

"Well I'm glad my unfortunate coincidence can bring you so much joy."

Ronnie laughed and started the car. "You are most certainly a man of coincidences."

"What's that supposed to me mean?"

"We're in the Excelsior," he said, checking his mirror, then looking at me before pulling away from the curb. "Just a few blocks from where your buddy Jerry Garcia was born."

＊　＊　＊

We were in the far south of the city, and traffic on the freeway heading north was slow. As we crawled along the 101, Ronnie cranked Nirvana again—

which was fine, as I needed to think. When I'd gotten as far as I could with that, I turned down the music and said, "We both agree that the bartender Abigail was lying about Keller," I said. "Right?" Ronnie nodded. "Only that doesn't make any sense either. Why send us to him?"

"Because she probably knew his reputation and figured there was no way in Hades we'd ever be able to get in to see him. She assumed we'd spin our wheels trying to get a meet, only to eventually give up. She didn't anticipate you having an ace in your deck."

"So what? We go back to Zeitgeist? Ask who really hired her?"

"Don't see much point. She'll only laugh in our faces, and we can't be sure we'll have the luck of the Isaac at the door this time—which makes me think maybe you should stay clear of that joint for a while. Anywho, whoever hired her is in the wind. It's like with Taylor. They'll have made it so we can't trace her back to them. Better to file away what we know and move forward."

"So, forget about Abigail?"

"Not completely—" he glanced over at me "—she did leave you with a lovely token of herself that I know I would like to remember."

An idea had crossed my mind, but I was hesitant to share it. Somehow Ronnie could tell.

"Talk to me, sport. What's on your noggin?"

"We're just spitballing, right?"

"No judgment for having notions," he said.

"What if the goal wasn't to see how I responded to being falsely accused, but to put me close to someone who could keep an eye on me?"

"Go on."

"Who am I working for right now? And I don't mean my private commissions."

He looked at me with narrowed eyes, and I knew he understood. Ronnie was sharp.

"It's a leap," I said. "I know. But think about it. You said yourself it's too much of a coincidence that seven years ago Martin Zorn and Faith Chadwick constructed an Operation Midnight room to blackmail Joe, and now here's the exact same room with a girl from The Nest being used to blackmail your client. What if Zorn is somehow involved? Maybe not directly, but peripherally. The Excelsior house, we know it's tied to your case. They see me lurking, call their buddy in the police department to check it out. Maybe he's on payroll, or he owes them a favor, or—I don't know. But he decides to concoct a reason to have me brought into the station so he can determine what I'm really up to."

Ronnie didn't say anything. His lips were puckered and he was squinting. Traffic was still at a crawl.

"So Ocampo's in on it too?" Ronnie asked.

"No," I said. "That's where Abigail comes in. Zorn needs Ocampo—or whoever was on duty—to believe the complaint was legitimate."

"Why, though?" Ronnie said. "To turn you into the human equivalent of a cardboard cutout in their training exercises?"

"No—well, yes—but only to keep an eye on me."

Ronnie was wincing and shaking his head. I was losing him. But at least he hadn't accused me of going full conspiracy nut—yet.

"I know it's a stretch," I said, turning in my seat. "But hear me out." It was starting to come together for me and I was getting excited. It was the same feeling I got when the plot for a novel fell into place—though I wasn't going to say that to Ronnie. "The night Ocampo and Zorn came to see me, Ocampo said Zorn had proposed to her that they start using civilians in their sessions. They'd never done that before, and she dismissed him. Then the day before the exercises were to begin, I end up at the station."

"Doesn't mean he engineered it," Ronnie said. "But . . ." He took another deep breath and I waited. It was making sense to me, more and more, and maybe to him too.

The cars ahead of us began moving, and we crept forward a few lengths, only to stop again.

"Could be," Ronnie said, "as you said, that Zorn was simply doing some-body a favor, without knowing what it was connected to." He looked at me and shook his head. "But no way he would have hired Abbs directly—or set up the flashing stunt. It's not even amateur, it's just plain weird. More like a prank than a setup. At best, he got a call with your name, slipped a couple unies each a few bills, and told them if a report came in about an artist play-ing Peeping Tom to pick him up. The rest was arranged by whoever called in the favor."

"That's a hell of a coincidence, then, don't you think? Zorn doing a favor for someone running an operation just like the one he ran with Joe? *And* Taylor's connection to The Nest?"

"Someone could be using him."

"Or are you just making excuses so you don't have to admit that all those years ago *he* used *you*? What if Zorn isn't just doing a favor, but is actively involved in the blackmail? Even running it? I mean, you say he's a crusader. Is that really the kind of thing you give up? What if he just learned from what went wrong with Joe and refined his approach to taking down pedophiles?"

Ronnie turned and eyed me. It was not a comfortable moment.

"Sorry," I said. "I just—"

"Don't be sorry," he said. "It's a good question—the right question. And I'm glad one of us had the stones to ask it."

We began to inch forward, and for the next few minutes, as traffic crawled along, we didn't talk. I could tell Ronnie was wrestling with all the possible scenarios that his well-honed, puzzle-solving brain was capable of. The music was still turned down, so I reached over to turn it up. Cobain singing *All Apologies*. Ronnie smiled.

30

BEWARE THE HIPSTER DONUT

After getting off the 101, traffic across the city only got worse. The bridge wasn't much better, and by the time we exited in Mill Valley, Ronnie was feeling pressed for time.

"Sorry to do this to you, sport, but I need to be way the heck up in the North Bay and I can't be late. I'd love nothing more than to witness your receiving an arm-twisted apology from the Mill Valley PD, but I ain't got the time. You'll be fine. I chased this all the way up to the top brass out here and made sure the chief knew his people were playing keep-away because of an old grudge with your brother, so if they don't act at least a tiny bit contrite, then throw some weight around—" he chuckled "—but maybe not too much."

He'd pulled alongside a high metal fence with razor wire winding along the top and stopped the car. "Listen," he said. I looked at him. "I'm not brushing off your theories on Zorn. I'm going to do some nosing around."

"I'm not invested in being right."

This made him smile.

"Meantime," he said. "The day you were drawing on Naples. You were taking photos, yeah?"

"Yeah. To finish the drawing from."

"You remember anything curious in them?"

"No. But I can't say I was looking."

"You still got 'em? Negatives too?"

"Yeah, I keep a file cabinet of all my reference photos. Prints and negatives."

"Maybe I swing by and we have a look?"

"Any time. I've got a few good bottles stashed away. Would be more than happy to crack one open with you—assuming of course Larissa hasn't drunk them all."

He laughed. "It's a shindig then. I'll check in with you tomorrow." He threw his chin toward the impound lot. "You sure you're good to handle this on your lonesome if I drop you and continue on?"

"I guess so . . ." I peered around and saw the entrance in the fence, also lined with razor wire. "How about we say that if you don't hear from me in three hours, you come back for me?"

Ronnie guffawed, then I got out of the car and he laid a little rubber peeling away.

*   *   *

The impound lot was not the police station, but a subcontractor for the county, and there was no apology waiting. Only a form to sign and a bill for nine hundred and ninety-nine dollars.

"For what?!?"

"Three days storage at three-oh-six a day, plus tax."

"Storage? But it was held here by mistake."

The woman behind the glass couldn't care less. She was maybe fifty, but she looked like she'd spent about a hundred years in a sealed room chain-smoking unfiltered cigarettes. "You can take it up with the PD over at the station, but if you go past four I gotta charge you another day."

I was annoyed. But what were my options? Even if I somehow managed to get the cops to apologize, they would surely only shrug their shoulders at the fee, saying it was policy and out of their hands, leaving me to return to the lot with another day's charges. On top of that, I had no car to even get there. Eventually, if I made enough noise, I might get the fee refunded, but at the moment my only choice seemed to be to pay the bill and get my car. I handed over my credit card.

The woman took out the manual credit-card swipe machine and flipped through my paperwork.

"Oh, right," she said, her raspy smoker's voice rising, and for a moment I had hope that maybe she'd found a note in my file to waive the fees and, despite her surly attitude, would actually honor it. "You're the one with the yellow Miata."

"Yep."

She shook her head and grunted. "You know you left a perfectly good cut of steak and a bunch-a other groceries in your trunk?"

"I do," I said. "Including a nice bottle of wine."

"I don't know why you'd do somethin' so stupid," she said, crumpling up the slip she'd put in the slider and fitting in a new one. "That mess stunk up half the lot. We had to get in there and clean the damn thing."

"Thank you," I said.

She looked up at me over the tops of her glasses. "You ain't gonna thank me when you find out what it cost you. Another two hundred. Cleaning ain't free."

* * *

Eleven hundred and ninety-nine dollars later I was driving away from Mill Valley back toward the city. Which got me thinking how much the car was actually worth. It was surely more than that, but probably not much. At least it was my car, though—and it didn't smell like rotten meat. Problem was, it didn't have any license plates. In yet another gracious act by the police, they'd been removed.

"Where the fuck are my plates?!?" I'd demanded in the lot.

"It's what we do with stolen vehicles," the woman told me. "We remove the plates so you're not pulled over again. You'll need to order a new set of your own plates from the DMV."

"But the plates *were* mine! Since the car wasn't actually—" I stopped, knowing that any attempt to reason with her would be useless. "So what does this mean for me right now?"

She clucked and moved her head as if she'd just seen a cat almost get run over by a semi. "You're lucky," she said. "Normally we won't release a vehicle without at least a confirmation of new registration, which can take weeks to process."

"Weeks? And I would still have to pay the daily storage fee?"

"I believe that's what they call a paradox wrapped in a conundrum," she said, then burst out laughing. "Most of the time, owners just sign the vehicles over to the county and we sell 'em at auction."

"Sounds like a racket."

But her humor stopped at her own jokes. She stepped back, looking offended. "What are you accusing me of?"

"Nothing," I said. "But you're saying I can still take my car? Even though it has no plates?" I was starting to worry what I might do if she said no.

"You must have some guardian angel over there at the station," she said, looking at her clipboard. "Says here you're authorized to take possession of the vehicle with temporaries."

And by temporaries she meant a sheet of paper taped over the license plate holder with my license number—as in the very same number that had been on the plates they'd removed—written in ballpoint pen. There was one on the front and another on the back, and both were so illegible that I hadn't even realized they were there until I bent down to look. I didn't see how they were going to keep me from being pulled over, and I cringed at the thought of trying to explain them to any cop who did. But I didn't see any other option. I needed to get away from that woman and her warped domain—and apparently Marin County—as quickly as I could. So if she was going to let me drive out of there with two flimsy sheets of paper taped to my car, then I would take it and go. My poor car, though. Two slices in the roof, and now this.

"Yeah," I said. "Guardian angel." I opened the trunk. "Who I see also cleaned out my bottle of wine."

She grinned.

Before I got arrested for a third time—for what would not be a misunderstanding but a willful assault on a county employee—I set off for home, driving the speed limit the whole way.

*   *   *

Back in the Mission I found parking easily enough in one of the cheater spots close to my place, then I went upstairs to wash up and see if Larissa was home. She wasn't. I went back outside and walked the three blocks to where I'd parked the rental car. From halfway down the block I could see the paper flapping under the wiper, and when I got close, confirmed it was a ticket for not having a parking sticker. It was the day that just kept on giving.

I filled the tank on the rental, then drove it to the shop downtown and returned it easily enough, though with yet one more charge on my credit card.

The Powell Street BART station was just down the street, which would get me home in no time, but there was a place I wanted to check out, and if I was right, it was only a few blocks away. And where I assumed Larissa would be: The Arcade.

I didn't know the address, but I remembered Larissa saying it was in an old Deco building. As far as I knew, there were only a handful in that area, remnants of what had once been the old Film Exchange. One row was on Golden Gate, and another around the corner, on Hyde.

The Film Exchange was a unique era of movie history. In the early days of cinema, theaters had to purchase any reels they wanted to show. By the turn of the twentieth century, exchanges became the first rental shops, though

Old Film Exchange, Hyde Street, San Francisco

only for theaters. Problem was, back then film was made of nitrate, which was highly volatile and extremely dangerous in large quantities. Archives were constantly catching fire and causing buildings to explode. So the Exchange houses had to be built like giant vaults with concrete two feet thick to keep from blowing up the entire neighborhood. Come the forties, nitrate was replaced with non-explosive acetate, and the exchange businesses faded. But most of the buildings remained, many of which were gorgeous examples of the Deco era.

I walked Market Street, then cut up Golden Gate into the Tenderloin. It was early evening and the sun had found its way through the fog to shine brilliantly over the rooftops. The light on Saint Boniface made me feel as if I were in Rome. A half block later, I didn't feel that way anymore. The sidewalk was a minefield of human shit, half-naked junkies, and a trio of swaggering young men in low-hanging pants stepping into my path to size me up. Rome for sure had its grit, but the Loin could boast its own distinct abrasiveness.

Just past Leavenworth on Golden Gate I came upon the first of the two-story buildings that had been the earliest of the Film Exchanges. Two blocks away, on Hyde Street, were more. And it was there that I found The Arcade.

The exterior was perfectly preserved. So thoroughly Deco I felt like I was stepping into the Valley of the Kings. And I thought it funny that within two blocks I'd experienced the Tenderloin as Italy, then Egypt. A confluence that felt uniquely San Francisco—like being able to stand on the corner of Naples and Peru.

Inside, the space was simple and open, lined with long shared tables holding at least thirty computers. Not dissimilar to the office of Insta-Pet—though smaller and without the glass handball court. And instead of photos of their humble leader, the walls were covered with murals of eighties video games, a rolling collage of every game from my youth: Pac-Man, Donkey Kong, Centipede, Mario Bros, and my favorite, Galaga. Plus many more. There weren't any actual machines, though, which I found disappointing, but I supposed made sense given that it was supposed to be a place of learning. Still, I thought there should at least be a few for authenticity—and also because I wanted to play. At the computers were ten or so teens, and walking the aisles behind them were several young adults observing and answering questions. Larissa was one. Her face lit up when she saw me.

"Well look who's in the house!" she said, coming toward me. "What are you doing here?" She was smiling, and both her question and demeanor surprisingly lacked sarcasm. I guessed it was because she was in her element.

"I returned the rental car down the street, so thought I'd come check this place out. I love these old Deco buildings."

Just then, Kai came bouncing down the stairs from the second floor.

"Hi Mister Hopper," he said to me. Then, to Larissa, "Jeep's in the lot by The Nest. I'm heading over there now and can get you the keys."

I hadn't taken much notice of Kai when I'd met him in my flat. Seeing him now, though, I thought him an odd character for a place like The Arcade. Handsome and fit, his thick brown hair was parted perfectly to the side in what used to be called the Harvard Clip, a cut made famous in the early sixties by JFK. He wore a light-blue button-down tucked into designer jeans, leather cowboy boots, and a brown belt with large die-cast buckle of a bucking bronco. He was too old to be a resident, at least twenty-five, so I assumed he was another volunteer.

Larissa turned to me. "How are you getting home?"

"BART was the plan."

"I can drive you. Want to go over to The Nest and meet Faith? I'm sure she'd love to meet you."

The idea that I might meet the infamous Faith Chadwick had never crossed my mind. But Larissa didn't know any of the stories I'd heard. And I had to admit, I was curious. "Yeah," I said. "Okay."

"Take your time," Kai said. "I've got some boxes to unload. Find me over there when you're ready. Good to see you, Mister Hopper."

"You can call me Emit," I said.

He said okay, then dashed off.

"The Nest is just across the street," Larissa said to me. "We can take a quick detour and see Tally on the way."

So we set off through the Tenderloin on foot.

"Isn't The Arcade awesome?" Larissa said as we walked along Hyde Street. "I love that the computers are completely free for kids, and that all the adults are volunteer. That's totally how all cultural institutions should work."

"And Kai's a computer teacher too?" I asked.

"Actually, Kai's the general manager of The Nest. He's one of the few employees. Most of the positions are staffed by residents, which is how they earn their keep. It's one of the cool things Faith does. She gives kids responsibility and purpose, so they feel pride in the shelter. But the more sensitive stuff like personal files and financial records, she can't let just anybody have access to. So that's Kai's job. Or at least one of them. It seems like he does everything, including now managing The Arcade."

We crossed Hyde Street at Eddy, just on the edge of Little Saigon, then Larissa pulled me into a tiny storefront barely big enough to hold four people. There was a display case with a small assortment of donuts, and behind, room for an espresso machine, cash register, and Tally. Seeing us, Tally threw her hands in the air and yelled, "Yay!" then ran around to give me a hug. "You came to see me!"

"Hi Tally."

"I'm taking Emit to meet Faith," Larissa said.

"So cool! You want a donut?" She didn't wait for me to reply. "You *have* to have a donut." She ran back around the counter. I looked in the display case. "We have chocolate Cajun spice, rosemary green tea, maple bacon—"

"Ooh," I said. "Maple bacon."

"Oh yeah, baby," Tally said, using tongs to grab one of the yellow donuts with maple glaze and chunks of bacon. "No loser vegans here." She put the donut in a folded small sheet of cellophane and handed it to me. "Just kidding," she said. "Vegans are awesome!" Then she stuck out her tongue.

I pulled out my wallet, but she waved me off. "No way, bub. First hit's free."

I put a five in the tip jar.

"Aw, much appreciated. But beware. After this, you'll find yourself wanting to wear pegged jeans and beanie caps. And before you know it, you'll be a full-on hipster."

"Beware the donut," I said. A couple had come in behind us—dressed exactly as she'd described—so I moved out of the way. "Thanks Tally. See you later."

"Bye babe," Larissa said. "I'll pick you up at your place in an hour."

Tally gave us an open-mouthed, wide-eyed wave goodbye, then turned to her customers. Larissa and I hit the sidewalk of the Tenderloin again. I ate half my donut. Larissa ate the other half.

*   *   *

The Nest was in the Midori, the former SRO not even one block down from Tally's bakery, and just across the street from The Arcade. An old awning with the name still hung above the entrance, and a placard on the front noted that the building had formerly been known as the Hotel Lafayette, and was now officially a historic landmark. Inside, the entry looked exactly as I imagined it had when it first opened in 1928: two stories high, with a pale yellow mezzanine of arched alcoves and wrought iron railings. On the left side was a reception desk, on the right a sitting area, and between, a short hallway leading into the building. Several large potted palm plants adorned the space, giving it a feeling of an exotic hotel for foreign correspondents during war time.

As we approached the desk I found myself confused. The story I remembered was that Joe Chadwick had been killed at the Midori, which had been a separate building from The Nest, under construction at the time.

"Is this maybe not the original location?" I asked Larissa. "Or are there multiple Nests?"

"Yeah," Larissa said, "there are two. The original Nest is a few blocks away, but it's much smaller. This is the building Faith converted after Joe died."

Now it made sense, but I was also a little creeped out by the fact that

Faith had used the building where her husband had been killed to house the kids he'd been abusing. Or maybe it wasn't creepy. I couldn't decide. Mostly I guessed it played well with the press.

Tending reception was a young man with a foot-high Mohawk. He was leaning back with his chair against the wall and his feet up on the desk.

"We're here to see Faith," Larissa said. "Larissa Huxley and Emit Hopper."

The young man leaned forward, picked up the office phone, and dialed an extension. Wearing a sleeveless denim jacket loaded with raggedly sewn patches and safety pins, he was by far the most interesting receptionist I'd encountered in a long time.

He said our names over the phone, then hung up and pointed toward a door at the end of the short hallway. "I'll buzz you in."

Larissa thanked him, then the kid said, "Hey," and I looked. He stood up to reveal he was at least six-five, and as thin as a rail. With the added foot-high Mohawk, I wondered how he was able to stand in most rooms. But it wasn't his height he was showing me. He was tugging out the bottom of his patch-covered jacket. Alongside poorly sewn patches of the Dead Kennedys, the Misfits, and Black Sabbath, was a square piece of canvas with a high-contrast image of my younger, but still recognizable, smiling face, display-ing a blacked-out tooth—a simplified version of FurTrading's one and only album cover. He bobbed his head and flashed what most people thought of as the rocker sign for the devil—index and little finger extended—but was actually a gesture made popular by the heavy metal singer Ronnie James Dio, who'd gotten the sign from his Italian grandmother, who'd used it to ward off evil. I flashed it back. Larissa was unimpressed.

The door buzzed and we went through. While the entry still felt like a 1930s hotel, the interior had been completely modernized. Most of the first floor was now one large communal space with three distinct areas. One third was an enormous shared kitchen with every appliance you could think of. There were three industrial stoves, three glass-fronted refrigerators, and three dishwashers. There were four stainless steel kitchen worktables, a wall of shelves with dish- and glassware, and dozens of pots and pans hanging from multiple racks. There were microwaves, toasters, blenders, knife racks, you name it. Another third of the space was a living area with four puffy couches, two large-screen TVs, and a dining table that could easily seat forty. There was a foosball table, a pool table, and an air hockey machine. The last third looked like a classroom or presentation area. A dozen or so folding chairs were set up for a small audience, and dozens more were stacked against a wall next to a floor-to-ceiling whiteboard. One portion had a hand-written organized list of names, room numbers, and chores. Another was a mess of cartoon drawings of what I guessed were the residents making fun of each other. And another was a list of "The Ways to Be," what I took to be the house rules to remain at The Nest. They were straightforward enough: *Be Honest*; *Be Accountable*; *Be in the Moment*; and more of the like. No different, I assumed, from any of the basic tenets one might find in any community aimed at creating moral stability. There were also more kitschy, motivational slogans on hand-painted signs placed around the space: *Today Is Not Yesterday*; *Choose Now*; *You Can Do This!* Hanging around were maybe ten young people, male and female. No one paid us any mind.

Larissa had clearly been here before. She led me through the main communal space to a set of double doors that reminded me of a hospital. On the other side were the administrative offices. Just then, we saw Kai enter from another doorway at the far end. He was coming in backward, using his shoulder to push open the door, carrying two large boxes.

"We can help with those," Larissa said.

"It's cool," Kai said. "We got 'em." Following behind him was a procession of three other young people, each carrying a box.

Kai went into an office with an open door, and his crew followed. Larissa and I watched as they silently set the boxes against a wall, then walked past us out of the room.

"I'll be in the basement," Kai said to us. "Grab me when you're done and I'll set you up."

"Sure," Larissa said. "We just want to say hi to Faith."

"Cool."

"Oh, honey, wait," a woman said, stepping out from behind the desk. She saw us, and a huge smile appeared on her face. "Well, look who it is! I'll be with you two darlings in one sec. Hon——" she turned back to Kai "——you make sure you tell those boys at the printer they owe us another run of mailers after what happened last time. You'll remember?"

Obviously Faith Chadwick. Though not the villainess character I'd expected. Pear-shaped is a common description for women of a certain build, but Faith Chadwick was the opposite—an inverted pear. She had a barrel-shaped torso with wide shoulders, thin hips, and skinny legs. She wore a yellow blouse patterned with small white cartoonish birds, and had a sweet round face and a medium cut of wavy brown hair. The half-glasses on a beaded string made her look more matronly than she actually was, but when she took them off to rest on her more than ample chest, she looked almost girlish. Based on what Ronnie had told me, I believed she was mid-forties, but with her smooth skin and big puffy cheeks she could have easily passed for a decade younger.

She took hold of Kai's shirt collar and straightened it, then smoothed out the fabric of his chest. The shirt didn't need pressing, but that's not why she was doing it. Kai stood there dutifully.

"You'll also make certain to confirm the car with Ronaldo so we won't be delayed tomorrow?" she asked.

"Of course," Kai said. Then, after receiving his preening, he dashed out of the room without making eye contact with Larissa or me.

Faith turned to us and for a moment slid the pair of reading glasses onto her face. "Well well well, Miss Larissa," she said, taking Larissa's hands but looking at me over the tops of her glasses. "Look what delights you have delivered to my door." She removed her glasses again and let them rest on her bosom. "Emit Hopper, as I live and breathe." Her manner was Southern, with an accent I was certain she could turn up or down depending on how much charm the situation called for. She was laying it on thick for me. "A pleasure to meet you, my dear."

"Nice to meet you as well," I said. I wanted to say I'd heard only good things, but that wasn't true. And I did my best not to let that cloud my first impression. Instead, I said, "Larissa raves about the work you're doing."

"Well, we should all listen to Larissa more, then, shouldn't we?"

"That's what she keeps telling me."

"We won't take up much of your time," Larissa said. "Emit stopped by The Arcade, so I thought I'd bring him by here."

"What do you think of our newest venture?" Faith asked. "Such a gorgeous building, isn't it?" But she didn't give me a chance to answer. She jumped back and exclaimed, "Oh, my! I've just had the most splendid idea." She stepped forward, wide-eyed, mouth agape. "Why don't you draw it?" She looked at Larissa, then back to me. "That *is* what you do, isn't it?" She waved her hand. "Oh, I know, you're one of those outrageous creative talents who do everything—books, music, TV—" I assumed she was conflating Brian and me into one person, but I was used to that "—but cityscape drawings, those are what you're most famous for, am I right?"

"True," I said, even though it wasn't exactly. "And you're also right that The Arcade is a beautiful building."

"Then it's settled," she said. "We have our annual holiday fundraising auction coming up next month. We can auction it off there. I'm absolutely positive it will go over splendidly—you know we have quite a few big names on our board, and more than a few deep pockets. I've no doubt it will bring a fortune." She called over my shoulder to a young woman who I only now saw at a desk behind me. "Kate, dear. Put Mr. Hopper down for our live auction." She looked back to me. "The live is the best place to be. We do a silent bid for show tickets, dinners, vacation houses, you know, the standard fare. But the live auction is where we can get the fervor going. With the right offering, we can bring in five times over value people get so carried away. And anyhow, it's for charity, so it's all for the greater good."

I occasionally donated art to auctions, and had been in my share of live as well as silent events. And she was right: at an affair such as hers, the number of potential art sales that might come as a result of the exposure could well be worth the effort of donating one drawing. That said, I was already doing the drawing for the Conservatory of Flowers for free, plus I had plenty of paying work, and—call it being a stickler—I preferred to be asked.

Now wasn't the time to parse out little things like common courtesy, though. I'd known Faith Chadwick for all of two minutes, and I was already certain she wasn't one to take no for an answer. "I can get details from your staff later," I said, figuring I could more easily beg off when Larissa wasn't standing right beside me—and safe in my own home. Though I doubted if I'd be able to get out of it even then. Faith didn't come off as the kind of woman to let go of you once she had you ensnared—and she was obviously good at ensnaring.

*

31

PREPPING FOR SAFARI

asements are uncommon in San Francisco houses, but a lot of the older downtown buildings have subterranean levels. There's also at least one set of underground tunnels that I know of, underneath Jones and O'Farrell Streets. In the days of prohibition, J. J. Russell Cigar Shop had one particular cigar on the menu, which, upon ordering, granted access to a trapdoor leading to the basement where the non-teetotaling patron could buy bootleg booze. In the event of a raid, multiple tunnels offered escape out of the speakeasy, leading under the street and up into buildings as far as a block away. The basement of the Midori didn't appear to be an old-time bootlegger's hideaway, but it very well might have been a gold miner's delight. A walk-in bank vault, replete with floor-to-ceiling door and large tiller wheel, led into a multi-chamber repository. Walls of various-sized brass safety-deposit boxes lined the walls. But money wasn't what The Nest was keeping in safe storage.

"It's where we keep all the alcohol," Kai said. "Residents at The Nest are required to be sober, but we host a lot of fundraisers, and, as Faith likes to say, the best way to loosen checkbooks is through a martini glass. So we stash it all here. Better to not create temptation, you know?"

After seeing the punk rocker at the front desk, Kai seemed an even odder character for The Nest than he had before. With his button-down shirt, preppy haircut, and cowboy shoes and belt, I wondered how it was that a young man like Kai had come to be the general manager of a youth shelter in the most seedy district of San Francisco.

"This one's for the jeep," Kai said, handing Larissa two sets of keys. "And this one's for the lot on the corner." He'd gone into one of the safety-deposit boxes and picked out two sets from dozens. "You're welcome to borrow her, but I don't think she's got much gas."

"Thanks," Larissa said. "I'll bring it back full."

Walking back toward The Arcade, I asked Larissa where she and Tally were going.

"The Madonna Inn," she said, with surprisingly no resistance. "In San Luis Obispo. You know it?"

I did. It was a classic lover's getaway. A large hotel with a famous pink communal dining room and over a hundred themed guest suites, such as the Caveman, with giant rocks in the middle of the room, and the Yahoo, with a stagecoach for a bed. I knew because I might have been there a few times, back when I was living in LA—and had possibly been banned for streaking through the pink dining room. Which I told Larissa.

"Of course you were," Larissa said, rolling her eyes.

"You guys staying through Thanksgiving?" The holiday was just a few days away.

"Yeah—is that a problem?"

"Why would it be a problem?"

"I don't know, the whole dad-uncle thing?"

"You don't owe me anything," I said. "You know which room you're staying in?"

"The Safari. It's got a rock waterfall as a shower."

On the corner of Hyde and Turk, just down from the Midori, was a fenced-in lot for private parking. Larissa used one set of keys to let us in, then led us to a red Jeep Wrangler so shiny it looked fresh off the dealership.

"Coooool," Larissa said, seeing the jeep. Then she took me on what might be the most jaw-clenching ride through San Francisco I'd ever experienced.

*　*　*

"Did Kai know what kind of driver you are when he lent you his jeep?" I asked when we'd finally parked in the Mission. We were stopped, but my hands were still braced against the dash.

"What? I got us here, didn't I?"

"You drove up two one-way streets—the wrong way."

She shrugged and got out.

She'd said she was only stopping by for a minute, then was heading out again, so I had her pull in front of the garage for ease—and also to save myself from what was sure to be a harrowing experience of her looking for parking.

"I just need to grab some clothes," she said as we climbed the stairs. "But first I have a gift for you."

286

Larissa led me into the studio, and from a large bag that hadn't been there that morning, she took out a small box with the word Casio printed on top and handed it to me. The packaging had already been undone, so I opened the lid to find a sleek red metal object the size of an eighties audio cassette.

"It's a digital camera," she said. "I know you love your Pentax, but I've used that thing, and for the work you do, this will be much more efficient. The disk holds, like, a thousand shots. And if by some crazy chance you fill it up, then you can simply pop it out and put in another. Which means no more loading film or sending out for developing. You can take more photos, more quickly, then import them into a computer and archive them."

I inspected the device. Small and lightweight, it was a fraction of the size of my manual camera. I found the power button and pressed it. A small shutter guard opened with a whirring sound, revealing the lens, and the back of the device lit up, displaying whatever the lens was pointed at.

"So what about prints?" I asked. "When it comes to finishing drawings, I don't think I can work off this tiny screen."

"You can totally make prints. All you have to do is get a printer and you can make them here, on regular paper. But you won't need to. Not with this—" She took another object out of the bag. A flat, rectangular plastic object with rounded corners. Half milky white, half blue, it looked like a large cookie that had been dipped in blue chocolate.

"A laptop?"

"An iBook. It's basically a kid's toy. But for your purposes it'll serve you fine. You'll be able to download all your photos onto here, then view them on screen." She slid the laptop back into the bag. "You don't need to worry about the computer right now. I can help you set it up when I'm back. You can start using the camera, though. I made sure the battery was charged, so the next time you head out to draw you can take as many photos as you want."

"Amazing. Thank you."

"Yeah?" She looked surprised. "I expected to have to drag you kicking and screaming into the future."

"Admittedly, I can get stuck in my ways," I said. "But it's a tool, and I like tools. So I'm happy to try." I gestured toward the computer in the bag. "This all looks expensive, though. And I'm not exactly rolling in the cash right now . . ."

"I told you, it's a gift."

"Why?"

"Because I'm happy and I'm trying to show it. Don't get all annoying and make me regret being nice."

I laughed. "Fair enough. Okay. Well, thank you. This is very thoughtful. And generous."

She waved me off. "Doesn't matter. I can afford it."

"Yeah? Colleges now paying smart students to attend?"

"I may have written a few pieces of useful code," she said. "And licensing royalties are a beautiful thing. You understand."

"I used to," I said. "Back when my album and books were in print, and people did more than ask me for free drawings."

To which she made a mockingly sad face and played the world's smallest violin.

* * *

Larissa grabbed her bag and rushed off to pick up Tally, and I worried for everyone on the road between my place and the Madonna Inn. Then I ordered Indian food. Someday I would get around to going to a grocery store.

I checked my messages. Two. The first was from Ben Mori, the man I'd met at the plaza outside Nihonmachi Mall, wanting to buy the Peace Pagoda drawing and commission another of the Telephone Building. The second message was from Inspector Zorn. "Aquatic Park. Ten a.m. tomorrow." No call from Brian. Which was hardly a surprise.

I'd already been feeling uncertain about working for Martin Zorn, and after my excursion with Ronnie to the Excelsior I was even more uneasy. The idea that he'd not only engineered the complaint at the museum but might be a significant part of a blackmail operation was more than a little disturbing. Of course, it was only speculation—on my part. And, thinking about it again, I was surprised by how much Ronnie had entertained the idea. It all sounded a bit outrageous. But of course, so were secret spy rooms copied out of a CIA Cold War handbook. And then it occurred to me: If my theory was in any way correct, did Zorn or the people who'd set me up still think I was a threat? Suddenly my hanging around with Ronnie was looking less like a helpful partnership, and more like proof that I was exactly what they'd suspected me of being: a spy.

My knee-jerk reaction then was to keep as far away from Inspector Martin Zorn as possible. Which was followed by the opposite thought, to not do anything to make him suspicious. The old adage of keep your enemies close.

Which I supposed was essentially what he was doing with me. I decided to sleep on it. With a belly full of Indian food.

I had one last thing to do before settling in for the evening, though. I went to my file cabinet and found the folder of reference photos from the Naples Street commission. I'd had four 12x16 enlargements made, and only two included the house Ronnie had linked to the bank account which issued payments to Taylor. To my surprise, in one of the enlargements I saw something I hadn't seen before. Unfortunately, it wasn't to do with the house with the palm tree, but with the house on the other side of the one I'd been paid to draw. A face in the window, peering out. The nosy neighbor who Ronnie had spoken to. Hardly a surprise. And I was guessing probably not who had set me up at the museum.

I then took out the complete stack of smaller 4x6 prints that came standard with getting film developed. My usual way of working was to look through those 4x6's to choose which shots I wanted to work from. Then I would send out the negatives to have enlargements made. Using a loupe to view the small photos more closely, I gave each a careful look. Since it hadn't been my main subject, there weren't that many with the palm tree house. It only appeared in the medium and wide shots, which I always took several of to make sure I had more of the scene than I might possibly need. As I pored over each photo, I hoped that Mrs. dela Cruz wouldn't be my only discovery—and lo and behold, I found two photos that had definitely caught more than I'd realized at the time. In one, a wide shot that showed half a dozen houses on the block, two people were coming out of the front door of the house with the palm tree. In the next photo, a medium shot with the palm tree house at the edge of the frame, one of the pair was looking directly at me. The loupe magnified the small faces, but it was hard to say if they might be recognizable, even to someone who knew them well. One thing I could tell for certain, they were both young women.

I checked the rest of the photos twice and found no other shots with the pair—though I did find two more with Mrs. dela Cruz. Then I called Ronnie and got his messaging service. "Tell him it's about the photos."

It was late when he called back. I'd long since eaten and was settling in front of the TV to a rerun of *Law & Order*—the one with Jerry Orbach, not any of the annoying spin-offs—when the phone rang.

"Talk to me, sport, whaddya find?"

I told him.

"And you can't make 'em out?"

"Not without making larger prints."

"And you don't remember seeing them?"

"No. But I don't see why I would have. I had no reason to think the house was anything but a regular home in a residential neighborhood. A couple of teenagers coming out the front door would have been normal. You want me to take the negatives to be blown up tomorrow?"

"Yeah," he said. "Ring me when in hand. We'll see what you got."

*   *   *

The next morning I woke having decided I would go to the Aquatic Park and continue to play my role after all. I wanted to say that it was because, as I believed Zorn was, I was also playing the game, but really it was because I believed that if the exercise proved to be the same as the last two, my interactions with the potentially dirty inspector would be minimal—and that a drawing of the Maritime Museum and popular swimming cove would probably sell.

Packing up my gear, I swapped out the Pentax for the new digital camera and made a joke to myself that this was what having kids was for, to help bring you into the future.

As I was heading out, I remembered the Miata and grabbed a Sharpie. My current license plates looked like they'd been made by a child. Out on the street, I traced over the letters and numbers to make them more visible. They still looked like a grade-school art project, but for the moment would have to do. I made a mental note to call the DMV when I got back home.

I was leaving early because I wanted to take the negatives from Naples Street to be printed. I drove downtown to Photoworks, the high-end photography shop where real photographers had their work done, and where I never went because I was too cheap.

Same-day prints were double the price, but I was fine to pay. I ordered two 12x16s of the two frames I'd marked, then headed to the north side of the city for my job as a civilian extra in a police training exercise led by a dark-crusader cop. Life had certainly taken a strange turn for me.

*   *   *

Aquatic Park Cove is a small beach just off of Ghirardelli Square, on the edge of Fisherman's Wharf, both heavy tourist destinations. A set of semicircular cement bleachers faces the water, looking out past the C-shaped pier to the

Golden Gate Bridge and Marin Headlands. On the far side of the cove is the Dolphin Club, locally famous for its swimming and rowing teams, and in the center is the Maritime Museum, a WPA-era building built to resemble the bow of a ship.

Same as when I'd arrived at the Peace Pagoda, I wasn't sure where I was expected to set up. Ocampo had said the locations would get increasingly more complex, and this was definitely a larger and more expansive area than the others. Dozens of people were sitting on the bleachers and on the beach, as well as walking the path that led out to the pier and over the hill to Fort Mason. I decided to go where I could make the best drawing, which ended up being at the far end of the stone seawall running alongside the walking path. Starting at the beach, it rose in height as it progressed along the walkway. At its max, the wall was about seven feet high. I climbed down the tiers to the lowest step, at water level, beside the line of jagged rocks, and faced inland for a view of the beach and museum, with the bridge at my back.

The day was surprisingly nice; windy, but that was to be expected, especially out at the water. And cold. Fifty-five at best, which felt like forty-five in the wind. Such was San Francisco weather.

I had my French easel, but there wasn't any room to set it up. Also, I had the stone tiers to act as shelves, so I took what I needed from the box and made myself at home. I began by using my new digital camera. I took dozens of photos, looking at each one on the small screen to see how they might work as reference shots. It was so convenient I was instantly convinced I would never use the Pentax for plein air work again.

I worked two and a half hours and got a solid line drawing started. The forced time of my new job was helping me get my stamina back. I'd been able to lose myself in rendering all the rocks and brick, and the time passed easily. Not once did I see Martin Zorn, which was fine with me. He may have passed by and I'd missed him, but if so, he chose not to speak to me. I wondered if that meant anything.

After being out in the elements all morning I was tired and not up for any more plein air work. The rest of the day would be in the studio. But first I needed to collect the photos. I took Van Ness back downtown and picked up the prints of Naples Street. After paying, I immediately slid them out of their folder and looked at them there in the shop.

"They up to your professional standards?" the clerk asked sarcastically.

I would have said he was being an ass, but he had a point. While the

9th Street, Oakland, CA — Commissioned by Peter Sullivan

photos were expertly printed, as far as being art, the shots were—as Larissa might have said—terrible. I didn't care enough to explain that I was a crappy photographer on purpose because I shot only for reference, so I just said, "They're perfect. Thanks." Then studied the photos.

The girls were definitely more legible in the enlargements. Of the two, the medium shot with the girl looking up was the best. You could see both girls' faces clearly, especially the one looking directly at the camera. They were normal-looking girls—meaning not made-up like prostitutes—dressed in matching uniforms of white blouse and blue skirt, which bolstered the neighbor's claim of a church group. I didn't recognize either of them, but guessed one was maybe twelve, the other fifteen.

On the way home, I also stopped by Falletti's to pick up the rolls of film I'd dropped off the day before. It was proving quite a day for photos, which

Vedanta Society, San Francisco

I found ironic since, now that I had a new digital camera, this would likely be the last time I did any developing for a while, if not forever.

I also did a crazy thing called grocery shopping.

Back home, I immediately phoned Ronnie. He answered.

I described to him everything in the photos, from the girls' expressions to their clothes looking normal. "Or at least not like Taylor had looked the day you and I picked her up."

"Good work, sport. I'll have a look. It's been a while since I worked the street, but who knows, maybe we'll get lucky again and I'll recognize one. Hang tight. I got a busy day, but I'll get at you when I can."

I took a short nap, then made lunch and got to work in the studio. I had a handful of drawings in process and took out two: Old Oakland, which was from the suite for the developer, and almost finished; and the Vedanta Temple, which I'd barely started. Once again I decided to put off Gough Street for another time. I worked all day, finishing Old Oakland, and progressing the linework on Vedanta to near completion. Just after ten I wrapped up. It

had been a solid twelve-hour workday, and I felt good. I opened a bottle of wine and on the second glass called Ronnie. I was feeling like we'd become friends, and so why not call? I got his messaging service. "Nothing important," I said. "You don't even need to tell him I called."

A half hour later, he rang me back. "What's up?"

"Nothing. Just—I don't know. Thought I'd see how things are going."

"Well aren't you a dear. I've been working steady. Trust me, I want to see those prints, for sure. I'll hit you up tomorrow, yeah? You good?"

"All good."

"Rock on. I'll catch ya." And he hung up.

✳ ✳ ✳

The next morning I went back to work. I had just put a second layer of wash on Vedanta when around eleven, Ronnie called.

"Got some time for me today?"

"Of course."

"Your place, one hour. We can meet in your washeteria."

At noon I went downstairs to the laundromat, the photos in my bag. Ronnie wasn't there yet, but Betty was—mopping.

"Shit," I said, rushing inside. "The water main?"

Betty looked up as she heaved a soaking-wet mop into the ringer and shook her head. "No. Valve is good. This was a niño with a soda."

"Phew," I said. "Had me worried." I dropped myself into one of the plastic bucket seats. "Let me guess. Double-wide-stroller-woman—even though she only has one kid—who likes to pretend the machine ate her quarters?"

Betty grinned and tugged at the handle to wring out the soda-colored water.

"I assume the heating unit got replaced, no problem?"

"Only problem would have been if you'd stayed to help." She slapped the mop back onto the floor and motioned for me to lift my feet so she could reach under the seats.

As I did, Ronnie walked in—with Ocampo behind.

I was surprised, but tried not to show it.

"You guys want to talk in the office?" I said, standing. If it had just been Ronnie, I would have happily taken him upstairs. But Ocampo hadn't won me over enough to be invited into my home—which I supposed Ronnie knew, and was why he'd called the meeting at the shop.

They said yes to the office, and I motioned toward the back of the shop for them to go ahead.

Betty snagged my arm before I could follow.

"They look like police," she whispered. "What did you do?"

"You don't want to know."

I followed Ronnie and Ocampo into the office and closed the door.

"Our friend here has something to tell you," Ronnie said to me.

I looked at Ocampo.

"I'm the one who reported your vehicle stolen," she said.

For a moment I just stood there. Finally I asked, "Why?"

"As a way to connect you with Ron."

"Okay . . ."

"Your being picked up at the Legion was bogus," Ocampo said. "I knew it from the start. Calls like that, especially out in the Richmond, generally don't get past the desk sergeant let alone warrant a response. Maybe if there'd been a busload of children involved and the museum staff was making a stink. But even then, fifty-fifty whether they would have bothered to send a patrol car. And to bring you in—you would've had to have been buck naked and running around like a lunatic for that to happen."

"Cops hate writing reports," Ronnie chimed in.

"Which is why I asked the pair who collared you why they'd bothered, and they said there'd been word on the street of a flasher escalating around town, posing as an artist."

"Heard from who?" I said. "Inspector Zorn?"

"They weren't forthcoming. Rumor, was all they said. So I asked around, and no one else seemed to have heard the talk, and there was no mention of it at any morning roll call."

"So it had to be him, right?" I looked to Ronnie. "He engineered my arrest at the Legion?"

"Can't say for sure," Ocampo said. "But it's looking highly circumstantial. First there was Zorn's suggestion to use civilians for the training exercises, which struck me as strange. Zorn has never once volunteered to run point on training before, let alone attempt to innovate. Then there's the timing of you ending up in my tombs a day before the training period was to commence. That was too much. I knew something had to be up."

"So you reported my car stolen and had me arrested?"

"When I learned you'd be north of the bridge, I had the idea to connect you with Ron." She looked to Ronnie. "I figured if anyone could sort out Zorn, it would be you."

"Still," I said. "You set me up. Just like Zorn did." She didn't respond. I looked to Ronnie. "And you too—she set you up too!" I was hoping to get him on my side, but he just sat there, cool as ever. I turned back to Ocampo. "You're really something, you know that? You know that stunt cost me twelve hundred bucks to get my car out of the pound? Fifteen if you count the rental—no, sixteen with the parking ticket."

"It was never supposed to go down that way. I'd asked the Mill Valley PD to alert me when they picked you up. The plan was, I'd call Ron to spring you, then you'd get your car back in the morning, no charge. I couldn't have foreseen the bad blood with the desk sergeant and your brother." She laughed. "He must have seriously screwed that woman over."

"But why all the cloak-and-dagger? Why not just tell Ronnie straight up you were suspicious of Zorn and ask for his help?"

"Because I would have ignored her," Ronnie said.

"But I knew he wouldn't be able to resist you," Ocampo said.

Ronnie snorted.

"If that's supposed to flatter me," I said, "it's both weird and not working." I tried to shake it off. "So, what? You imagined Ronnie would be so charmed by my presence that he'd feel no choice but to help?"

"Something like that. Mostly I knew he wouldn't be able to resist the puzzle. He would instinctively know your collar at the Legion smelled funny, then there'd be the screwed-up stolen vehicle report. One out-of-the-box incident he might be able to let slide. But two . . . Add that to your colorful career history, and I was sure I was dangling a hook he couldn't help but bite."

"She seduced me," Ronnie said. He seemed genuinely amused.

"If it'd all turned out to be nothing," Ocampo said, talking to Ronnie, "then you would have solved the Emit puzzle, and that would have been that. But if the clues led to Inspector Martin Zorn, I knew you'd be in too deep to let it drop."

"So then you knew the case he was working?" I said. Then I caught myself. I quickly looked to Ronnie, worried I might have betrayed a confidence.

"It's okay," Ronnie said to me, seeing my concern. "I filled her in. Which is why we're here. Taylor rang me. She got a page for a date. Two this afternoon. I want to stake it out."

"I could give you a couple unies in plainclothes," Ocampo said. "But I'm not so sure we should. We've got to be careful. It's such short notice. We can't be sure who's in with Zorn. We choose the wrong team and we could blow this whole thing."

"I agree," Ronnie said. "Which is why I'm telling you, and only you. And why our celebrity artist here is going to assist."

"You want me to go on a stakeout?" I said.

"Just do what you've been doing with the training exercises. You've got that fancy portable easel. Set up, draw, and if anybody questions, you got a reason."

"But if this all started because someone at the Excelsior house suspected me, then won't my being there be like a giant red flag saying 'We're on to you!'?"

"That could work in our favor," Ocampo said. "Flush 'em out."

"Would prefer it not go that way," Ronnie said. "But I agree, if they do recognize you, we'll have them running scared. Either way, we'll spot 'em coming and going, and we'll have the room. Still, better to play it safe. Let's have you arrive after the party begins. If you're there before, and the cinematographer does see you, you'll definitely spook them again, and they could abort."

"We'll keep it simple," Ocampo said. "A three-team post. Ron in one car in the front, me in another at the rear, our player here on the street."

"I need to swap vehicles," Ronnie said. "Don't want the Mustang sticking out as yet another red-flag parade."

"Take mine," Ocampo said. She handed him her keys, then looked at her watch. "It's 12:15. We've got one hour forty-five to get in place. Emit, can you ride me to dispatch so I can get another car? While I'm there, I'll see if I can line up a quick safe house for the girl to rendezvous after the meet."

"Got you covered on that one," Ronnie said. "A loaner from a pal who's out of town. A half mile from the site."

"Good. I want eyes on Taylor from the moment she leaves the building. Once she's secure, I'll get in a team in place to take down the room."

＊　＊　＊

Ronnie left in Ocampo's car to get to the building with enough time to find parking with a good line of sight. Ocampo and I headed for the Miata.

"You really need to get a new car," she said, seeing one of the two strips of duct tape half-peeled from the canvas roof and flapping in the wind.

"I'm offended you didn't notice my stylish new license plates—they were a gift from you."

As we got in, I wanted to ask her for an apology. Instead, I asked her to reimburse me for how much her Stinson stunt had cost. "Call it field expenses, or whatever satisfies the city bean counters," I said. "But either way, I'm out some real money because of what you did. And we both know I've done nothing wrong."

I started the engine and began to drive.

Ocampo hadn't replied, so I kept talking. "Both you and Zorn have been using me as a pawn, which, I have to say, is taking everything I have not to be sincerely pissed off about. The way I see it, since I'm already on the city payroll with the training exercises, the least you can do is find a way to reimburse me. I mean, I've essentially been working undercover. So deep, I didn't even know it."

Ocampo laughed. "That's quite some logic you have going. How about you look at it this way: You're out, what? Fifteen, sixteen hundred? That's not even what Ron Gilbert charges for a day."

"You mean because he's been helping me for free to solve the setup at the Legion? That one of *your* inspectors orchestrated? Now who's playing with twisted logic?"

She'd been smiling, but now her face turned serious. "Listen," she said. "Ron's a decent guy. And he's got a lot of friends. But there are also more than a few people in the department who are happy he took early leave, if you know what I mean."

"Like Inspector Zorn?"

"What do you know about why Ron left the force?"

I was careful with my answer. "Not much," I said. "Ronnie's pretty tight-lipped when it comes to sharing information." Ocampo was playing at being my friend, but she'd already played me for a fool—twice, at least. I wasn't going to let her do it again. So I did my best to play too. "I got the feeling he didn't fit in very well," I added, and saw her eyes sharpen with interest. "You said it yourself, Ronnie likes puzzles. I think the everyday life of a cop was too mundane for him. He got bored of the run-of-the-mill and wanted to find cases he could look at sideways."

That seemed to work. She could tell I'd gotten to know him well enough to pin his character, but she couldn't be sure how much more he'd let me in.

"Ron told me about the house in the Excelsior," she said. "You have a chance to look at the photos?"

This took me by surprise. I hadn't had a chance to ask Ronnie if he'd wanted to see the prints, and since he hadn't brought the subject up, I took it to mean he didn't want Ocampo to know. And something about the way she asked made me think he hadn't actually told her. He'd surely told her about the house, since that's how the two of them had worked out that it was likely Zorn who'd tasked the two cops to bring me in, but her asking about the photos felt to me that she was playing a hunch. Ocampo was smart. She'd orchestrated luring Ronnie into her game, which was no easy feat. Putting together that I had reference photos of Naples Street and that I'd given them a second look after visiting the house was child's play in comparison. So I played a hunch of my own and told her I had looked at them, but found nothing. "Not even someone flashing her boobs," I said. And we both had a laugh. But I don't think she believed me.

32

THE MAN BEHIND THE MIRROR

I dropped Ocampo at a city car lot on Bryant Street, then returned home. I was driving more than I normally did and was really getting sick of looking for parking, and seeing that I'd be turning right around to leave in half an hour, I parallel-parked in front of my garage. Admittedly, I was taking more and more advantage of things that were no longer mine—sleeping in the unit I'd sold but was being paid to look after, and parking in front of the garage I owned but charged exorbitant rent for someone else to call theirs. Granted, the second floor was owned by a Chinese investment firm that was likely keeping the place empty in order to drive up housing prices by taking inventory off the market, and the couple renting the garage didn't even keep a car inside, just two Cannondale racing bicycles they hardly rode—and which I could have probably squeezed the Miata in alongside if I'd wanted—but still, no matter how I justified it, I couldn't help but think that at some point overstepping was going to bite me in the ass.

Upstairs in the studio, I was gathering my supplies and feeling uneasy. The address we were staking out was not the same as where Taylor had taken us a few days before, nor was it any of the addresses that had been on her pager when she'd shown Ronnie, and I couldn't help but wonder how many of these secret recording rooms existed at any given time. That there was even one was a disturbing thought. But more disturbing was what we were about to do. We weren't just following any old prostitute who'd been called to turn a trick, but a teenager who'd been paged to have sex with a paying adult in order to be secretly recorded. How was it that neither Ronnie nor Ocampo was finding this at all troublesome?

None of this was sitting well with me. However, not going out of principle wasn't going to stop it from happening. Plus, I'd agreed to help, and

I didn't want to leave Ronnie hanging. So at 1:45, with drawing supplies and new digital camera in hand, I got in the Miata and headed to the stakeout.

*　*　*

The address was on Golden Gate, at the corner of Steiner, in the Western Addition. As I drove past, I saw that the building we were to watch was across from the Chateau Tivoli, a historic Victorian that at some point had been converted into a bed-and-breakfast. The Tivoli was exactly the kind of place I might draw. I could easily set up across the street and have it appear as if I were drawing the hotel, while having a clear view of the apartment building entrance. Still, I was uneasy. On the drive, my moral concerns had turned more practical. What if we were being played? What if Taylor had double-crossed us? Who knew what these people might do to protect their criminal enterprise. We were only a three-person team—and maybe not even that. Ronnie I trusted; Ocampo not so much.

I found parking on Golden Gate, just past Fillmore. It was five minutes after two. Walking up the block toward the building, I heard a whistle. I looked around and saw Ronnie in the driver's seat of a black Crown Victoria. Ocampo's car. The window was rolled down, and he waved me over.

"Seems we got a bit of luck," Ronnie said as I got close. "The Tivoli is a ruse better than we could have hoped for. Looks to me like you can set up your rig almost directly across the street from the front door of our site and have it look as if you're doing your thing for the chateau."

"I thought the same," I said, bending down and leaning my arm on his door. "You been here long? See anyone of any note go inside?"

"Only Taylor and a man I'm thinking is her john. Late fifties, trim, salt-and-pepper hair. Black Armani suit. When you see him come out, don't take any pictures. I already got his image, and he's gonna be twitchy after the deed. After Taylor exits, though, you snap away at anything that walks. What are you using to shoot?"

I reached into my pocket and showed him my new digital camera.

"Well look at that," he said. He held up the exact same model.

"If you're shooting too, then why do you need me?"

"'Cause I'll be leaving with Taylor. I don't want her out of my sight, in case she pulls a runner. Moment she comes out I'll scoop her up and take her to the safe house. You stick here for as long as it takes. Ocampo will stay too. Your jobs are to spot the cinematographer. Someone is behind that mirror up there running the camera, and they ain't gonna stay there all day."

"Where is Ocampo?" I asked. "You see her?"

"As a pass-by. She'll have taken point on the rear exit by now. You're on point for the front."

"Got it." I was about to go, but hesitated. "Tell me," I said. "Do you not see a little bit of irony here? Of the past repeating itself? Of Martin Zorn having let Crystal go with Joe Chadwick so he could record her? Only for it all to go to shit? I know this isn't the same, but . . . Taylor *is* only fifteen."

Ronnie nodded. "You're not wrong. But what do you want me to tell ya? We got kids turning tricks for smack and someone filming them to blackmail johns. The game's too messy. Even the good guys are gonna get a little dirty."

"Yeah," I said. "But shouldn't we have tried to get the cameraman before the sex instead of after? I mean, we're basically complicit in a minor prostituting herself."

"I hear ya. And I know this isn't going to satisfy you, but this trick she's turning, it's nothing she hasn't done before, wouldn't have done anyway, and won't do again. Stopping her from coloring outside what we both agree are the pretty lines isn't going to save her."

"You're right," I said, looking up the street, then back. "It doesn't satisfy me."

"Sorry, sport. And hey, if this ain't your game, then no problemo. I know I said you owed me a marker, but this is a different league. You're a good egg, and I trust you. But you don't owe me nothin'. If you're feelin' off, then take a pass. I'll still respect you in the morning."

"But you need me, right?"

"Brother, this ain't D-Day. You do what you gotta do."

"No," I said. "I'm in. So you don't want me to photograph the john?" I said, confirming my assignment. "But you do want me to photograph everyone else who comes and goes?"

"Only those who leave after Taylor. Remember, the cockroach behind the camera thinks Taylor doesn't know about the recording room. He—or she—is going to let our girl do her thing, and only after she leaves will they scurry out of their hole. We don't know how long the john's rocks are gonna take to get off, but I'm guessing he's out that door just before three. After that, I told Taylor not to dawdle. No fussin' with her makeup, and definitely no gettin' a fix. I want her out of there ASAP. That'll be your cue. Moment you see Taylor exit, you go on high alert."

"Got it."

I stood. But just as I did, Ronnie said, "Hey." And I bent back down. "I'm glad you're staying. But remember, this ain't a training exercise. You're in the game for real this time. If we're going to take our shot, let's make it count. Ocampo's got the rear and you got the front. If you catch our cinematographer on camera, you circle round and give Ocampo a sign. If she gets him, she'll do the same for you. Then we'll all meet at the rendezvous point. But neither of you leave until you get this fucker on film? You understand?"

"I do. But how will I know for sure who the cinematographer is?"

Ronnie chuckled. "Guess you're just gonna have to use that brain of yours."

*　*　*

It was two twenty when I had my easel set up and was ready to draw. I was on the southeast corner of Golden Gate and Steiner, catty-corner from the Tivoli, and directly across the street from the building I was staking out. It was a decent angle to draw from, but I barely noticed. Nor did I care about the light—which was terrible. I could barely focus enough to draw. I had to take several deep breaths to do more than just stand there. And once I got myself working, I didn't even try to do a pen drawing. I took out my sketchbook and made only rough pencil sketches. I'd been less distracted when I was fifteen and drawing a nude female figure model for the first time.

Eventually I did start a pen drawing, homing in on the top turret so I wouldn't have to worry about the perspective of the entire building. At two fifty-five—pretty much exactly when Ronnie had predicted—a man matching the john's description left the building. I watched him out of the corner of my eye. He was nervously glancing all around—also as Ronnie had predicted—and I was glad I wasn't trying to photograph him. He definitely saw me, and if I'd even been holding a camera, he for sure would have been paranoid I was taking his picture. I didn't make eye contact. I just kept drawing and didn't look up again until I knew he was out of sight.

Fifteen minutes after that, Taylor left. She headed west out the door, then turned the corner up Steiner. If she noticed me, she showed no sign. A second later, I saw Ronnie's Crown Vic pull out of its spot after her.

I kept working. The moment Ronnie drove off, something in me clicked and I became laser-focused.

Five minutes later, a car roared up beside me and screeched to a halt. On the dash was a spinning red light, and at the wheel, Ocampo.

"You see him?" I asked. "Did you—"

"Got an emergency call," she said. "It's all on you. Tell Ron I'll find him."

Then, without any more information, she punched the gas and sped off. Leaving me on my own to stake out a building where, inside, was likely someone who already thought I'd been spying on them, and had responded by calling their inside man on the police force to set me up to be arrested.

With no one covering the rear of the building, I wondered how long I would stay until packing it in and calling the operation a loss. A very long fifteen minutes later, I had my answer. The door of the apartment building swung open, and someone stepped out. My Casio was placed in the partially opened drawer of the French easel, as easy to snatch as a pistol from a holster. I whipped out the compact device, pressed the power button, and began shooting—only to realize the hobbled old woman in the babushka scarf with the barking terrier wasn't our cinematographer. However, the person holding the door for her and stepping out immediately after, I was pretty damn certain was. Because I recognized him—and he most certainly recognized me.

Chateau Tivoli, San Francisco

33

TAYLOR

"You sure?" Ronnie asked.

"Look for yourself." I showed him the digital camera. "I'd paused from snapping pictures when I saw the woman, but the moment I realized who was behind her, I just held the shutter button down. These cameras are crazy. I probably got twenty shots of him in just a few seconds. He looked directly at me. Our eyes locked and there was clear recognition on both our parts. Then he immediately turned tail and took off in the other direction. But as you can see—" I zoomed in on the photo on screen "—there's his face. Plain as day."

"Yeah," Taylor said. "Totally. That's Kai. He's the manager at The Nest. He looks all super-preppie, but he used to be a street kid, like, ten years ago. I heard he did some pretty fucked-up shit too. Like, cut up a bunch of kids because they tried to steal his shoes. He did a couple years in juvie, but then Faith took him in. She's got a thing for the hardcore messed-up types. Which I guess worked for him because now he's all Lord of The Nest and Chadwick's little bitch boy. I can't believe that fucker's been filming me. I'm totally going to cut his shriveled little cowboy balls off."

"Double confirmation," Ronnie said. "That's good enough for me."

"And we're sure this can't be a coincidence?" I said. "I mean, I have to ask. Could he have been there visiting a friend? I just don't want to jump to any—"

"You said he's also been hanging round your house, though, right?" Ronnie said.

"Yeah, because Larissa met him through volunteering at The Arcade."

"Another of Faith Chadwick's philanthropic enterprises. No, sport. I think we found our auteur. And his seeing you means he knows you're on to his game. Question is, what will they do about it?"

"And by 'they,' you mean Inspector——"

Ronnie threw up a hand to stop me. He turned to Taylor. "Is there anything else you haven't told us? If so, now's the time."

"Nothing," Taylor said. Ronnie and I stared at her. "What?" she said. "If there was, I'd tell you. Now that I know that pervy little asshole Kai has been jerking his pud while watching me fuck, I'm not keeping anyone's secrets."

"What about anyone else at The Nest?" Ronnie said. "Is there anyone who has always seemed a little off?"

"They're all a little off. That's how they got there." She looked at me. "And I know what you were going to say. I don't know if Zoro's bent, but no way Faith is. She can be a controlling cunt sometimes, but she's a fucking saint." She shook her head and scoffed. "God-fucking-dammit. This totally sucks, you know that? I actually liked that little prick."

* * *

"This is crazy," I said to Ronnie. We were preparing to leave the house. Taylor was in the bathroom. "So what do you think? Is Faith Chadwick involved?"

"Maybe," Ronnie said. He was leaning with his back against the window-sill, fingers to his chin. Every few minutes, he'd turn and peer anxiously out to the street. I hadn't known Ronnie for long, but this was the only time I'd seen him stressed.

"You looking for Ocampo? I told you, she had an emergency call."

"At your shop," Ronnie said. "After I left. She give you the scoop?"

The question was vague enough that I could have asked what he meant, but I didn't need to. And anyway, I thought of Ronnie as a friend, so there was no need to play dumb. "Only so far as to make insinuations," I said. "Mostly she was fishing to see what I knew about you."

Ronnie nodded.

"I kept my mouth shut," I said.

"Appreciate that, sport." He exhaled frustratedly out his nose. Then he turned back to me. "Something I might have left out when ol' Mary Jane got my tongue wagging at Jerry's place. There's a contingent in the SFPD who think I killed Joe Chadwick. And Ocampo's probably one of them."

I had deduced something close to that. Given the trap Zorn had led him into, and—to use Ronnie's word—the hinky nature of the scene, the cover-up, and his leaving the force shortly after, it stood to reason there'd be suspicions.

"So why did you go to her then?" I asked. "With Taylor and the stakeout today?"

"Because she was the one who started the ball rolling."

"You mean with engineering our meet?"

He nodded.

"But I thought the reason you weren't pissed at her for putting us together was because it meant she was investigating Zorn, which meant you could trust her. Was I wrong?"

"That's one of the hands I'm playing."

"Okay. So . . . what's another? That you involved her because you think *she's* the dirty cop? But if that's true, then . . ." I was getting turned around.

"Then it's a double bluff," Ronnie said. "She could have known about my client long before he'd come to me, and been using my suspicion of Zorn to distract me and pull me close."

"Which would mean it wasn't Zorn who brought me in, but Ocampo?"

"Or both."

"So now they're working together?"

He shrugged.

It sounded overwrought to me, and I wanted to tell him he was maybe leaning a little too far over to be looking at the situation straight on. But Ronnie was the pro, and he'd been willing to follow me down my share of lopsided rabbit holes, so I figured it only fair to follow him down his.

"Okay," I said. "Let's play it out, then. If Ocampo and Zorn are working together, then bringing me in I can understand. But why bring *you* in? If the whole point of them keeping me close was to make sure I wasn't working as a spy, why put me with a private detective—*the* private detective who's working the case?"

"For exactly that reason. Because I was already involved. Chasing down the Midnight Climax rooms for my client. They knew I was me and I'd get to them eventually. So instead of waiting, they pulled me in to take control of the game."

"To neutralize you? Like Zorn did the night of Joe Chadwick's death."

"It'd be a risk," Ronnie said. "You don't tap in a dangerous player who can hurt you unless you plan to take them down for good."

"And so by letting Ocampo in on today's stakeout, you were what? Looking to take her down first? Take back control? Or . . . ?"

"I had to know where she stood. If Ocampo was playing it straight, then we'd be on the verge of finishing this thing. But if she was playing it crooked, and today was a setup, then we were gonna be even further back on our arches than when we started. And I gotta tell ya, her racing off like that, it reeks of my having bet on the wrong horse." He shook his head. "Damn. Usually I'm pretty good at cutting through the layers of smoke. But this Zorn and Chadwick thing . . . When it comes to those two, I'm always missin' the pitch, not knowing whether the sun's going up or down. Which is why I should've known, when this bird circled back around . . ."

I was used to Ronnie's mixed metaphors, but this string of unrelated expressions was impressive. Still, I understood what he meant—and why he was worried. Either Ocampo was a good cop and wasn't with us at the safe house because there truly had been a police emergency, or she was even more bent than we'd thought Zorn was, and, at that moment, was busy wiping her fingerprints off a blackmail operation—if not having alerted a hit squad that the three people who were on to her conspiracy were now gathered tidily together in one house. Until that moment, I'd been feeling like I was humoring Ronnie's lying on his back and looking at this thing upside down, but the more I thought about it, the more plausible it seemed. What proof, really, did we have against Martin Zorn? None, it was all speculation. Ocampo could just as easily have been the one behind my setup at the Legion, and was using Ronnie to hang a frame around his former partner to draw attention away from her. And while I didn't know the players as intimately as Ronnie did, of the two, I knew for certain that Ocampo had already played me—twice. Whereas all Zorn had ever done was have a little laugh with me one night outside my shop.

Ronnie looked through the curtains again. "Dammit," he said. Then he looked toward the bathroom. "What the shite is that kid doing in there? We need to—no, don't tell me—"

Ronnie ran to the bathroom, tried the door. Locked. He pounded. No answer.

"Fuck," he said, running past me. "Outside, come on."

We darted outside. The house was a two-story Queen Anne, one of the rare inner-city homes with a carport on the side.

"Check the street," Ronnie said, running around the side of the house.

I hit the sidewalk, looked left and right. No sign of Taylor. The park was directly across the street. I scanned best I could, but much of the view was blocked by eucalyptus trees.

Ronnie joined me on the sidewalk. "Bathroom window is open. Any sign of her?"

"No."

"Damn," he said. "Leave it to me to pick the one house in San Francisco where you can actually escape through a bathroom window."

*   *   *

Ronnie said we should divide and conquer.

"I know the Loin," he said. "I'll look for her in the usual spots. You go to your place. Tell your girl Larissa to stay clear of anything to do with Chadwick."

Luckily, Larissa was two hundred miles away at the Madonna Inn with Tally, so I didn't have to worry about her.

"What about The Nest?" I said. "Maybe Taylor really is going to cut Kai's balls off."

"Maybe. Stick close to the phone. I'll check in ASAP." And he took off jogging down the sidewalk.

I drove home in a daze. Next thing I knew, I was circling my neighborhood. Of course there was no parking, and between all I'd just witnessed and my having handwritten license plates, I'd had enough. I parked in the garage—with more than enough room beside the bicycles.

Upstairs I considered phoning Larissa at the inn to tell her to stay there until she heard from me, or to go to Stanford, or maybe stay with Tally, only to realize that Tally was also affiliated with Faith Chadwick and The Nest, and wasn't sure then what I should do. The question was, how close still was Tally with Faith? I knew she didn't live at The Nest anymore, but her bakery was right there in Chadwick Village, and Tally had called Faith "the mother she wished she'd had." Had she and Kai both gotten close to Larissa as a way to get close to me? If that was the case, then was the trip to San Luis Obispo a ruse to separate us?

I was already feeling bad; now I was feeling worse. And Ronnie's having run off wasn't helping my paranoia. We were all divided, like antelopes having been separated from the herd. The question was: Who were the lions?

I went to the kitchen for something to calm my nerves. Not booze. I needed my wits sharpened, not dulled. I found a tin of chamomile tea and put a kettle of water on to boil.

I tried to sort out what I knew—or thought I knew. Seemed the closer I got to pegging someone as a villain, the less sure I could be. I decided the only way to sort this out was to write it all down. I fetched a notebook from the studio, then settled onto a stool at the kitchen island and began making a list of everyone involved:

- Inspector Martin Zorn. It made sense that after someone in the Naples house saw me drawing, they'd called their cop friend, who then engineered bringing me in to keep me close. But what proof was there that it was Zorn? None. And if it was true, who was he protecting? Himself? Ocampo? Faith Chadwick? Me?

- Lieutenant Ocampo. She'd been the one who put me in the training exercise in the park—and lied about why—then called in the phony stolen report on my car—another deceptive move that smacked of the same absurdity as the lewd behavior complaint at the Legion. Had she been the one behind it all along? Playing the good cop by laying all the blame onto Martin Zorn—a man she knew Ronnie had a history with? Then, as Ronnie had proposed, brought him in to take control of the game? Or, was it as straightforward as she'd claimed? Connecting me with Ronnie because she didn't trust Zorn, believing he was the only one who could help? Whatever the case, Ocampo proved that she could be a highly skilled manipulator. The question was: For what purpose?

- Ronnie Gilbert. Ex-cop turned private detective, and the only one of the lot I actually trusted. But if I were to follow his method of looking at things straight on, I needed to question his motives with the same rigor as I questioned everyone else's. Starting with the events surrounding the night of Joe Chadwick's death. Beyond his version of the story, what proof did I have that the night had gone down as he'd said? There was the public version, which I had no doubt was sanitized. The question was, in which direction did the truth more closely lean? Ronnie had certainly come off as genuine that night in Stinson, smoking a joint with me and sharing a bottle of tequila, and I hated doubting the closeness I felt with him. But at the same time, why would a guy whose business was keeping secrets choose to confide in *me*? I mean, I knew he had a soft spot for rock and rollers, but I was a stranger. Why admit that he'd tampered with evidence and instructed a witness to lie in a homicide? Unless he was maybe doing the very thing he'd insinuated Faith had done, which was to make me complicit in order to neutralize me. But in what universe was I a threat to Ronnie Gilbert?

- Faith Chadwick. Real estate developer, philanthropist, and widow. Hers was a classic rags-to-riches story with a subplot of Greek tragedy. And according to everyone—everyone but Ronnie, that is—she was a saint. The woman I'd met was certainly a master at roping people in, but did that make her a blackmailer? Abusing the very kids she was working to save? The prospect sounded outrageous. And there was zero proof. Except for—

- Kai. Ex-street kid who now worked at The Nest. A clean-cut young man who at first had barely made an impression on me, yet appeared to be the cameraman filming the very girls he was supposed to be helping—but again, so it seemed. I'd only witnessed him coming out of the building. It wasn't as if he'd been carrying a tripod and video camera. He had turned and darted off, which only more pointed toward his guilt. But what if he too was being set up?

- Taylor. A fifteen-year-old street kid turning tricks for money and drugs. She seemed sincere, but who knew what she was after—plus, she'd done a runner. That did not bode well for her motives.

- Tally. Another Nest success story who, like Taylor, had nothing but good things to say about Faith Chadwick, and, while seemingly sweet as pie, had seemed to quickly befriend Larissa, right alongside Kai. And who had now taken Larissa hundreds of miles away—assuming that's even where they'd gone.

- And since I was listing everyone, I had to add one final name: Larissa Huxley. An eighteen-year-old stranger who talked her way into my home. That a blood test proved 99.8 percent positive that either Brian or I was her father seemed pretty solid evidence that she wasn't involved in some complex blackmail conspiracy. Not to mention that she was on record as a genius. Though given that her field was questioning the nature of social ethics, I supposed being an evil genius wasn't wholly off the table. Though not necessarily relevant to the situation at hand.

The kettle began to whistle. I poured half a mug of boiling water, added a splash of cool, and set a tea bag to soak. Chamomile tea. Supposedly calming. I wondered how many vats' worth it would take to actually work. That's when I heard the front door open and close.

* * *

I moved down the hallway and hovered at the top of the landing. A few seconds later I saw Larissa rounding the stairs—alone. I couldn't believe it.

"You're back early," I said, trying not to sound alarmed. "You all right? Where's Tally?"

"Well you're just full of questions, aren't you?" she said. She walked past me and threw her bag onto the pew.

"I need to talk to you about something," I said.

She looked at me. Her face was puffy. She'd been crying.

"Shit," I said. "What happened?"

She crossed her arms. "What do you want to talk about?"

"Let's go into the kitchen. I'll make you some tea."

"Are you freaking serious? Who are you, Grandma Emit?"

I stared at her. "Something terrible is going on," I said. "Is that why you're home?" —*Home*, I'd said it without thinking. "Is that why you're upset?"

"I'm upset because I borrowed a car and paid for a cheesy theme room and bought tons of food and did whatever she wanted only for us to end up getting into a fight."

"What did you fight about?"

"I really don't see how that's any of your business. Don't you think maybe you're taking this potential-dad thing a bit too far?" She reached to pick up her bag. "Whatever. I have to go."

"No," I said, putting my hand on her bag to stop her. "Please. We have to talk."

She wanted to fight with me, so I said it again. "Please. It's important." Luckily, my eyes conveyed enough that it worked.

We went into the kitchen and I told her everything. It took almost an hour. When I was done, whatever disagreement she'd had with Tally was gone from her mind.

"I'm sorry to have to ask this," I said. "But, Tally—do you think there's any way she—"

"No," Larissa said defiantly. "No. She's got nothing to do with blackmail. I'm positive."

"How can you be sure?"

"Because I just am, okay? Anyway, she doesn't have anything to do with The Nest anymore. She's her own person with her own life."

I let it go. But only for the moment, and not all of it. "And your fight?"

Larissa laughed. "You really don't stop, do you?" She shook her head. "It was nothing. Just a stupid disagreement." She looked down, pulled out the fabric of her hoodie, and stared at one of the stains she'd turned into art. "Apparently I can be difficult," she said, looking up to me. "Or at least that's what I'm told."

"Love is hard."

She snorted. "Great. Now you're going to offer me romance advice." She'd wanted it to be shitty, but there was no fire in her and the comment just came out sounding sad.

"No," I said. "No advice. Just saying love is hard."

"Well, that's good. Coming from a thirty-seven-year-old divorcee who has no idea how many illegitimate children he's fathered and doesn't even have a girlfriend—why is that, anyway?" This time she had plenty of fire. And it came out just as shitty as she'd intended.

I'd had enough. I opened my mouth to lay into her, but luckily the doorbell rang before things got truly nasty.

*　*　*

I went into the studio, opened the bay window, leaned out, and looked down to see who it was. Then I ran downstairs. At the gate was Taylor, hunched over by the weight of a large hiking backpack slung over one shoulder.

"I wasn't running away," she said as I opened the gate. "I just needed to do something."

"Was it castrating Kai?" I asked, looking up and down the street as I let her in.

"In a way."

Upstairs, Taylor dropped her large pack onto the floor. "Is Ron here?"

"He's out looking for you," I said. "We should call him."

"Already did," Taylor said. "Half an hour ago. Got his service. Woman told me to come here."

"I'm glad you did—come here, I mean. And that you called Ronnie." I gestured toward the studio. "Come on in."

We could see Larissa in the kitchen at the far end of the flat.

"Who's that?" Taylor asked suspiciously.

"My daughter," I said, keeping things simple—though it did feel strange to say.

I flashed Larissa a thumbs-up, then a single finger to tell her to give Taylor and me a moment alone. She moved her head to say she would.

"Where did you go?" I asked Taylor.

Taylor picked up her large backpack, carried it into the studio, then dropped it down beside the couch.

I followed her in.

"So you're an artist, huh?" she said, looking around my work space.

"Yeah."

"That's cool. I used to like to draw."

"So where'd you go?" I asked again. "If you weren't running away—"

Just then, the doorbell rang again. Taylor looked worried.

"It's all right," I said. "It's probably just Ronnie." I had no idea if it was, but I hoped so. I looked out the window. It was him—and Ocampo. She sure did have a knack for surprises.

I turned and saw Larissa coming down the hallway, pointing toward the stairs. She raised her brows, and I gave her a thumbs-up to go down.

I heard Ronnie's voice at the bottom. "I got a message that—"

"She's here," Larissa said. Then she introduced herself.

Taylor looked relieved to see Ronnie walk into the studio, then suspicious to see Ocampo. I was equally suspicious.

I looked to Ronnie, but he went straight to Taylor.

"You okay?" he said to her.

"Yeah," Taylor said. "Sorry to bolt. I had something I needed to do." She slid her backpack between her legs and began to open it. "I want out," she said. She looked up and stared at Ronnie with a look both plaintive and defiant. "Like out, out. As in, school and a place to live and a life away from here kind of out. Can you help me?"

"Yeah," Ronnie said. "I can help you. But it ain't going to be easy—and you gotta help me first. And I mean all the way, as in whatever it takes. You willing to do that?"

"Yeah," she said. "Whatever it takes." She began removing plastic boxes from her backpack and setting them on the coffee table. "Which is why I got you these."

Ronnie stepped over, and she handed him one of the boxes.

I looked to Ocampo. She was keeping oddly quiet, and I wondered how it was that the last time I saw Ronnie he'd pegged her for playing for the other side, only to have him show up two hours later with her in tow. She glanced at me but betrayed nothing.

"Damn," Ronnie said, and Ocampo and I looked. He'd opened one of the boxes to reveal a set of five small camcorder tapes. Each labeled with handwritten initials and dates. Taylor had stacked four more boxes onto the table, which made twenty-five tapes.

"There were more," Taylor said. "But these were all I could fit in with my stuff. Along with this—" She pulled out a silver metal box. "I don't know if it'll be any help, but it was with the tapes, so I grabbed it."

"It's an external hard drive," Larissa said, stepping forward and taking it.

"Is it useful? Or should I have taken more tapes?"

"We'll have to see what's on it," Larissa said, then left the room.

"Where did you get all this?" Ronnie asked.

"The Nest used to be an old hotel," Taylor said. "And it's still got a safe in the basement. Like, one of those full-fledged bank vault rooms with the walk-in door and big spinning wheel. They still use it, but mostly to store wine since the building is full of delinquents. There's also all these old safety-deposit boxes. And they still use them. Once you get a bed at The Nest, you also get a box. Since Kai is the manager, he's in charge of the vault, and because I may have let him fuck me once or twice, I know where he keeps the combination and keys to all the boxes. I went into his and found these."

"You took a doozy of a gamble going back there," Ronnie said.

"Why?" Taylor said. She looked at me. "Just because Kai saw you today doesn't mean he knows I'm on to him—or at least he didn't before I stole his shit."

"He saw you?" Ronnie asked.

"Only as I was leaving. He was coming in."

"You guys talk? What was your interaction like?"

"I wanted to kick him in the balls so hard he could feel them in his throat," Taylor said. "But I didn't. I just said 'Hey,' and kept going."

"So he didn't seem suspicious?"

"I didn't stick around to ask about his feelings. But I could tell he was rattled. Which was why it was good I went when I did. If he'd caught me in his room or in the vault, then I would have had some serious explaining to do. But I was in and out, no problem. Which is why I bolted from the safe house. I wanted to see what he had stashed before he had time to move it, and I knew you'd never have let me go. And look—" she gestured at the boxes of tapes "—I was right. Totally paid off."

Ronnie nodded. "This is good," he said. "You did good." He turned to me. "In other news. Something you need to know." He looked to Ocampo.

She'd been hanging back and listening. Now she finally stepped forward and spoke. "I know what happened at the museum."

34

CIRCUS AT THE MUSEUM

wanted to make a sarcastic comment like, "Let me guess. You paid Abigail to flash me because, all this time, you've really just been a die-hard fangirl, and couldn't think up a better icebreaker to introduce yourself," but the air was too tense to risk sarcasm. So I kept my mouth shut.

"Call I got while on our stakeout," Ocampo said. "That I rushed off for." She glanced at Taylor, then hesitated.

"Seriously?" Taylor said.

"Let her hear it," Ronnie said to Ocampo. "She's all in."

He gave Taylor a look that said not to worry, that he knew she was one of us. And by her reaction, if she hadn't been committed to trusting him before, she was now.

"Naples Street," Ocampo said. "House isn't a brothel. It's a shelter."

"Shit," Taylor broke in. "I coulda told you that." We all looked at her. "It's a sanc house, for kids rescued from fucked-up homes. So their families can't find them and kidnap them back."

"That's right," Ocampo said. "A Sanctuary House. Secret locations that hide children from excessively abusive families. No one has been able to prove Faith Chadwick is involved, but speculation has been that she funds these houses, as well as relocation programs, for abused kids. It's a shady gray area of the law, and highly controversial. In theory she's rescuing at-risk children, but some argue she's the one doing harm. They question whether these kids are there willingly."

"Must be something about the block," Ronnie mused.

No one else understood, but I did. The house next door, the one I'd had a commission to draw. Where years earlier, my client had hid from the Mormon church.

"The girls coming out of the house who you caught on film——" Ocampo said to me.

"I told her about the photos," Ronnie slid in.

"——they were kids from the sanctuary. They saw you across the street taking pictures, got worried, and reported you to who we can only assume was Faith."

"And Faith called her old pal Inspector Zorn," I said.

"Zorn tracked you down. Learned you took commissions, and wondered if maybe you'd taken on a special job to find a lost little Susie or Bobby that some desperate parent claimed had been taken against their will."

"Lots of p.i. work out there to hunt for these kids," Ronnie chimed in. "Plein air artist makes a damn good cover."

"Zorn told a pair of young patrol cops to roust you, see if they could find out if you'd discovered the sanctuary."

"And Zorn told you all this?" I asked.

Ocampo shook her head. "Roberts. One of the unies who picked you up at the museum. That was the call I sped off for today. Someone put Roberts in the emergency room. Hurt him real bad. Arm fractured in two places, three broken ribs, punctured lung, a face so swollen I could barely tell it was him. A bouncer from the Zeitgeist named Isaac."

I raised my eyebrows at Ronnie. He snorted.

"Gets better," Ocampo said. "Seems a while back Roberts and his partner Jantze collared an ex-stripper for possession. They didn't book her, on account of she was well-endowed. Instead, they kept her on a string and would occasionally come around for favors."

"Meaning blowjobs," Ronnie said.

Taylor guffawed.

"And," Ocampo said, "performing the occasional act of public indecency at a museum."

"So the two cops in uniform set me up?" I asked. "Not Zorn?"

"Zorn was only trying to find out if maybe you'd been sold a sob story by a weepy parent," Ronnie said.

"No parent wants their child taken away," Ocampo said. "But some of these hardcore abusers, it's also about power. They'll stop at nothing. At the same time, the whole sanctuary concept is pretty far out on the ledge. Faith basically kidnaps these kids, then she hides them. She sets them up with new names, new homes, new lives, sometimes in other countries. Most of the parents never see them again. There are a lot of people who argue it's not right, that she's playing judge and jury and cutting out the system. And I can't say I disagree. Even if she is doing good. No one's above the law."

"How does she get away with it?"

"Because it's only the parents who are up in arms. Not one kid has ever come forward to say they'd been taken against their will. Of course, some of these kids are young—as young as five. So who's to say they know what's right?"

"Or not being brainwashed," Ronnie said.

"Okay," I said. "Whatever the ethics of the Sanctuary House, you're saying Zorn had me brought in not to protect a pedophile blackmail operation, but to protect a secret shelter for abused kids?"

"About sums it up," Ronnie said. "It was the dynamic duo who turned the museum into a circus. They got the brilliant idea to play entrapment with you. Thinking it would be a gas to have Abbs flash her lovelies in a public place, then haul you in."

"Roberts said Zorn gave him hell for it," Ocampo said.

"And he told you all of this because Isaac kicked the shit out of him?"

"He needed to file an incident report. Only way to do that was to come clean. And anyway, Isaac was talking up a storm, preparing his defense. Seems Roberts had come around the Zeitgeist this afternoon and pushed Abigail one step too far. She whistled for the door, and now Roberts is in traction."

"So," I said. "Just to be clear, we're saying Inspector Martin Zorn is innocent here?"

"Crusader Zorn," Ronnie said. "To the rescue."

"Okay . . . But then how does that explain the Naples Street house being linked to the money that was sent to Western Union to pay Taylor? How can a house that's a protective sanctuary for kids also be tied to paying kids to have sex with pedophiles?"

"I think I can answer that," Larissa said.

We all turned to see her behind us in the doorway.

"You guys need to come see this."

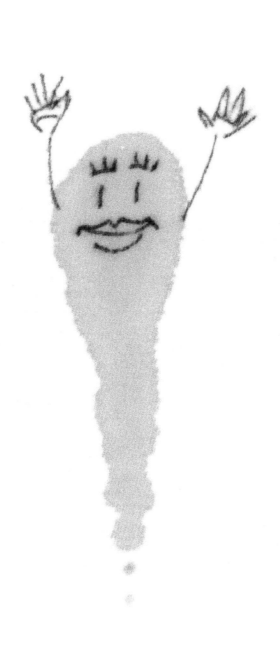

35

WHERE THERE'S SMOKE

"The hard drive," Larissa said. We were all in the kitchen, gathered around Larissa's laptop at the island. The silver metal box Taylor had delivered was plugged into Larissa's machine, as was another box, sand-colored, with a series of green, orange, and red lights. "It contains a lot of documents that I'll need more time to dive into, but there's a master doc that I think explains a few things." She pointed to a spreadsheet on her screen. There were four columns, each with a list of addresses. "Best I can tell, this is an overview of all the properties owned by Faith Chadwick. This first column lists her personal holdings. You'll see there's only a few. The second column are the properties owned by her LLC. An impressive list. The third column is what's owned by the foundation. Pretty much just The Nest and The Arcade. It's this fourth column that's most interesting. These are the properties held by a variety of shell companies. Over thirty. I did some quick poking around, and none of these trace back to Chadwick in any way."

"Meaning she's hiding them from her legal assets?" Ocampo asked.

"Seems that way," Larissa said. "Look here——" she pointed to one of the addresses in the fourth column "——that's the house on Naples Street, right? The sanctuary?"

"It is," I said.

"And bingo," Ronnie said. He'd pulled out his notepad and was comparing what he had written with what was on the screen. "Polk Street is on here, Golden Gate, and Bay Street—all Operation Midnight spots. The first two where Taylor took us, and Bay being where my client was filmed. The other addresses from Taylor's pager are listed here as well."

"Along with a disturbing number of others," Ocampo said. "All for making secret recordings, you think?"

"Naples isn't," I said. "Right?"

"And not the San Mateo address," Taylor said. "Or the Sebastopol. Those are also sanc houses."

"Are you sure?" Ocampo said.

"I mean, I've never been, but yeah, I'm pretty sure."

"Makes sense she'd have more than one," Ocampo said. "Supposedly the locations are constantly changing. Scroll down," she said to Larissa. "There are addresses all across the country. This must be her part of the network. She probably places kids in sites far from their original homes to ensure no one recognizes them. Can you get me a printout of this list?"

"What are you going to do with it?"

Ocampo flinched. "I don't see how that's any of your concern."

Larissa punched a key, and her screen went blank. "I also don't see why I have to give it to you."

"It's evidence of a crime."

"Is it? I see no proof of secret locations for recording sex for blackmail. All I see is potential tax fraud. But you're looking to go after the Sanctuary Houses, and I don't want to be a party to that."

"I don't see how you have much of a choice."

"So then get a warrant."

"All right," Ronnie said. "Let's just everyone cool their horses. Anything else on that hard drive of use?"

Ocampo and Larissa stared at each other for a long second.

"As a matter of fact," Larissa said, punching a key and immediately closing the document the moment her screen came back to life, "there is." She opened another spreadsheet. This one had multiple columns, two of what looked like abbreviated names, several of dates, and one of what appeared to be dollar amounts. There were dozens of entries. Larissa pointed to each column as she spoke. "I believe this is a list of all the men blackmailed, the minors they had sex with, the date of the sex, the date of the blackmail, the date of the payment, and, finally, the payment amount."

"Way to bury the lede, kid," Ronnie said. "Holy crap on crapola—this is it!"

"There aren't many payments," I said. "Don't you think that's weird?"

"What's also weird," Larissa said, "is that there aren't very many blackmail dates either. Look—" she pointed to the first row of dates "—almost every john has an initial date, what I'm guessing is the date of sex. But from there only a few have entries."

"So you're saying that dozens of men were recorded having sex with minors," Ocampo said, having put aside the confrontation, "but only a few were blackmailed?"

"And even fewer paid out. Look. Of the roughly fifty men recorded, only eight were blackmailed, and of those, only two have what appear to be dollar amounts in the payment column. One is empty, and the other five are just symbols, which I haven't yet decoded."

"They're non-cash payments," Ronnie said. "Look at the one on—" he leaned forward to read "—July twelve this year. Payment entry reads 30G3. When did The Arcade open?"

"Just a couple months ago," Larissa said.

"G3," Ronnie said. "That's the new Mac desktop, right? How many machines they got in that new free computer center there?"

"Roughly—" Larissa flinched "—thirty." She looked back to the screen. "30G3—they blackmailed someone for computers."

"Payment in another fashion. And the first column of entries, we're thinking those are abbreviations for the johns' names, yeah? Well, the one with the empty payment, GJ, that's gotta be my client. And the dates—" again he consulted his notebook "—they line up. First entry is his rendezvous with the playmate, second is when he received the surprise package."

"But no entry of payment?"

"Because he hasn't been tapped yet."

"What's your guy do for a living?" Ocampo asked.

"Exactly," Ronnie said. "He works for the EPA, the Environmental Protection Agency. When the videotape he received didn't specify an amount, I figured they were angling for political sway. Thing is, he oversees an office handling thousands of cases, up and down the state, so there was no way to know which he was going to have his arm twisted for. But now I think I get it." He paused to look at each of us. "Mission Bay. The development off of Third Street. Chadwick's heavily vested there."

"But you said your guy hasn't been contacted with demands. Why would Chadwick wait?"

"'Cause, like everyone else, she thought Willie was going to sweep the election. Which is why she sent the tape, to set the blackmail in motion. Then Ammiano made everyone flinch, and suddenly she doesn't know which way the political wind is going to blow. Mission Bay is Willie Brown's legacy project. If he goes down in the run-off, Ammiano is likely to tank the expansion, and there'll be no point in blackmailing my guy. She'd be wasting a play. But if Brown gets another term, then the fight to build is still on, and she can resume her plan to activate my guy. 'Sign off paving over wetlands, or else the world sees a movie of you shtooping a teenager.'"

"And all these other entries?" I said. "The ones with only dates of sex and no dates of contact? You're saying they're johns she's waiting to blackmail?"

"If so," Ocampo said, "that's a lot of entries she hasn't tapped—most. If she has plans for every one of these names, then that's one hell of a web she's got spinning. But I don't see what else it can be. Otherwise, why go through the trouble of recording these men and not follow up with the blackmail?"

"My guess is insurance," Ronnie said. "Seems pretty clear Chadwick isn't in this to hold pedophiles accountable, or even for straight-up extortion. She's in it for political maneuvering. Ask me, there's no master plan for these guys, she's just preparing for any future roadblocks she might hit—EPA, zoning board, Congress—and lining up advance leverage." He shook his head. "I don't mean to compliment her, but it's brilliant. Who knows the names behind all these abbreviations. Could be judges, cops, senators, anyone in power who one day she might need to have sway over."

"And so, to be clear," I said. "We're accusing both Faith and Kai, right?"

Ronnie inhaled deeply through his nose. "The bronco-kid is definitely involved. Seeing him come out of that building today—and now all those tapes—he's in it up to his Kennedy haircut."

"And Faith is definitely aiding the Sanctuary Houses," Ocampo said. "Plus, she's the powerbroker, and the obvious connection to Zorn—because who else could persuade him to look into you over the Naples house? And with the bank payments to Taylor, it means the blackmail and the Sanctuary Houses are linked. It's perverted, but a secret network like that—housing, feeding, and giving these kids new lives—all costs money. Faith funnels in some cash of her own, but a little blackmail grease here and there would definitely help keep the wheels turning."

"So Faith is the mastermind," I said. "And Kai is her second, carrying out her orders."

"She figures these kids are turning tricks anyway," Ocampo said. "May as well use a few of them to her advantage. She takes out a few pedophiles, strong-arms a few political favors, and saves some abused children, all in one. She probably looked at the balance sheet and saw the wins coming out ahead of the losses and thinks herself a hero."

"Your logic ain't faulty," Ronnie said.

"Fucking bitch," Taylor said.

"So is this enough?" Taylor said, pointing to the computer screen. "To take her down?"

"It's a start," Ronnie said.

"And you'll honor our deal?"

"I'll drive you to college myself."

"Can you also give me a place to stay? The Nest was the only place I had to go. And I'm sure as shit not going back there. And I can't be out on the street. You gotta get me somewhere safe. When Kai finds out I took all this, who knows what he'll do."

"Don't worry," Ronnie said. "I'll get you far away from here." He turned to me. "I can take her to my place up in Russian River. But there's something I need to chase down first. You mind putting her up for a bit?"

"Not at all." I looked to Taylor. "You can stay up here, or if you want some privacy, you can stay in the flat downstairs."

"You're going to talk to Zorn," Ocampo said to Ronnie. "Aren't you?"

"I need to know what he knows."

"You should let Internal Affairs take care of it."

"I'm serving up Chadwick to you on a plate," Ronnie said. "And anyway, I'm not asking."

Larissa handed Ocampo the hard drive. "You weren't going to leave here without it, and I'm not in the mood for any more fights today."

Ocampo took the drive, but she didn't say thanks.

"But so you know," Larissa said. "I made a copy of everything on it."

The two stared at each other. Ocampo didn't like it, but she had the drive, which was what she wanted. And she knew there was no way she was going to win this one.

"Fair enough," Ocampo said. "But you keep it to yourself. I don't want to see any website exposés. We clear?"

"Yep. But only so long as you don't go 'accidentally' misplacing that drive."

Ocampo turned to Ronnie. "Between this and the tapes, I can hopefully get a warrant on the Golden Gate location. See if we can snag that camera room before Kai torches it. Then we'll go from there."

She and Ronnie moved toward the front of the flat.

I gave Ocampo a shopping bag, and as she gathered the boxes of tapes, Ronnie looked at me and, throwing his head toward Ocampo, said, "You're wondering how I went from thinking she'd sold us out to her and I being best pals?" He didn't need me to say I'd very much been wondering just that. "When you and I parted," he said, "I took off after Taylor and put the scanner on in Ocampo's Crown Vic. I heard the chatter about Roberts getting his clock cleaned, then the order to pick up Isaac at the Zeitgeist, so I took a gamble and went to sf General to intercept. I told her I knew the perp who'd laid Roberts low and would do a little quid pro quo if she took me in the room when she did the unofficial interview. He was doped up and looking like a rag doll, but everything he said fit. That's when I got the page that our girl here made contact with my service and was sent to you."

Ocampo had gathered the tapes and was now standing right there. I was hesitant to ask, but at the same time, the stakes were too high to worry about hurting anyone's feelings.

I glanced at Ocampo, then looked back to Ronnie. "And that was enough to make you believe she isn't in on it? We're letting her leave with all the evidence. What if you're wrong?"

"Shortest distance between two points, sport. And Ocampo bent is not the straightest line."

I inhaled deeply through my nose and exhaled quickly.

"Here," Ocampo said. She handed me one of the boxes of tapes. "Twenty tapes will be just as convincing to a judge as twenty-five. And if these four boxes mysteriously disappear, then you've got one for insurance, and—" she glanced at Larissa "—you've got a copy of all the files."

I took the box and nodded.

"I'll want that back once the d.a. gets involved," Ocampo said. "We're going to want to identify as many of those johns as we can."

"So we good?" Ronnie asked me. "You on board?"

"Aye aye, captain."

Ronnie clucked and turned to Taylor. "Hang tight, kid. You're in good hands. I'll be back for you in a bit."

Then Ocampo and Ronnie left; Lieutenant Ocampo to take the evidence Taylor had retrieved to a judge, and ex-sergeant Ronnie Gilbert to confront his former partner Inspector Martin Zorn for the first time in seven years.

* * *

With Ocampo and Ronnie gone, and having seen damning evidence against Faith Chadwick, Larissa was looking a little shell-shocked. Taylor, too, was unsure what to do. So I said I'd order us all some dinner. I asked Taylor what

328

sounded good, and she said Chinese, so I called it in, ordering enough for ten. Taylor asked if she could take a shower and I said of course. I gathered everything she'd need, then led her down to the second floor to give her something I wagered she rarely got: space to herself.

"Here you go," I said, handing her a towel and my travel Dopp kit. "There's not much down here, but the water is hot and the bed is comfy. I'll come get you when the food arrives. And—" I wasn't sure how to say this exactly, so I just said it "—I'm really sorry for what's happened."

"Why? You didn't do anything wrong." She smiled. A bright and sweet smile. And, for the first time, she looked like what she was, a kid. Her hard exterior gone, all I saw was a young person who had been hurt and lied to. "Way I see it, you're the hero."

I said I didn't know about that. Then I left her to rest and went upstairs.

When I'd taken Taylor down to the vacant unit, Larissa had been deep in reviewing the contents of the drive she'd copied, but when I returned she was gone. As was her laptop. On the counter was a handwritten note:

Going to find Tally. Need to tell her what's going on.

Shit. Tally. Larissa had sworn there was no way Tally could be involved. And the more I thought about it, the more I was inclined to agree. Still, given all the revelations, it was hard to know who to trust. Mostly I was just worried for Larissa. She was in love, and I didn't care how much of a genius someone was, love can make fools of us all.

I called Ronnie, assuming I would get his service, and did. "Tell him Larissa went to find Tally." I wasn't sure what he was supposed to do with that information. But I wanted him to have it.

I was feeling on edge. Everyone had run off to connect with other players, and once again all the antelopes were divided. But then I realized I had my role too. I'd wait for the food to come, find a good movie on TV, and do everything I could to make Taylor feel a part of this unusual family.

* * *

When forty-five minutes later the food came, Larissa wasn't back. I closed the front gate and set the bags in my entry, then went up to the second floor, calling out as I climbed the stairs. I didn't want to surprise Taylor if she hadn't finished showering. There was no reply. At first my heart sank with the thought that she'd bolted again. She'd seemed so earnest in wanting help that it never occurred to me that I shouldn't leave her alone. I saw the bedroom door was closed and felt relieved. She was probably just napping.

Sanchez Adobe, Pacifica, CA — Patron asked to be unnamed

I knocked lightly on the door. "Taylor? Food's here if you want to eat."
I knocked louder, then cracked open the door. She was there, on the bed,
surrounded by pillows. I figured I'd let her sleep. Then I saw the works.
Beside her on the bed, a spoon, needle, and small bag of what I assumed
was heroin. I went in, put my fingers on her neck to feel for a pulse. She was
alive. She was on her back, though. I rolled her to her side so she wouldn't
aspirate. Then I gathered the works and took them upstairs with me. She may
have wanted out, but she was going to have a harder time than I'd thought.

I ate alone, feeling sad. There were too many broken lives. Too many
people taking advantage. I thought about Taylor and wondered how someone
climbs out of a life like that. Then I thought of Tally and wondered how she
would take the news about Faith Chadwick. I wasn't sure Larissa had made
the right decision in going to see her. Taylor was hardened, deep in the life.
But even for her, learning that she'd been betrayed had been a disappointment. How would Tally—who idolized Faith and credited her for giving her

the loving family she'd never had—respond to the information that Faith and Kai were pimping out girls from The Nest? Heartbreak was the only word I could think of. I was worried for Tally, and I was also worried for Larissa. Tally's world was about to crumble. Which meant Larissa's would too.

*　*　*

I was cleaning up dishes when I smelled the smoke. I lived in the Mission, where fires were common. The neighborhood was loaded with old wooden buildings with equally old knob-and-tube electrical that would fray and spark behind the plaster, and next thing you knew, the building was ablaze. I went to the French doors to step onto the deck to see if the fire was visible above the rooftops, only I didn't need to. As I got close to the doors I felt heat and a second later saw flames jump up on the other side of the glass. Then suddenly smoke was filling the room and I realized it was my building that was on fire.

I flung open the doors but that was a mistake. Flames shot up from beneath the wooden planks. There was no going down the back stairs from the deck—it was the stairs that were on fire. I ran to the front of the flat. I was barefoot but not thinking of shoes. I was thinking of Taylor, unconscious on the second floor. I snatched the keys and flew down the stairs. I flung open my door and somehow managed to get the second-floor door unlocked and open in a single motion. I ran up the stairs two at a time, but the air was stifling and I began to cough. Come the landing I was engulfed in sooty black smoke. My lungs burned and my chest seized up. Instantly my vision crackled. I tried to move forward but kept falling. I tried to call out but couldn't speak. I made to stand and collapsed to my knees. The smoke was thick and toxic. Crawling, I was halfway to the bedroom when I heard a crash and thought the ceiling had collapsed and wondered if the floor was next. My stomach seized and I was coughing and retching and my vision became a tunnel. All the strength left my body and my face hit the floor. Then I felt a pair of hands on my shoulders, and next thing I knew I was outside on the sidewalk. My gate was busted open and firefighters were rushing past me. I tried to tell them there was someone inside, but I just started choking. An oxygen mask was thrust over my face and the world went black.

*　*　*

I woke in the back of an ambulance. The back doors were open and beyond was a carnival of fire trucks and firefighters and cops and my building burning. The façade looked normal, but from behind, flames shot twenty feet into

331

the air. I still had the oxygen mask on. I left it. My throat felt like sandpaper. "How you doing?" I hadn't noticed, but there'd been an EMT there in the truck, behind my head. "Let's sit you up."

I took the mask off and tried to talk. I started coughing. It hurt like hell. I couldn't seem to get any air in my lungs, and I thought I might pass out again.

"Here." The EMT put the mask on me again, and I managed to breathe.

Once I calmed, I took it off again and managed to get out a few words. "Second floor, bedroom. Girl."

The EMT moved to the doors of the truck. "Charlie!" she called out. A fireman about ten feet away turned. "He says there's a girl on the second floor."

The fireman gave a thumbs-up with his heavily gloved hand, then took up a walkie-talkie from his belt and reported it.

I put the oxygen mask back on and lay back down.

I must have passed out, because I woke to Larissa's face looking down at me. "Fuck. Is he——"

"How long——" I managed to say, pulling away my mask.

"You were only out a few minutes," the EMT said. "Here, look at me." She spread one of my eyes open and shined in a pen light. "How many fingers?"

I saw two, so I said two.

"Good."

She put a couple drops of liquid in each of my eyes, and only by the instant relief I felt did I realize how much they'd been stinging. I was feeling like I might be able to breathe, so I took off the mask, then slowly, carefully, tried to fill my lungs on my own. If I breathed too deep, it felt like a thousand shards of glass. So I kept my breaths short.

"What the fuck happened?" Larissa asked. She was on high alert.

"You okay?" I asked.

She started laughing. "Am *I* okay? What the hell is wrong with you? Where's Taylor?"

"I don't know. She's . . ." I pointed toward my burning building.

"Ron!" Larissa called out. She'd turned toward the open doors, then turned back. "Ronnie's here," she said to me.

I managed to sit up. "I'm okay," I said. "I want to see."

Larissa helped me to the edge of the gurney.

"Stay close," the EMT said.

"I just want——" My throat seized. I pointed to the edge of the truck.

Larissa and the EMT helped me down. I sat on the back of the ambulance with my bare feet on the pavement. Multiple hoses were shooting arcs of water onto the roof of my building. Ronnie came over.

"God damn, sport, what happened?"

I started shaking my head.

"I couldn't get her out, Ron. I tried, but—" I started coughing. It felt like the fire was in my throat. "She'd been shooting up. Then the fire and—" I started crying. "I just—I couldn't get her."

"It's not your fault," Ronnie said. His hand was on the back of my head, the other on my shoulder. "It's not your fault, buddy. You did everything you could."

"I'm going to see what I can find out," Larissa said, and she disappeared into the hellish circus of rescue workers.

After a minute, I pulled myself together. "Did you find Zorn?" I asked. "Is he part of it?"

"I found him at the TL station. He was as shocked as we were—more so. His legs literally gave out. I can tell you about it later. Short of it is, I believe him." He looked around. "He should be here any second. He was right behind us." He threw his chin toward the burning building. "Was it Taylor? Did she get high and set the place on fire?"

I shook my head. "No. She was passed out cold. Even so, I took her works. I have no idea how the fire got—" I started coughing. When I finally stopped, my vision was twinkling. I had to take a moment before I could continue. "Could have been the shop, I guess. We had a heating element go in one of the dryers, so—" I started hacking again. Every cough felt like a belt sander on raw skin.

"It's all right," Ronnie said. "We'll get it sorted. Save your breath for breathing." Then we watched as firefighters ran hoses up the second- and third-floor staircases. After a minute, Ronnie looked at my bare feet and said, "You need some shoes, sport. Hang tight." Then he too slipped into the chaos.

* * *

I just sat there watching my home go up in flames. Two weeks ago my biggest problem had been calculating how many drawings I needed to make to pay for the extravagant renovations I'd splurged on. And like a fool, I'd thought those were actual problems. I would have chastised myself for having been so self-absorbed, only that would have been equally as indulgent. Instead I thought about Taylor. Her life ruined before it had even had a chance to get started. And I found myself making a bargain. The entire building could burn down, and every one of my drawings could be lost, just so long as she got out. But I also knew it was a beggar's plea. Because as much as I wanted her to have been rescued moments after me, I knew how badly I'd been affected from being inside for only half a minute. I'd been lucky to have been pulled out when I was. She'd been there before me, and long after.

And as if to prove me right, just then a firefighter emerged from the second-floor doorway. Followed by another. Between them they held a stretcher, a white cloth draped over a body that I knew was Taylor's.

"No," a voice said beside me. I turned and was surprised to see Tally. She was also watching the body being carried out. "No." Her voice rose as she said it over and over again. "No, no no no no!"

I realized then that we weren't seeing the same scene—she thought they were carrying out Larissa.

"Tally," I said, but my voice caught in my shredded throat and I began coughing.

She turned to look at me, terror in her eyes.

"It's not," I tried to say, but couldn't catch any air. Then another voice cut in.

"They ain't the height of fashion," Ronnie said, coming toward me holding a pair of large boots, "but they'll—"

He stopped, looked at Tally. She looked at him.

His face dropped. "Crystal?"

36

CRYSTAL LAKE

Tally went instantly pale, then turned and ran off.

I tried to call out, but again ended up coughing.

"What was she doing here?" Ronnie said, handing me the boots.

"That was Tally," I managed to say, once I got the coughing under control. "Larissa's girlfriend." It was all I could do just to breathe. "She must have thought Taylor was Larissa. We have to go get her."

"Tally?" Ronnie said. "No. Whatever she's calling herself these days, that was Crystal Lake. The kid who shot Joe Chadwick."

"But——" My mind was not working well enough. "No," I said. "How can that be?" My words were hoarse, and I could barely get them out. "You said Crystal had blond hair. I remember. You said the image would stick with you forever. Of her angelic platinum white hair, stained with clumps of——" More coughing.

"Hell of a memory you got there. And you're right. Only the platinum was a dye-job. So yeah, I see your confusion. I never said the kid was Asian. I can see how you'd assume otherwise. And anyway, she'd told you her name was Tally. But no, that girl, no question. That's Crystal Lake."

I leaned back against the side of the ambulance. A long ladder was being extended from the top of a fire truck to the roof of my building. Spouts of water continued to arc toward the flames. "This is really fucked, you know that?" I squeezed the bridge of my nose with one hand. My head was pounding. I slipped on the boots. They were too big. Which was better than too small. I made to stand; Ronnie helped me. "Why did she lie? Do you think she's involved?" I still couldn't believe it.

"I don't think so," Ronnie said. "And I don't think she lied. I think she's just been trying to live her life."

335

Seemed a bit coincidental to me, though. Both her and Kai getting close to Larissa.

"And Zorn——" I started to say, only to spontaneously begin coughing again. "You say he claimed not to know what Chadwick was up to. You really believe him? That he had absolutely no idea at all about——" And once again I started coughing. My throat was destroyed.

Ronnie waited until it passed, then he said, "Zorn was completely in the dark about the Midnight rooms. I saw his face. Looked in his eyes. He didn't know. When I gave him the lowdown, he freely admitted to having set the unies on you at Chadwick's request. Everything Roberts already told us plus what we'd deduced. When you were out drawing on Naples, a couple-a kids from the sanc house got spooked by a guy across the street with a camera. They told Faith, then Faith told Zorn she was worried the house might be compromised. Our boy thought he was helping to protect a shelter for abused kids. As for the circus at the museum, Zorn had nothing to do with Abbs the bartender and wanted to kick the shit out of Roberts and Jantze himself for the idiocy they'd pulled."

I still wasn't buying it. Ronnie was as sharp as they came, but when it came to Martin Zorn, he had a tendency to——as Ronnie himself might have said——grab the blade instead of the handle. But now wasn't the time to push it.

"And Tally——Crystal?"

Ronnie looked off in the direction she'd run off, as if he might see her and get a sign, but of course she was long gone. He sighed and shook his head. "That one's a twister," he said.

"I can't believe I let her die," I said.

"You didn't let anybody do anything," Ronnie said, understanding that I meant Taylor. "This ain't your fault."

I just stared at my building, smoke billowing from the roof.

"I know it's no consolation," Ronnie said. "But she'd already put herself into dreamland with the smack. She was probably so sedated, she didn't feel a thing."

He was right, it wasn't any consolation. But for a hard-boiled guy who didn't always have the most tact, Ronnie really did try.

* * *

"You okay?" Ocampo said as she hurried toward us. "What the hell happened?" Larissa was with her. Ocampo had on an SFPD windbreaker, her badge clipped visibly to her belt.

"Not sure," Ronnie said. "You see Marty?"

"Zorn?" Ocampo said. "He's here?" She looked around, then back. "And the 10-54?" She was talking about the body taken from the second floor. "Taylor?"

Ronnie sighed and nodded yes.

"Damn," Ocampo said. "Poor kid. Think maybe it was Chadwick's sidekick? Kai? Retaliation for stealing the tapes and drive?"

Ronnie's head jerked back. "Would be a hell of a response, but—yeah, suppose we can't take it off the table. If he knew Taylor had come here, he might think he could take out the evidence and the witness with one strike of a match."

Ocampo snagged a firefighter hurrying by. Showed her badge and asked what he knew.

"Point of origin appears to have been ground level rear exterior staircase," the fireman said, first addressing Ocampo, then looking to all of us. "Currently unable to identify the source material, however, an accelerant was most certainly involved. Based on first assessment of burn patterns, my thought is rags and gasoline. The exterior structure was new material, so slower to catch, however, the building is ninety years give or take. And these old wood structures go up like tinderboxes. Ground and second floor rear were worst hit, where the event began. We arrived as acceleration progressed to the third floor. As of a few minutes ago, we were able to contain momentum and stop spread to neighboring buildings. Barring any sudden changes in wind, we should be able to prevent further escalation."

"Is any of the building livable?" I asked.

"As noted, sir, the rear received the greatest impact. All floors, rear to midway, are unreachable. Third floor we've managed to prevent spread to the front rooms, though due to smoke and water exposure, no part of the structure is inhabitable. However—" he cocked his head, appearing mildly amused "—the section left most intact is the laundromat. Pressure from the heat caused the water main to blow. You been having trouble with your regulator valve lately?"

I nodded. "Had it burst on me a few weeks ago."

"Yeah," the firefighter said. "Been seeing that a lot in this area lately. puc has been rerouting source lines as they upgrade piping. Has been messing with the pressure in these mid-range commercial businesses, causing surges. Enterprises such as yours use a smaller-volume line than major industrial, but much higher than your standard residential, so when they break, you've got what equates to a gushing fire hydrant inside your building. It's a nightmare when it happens on a normal day, but in an event like this it's a gift. The water surging from that line bought us enough time to prevent the entire structure from being lost, if not half the block from being contaminated. You can thank the PUC for falling ass-backwards into being helpful." Then he tipped his large hat and hustled back to work.

"So the laundromat saved the neighborhood," Larissa said.

I couldn't tell if she was making a joke or trying to make me feel better. In any case, I didn't care. I grabbed her and hugged her. Because as much sadness as I felt for losing Taylor, I was glad Larissa wasn't the one lying lifeless under a sheet.

*　　*　　*

"Come on," Ocampo said. "Let's get you inside somewhere. There's nothing you can do here."

"So Zorn didn't find you?" Ronnie said as Ocampo led me to her Crown Victoria. She and Ronnie had taken their own cars back. "He was supposed to be right behind us. How'd you know to come?"

"Same as you," Ocampo said. "Heard the 528 fire call on Guerrero go out over the radio. As for Zorn, I haven't seen or heard from him all day." She opened the driver's side door. "Why? How much did you tell him?"

Ronnie hesitated. "Everything."

"Jesus, Ron."

The four of us were standing beside the car, Ocampo with her hand on top of the open door. I was still wearing someone's oversized boots.

"I went with my gut," Ronnie said. "And I believe him."

"And how'd that work out for you? He was also supposed to follow you here. Which he obviously didn't. So I'll take your belief as far as I can throw it. You may have given him a pass, but as far as I'm concerned, Zorn is nowhere in the clear. He's way too in bed with Chadwick to be clean. And now you've given him everything we got—*and* he's in the wind."

"Crystal knows everything too," Larissa said. We all looked at her. She'd called Tally Crystal, intentionally, so we'd catch it. "Yeah," she said. "I know. She'd already told me everything about the night with Joe. I didn't care—and still don't. That night changed her life. It made her a different person. Which is why I thought she deserved to know the truth about Faith. But she didn't take it well."

"Like how not well?" Ocampo asked.

"As in she totally freaked out. We were at her apartment in the Lower Haight and she ran out. I thought maybe she might have gone to The Nest to confront Faith, so I went to look. But she wasn't there."

"That was a hell of a risk," Ocampo said.

"I said the same," Ronnie said.

"I know," Larissa said. "But I still had Kai's jeep, so I thought if I saw him, then I had a good excuse, which was that I was returning it."

"Was Chadwick or Kai there?"

"Not that I saw. But I didn't go inside. I only asked at the front desk if Tally had come in. From there I went to the Tenderloin police station to look for Ronnie. I knew he'd gone to talk to Inspector Zorn."

"That's where we connected," Ronnie said. "I'd gotten there an hour earlier. Enough time to have a heart-to-heart with Marty. Not long after our computer whiz here showed up we heard the 528 call come in, and the address. Larissa and me took my car, Zorn got in his own. The three of us were to race right over in tandem, but, as you can see, Zorn must have diverted."

"All right," Ocampo said, looking away for a second. I looked too. Fire-fighters were on the roof of my building. Swinging axes. "We have to find Zorn," she said. "And the girl."

"On it," Ronnie said. Then to Larissa, "You're with me."

"What can I do?" I said.

"You can try not to get yourself killed," Ocampo said. Then, as Ronnie and Larissa hurried off together, she added, "Come on. The manager at the Mark Hopkins owes me a favor. You can get a shower and a bed on me." She motioned to the passenger door. "And for once you can ride in the front."

37

GONE

As promised, Ocampo got me a comped suite at the Mark Hopkins hotel on Cathedral Hill. I ordered chicken soup and herbal tea with honey and loaded both with ice to try and ease the worst sore throat I'd ever had. Neither worked. I undressed and stuffed my smoke-drenched clothes inside a laundry bag, and only after I'd showered did I realize how wretched they smelled. So much that I called a porter to take them away. I lay down and passed out. I shouldn't have been able to—and didn't want to. Everyone but me was out there doing something: firefighters were extinguishing the blaze that was destroying my building, Ronnie and Larissa were looking for Martin and Crystal, and Ocampo was doing who knew what, but I hoped it was arresting Faith Chadwick and Kai whatever the hell his last name was. While all I was doing was lying clean and safe in a posh hotel room.

I woke up to the phone ringing just before 4 a.m. I tried to speak, but my throat seized up.

"They're safe," Ocampo said. "Larissa and Crystal. Ron's got them. Get some sleep. We'll connect tomorrow." Then she hung up. My mind was barely working, but I'd heard the word *safe*. So I went back to sleep.

* * *

At ten I woke with a pounding headache and razor blades in my throat. I was able to get down a little of the tea from the night before, then managed to order fruit and yogurt and iced coffee—and a bag of throat lozenges. When I opened my door to let the cart be wheeled in, I saw there was a uniformed cop stationed in the hallway.

Wearing a robe, I sat in the window overlooking San Francisco. It's a strange thing to have your home destroyed. What do you do? Where do you

Swedenborgian Church, San Francisco — Commissioned by Rena Macapagal and Colin Sebestyen

go? I supposed for people who had families and regular jobs, while they might have to live out of a hotel or a relative's guest room, they would also have routines such as school and work which they could resume and find some sense of normalcy in. But my entire life had been in that building. Even if I'd been so bold as to think I could go out and resume drawing commissions, I would have to first buy new supplies. And with what money? I had no bank card, no identification, no anything—hell, I didn't even have any clothes. I suddenly found myself even more grateful for Ocampo having put me up in such a swank hotel, when she could have just as easily put me in a seedy motel in the Tenderloin—or not helped at all and left me to fend on my own.

* * *

An hour and a half later I opened the door to let in my friend Adam Levy. He looked at me in my robe and the cop in the hallway and said, "So you finally went in for witness protection. I always knew you'd cave eventually."

"That's not funny," I managed to get out, in a soft, hoarse whisper. Then I looked at the cop. "He's joking."

Adam walked past me and I closed the door behind him. "Man alive. What happened?"

I popped my thousandth cough drop. "I wish I had the voice to tell you," I said. "But I can hardly—" Then, as if to prove my point, I began coughing. Each cough was an excruciating pain unlike any I'd ever experienced. It felt as if the skin inside my throat was being peeled off in ragged strips. "Clothes?" was all I managed to say after I'd recovered.

Adam slid a kid's backpack from his shoulder, one he'd probably had since the first grade. He was almost a foot shorter than me, and easily fifty pounds lighter, but he'd said he'd bring me some clothes. "I found some old basketball shorts with a stretched-out elastic waistband," he said. "And an oversized sweatshirt that someone must have left after a party. Oh, and an old pair of flip-flops—though I doubt those will fit very well."

"They'll be fine," I said.

"I can't believe someone set your building on fire," Adam said. "I drove by on the way here to make sure you weren't pulling my leg. You haven't let your insurance lapse, have you?"

"No," I said. "Paid up."

"Well, at least there's that."

I shrugged. We'd see. My insurance company had been my first call after Adam. I didn't know my policy number, and the agent taking my report didn't seem to grasp that it wasn't something I was able to access. I was told I'd need to go in to an office to verify my signature—with an ID I also didn't have—before a claim could be filed. The conversation inspired little confidence that the company would help me get back on my feet let alone cover what was quite possible the retaliatory act of an arsonist blackmailer. Also, there was the second floor to deal with. Which I didn't own. Despite having been employed to look after the unit, there'd be no denying that I'd overstepped by using it, seeing that's where Taylor's body had been recovered. If that wasn't cause for my insurance company to not only deny my claim but turn around and sue me, I didn't know what was. But there was nothing I could do about any of that at the moment. And if I was going to use my voice to explain anything to Adam, it was going to be the story of the past two weeks—and who Larissa was.

"Criminy, man," Adam said after I'd managed to get out the basics. My voice was barely audible by the end. "Well, crap. The least I can do is buy you a set of new clothes. I'll use the company credit card, and we can deduct it from your next advance if you ever find your way to write anything again."

"Always a pal."

With Adam dressed as he always was, in jeans, a fitted button-down, and a tailored blazer, and me dressed like a teenager who'd been left too long to live on his own, my old friend and I left the hotel. The cop outside the room didn't try to stop me, but he did radio in that I was leaving.

Adam took me shopping downtown, paid for my new clothes, bought me lunch, then, back in the hotel lobby, gave me a handful of hundreds. "Walking-around money," he said. "You'll pay me back when you're on your feet again."

Thanksgiving was the next day, and Adam asked what I was doing. I told him nothing. "I'm heading down to Palo Alto," he said. "It'll be twenty of the Levy clan, but you're welcome to tag along. They'll have so much food, one more mouth isn't going to make a difference. And with the way my family yells over each other, you wouldn't be able to get a word in even if you could talk."

If it had been a normal Emit–Adam interaction I would have made a snarky comment, but this was anything but normal. So I hugged him and managed to say, "Thanks for being my weird family." Which he didn't know what to do with, and which also felt right to me.

* * *

As I passed by the front desk I thought I saw the concierge eye me and pick up the phone. But given that twice in the past week I'd been falsely arrested, and the night before my house had been set on fire, I may have been slightly paranoid. On my floor the cop was still stationed outside my door. Seeing me coming down the hallway, he did as he'd done when I left, bending his neck to speak into the radio attached to the upper portion of his vest.

"Mister Hopper," he said to me as I slid the keycard into my door. "Lieutenant Ocampo requests you remain in the room until she arrives." And of course, no, he couldn't say why.

A half hour later there was a knock at the door. I looked through the peephole to see Ocampo and another uniformed cop. I opened the door.

"Have you seen or heard from any of them?" Ocampo said to me, pushing her way in. Her voice was firm and authoritative.

I shook my head as the cop went to the bathroom and turned on the light. I'd exhausted my voice with Adam, and my throat felt like it had been scraped with a broken bottle. I opened my hands and did my best to convey the question, "What happened?"

"You sure?" Ocampo said. "You didn't meet with any of them while out on your shopping spree? Not Larissa, not Ronnie, not Zorn or Crystal?"

Now I was annoyed. *Spree?* What the hell was I supposed to do? Live in a bathrobe? If I'd had a voice I would have said, "What the fuck did I just say? No, I haven't seen them. Now tell me what's going on." Instead I reached for the hotel stationery and a pen. But my body language must have conveyed all of my intentions.

"You need to sit down," Ocampo said. "There's been a development."

I looked at her, then the cop. The cop had checked the bathroom, bedroom, and closet, and was now standing perfectly still, watching me. I took the pad of paper and pen to the sitting area and sat on the stiff Elizabethan sofa. Ocampo sat in one of the equally stiff regal chairs opposite me. "Order us some coffee, will you?" she said to the cop, who moved to the phone, picked up the receiver, and pressed the button for room service.

"Faith Chadwick and Kai Sjugard are dead," Ocampo said. "Shot at the Chadwick residence at approximately midnight last night. Roughly an hour after our little band of misfits parted outside your burning building."

*   *   *

The doorbell to my suite rang again, and the cop answered it. A hotel porter wheeled in a cart with a pot of French press coffee, three dainty cups, and a set of milk and sugar. Also on the tray was a plate with a metal dome. He pushed the cart over to where Ocampo and I were sitting, pressed the plunger on the coffee, then lifted the dome to reveal a plate of freshly cut fruit and melon. Then, without an expectation of a tip, he turned and left. The cop and Ocampo immediately poured themselves coffee and loaded their small porcelain cups with cream and sugar. They looked like lions over a fresh kill. I waited until they backed away from the carcass, then took a piece of cantaloupe. It felt soft and cool on my burning throat.

"You obviously have questions," Ocampo said. "I won't make you write them. Here's what we know: At approximately 12:15 this morning, officers responded to a 216, shots fired, corner of Jackson and Laguna. Residents reported hearing roughly a dozen shots in succession. No evidence of foul play was found on the street. Officers then encountered Inspector Zorn on scene. He exited from the front door of what was later determined to be the residence of Faith Chadwick. Officers did not question his presence, though they did wonder why an inspector had been called out, especially at that hour. You may not know this, but as a rule, inspectors and sergeants don't like to leave their desks unless there's a confirmed 187, homicide. However, with the neighborhood being Pacific Heights, officers assumed one of the residents had connections, so the irregularity was dismissed. The inspector immediately confirmed this assumption when he informed officers that the resident was a personal friend and called him directly, and he——"

I was waving my hand, and she paused. I scribbled on my pad: *I thought you were looking for Zorn?*

"Yes," Ocampo said. "I'd put word out to all stations to have Inspector Zorn radio in if any officers made contact. But I kept it low-key. I didn't want to ring the alarm bell too loud. Roberts and Jantze aren't the only friends Zorn has. And at the time I had nothing to pin on him. I just needed to find him and keep him contained."

I scribbled quickly, then flashed the pad: *Had nothing on him—AT THE TIME?!?*

Ocampo moved her head quickly. "Let me finish," she said. "When officers encountered Inspector Zorn on scene, he reported that he had spoken to this friend at the residence and that she believed the shots had been fired from a moving vehicle, not at any house, but in the air. Officers inquired as to whether the inspector wanted a search conducted along the street for shell casings, at which time the inspector laughed off the report, saying he believed the incident was not gunfire but firecrackers, adding a joke about the 'specific whites' of the area not knowing the difference. He then instructed officers to leave the scene. At which point the officers radioed in an all-clear and left the area. Thirteen hours later, shortly after 1 p.m. this afternoon—" Ocampo looked at her watch "—approximately three hours ago, a neighbor reported a potential break-in at the residence of Faith Chadwick—at the corner of Jackson and Laguna. Officers responded to find a broken windowpane on a rear door and the door ajar. Officers entered the premises and proceeded to the third floor, where they discovered the bodies of Faith Chadwick and Kai Sjugard in the master bedroom. Both were unclothed. Chadwick was in bed, Sjugard on the floor. Preliminary assessment suggests he had been reaching for a gun in a bedside drawer, which was determined to have been unfired."

"Who?" I made to say, the word barely audible.

"One weapon was used to kill both victims. Caliber is not a match to Inspector Zorn's service pistol. At the moment we cannot say who fired the weapon. Initial report from the inspector on scene suggests the evidence points to the incident being a robbery gone wrong."

I laughed, even though it made my chest feel like a bag of broken bottles.

"And so I ask you again," Ocampo said. "In the three hours you were out, did you have any contact with either Larissa, Crystal, Ronnie, or Zorn? And in case you're wondering, yes, you were being followed. For your protection. But you've also participated in training exercises, and you know that not every interaction can be observed."

"No," I managed to say, my voice no more than a whisper. From there I took up my pad. I tore off the top sheet of scrawl and wrote on the next sheet: *I swear. No contact. What about Sausalito? You said they were safe?*

"As of four this morning, this was my understanding. However, following the discovery at the Chadwick residence, I had Mill Valley PD call on Ronnie's houseboat, and there was no one home. And according to neighbors, no one has been there for at least a day. Certainly not two young women. And Ron Gilbert has not checked in with his answering service."

I nodded. Ronnie had said the houseboat community was a gossipy bunch, so they would definitely know.

And Zorn?

"Inspector Martin Zorn has not been seen since the encounter with officers at the Chadwick residence at 00:15 this morning."

After the shots were reported?

Ocampo pressed her lips together.

Why didn't you know about the incident earlier?

"Are you referring to the shots fired at the Chadwick residence?"

I nodded.

"As I said, Inspector Zorn is a personable guy." She exhaled through her nose and quickly shook her head. She'd been being very formal, which, considering the situation, I wasn't taking personally. But now her tone became more casual. "I don't know. I'm thinking the unies probably told Zorn I was looking for him and probably made some joke about how you can't trust something that bleeds for seven days and doesn't die. I may be a lieutenant, but the police force is still an old boys' club."

So, nothing complicit? I wrote. *No one trying to help him get away?*

"I don't think so. Though now that the murders have been discovered, the bell is full-on rung. There's going to be a serious investigation by Internal Affairs. The D.A. will not take the killing of a high-society figure like Faith Chadwick lightly. It'll take time; but if Zorn or the officers on scene were in any way involved, we'll eventually get to the bottom of it."

My head was pounding, mostly from all the toxic smoke I'd inhaled, but also from lack of caffeine. So, despite how much my throat hurt, I poured myself some coffee, though only half a cup. The rest I filled with cream. I drank carefully, then managed to say, "Faith and Kai. Lovers?"

"Apparently."

I took up the notepad again. *Tell me honest. What do you think? Did Zorn kill them? Then go after Ronnie and the girls?*

"All I know is we have two dead bodies and four missing persons: an ex-cop turned private investigator; an ex-member of The Nest; a current computer genius; and an active SFPD inspector. All of whom had connections with the victims."

Let me guess, don't go out on any more shopping sprees?

"And maybe stay away from the windows."

Atlas Stair Building, 22nd Street, San Francisco — Commissioned by Ashley Gunn. Ashley was calm but resolute when she first came to the studio. She said she'd had enough of San Francisco. She'd come in her twenties, believing the city was a place of open-mindedness and acceptance, and now that she was in her thirties she was disillusioned and ready to leave. When a few weeks later she returned to pick up the drawing she was angry. Seemed the day before, she'd found a patch of freshly poured concrete on the sidewalk in her neighborhood. Feeling she could finally "put her mark on this town before leaving," she'd signed her name: A. Gunn, '99. Then, the next day, on her way to see me, she noticed someone had also written in the wet cement. They'd scratched a line through her name and wrote: Fuck the NRA. *She said she couldn't get out of the city fast enough. She lived across the street from the Atlas Building, which she'd always loved waking up to, but was now more than happy to never see again, other than as a drawing.*

38

THE HALL OF JUSTICE

I passed the evening in an anxious and restless state. My thoughts were spinning off in a thousand different scenarios. Some strange, some bad, some worse. It was the flip side to having a creative mind. When poisoned with fear, it was a nightmare machine. I decided to put it to work. I took up the pad of hotel stationery and began outlining everything that had happened, everything I thought I knew. I wasn't trying to solve any mystery, and I wasn't thinking of writing a future book. I was just trying to tame the beast.

When I ran out of paper, I called down and managed to convey that I needed more. I was also hungry, but could barely swallow, so I ordered mac and cheese and let it congeal to room temperature before attempting to push it down my throat. When the writing became exhausting I dialed up pay-per-view movies but still couldn't concentrate. Every hour that Larissa, Ronnie, and Crystal remained missing was a ratchet-turn higher in anxiety.

When the phone rang just past ten-thirty, I had simultaneous feelings of relief and terror. It was Ocampo. "You need to get down to 850 Bryant. ASAP." As I hung up, there was a knock on the door. I answered it while tying my robe. It was the cop stationed in the hallway. Different from the one earlier. Shift change, I assumed.

"I'm to escort you downtown," she said.

I closed the door and got dressed.

* * *

Eight-fifty Bryant is San Francisco's Hall of Justice, which is Police Department headquarters and County Superior Court. A police cruiser dropped me in front as if a taxi. Inside, I walked through the metal detector, then took an elevator to the fourth floor. When I stepped out, Ocampo was there waiting. Her call a half hour earlier had been brief, but not as brief as her simply telling me to come. She'd also told me they were all right—Larissa, Ronnie, and Crystal. Though she hadn't mentioned Martin Zorn.

"So what—" I started to say.

"Better you hear it for yourself," Ocampo said. She set off down the hall and I followed.

The hallway was gray and busy with cops in uniforms and men and women in suits. With all the commotion, you wouldn't have guessed that it was almost midnight on Thanksgiving eve, and I wondered what the place was like in the middle of the afternoon on a regular weekday.

Ocampo put her hand on a door handle but stopped before opening. "Technically," she said, "you shouldn't be in here. I'm playing the card that you're a family member, but even that is stretching it thin. If this ever goes to trial, you could be considered a co-conspirator, which would make what I'm about to do a criminal act."

I just stood there. I'd come all this way, on her invitation, and after all that had happened, felt I had a right to be let in on whatever was going on. I understood that she needed to give her little speech, if for no one other than herself. But I had no patience for it. And I'm certain the look on my face conveyed just that.

"I know," she said. "But I have to at least pretend I'm trying to play by the rules."

Then she opened the door and I followed her inside.

*   *   *

The space was just as I'd seen in movies and on countless TV shows: small, dark, and bare, with one large pane of glass—which I presumed was one-way—looking into an interrogation room. Inside, at a table, were three people: Larissa, a man who fit the bill perfectly for a high-priced attorney, and another man who was obviously a cop. The roles in this building were so well cast that it gave me an uncomfortable feeling that there was only one way this could go.

"I've already answered that," Larissa was saying. The interview had already started. "Rephrasing the question isn't going to change the answer."

Ocampo leaned close and said, "You haven't missed anything important."

"Tell me again," the interviewer said. "Why did you leave your house?"

"A," Larissa said, "it wasn't my house. And B—"

Larissa's lawyer whispered in her ear.

Larissa rolled her eyes, but nodded her head. "I get it," she said. Then, putting on the largest and fakest smile she could, turned back to the interviewer and said, "I left Emit Hopper's flat because I wanted to inform Crystal Lake that I had been presented with evidence that Faith Chadwick and Kai Sjugard were exploiting young women from The Nest to extort political favors from powerful men."

"And this is evidence which you received from Taylor Greene? Who had purportedly taken videotapes and a computer from a vault in the basement of 240 Hyde Street? The former Midori Hotel, now home of The Nest Youth Center?"

"A hard drive," Larissa said. "Not a computer. And yes, which Taylor removed from Kai's safety-deposit box in the basement of The Nest—or at least that's what she said she did."

"And this is the evidence which you have handed over to the District Attorney's office in electronic form?"

"This is the drive that Lieutenant Ocampo took from Taylor. What she did with it, I don't know."

"And where are the originals of these documents?"

"There are no originals. They're all—" she turned to her lawyer "—do I really need to give this guy a tutorial on electronic data?" The lawyer tilted his head. Larissa turned back to the interviewer and once more put on a fake smile. "The files have metadata which will link to the source machine on which they were originally created. Someone who knows more than you will understand."

The interviewer stared at her, then decided to move on.

"And were you able to locate Miss Crystal Lake? Who I understand you knew as Tally?"

It went on like this for another hour. That Larissa didn't grab the interviewer's head and rattle it back and forth was a testament to a patience I wouldn't have bet she had. The gist of her story was this:

Larissa drove Kai's jeep to Tally's place on the Lower Haight. Being lovers, Tally had already confided in Larissa her former identity as Crystal, and her role in Joe Chadwick's death. Larissa only cared for her all the more for it. Which is why she believed Tally deserved to know the truth about Faith Chadwick.

Tally hadn't taken the news well, though. She'd run off.

Larissa was afraid that Tally would go to The Nest and confront Faith, so she drove there in Kai's jeep, hoping to stop her. When Tally failed to show at The Nest, Larissa went to the Tenderloin police station. She knew Ronnie had gone there looking for Inspector Zorn, and after she inquired with the desk sergeant, both Martin and Ronnie appeared. Ronnie had already informed Martin of what they'd learned about Faith.

Martin professed to know nothing of Faith's blackmail schemes, and Ronnie said he believed him. Larissa was inclined to believe him as well. Larissa told them that Tally had run off. It was then that they heard the report of a fire in the Mission, and recognized the address as mine.

Ronnie and Larissa rushed over in Ronnie's car. Zorn said he would be right behind, however, he failed to show at the fire. Larissa did not know where he went. The Tenderloin police station was the last she had seen of Inspector Zorn. Approximately twenty-eight hours earlier.

As for Tally, Larissa couldn't account for her every step because she hadn't been with her, but as she later came to learn, Tally had walked around her neighborhood, the Lower Haight, to process all she'd heard, then eventually returned home. Finding Larissa gone, and wanting to apologize, she then walked to my place in the Mission, roughly fifteen minutes away, only to see the building on fire and a body being carried out. Thinking the body was Larissa, Tally once again ran off.

Larissa and Ronnie went after her. They again thought to try The Nest, and this time found Tally in the Tenderloin, on her way to confront Faith.

Upon seeing that Larissa was alive, Tally had broken down in tears of joy.

Larissa and Ronnie had come upon Tally on the street, so Larissa was unable to say whether Faith, Kai, or Martin were inside The Nest.

Ronnie, fearing for the girls' safety, quickly whisked Larissa and Tally away. Suspecting that Kai had set the fire that had killed Taylor, and that he was an ongoing potential danger, Ronnie took them to Monte Rio, a small town two hours north of San Francisco, along the Russian River, where he owned a remote cabin, off the grid, with no phone or Internet.

Larissa was unable to say what time exactly, but she guessed it had been around two or three in the morning when they arrived in Monte Rio. "The place is pretty rustic," she'd said of Ronnie's cabin. "It's literally powered by generators." Ronnie got them comfortable, then drove into the one-road town, looking for a pay phone that worked. He called Ocampo to report that the girls were safe, though apparently he didn't say where. When he got back to the cabin, he informed the girls that I, Emit, was also safe, recuperating at the Mark Hopkins Hotel, and that Ocampo would pass the message on to me that they were all also safe.

The next morning Ronnie went into town again to buy supplies and once more check in by phone with Ocampo. When he returned, he said there'd been no updates. This, she now understood, was before the bodies of Faith and Kai had been discovered. "As far as we knew," Larissa said, "Faith, Kai, and Martin were all alive and out there doing whatever they might be doing. We all agreed it was best to stay put. And anyway, Tally was still pretty upset."

That evening, the Monte Rio sheriff came knocking. Ocampo had traced the calls Ronnie had made to a Russian River pay phone and sent the sheriff to find him. The sheriff knew Ronnie and the location of his cabin. He informed Ronnie that Faith Chadwick and her young lover had been murdered. Ronnie immediately called Ocampo. She confirmed the deaths of Faith and Kai and informed him that Martin Zorn was still unaccounted for. She also suggested that he and the girls return to San Francisco to make a formal statement, at which point they packed up and returned. And now, here they were.

It was at this point that the interviewer began backtracking, asking the same questions again, and Larissa looked at her lawyer and said, "You need to stop this," to which the lawyer announced that his client would be answering no more questions for the time being. The lawyer motioned for Larissa to stand, which she did, and, without protest from the interviewing cop, escorted her out of the room.

I asked Ocampo what would happen next.

"She's done nothing wrong, so it will take a few minutes to process her out, but then she's free to go."

"What about the others?"

"Same." She smirked. "Larissa hired her hot-shot firm to represent all three of what I'm calling the Merry Trio—which I'm guessing she'll do for you as well."

"For me?" I said. "Why would I need a lawyer? Why would any of us need one?"

"You'll need to give a statement regarding the fire and Taylor Greene," Ocampo said, not answering my question. "But it can wait. For now, everyone's holding their breath for the other shoe to drop."

I didn't have to ask what—or, rather, who—the shoe was. It was Inspector Martin Zorn.

Menlo Park, CA — Patrons asked to be unnamed. A retired couple who requested I hand-deliver the drawing, then surprised me with a home-cooked dinner and sent me home with a cherry pie.

39

AFTERMATH

I've had a fair number of interesting Thanksgivings over the years. At eighteen, during our first year in Los Angeles, Brian and I dressed in drag and dined at an all-you-can-eat Indian buffet. This was before the band had any legs, when we were living hand to mouth. We ended up closing the place down and getting drunk with the owners, a couple from Mumbai who'd been married for fifty years. There was another year that I celebrated America's pilgrim holiday in a small northern Thailand village with an ex-u.s. marine named Roy. Instead of turkey, we roasted a wild boar that he'd caught and killed, and that I'd helped him tie to a spit. There have been other unconventional celebrations of holidays too, but Larissa and I dining with Adam and the Levy family, as seemingly normal as it was, would rank pretty high on the list of memorable Thanksgivings.

To start, I could still barely speak. Which, despite Adam's having been spot-on about a room full of lively people talking loudly over each other, did not mean I was able to get away with sitting quietly. This was family. Everything these people had to say to each other had been said a dozen times before. Whereas I was a novelty, and they had more than a few questions: Why did I not write books anymore? So I used to be a rock star? Why do kids these days like such terrible music? Someone burned my house down? Why did someone burn my house down? Luckily, I had Larissa to deflect. I'd seen her be social, but she could also be slightly awkward and at times abrasive. But she fit in perfectly with the Levy clan. Yelling across the table right along with the lot of them, it was as if she'd been there with Adam's mother and his aunts and uncles growing up on New York's Lower East Side, or with Adam when he was eight years old and traded a page he'd torn out of a magazine to a boy in his class for a new toy truck, only to have the teacher call his parents

355

to warn them that their son was on the road to becoming a con man. It was as if she'd always been part of the family, and for that I was truly thankful.

*　*　*

The weeks following were many things. One being my thirty-eighth birthday, which I celebrated alone, in Steven Thorn's house—formerly Jerry Garcia's—above Stinson Beach, with a bottle of Russian River Pinot, a New York strip, and intermittent soaks in the hot tub. The other, more significant event, was the lead-up to the end of a millennium. The year 2000 was coming—at least for the Western world—promising to be the New Year's to end all New Years. And along with it was the dreaded Y2K, the fear that computer systems around the world would fail in succession with each changing time zone. People were maxing out their daily ATM withdrawals, anticipating the crash of the international banking networks, while others were flying to remote islands in case the computers controlling nuclear power plants malfunctioned and set off worldwide meltdowns. I'd expected Larissa to roll her eyes and call them all idiots. But she'd just nodded and said, "It's a real thing. But programmers have been working on it for a long time. They've been recoding all the two-digit yearly formats to a four-digit system. Everything's going to be fine." Which somehow gave me hope for everything else.

And by everything else, I mean quite a lot.

The aftermath of what ultimately came to be known as "The Nest Murders"—among many other more-colorful titles, which I'll get to later—was a chaos equal to, and yet entirely different from, the chaos of the two weeks that led up to them. The best way for me to explain the time between Thanksgiving and New Year's is to divide the events into two categories: the public, and the private.

I'll start with the public.

Reports of Faith Chadwick's murder were front-page news. "Philanthropist and Young Lover Gunned Down in Love Nest." That the forty-seven-year-old head of a charitable organization whose mission was to help troubled youth was sleeping with a twenty-four-year-old former resident became an instant and easy scandal. The irony was that the smear campaign ended there. There was no mention of abuse of minors within The Nest, blackmailing of pedophiles, or the use of Operation Midnight Climax rooms. Allegations that Faith may have been involved with the highly controversial network of Sanctuary Houses resurfaced, but only as a recycling of old speculations to

356

help stir the pot. In the cafés and on the streets, San Franciscans relished the gossip of Faith's illicit yet shallow affair, with no idea the depth of scandal they could have been savoring.

It seemed shocking, but when you looked at the actual evidence against Faith and Kai, it made sense. The tapes Taylor had provided, which Ocampo had taken to a judge, had no direct link to Faith Chadwick and could not be identified as having been filmed in any of her properties. Investigators might attempt to track down the girls in the videos, but even then, what would they say? That they'd received an anonymous message on an untraceable pager to appear at an address? And even if they managed to remember the addresses after so much time, and those addresses could be linked to those on the list of shell holdings on the spreadsheet on the hard drive, the connections would be only circumstantial. Prosecutors would still have to prove that Faith not only knew, but actively coordinated the recordings—and this was assuming any of the girls could be found. The judge hadn't even signed off on a warrant for the Golden Gate property, citing insufficient cause. He had said that if Ocampo provided an affidavit from Taylor stating she'd met a man for paid sex in that room, he would consider authorizing a search, but of course all of that was moot now that Taylor was dead.

After the killings of Faith and Kai, investigators had been able to search The Nest with the premise that one of the residents may have committed the murders, which gave them cause to open all of the safety-deposit boxes. But along with finding no evidence pointing to a murder or robbery suspect, they also found no evidence linking Faith or Kai to any criminal activities. Whatever tapes and additional evidence might have previously been in the vault had been removed, presumably by Kai, after he'd discovered what Taylor had taken.

Even the hard drive ended up going nowhere. Financial analysts were poring over the spreadsheets—as was Larissa—however, at best, it was looking like the only crime those documents could prove was that Faith was guilty of tax evasion for hiding a significant number of properties in shell cor- porations. Even the argument that the properties were being used as Sanctu- ary Houses was little more than conjecture. The underground organization was thought to be a network made up of many arms with no head. While suspected of being a significant contributor to the cause, Faith was only one arm, and the moment her death was announced, the other arms would have severed all connections that might connect back to them. Then there was the provenance of the digital files, which couldn't be authenticated. Taylor was dead, and so couldn't testify as to where she'd gotten the drive. And even if, as Larissa claimed, a digital footprint could be traced back to computers at The Nest, the place was accessible to hundreds of less-than-trustworthy young people, many of whom were good with computers. Anyone could have created those documents in an attempt to discredit Faith. I hated to admit it, but when I looked at it from the side of the prosecutor, all of what I'd believed to have been indisputable and damning evidence amounted to little more than scraps of innuendo about people who were no longer among the living to defend themselves.

As for the murders, in short time the initial ruling that the deaths of Faith and Kai were the result of a burglary gone wrong quickly became official. And again, when looking at the evidence, it was hard to fault investigators for their conclusion. Faith Chadwick's house had in fact been ransacked. Works of art, jewelry, silver, and all the valuables one would expect to go missing after a burglary were gone. A safe had been opened and emptied. Even Kai's wallet had been taken from his pants pocket.

Then there were the politics. Mayor Brown's project had been heavily invested with the Chadwick Development firm on the Mission Bay project, a fact which the Ammiano campaign attempted to exploit as a political scandal, calling out Willie and his cronies for "continued flagrant abuse of back room deals and blatant disregard for public good." But it was all political theater. There was no sound reasoning for how the murder of Faith was in any way related to the election or corruption. For the administration's part, Mayor Willie Brown gave an impassioned, yet brief and ambiguous speech about the deep sadness he felt for the loss of Faith Chadwick, "a true San Franciscan," and left it at that.

There was another angle, though: Inspector Martin Zorn, the San Francisco police officer who had been close with Faith Chadwick and The Nest, who had gone missing the night of the killings and not been seen since. This fact had not been immediately released. Not until Friday, December 10— two and a half weeks after the murders, and four days before the runoff election—did it become public. And even then the news was dubious. It came not as an announcement, but as the report filed by the officers who had responded to the shots-fired call the night of the murders, which included their account of having encountered Inspector Zorn outside the property, leaked by an 'anonymous source within the police department' to a reporter at the *Chronicle*. This of course raised more than a few brows, and it didn't take much imagination to think the timing of the leak was political, instigated by the Brown administration in an effort to wipe away any aspersions Faith's death might cast over the runoff election. And nobody was feeling shy in saying so. The *Chronicle*—while simultaneously publishing the report—flat-out called the move "An Abuse of Reign to Further Reign."

The strategy worked, though. In response to the leaked report, and under fire from the public, the District Attorney's office released a statement saying that "The matter of Inspector Zorn was being taken very seriously, and had been kept confidential while being investigated internally." Adding, "The investigation into the deaths is now unofficially being centered around the missing inspector." And instantly, all those who'd believed the burglary conclusion to have been a cover-up now had a new culprit to point to. Not the amorphous political power machine, but a very real and defined police inspector within that machine. The scenario formed itself: Martin Zorn had been cozy with the Chadwicks from his first days on the force. He'd moved to the Tenderloin and volunteered at The Nest in his off-duty hours. He was known to bring kids from the street into the shelter rather than put them into the system. All upstanding and noble deeds, if not for the fact that he had been on scene seemingly at the same time as shots had been reported, and was now missing. The conclusion was an easy one to draw: Martin Zorn and Faith Chadwick had been lovers. He discovered she was having an affair with her younger subordinate Kai, and, in a fit of jealous rage, killed them both.

As for explaining the robbery, of course it was staged. If not by Zorn himself, then by professional thieves who Zorn invited in—because of course a police inspector would be cozy with more than his share of unsavory characters. One opinion headline read "Thieves Lucky Day," followed by an imagined scenario of a thief in his pajamas preparing for bed, only to get a call from Zorn offering a house full of valuables. "You'd be doing me a solid by clearing the place out," the imagined inspector had told him.

When the election was over—with Willie having emerged victorious—and Zorn nowhere to be found, fervor for these sorts of wild speculations only grew as editors found themselves desperate to fill the void in the news cycle. The mayor, now secure in having had his crown polished and returned, also took an opportunity to take a potshot at the police department for their mishandling of evidence and potential obfuscation. But that too was theater. All of which resulted in an even more painful ironic twist, which was that the spotlight turned even further away from Faith and the chance of exposing her criminal activities. Occasionally, speculation of Faith's potential connection to Sanctuary Houses would stir, but with the absent Inspector Zorn as an easy go-to villain, editors, as well as the public, were more inclined to focus on Faith as a tragic hero. When alive, she'd been attacked the same as all high-profile figures are, called a calculated climber, and even compared to a Southern plantation owner. But in death, she was the rags-to-riches symbol of the Western spirit, a symbol of feminism oppressed by the patriarchy, and a slew of other overblown and trite attributions. The short of it being, the police department officially changed its ruling from Homicide During the Commission of Burglary to Domestic Homicide, and all hope that the criminal deeds of Faith Chadwick would come to light disappeared as quickly as Tom Ammiano's name from voters' lips. Faith Chadwick and Kai Sjugard were the victims, and Inspector Martin Zorn was the killer. And with the inspector gone—having avoided capture through either the ineptitude or willful disinterest of the police—there was no evidence to refute the conclusion. This was nothing more than a run-of-the-mill killing by a jealous lover. A crime to fit neatly into a box.

*   *   *

That was what happened in public. Then there was the private, meaning all that transpired between me, Ocampo, and—who the lieutenant called "the Merry Trio"—Ronnie, Larissa, and Crystal.

For my part, I'd been annoyed by the burglary conclusion, but even more so by the final declaration of a lovers' quarrel. Which is what the D.A.—as well as the press and the public—all took to be fact. It was too close to what I believed was true, making it that much harder to refute. I believed that yes, Martin Zorn had shot and killed Faith Chadwick and Kai Sjugard, then staged the burglary. What I didn't believe was the motive. And motive was everything. It meant the difference between Martin having been a common jealous lover versus having been a disillusioned cop who, for years, had been manipulated by Faith, and had finally meted out his own brand of justice.

I believed that after Ronnie told Martin of our evidence against Faith, Martin's world imploded. He finally saw the truth, that Faith had used him to set up her husband, Joe, possibly even kill him, and had gone on to take advantage of the young women she had been claiming to protect. Whether Joe had in fact been a pedophile and was in on the abuse with Faith, or she had simply wanted to get rid of him to have all the power, I didn't know, and almost didn't care. The point was, she had manipulated Martin. She'd taken his unbridled need to do good and used it to do harm, and for the next seven years continued to exploit him. And once Martin was faced with evidence provided by his ex-partner—who Faith had also coerced him into manipulating—the denial he had been so good at maintaining finally gave way, and he snapped. He went to Faith's house and killed her.

So in that way, Martin had, as everyone assumed, killed out of rage. Just not the rage they thought. And the consequence of that mistaken detail meant not just a difference in how the public saw Martin, but in how they saw Faith. It was a contrast as stark as they came: between hero and villain.

Next was Ocampo. She knew there was a link between the recording room where Joe Chadwick had been shot and the Midnight rooms where the underage blackmail recordings were being made, but whether she knew the full backstory of Martin having constructed the original Midnight room for Faith, I couldn't say. I knew Ronnie filled her in on some of the details, but I doubted he gave her all. And neither of them was telling me. Having met Taylor and seen the documents on the hard drive, Ocampo had been convinced that Faith Chadwick was involved with the Sanctuary Houses. However, from there her suspicions wavered. The tapes and drive hadn't been enough to convince a judge, and, as a cop, she too had been inclined to focus on what she could prove. "The best we can do at the moment," she said to me that night at the Hall of Justice, "is to find Zorn." And on that front she had more than a few questions. Starting with the Merry Trio.

Her problem was that Ronnie and Crystal's stories were the same as Larissa's—as in, "*exactly* the same," she'd said. Implying that they were too much so. I might have countered with something like, "Isn't truth always the same?" had her comment not rung a disturbing bell. It made me think of the story Ronnie had told me about the night Joe Chadwick had been killed, about how he had coached Crystal on what to tell the police, so that her story—the version Ronnie had invented—would ring true without contradicting the scene. I didn't tell Ocampo this of course, nor was I saying I didn't believe the trio. Only that I understood how she might think there was more to the story than what they were telling.

As for her thoughts on the missing Inspector Martin Zorn, when I asked her if she thought I should be worried—if any of us should be—she said she didn't think so. "He's got nothing against any of you," she said. "But we also can't close the book on this thing until we find him. I have every state-wide agency reviewing toll-booth videos, airport surveillance, train and bus station cameras, you name it, looking for our damn inspector. I've got beat cops interviewing junkies and hookers in case he went to the street for help. But this guy is nowhere to be found. He hasn't been to his apartment, hasn't used his credit cards, hasn't shown his face in one regular haunt. I'm starting to think he threw himself off the Golden Gate."

Only, Martin Zorn hadn't killed himself—at least not yet. He would take twenty years to get around to doing that. And that he ultimately would is either fitting or ironic, I've yet to decide which. But of course, at the time we had no idea what had become of him. He could have taken his own life as Ocampo had suggested, fled to Mexico—where he'd slipped away after the death of Joe Chadwick—or, some speculated, been kidnapped from the Chadwick residence, killed, and buried in any number of the abandoned mines in the Headlands in order to make him appear to have been the murderer. Such was the extent to which no one knew what to make of Martin Zorn's disappearance.

Ronnie was less concerned.

"My job was to track down who was blackmailing my client," he said. "And I did that. The rest is up to the people who get paid to care."

I wasn't sure I believed him, but I had other questions.

This was two days after Thanksgiving. Martin Zorn had been gone three and a half days, and already it seemed consensus was that he was never coming back. Ronnie had phoned, inviting me out for a sail on the bay. "Feel the wind in your hair," he said. "Will do us both some good."

I met Ronnie in the Sausalito Marina and we boarded a forty-foot sailboat being lent to him by a friend. The friend wasn't there, but his small crew was, three young people who managed the ship's rigging and paid us no mind. While they navigated us out of the harbor, Ronnie remained his tight-lipped self, and I joked that if he wanted to buy my silence he didn't have to dump me out at sea, just give me a place to live. Once we were on the water he opened up, starting with a bottle of something called Eagle Rare bourbon. He poured us each a fat glass. The bay was relatively calm, but even still, the boat bobbed up and down in the undulating waves. "You might not want to spill any of that," Ronnie said about the whiskey. "It runs about seventy-bucks a shot."

We managed to down two shots each, spilling only maybe twenty dollars' worth, then moved to the deck and sat in two fixed chairs under the mainsail. The crew was far enough away and the sounds of the water loud enough that we might as well have been alone.

"It's over, sport," Ronnie said. "The evidence we had wasn't enough, and whatever more there may have been is gone."

"You think that's why Martin killed them?" I asked. "Because he thought they'd never be brought to justice? Or was it because he finally realized how evil Faith was and took revenge?"

"I can think of another reason."

He gave me time to mull it over, then the answer came to me. "The Nest," I said. "He did it to save The Nest. If Faith was prosecuted, all the good she'd done would be destroyed. And if she wasn't prosecuted, she'd keep on doing harm. That's what you're saying, right? That you believe Martin Zorn really was innocent, so much so, that, in the end, even by murdering two people, he was still trying to be the crusader?"

At first Ronnie didn't answer. He just stared out at the horizon as the boat rocked up and down in the waves.

Eventually he said, "I'm saying I think Martin Zorn is a tragedy."

"If you ask me," I said, "the real tragedy is that Faith Chadwick is going down as a saint."

"Maybe. But at least it's over."

I wanted to say: "But it's not. How can it be? With Zorn still unaccounted for?" But I knew what he meant. That this chapter of Operation Midnight Climax, Faith's chapter, of manipulating young women to extort favors from influential men, was over, and that was no small thing.

As he was often so good at, though, Ronnie could tell this wasn't enough for me. "I know," he said. "But better not to tax your noggin with things you can't change. Thinking too much will put you in an early grave."

"So will not thinking enough," I said.

Ronnie snorted, then he reached into the pocket of his windbreaker. "Here," he said, offering me a small gift wrapped in newspaper. "It might seem like another less than adequate consolation prize, but if you ask me, it's about as useful as the original version." He grinned as I set to unwrapping. "You can mount it on the dash of a real car. If and when you ever find your way to getting one."

It was a yellow Hot Wheels Matchbox Miata.

Then there was Larissa. By that time she'd already gone back to Stanford. She'd taken an extended break to come up and meet me, and now she needed to return to her studies. She'd left straight after Thanksgiving, since Adam's family house in Palo Alto was only ten minutes away from her apartment.

"I'd let you crash with me," she said, "seeing that you have no place to live and how generous you've been, but I think my roommates would be weirded out."

I said it was fine, though I found it hard to fathom that Larissa had roommates.

As for Tally, Larissa said they would be taking some time away from each other.

"It was a silly whirlwind," she said, trying to dismiss their time together. But underneath the callous brush-off, I could tell she was heartbroken. "Anyway, she's got some shit to work out, and I need to get back to school."

I didn't ask anything more. And I didn't see Tally again. The last image I have of her is from the night of the fire, when I'd been sitting on the edge of an ambulance, unable to speak, watching as she saw Taylor's lifeless body being carried out of my burning building, thinking it was Larissa. Tears were streaming down her face and she was screaming, and I couldn't help but think of the terrible image Ronnie also held of her, sitting on the floor of a bathroom, Joe Chadwick's blood and brains in her hair. I'd only known Tally for a few days, and she had been nothing but sweet and open-hearted. The fact that death and horror were the end to so many of her stories was heartbreaking, and for years I would find myself thinking of her, and hope we might one day randomly run into each other. I still do.

Outside Adam's father's house I put Larissa in a cab and was told very clearly that this would not be a heartfelt goodbye. "We're like an hour away from each other," she said. "So no need to get all weepy."

Still, as she drove off, I felt a wave of sadness crash over me, as empty as the sky above the lonely sea I was being swept out to.

From there I took my own cab back up to the city and returned to the Mark Hopkins, where I was promptly informed that starting the next afternoon I would be responsible for all charges for the suite. I went to sleep, and the next morning, despite still being full from the Levy Thanksgiving extravaganza, ordered an excessive feast as one of my last free meals, and tried to work out where I might live.

40

A WASH OF GRAY

stayed at the Mark Hopkins for another four nights on my own dime while I hounded my insurance. I'd managed to get ahold of my policy and found a clause that held them liable for putting me up in a residence of "equal standard"—a term which was far too open to interpretation, but that ultimately got them to cough up for three months in a new construction loft in South of Market called the City Mews. Three months wouldn't be nearly enough time to sort out my building, but it was a start.

The fire was ultimately ruled arson and Taylor's death an accident, but the months I would spend battling with the insurance company over reconstructing my building made me pine for the days when my biggest complaint was having been accused of lewd behavior. There were the less-than-subtle suggestions that I'd set the fire myself to get out of paying back the second mortgage which I'd used to cover the renovations. An accusation which, beyond being offended by, I found ridiculous. That building was my entire life. Not just my home, but my studio and business. All of my artwork and every worldly possession I owned had been there. Why would I destroy all of that to leave myself with nowhere to live or work? I won't even bother sharing their answers.

The stickiest part, though, was explaining Taylor. Which was even stickier than I'd feared. My insurance company, as well as the one representing the entity who owned the second floor, were both threatening to sue me for criminal negligence. I did have a contract to look after the unit, but in no way did it give me the authority to let a homeless minor live there. The expensive lawyer Larissa had hired for me told me to "Think long and hard about how this girl may have ended up in your neighbor's apartment." Which, shy of being accompanied by a wink and a nod, told me that no matter how much

Cole Valley, San Francisco — Commissioned by Esther Stein. Long-time resident who liked to refer to the fog by a man's name, which I won't print here because I think it's annoying and refuse to perpetuate.

he charged an hour, things weren't looking good for me on the Taylor front. Still, I'd given my statement to the police explaining how and why she had come to be on the second floor, so I didn't see how I could give a deposition to the insurance companies saying anything otherwise. But, as Ronnie told me, "That PD statement ain't ever gonna see the light of day let alone get in the hands of an insurance company. Why? Because it's plutonium. There's no proof Faith Chadwick was anything but a darling saint in this town. Even the people who believe us wouldn't dare make unsubstantiated allegations." The end result being, I lied. I told the insurance investigators I had no idea how Taylor had gotten in and that I'd only learned her name from the police after her body had been identified. When asked how I could explain her being in a building only I occupied, I said simply that I couldn't, and didn't need to, since she'd had nothing to do with me. They knew I was lying, but had no proof. Even when they subpoenaed the police department, the official statement I'd given had conveniently been "misplaced."

I assumed this had been Ronnie. Only, when I asked him, he was incredulous. "If I were to have had any kind of hand in the sort of nasty business of making an official police report disappear," he said, "then that would be one hell of a marker you'd owe me. But no, sport, wasn't me." Then he suddenly remembered having heard of a new sushi restaurant that had just opened and realized he was feeling really, *really* hungry. "World-class chef from Japan," he said. "Supposed to be phenomenal. And expensive. You got your credit cards replaced, yeah? You feeling as hungry as I am?"

All of which was to say that the insurance companies ultimately had to let their threats of a lawsuit go and pay up on reconstructing my building. I wasn't proud of how we'd gotten there. But I also didn't think I deserved to be sued and denied a payout. Whether Taylor had been on the second floor or the third, Kai still would have set fire to the building—and yes, I believed Kai had set the fire. Though of course there was no proof. A condition which there seemed to be a whole lot of going around.

Despite having saved me from being implicated to the insurance companies, my statement getting "lost" really bothered me. It was one more document suggesting that Faith Chadwick was not who everyone believed her to be that was no longer in the world. And it wasn't just my statement. Everything seemed to have disappeared, including the tapes Ocampo had delivered to the judge. Which just made me sad. Taylor had given her life to get evidence against Faith, and none of it was ever going to see the light of day. I assumed this went far beyond Ronnie's pull within the police department, but was an extension of a deeper cover-up that had begun with the death of Joe Chadwick. I began to wonder who all might have been on that list of johns on Faith's blackmail spreadsheet. Faith had clearly targeted influential people. Even Ronnie had speculated that she'd probably gone after men within the criminal justice system as future insurance. Who's to say that someone with the power to decide the fate of that spreadsheet wasn't on the list? They saw their initials, recognized the dates, and pulled the same stunt Ronnie had pulled for me in regard to the insurance companies. I hated it, but I also would have been a hypocrite to fault them. When the cards had been stacked against me, I'd readily accepted the law being skirted for my own personal benefit. Without hesitation, I'd lied to save my own ass and let a document proving otherwise be destroyed. Why would I assume others with more power than me—and more to lose—wouldn't do the same?

Some might say that's a cynical conclusion—or one of an amoral person. What it made me think of was Larissa's studies, about the nature of ethics. How, within every human system, there seemed to be an inevitable gap, a contradiction between the laws a society writes and those it enforces, and between the values to which individuals claim to subscribe, and those they actually live by. Larissa and I never spoke of it, but it also felt like we didn't need to. The subjective natures of good and bad were at the heart of not just this story, but of so much of life. A gap we all exist in, of justification and manufactured reason. A wash of gray.

＊　＊　＊

Which, fittingly, brings me back to Inspector Martin Zorn, and also back to the public reaction to the deaths of Faith and Kai. In the days, weeks, and eventually months following Martin's disappearance, when even his face on every newspaper and nightly TV news program didn't lead to his capture, conspiracy theories grew rampant. Many believed the police department had intentionally let Zorn go, and there was at least one pair of reporters at the *Chronicle* who were not buying the jealous-lover story. In the wake of the election they doggedly pursued an expose on The Nest, attempting to prove there had been abuse—though, ironically, and painfully, not by Faith Chadwick, but by Martin Zorn. It seemed the prospect of a female philanthropist abusing her power over young teens was beyond their journalistic imaginations. They did, however, get their hands on the tapes Ocampo had delivered to the judge, which had previously, and curiously, gone nowhere. Once public, those recordings did lead to the arrest of several prominent

Bay Area businessmen—and, no surprise, one judge, which, as I had mused, explained why nothing had come of them earlier. I was shocked that the tapes hadn't been destroyed, and for a flicker of a moment thought there might be hope for the spotlight to turn away from Martin Zorn as everyone's go-to villain, only to find that hope just as quickly extinguished. Of the men on the tapes, most pleaded innocent, claiming either mistaken identity or lack of proof that the women were underage or even prostitutes. And even in the case of the one man who was caught dead to rights and struck a plea deal, the evidence he provided in no way connected the operation to Faith. Which of course it wouldn't. Resulting in the reporters never even considering Faith a suspect. And in short time, with the Zorn trail gone cold and what looked to them like a win under their investigative belts for exposing the men on the tapes, their pursuit of the story ended there.

As for anyone who might have been complicit in the blackmail scheme—people who, even if not fully aware of what they'd been participating in at the time, in the wake of the tapes going public had to have put two and two together—none stepped forward. Not the men who'd been blackmailed, not the girls at The Nest who'd had sex with the johns, not the carpenters who'd built and dismantled the spy rooms. It was hardly a surprise. If reporters had come sniffing around my door, I wouldn't have said a word. Not because I didn't want the truth to come out, but because I would have never involved Larissa, nor would I have outed Tally as Crystal. Having been a minor at the time of Joe Chadwick's death, Crystal's name had never been released to the press, and no way would I have wanted to expose her. Which means I would have done just as I had with the insurance investigation—same as the johns on the recordings had done—and claimed ignorance. As, I'm sure, would have each of the Merry Trio. Ronnie certainly wasn't going to talk. In part, I assumed, because of his association with the original Joe Chadwick case, another part because of his political relationships and career, but mostly because he was Ronnie, and he wasn't going to spill any of his beans simply because some newshounds came sniffing around his houseboat door. Larissa wasn't going to talk out of a general principle of "My life is nobody's damn business," and, I'm sure, also out of wanting to protect Crystal. And obviously Crystal wasn't going to throw herself to the wolves. But it was never even an issue. No reporters came nosing around, and not one of our names ever came up in journalistic investigations. Which, I had to assume, was the result of another ethically questionable maneuver by Ronnie, or possibly even Ocampo. Because there had most certainly been a trail—the statements made by all three that night at 850 Bryant, as well as the provenance of the tapes Ocampo had delivered. What had become of those documents, I can only assume. Washed away, like everything else, in the gray. An act of which I was also complicit. Seeing that I wasn't lifting a finger to color any of it in.

On the subject of reporting, though, Taylor's death did make the papers. As did the fire that killed her. However, the story received little more than an inch of column space on the second-to-last page, and, because my name carried a bit of recognition, Taylor didn't even get top billing. *Fire at Mission District residence of local artist and author believed arson. A homeless teen suspected of breaking and entering died when . . .* It was sad to me how much of the story was unknown, twisted, or blatantly wrong. And how easily erased was a life. And yet, again, it wasn't as if I were calling reporters to go on record and straighten it out.

There were others who wouldn't let the story die, though. In time, at least one indie filmmaker attempted a documentary on The Nest, as well as a slew of bloggers trying their hands as amateur sleuths. The problem was, all took the same view as the *Chronicle* exposé had, that Martin Zorn had been a duplicitous and charismatic cop who took advantage of teens he'd "rescued" from the street. Unlike the legitimate journalists, though, none of these storytellers even tried to bother with facts. Even the free weekly papers got on board. I remember one headline reading: *Zorn Takes Nest Cult to Guyana, Rebuilding Jonestown in his image.* And for a while, "Zorntown" became a local joke.

Ironically, as the absurdity of these stories grew, the basis of all the unsubstantiated assertions began to creep closer to the truth than anyone even knew. But only because they'd gotten lucky by exploiting a common taboo: *Nest Revealed As Secret Sex Cult Abusing Teenage Runaways.* Yes, actually, it was. But seeing that *secret sex cult* was puritanical America's go-to conspiracy plot, no one put much stock in it. I do have to admit, I took pleasure from those stories. I've never been much for supermarket tabloids about Elvis's UFO baby, or Hitler's underground Argentine bunker, but this was one time I was rooting for the nutters. Despite any actual proof, The Nest took on a legend of being one more in a long line of perverted San Francisco cults: Peoples Temple, Synanon, the Symbionese Liberation Army, the Purple People, the Family, and now The Nest. And the links to politics were certainly there. Photos of the mayor with Faith Chadwick, laughing it up at benefit auctions and standing arm in arm at inaugural ribbon cuttings, ran chillingly alongside historical photos of politicians shaking hands with the infamous Jim Jones. In the mid-seventies, back when Jones was considered a well-intentioned local religious leader, Willie Brown had been a California State Assemblyman, and the two had met on at least one occasion. Future San Francisco mayor George Moscone had also been close to Jones. Volunteers from the People's Temple had rallied support for Moscone's campaign, and, after winning the election, Moscone had credited the charismatic Jones as being instrumental in his victory. According to the self-proclaimed "truth-tellers who the government would like nothing more than to silence," this was simply history repeating itself. Just one more apple in a basket of prominent San Francisco community leaders proven to be rotten. One website still asserts that Kai was Faith and Martin's lovechild, bringing incest into the mix. Though, considering that in 1999 Kai was twenty-four and Martin was thirty-one, I'm not really sure how that was supposed to work. But the people who write these kinds of things, as well as the people who believe them, tend not to care too much for silly details like facts. Just look at one of the most popular shows on television at the time: *The X-Files*. We were in an era when everyone wanted to believe. I know I certainly did—at least when it came to Faith Chadwick and secret sex cults. And I still do.

Vedanta Society, San Francisco — Commissioned by Vic Geary, former drummer for the punk band

Noodlespoon, who'd quit music to become a swami, then quit religion to become a barber.

View Mount Davidson & Sutro Tower, San Francisco — Patron asked to be unnamed

(* Note from me: all those damn windows!)

SE BUSCA

MUERTO O VIVO

EL RESBALADIZO

$1,000,000.00

RECOMPENSA

PART 4

MAY – JUNE 2019
AMSTERDAM / SWITZERLAND

ZORNTOWN

Pine Street, San Francisco — Commissioned by Travis Mak. In the eighties, Travis opened his first tattoo parlor here in the heart of the Polk Gulch. Not in the storefront, but in the first-story apartment. "Made a killing off of inking trannies and rent boys," he told me, smiling with two gold teeth.

41

LAST SHOT, THEN YOU GO HOME

"So, who is it?" Danielle asks. "Who is Tulip?"

Danielle and I are in my studio in Amsterdam. Hours earlier, the body of former San Francisco police inspector Martin Zorn had been fished out of the Singel river, an apparent suicide. A Dutch prostitute, Kitty, had told Danielle that she'd seen another prostitute, Tulip, rush off with Martin over a week ago. Since then, Tulip had been missing, and, with Martin dead, I want to find her. Something Danielle just said, about her not being a crusader, has sparked a connection for me, and I believe I know who Tulip is.

"I told you," Danielle says. "I hate guessing games."

"I need to check something first," I say. "You have Kitty's number?"

"Yeah."

"Will you text her for me? Ask her Tulip's ethnicity?"

"I don't need to. I know."

"I thought you said you didn't know her?"

"I don't. But I've seen her. I told you, I'd planned on doing an interview."

"Okay. And?"

"Tulip's Asian."

"Specifically?" And when she doesn't immediately answer, I say, "Taiwanese? Chinese? Japanese—"

For once, Danielle looks embarrassed. "Honestly, I don't know. Chinese? I don't really know her."

"That's okay," I say.

"She still the person you're thinking of?"

"I think so."

"Congratulations," Danielle says. "So, what are you going to do about it?"

"I have no idea."

* * *

It's midnight and I'm at Winkel, the pub across the square from my subterranean home with—according to me—hands-down the best apple pie in Amsterdam, which I've eaten as my dinner, though without the usual pairing of Irish whiskey because I'm writing. I've been here all evening. Outside, the air is cold and the wind ferocious. Tree limbs are whipping around as if they're conducting a manic orchestra. Inside is warm and cozy, though, the small bar glowing dully with the soft amber light on wood. I'm the last one here, and the staff is cleaning up. This won't be the first time I've shut the place down, so I just keep working.

I've been going back and forth between outlining the events of those fateful two weeks of the fall of 1999, and writing bits of random scenes as they come back to me. It's the feverish beauty of inspiration, where the whole of a book is right there in your head. You know it will take months, if not years, to get it all down, but still you feel as if you might be able to write it all in one sitting.

Eventually the lights start turning off inside the Winkel, signaling it's time to go. I close my computer, but as I'm standing to pack my bag, Ingrid, who knows me as a regular, plops two plates of apple pie on my table, each with a scoop of vanilla ice cream, along with a bottle of Jameson and two shot glasses.

"Is leftover, so we have to eat," she says, sliding one of the plates of pie toward me and sitting down.

I sit as well. "If you insist."

Ingrid pours us each a shot of Jameson. She is six foot, blond, and all of twenty-two. Like many Dutch people I've met, she can switch to speaking English effortlessly.

"Cheers," Ingrid says, handing me the shot of Jameson.

Writing or not, it would be rude to turn down free booze, so I accept. "Proost," I say, then down my shot.

"You are creating your next masterpiece," she says, refilling our shot glasses again, though instead of drinking, she pulls her plate close.

"We'll see."

"No," she says, cutting off a chunk of her pie and mopping it around the melting ice cream. "I have seen you here working many times, and always you are very serious and frustrated. But tonight you have energy—and no whiskey. Until now." She grins and raises up her glass.

I raise my shot in return, then, for the first time in all the months I've been coming here, Ingrid and I have more than a surface chat. I learn that she's from Rotterdam, is here studying water-control systems, and is volunteering with an international agency in Bangladesh to implement damming techniques perfected by the Dutch.

"In Holland," she says, "over one quarter of the country is below sea level, making us Dutch the world leader in water-control technology." Then she goes on to explain how, in the 1950s, after a catastrophic flood killed thousands of people in the city, an innovative network of dams and levees was built. Her eyes light up as she explains what might otherwise be boring civil engineering details, only to suddenly pick up the bottle of Jameson and say, "Okay, last shot, then you go home."

* * *

Five minutes later I'm at my desk and back at the story. And next thing I know, I've gone all night having barely felt the Jameson wear off. And only as I see the sky growing light beyond what is a high window for me but a sidewalk-level window outside do I feel tired. My eyes are stinging, and while I'd like to keep going, I should get some sleep.

It's just after eleven when I'm woken by the sound of the little bell on the front door. Danielle, arriving after class.

"Don't tell me you're so depressed you can't get out of bed," she says, stepping through the curtain as I'm swinging my legs to the floor and yawning.

"Quite the opposite," I say. "Up till dawn, working."

"Good for you."

"You mind watching the front today?" I say. "I want to keep at this."

"Yeah," she says. "I can work on my laptop." And after hanging up her coat, she takes her computer from her bag and disappears back through the curtain into the front.

I get out of bed and put on clothes. I want to get back to writing, but there's something else I need to do.

After going to La Gelafferia, the ice cream shop that is pretty much directly above me, and getting a cappuccino for take-away, I return to Singelgebied, one of Amsterdam's smaller red light districts. I walk the narrow alley, drinking my coffee and looking at the women in their windows, who either smile and strike a pose for me, or glance up only to look away. When I spot Kitty, I step down the short set of stairs similar to those to my own shop.

"Hi, hon," she says, opening her door. "Want to have some fun?" She's wearing the same silk kimono as when Danielle and I came by two days ago, and, also as two days ago, she raises her arm against the doorframe, allowing the robe to spill open and expose her breast. Which I now understand is just what she does with everyone who comes to her door. No different from me repeating my standard line, "Have a look around, and if you have any questions just let me know," to each person who steps into my shop.

"I'm Emit," I say. "Danielle's friend. We were asking after Tulip."

"I remember, hon, doesn't mean we can't have some fun."

"Thanks," I say. "But I think my fun has left the building. I'm just wondering if you've heard anything about Tulip."

Kitty shakes her head. "No, but——" she throws her chin across the narrow alley "——a new girl's using her window."

I glance over. The red curtain is drawn and the red light is off.

"She's not in," Kitty says. "Works nights."

I look back. "Have you talked to her? Do you know if she's renting from Tulip?"

"I asked. Says she's never heard of Tu. She rented from the agency. But the girl's Russian. So who knows."

"Meaning what? I remember you saying that Tulip might have owed money to the Russians. You think gangsters gave her window to another girl?"

Kitty shrugs. "I only know I don't trust Russians. The men are thugs and the girls, they rip off the clients. Take their money, then don't perform. Gives us all a bad name."

"You said Tulip would bring the girls tomatoes from her garden, but wouldn't go for a pint. I also know she was going to talk with Danielle for the art project. She ever talk to you about her past?"

"Only that she worked some years in Zurich. I think maybe one time she mentioned Milan."

"She ever talk about San Francisco?"

Kitty shakes her head. "Tulip is good at telling stories. She likes to make everyone laugh. But always her stories are about funny people or crazy accidents. She never talks of herself."

"Danielle said she's Asian. Is that right? Is she Taiwanese?"

Kitty snorts. "Taiwan, Thailand, what do I know? Asian." Then her head jerks as she sees something behind me. I reflexively turn to look. A man. Sixties, white, beer belly. He slows to give Kitty a look. "Hi, hon," she says to him, striking her pose. "Want to have some fun?"

He keeps going, but I understand I'm hurting her business. "One last question," I say, "and I'll go. What about her other friends? Any mutual friends you two have that might know more about her? Is there someone you think I should talk to?"

The man had walked a few paces, then slowed, and is now glancing back. Knowing she has a live one, Kitty loses all interest in me.

"Listen, hon, you should ask that girl of yours. She knows the windows same as me. Now, if you're not buying——"

"Yeah," I say. "Of course." Then I step aside, and gesture to the guy that she's all his.

The man walks closer as I climb the stairs. "Thanks," I say to Kitty.

"Sure, hon," she says to me, with no care. Then, to the man, with all the syrup one might pour, "Hiya, top dog. Looking for some fun with Kitty?"

* * *

Back in the shop, I find Danielle working on her laptop. "Have a look around," she says as I walk in the door. "And if you have any questions just let me know."

"Yes," I say. "I do have a question."

"No," she says. "I won't draw you naked."

"You really think I'm terrible at closing sales?"

"You got an interesting piece of mail today," she says, handing me a postcard with a photo of a medieval village. On the back is a short handwritten note:

> *Sorry we didn't get to have that last drink together*
> *—— MZ*

Seems obvious the card is from Martin. And thinking back to what the police told me, of the note he'd left on the mirror of his hotel room—*I've gone for one last drink in the canal*—I can't help but wonder if this was his last attempt at a dark-humored double entendre. Above the message there's a return address, Bern, Switzerland—which I'm guessing is the location of the photo on the front—and a name: Francesca Molinari.

"Ever been to Switzerland?" Danielle asks.

"Nope. And I don't know a Francesca Molinari."

"Think that's Tulip?"

"Don't know. Sounds made-up."

"So does Emit Hopper."

I laugh. "The postmark is from Amsterdam," I say. "Yesterday. Which means Martin posted it here—possibly after leaving me and before shooting himself." The errand he had to run? I look at the front of the card again. "You can buy a million postcards of Amsterdam here," I say. "But I doubt you can find any of Switzerland. Which makes me think he brought the card with him. Which means maybe he planned the whole thing. From seeing me to his suicide."

Danielle puffs up her cheeks and makes a popping sound. "Bloke was definitely one twisted fuck."

I go through the curtain into the studio. I do a Web search for the address in Bern and open up street view. A charming three-story, very Swiss-looking building appears on screen. Could this be where Tulip is?

I lean back in my chair. There's been something else nagging at me: the wedding ring Martin had been wearing. It seemed too subtle to have been a prop. Which has had me wondering: Is there a Mrs. Zorn? Possibly a Mrs. Crystal Zorn? And possibly in Bern? Of course, Zorn wouldn't be their name, having survived on the run for twenty years. So maybe, Mr. and Mrs. Molinari?

I do an image search for Francesca Molinari. A thousand photos, not one of an Asian woman.

I think on what that might mean. Decide I can't know. Then book a flight to Bern.

*　*　*

"I need to leave town for a couple days," I say to Danielle, stepping into the front room pulling my small rollaboard. "Do you mind tending to the shop? If so, then no worries. It's not like business has been booming."

"You're going to Switzerland, aren't you?"

"I am."

She snorts. "Good luck."

I walk to Centraal Station, tugging my luggage over the bumpy cobblestones, and take a train to the airport.

Waiting to board, I take out my laptop and resume writing.

Without missing a beat, the words continue to flow with ease, and the more I write, the more I remember. Scenes come to life as vividly in my mind as if I were watching a film. Details such as Larissa's shirt-stain drawings, and the miniature replica Mustang Ronnie kept mounted on his dashboard—and the miature Miata he gave to me—each making me smile bittersweetly. But while I feverishly note these down, I'm also thinking about Crystal Lake, and whether she and Tulip, or she and Francesca Molinari—or all three—could actually be one and the same. Or if I just want them to be.

Flights from Amsterdam to the Swiss capital are frequent, and three hours after receiving Martin's postcard my plane is touching down in Switzerland, and a half hour after that I'm stepping off the train in downtown Bern. Using my phone, I see that the address is only a ten-minute walk, and while crossing Kirchenfeldbrücke bridge I find I'm looking out over the exact view featured on the postcard.

From the bridge I turn onto Weststrasse. As I walk along searching house numbers I wonder who I will find when I reach the one I am looking for. Will it be Tulip? And will she in fact be Crystal? And what are the chances? Martin had twenty years of life after shooting Faith and Kai then disappearing; Tulip could be anyone from any of those years. That said, Tulip being Asian does seem a coincidence, considering that—at least according to Danielle—Asian sex workers are rare in Holland. Not that it proves anything. Then I think, as far as coincidences go, how strange and tragic would it be if Tulip *does* turn out to be the sweet young woman I knew as Tally? To learn that her life had not continued forward as she or any of us had hoped, but that the whole time I've been living in Amsterdam she'd been only a short distance away, working as a prostitute. The thought makes me completely change my mind, and hope wherever Tulip is, here in Bern or elsewhere, that Crystal slash Tally is somewhere else, far away, with a life that has nothing to do with Martin Zorn; a beautiful life beyond what she could have ever hoped for.

The street narrows as it winds down the hill, and as I round the bend, the building I saw on Google Maps comes into view. Only then does it occur to me that I might have this completely wrong. If this house is—was—Martin's home, and there *is* in fact a Mrs. Zorn, then this may have nothing at all to do with the events of twenty years ago, but may actually be a sick joke on Martin's part. I may be knocking on the door to inadvertently be the bearer of bad news; the postcard having been Martin's last laugh, using me to deliver the message of his death to his wife.

I am at the house now. I open the wooden gate and walk through. I've traveled from Amsterdam to Bern on a hunch, and as I ring the buzzer I think, if Martin is just using me, I'll—

The door opens and I'm greeted by an Asian woman who smiles and says, "Hello, Emit. Nice to see you."

42

A PANTRY FULL OF SPIRITS

read her face, then read it again to be sure.

"I am Francesca," she says, stepping back and opening the door. "Please. Come inside."

I do.

Francesca is maybe thirty-five, and, within seconds, strikes an odd character, comprised of several contradictory traits. Her ethnicity is Chinese, but her speech is Italian, as is her name. She is dressed in casual, three-quarter linen pants and a loose sweatshirt, yet her manner is proper, and, as far as I know, up until a week ago, she was a prostitute.

"You were expecting Crystal," she says.

"I thought maybe," I say. "But . . ."

She smiles. "Martin hoped you would. In fact, he counted on it."

I glance at her hand to see if she's wearing a wedding ring. She is not. Nor is there any groove on her finger to show that she has recently taken one off.

"I know he is dead," she says. Her eyes turn heavy. "He informed me of his intention when he came for me in Amsterdam one week ago. I spoke to him on the phone not one half hour before he left for the canal. I suspect I was the last person to hear his voice. Please, come inside. Let me make you some tea."

* * *

I follow this woman who is not Crystal up a wide circular staircase, a rich, delicious aroma growing stronger as we climb. On the second floor, we step through an arched doorway into a spacious kitchen and dining area, both empty of furniture.

"You will stay for dinner, I hope?" Francesca says. "I am preparing risotto.

Though it still needs a bit of time. Please——" she touches my arm "——you may leave your things. We do not know each other, but I am sure we will be friends."

I set my shoulder bag atop my rollaboard and place the pair against a wall, then I stroll around the large, empty space. I can't speak for the rest of the building, but this area has been recently remodeled. The wooden floors have been newly refinished, the walls freshly re-plastered, and all the lighting modernized. At the far end of the room is a steel—and obviously new—spiral staircase, and I realize that at one time the building had likely been separate flats, and has now been converted into one single and very large home.

As for furniture, I was wrong. Facing one of the front windows are two small sofa chairs and, between them, a wine crate turned on its side. Which I suppose counts, but in a place of this size and stature, also doesn't. Even in the kitchen, which is equipped with high-end appliances, there is the barest of cookware visible. So much so that the cast-iron pot on the range, if not for the delicious smell emanating from beneath its lid, I might think was a prop.

"Please," Francesca says as she lights a burner under a kettle for tea—I see now that there is also a kettle. "Sit." And so I do, taking one of the two small chairs by the window. On top of the wine-crate-turned-coffee-table is a book—by me. My most recent novel, *Come to Light*. If the bookmark between the last page and cover is to be trusted, she has either finished it, or not yet begun.

"Yes," Francesca says, carrying over a tray with all the elements for tea. "You see I have been preparing for your arrival. Would you——" I move my book to the floor so that she can set the tray on the not-at-all-stable wine box "——thank you, dear." She straightens up and rests her hands on her hips. "I will say, I enjoy your stories very much. Are they true? Your wife disappeared in the wilderness? Then you chased the man you thought murdered her across Europe?"

"All true."

"But you also say that much of what you wrote in your previous book was fantasy. So how are we to believe anything you write?"

I laugh. "I think that's why they call me a 'post-modern, yet classically unreliable narrator.'"

She scrunches up her nose and grins with delight. "Is that what they call you?"

"I've been called worse."

"Oh, dear, me too."

The kettle begins to whistle and she moves off.

"I will say, " Francesca says from across the room, "I did not think it would work."

"What's that?"

She comes back to the window carrying the kettle. She pours steaming hot water into the cups and I reach out to steady the tray, which is wobbling atop the wine box.

"Martin's plan," Francesca says. Having finished pouring the water, she drops a pot holder to the floor and sets the kettle on top of it. Then she sits, daintily crossing her legs. "I believed it was too complicated. I said to him, 'Just tell the poor man what you want him to know!' But Martin insisted. 'No,' he said. 'Emit will prefer it this way.'" She holds up a tea bag. "Black good? I have only Earl Grey."

"That will be fine," I say, still unsure of what's going on.

She slips a tea bag into each of the cups of hot water. Then a curious look comes over her face. "Look at me," she says. "Making tea—on an occasion such as this! We should be drinking something stronger, do you not think? Would you prefer wine? Vodka? Gin? I may not have any furniture, but I have a pantry full of spirits."

"Eventually," I say. "But for now, tea is good."

"Then it is settled. You will stay for dinner."

It wasn't a question, but I reply as if it were. "If we're eating what I smell, then I don't see how I can resist."

"Excellent," she says, moving primly to the edge of her seat and lacing her fingers together in her lap—another odd character feature. "Because, my dear Emit, I have a story to tell. One that is only for you."

* * *

"To start," Francesca says, "you must understand that I have learned this story in its entirety only last week. Which—" suddenly she smiles and shakes her head "—I see now makes my telling difficult. Martin, he made me practice telling this story, over and over, correcting me when I had even the slightest detail wrong. So many times I am certain I will recite it perfectly. And yet, not once did we prepare for the explanation! Do you see? I have imagined sitting across from you—you, a storyteller!—for over one week now. But not one time did I imagine explaining to you how I have come to know what I know."

"Just start from the beginning."

This hits her like a gust of wind.

"Oh my—the beginning? What is the beginning? No, I think maybe best to be succinct. Our friend had a message for you, and I am the messenger. Better to focus on his intent. However, I will say, for all the years I knew the man you know as Martin Zorn—which were only a few—he wanted only to do right, and to make amends. What you see here—" she looked around "—this home, my new life—and you sitting across from me—is his attempt to make those amends." She takes a deep breath, smiles mournfully. "I know you thought poorly of him, and he understood. You should know he never thought poorly of you, nor did he expect you to forgive him. He wanted nothing more than for you to know his story. Which is why I ask that you listen to what I have to tell, and do your best to hear it with an open mind, and an open heart." She removes the tea bags from each of our cups, picks up hers, drinks, then sets it down. "To start," she says, "Crystal Lake did not kill Joe Chadwick. Martin did."

* * *

She pauses just long enough for this to sink in, but not long enough for me to respond. "The story Ronnie Gilbert told you of the death of Joe," she says, "the story only Ronnie knew—for it was designed for him—is only partially true. Yes, Martin built the secret recording room to catch Joe. And yes, it was his idea, though instigated by Faith Chadwick. Joe Chadwick, however, was not a pedophile. He had never abused any of the children from The Nest. The truth was, Faith Chadwick had political ambitions, and wanted her husband gone.

"Crystal Lake, whose real name was Kris Tao—you see? *Kris, Crystal, Tally?*—had been a fourteen-year-old runaway on the streets of San Francisco. She was using drugs and selling her body. Faith Chadwick had given her a home at The Nest. But Crystal was wild. She kept running off. After one too many arrests, Faith tells her no more. She will let the system do what they will with her. Unless Crystal helps with a plan. She is to flirt with Joe. He will refuse her, but she is not to give up. Slowly she is to wear him down, until he can resist no more."

Francesca pauses to hold up a finger. "Please know, Martin is unaware of the maneuvers of Faith. He knows only what he is told, which is the lie that Faith suspects her husband of taking advantage of the wayward children in their care. She puts on a tremendous show of being distraught. She plays the helpless victim, knowing that Officer Zorn, the ardent defender of good, will come to her rescue.

"Martin wants to arrest Joe immediately. Faith begs him not to. 'Think of The Nest,' she tells him. 'Of all the good we do. Do not let that be destroyed.' She says she does not want—cannot have—her husband publicly punished. 'The shame will destroy all the good we have done,' she tells Martin. No. There can be no trial. She wants only to have Joe out of the picture.

"Faith proposes blackmail. To confront Joe with evidence that will leave him no choice but to grant her a quiet divorce and total disinvolvement from the business with no protest. Because she is smart, she does not offer a method of how this evidence might be acquired, but leaves Martin to decide.

"As you surely know, The Nest was built in a converted residence hotel. The Chadwicks owned several buildings of this sort, and were at the time renovating one close by. Faith tells Martin it is on the upper floor of this building, in the penthouse, which is nearing completion, where her husband takes the girls for his exploits. Martin then formulates a plan. His idea is to take advantage of the construction and install a secret room where he can record Joe Chadwick in the act.

"Martin builds this room himself, and acquires all the equipment in secret. Time passes, then comes the fateful day. Faith informs Martin that Joe is acting skittish, that he has told her he does not know when he will be home that night. That he has an event at his club, or some other vague excuse that a wife always sees through. She cannot say for certain, but she believes Joe will be taking a young woman to the room that night."

"Hold on a minute," I say. "Apologies for interrupting. But did she tell Martin who the girl was?"

"No," Francesca says. "Faith knows, of course, as she has arranged it. For weeks, months possibly, she has instructed Crystal to flirt and tease Joe. Crystal undoes buttons on her blouse, fails to wear a bra, and puts on big, longing eyes, telling Joe she wants him to love her in all the ways only he can, until the man can take no more. But Faith tells Martin none of this. Only that she suspects Joe is taking one of the girls that night."

"So Martin never sat down with Crystal? Never told her what he was doing?"

"Not as I understand."

I put my hand to my chin. I've quickly allowed myself to be lured into this tale, and now I'm trying to track what Francesca is telling me with the story I think I know. For two days I've been meticulously writing down everything I can remember. I'd also managed to find the notes I'd written at the Mark Hopkins in the days following the fire, and so have been consulting those. But of course they don't cover everything, and certainly not granular details such as this. And the problem is, when Ronnie told me the story, aside from it having been twenty years ago, I was stoned. Still, if I'm going to adequately write this book, I damn well need to have what I believe is my version straight.

"Please," Francesca says with a smile. "I can see you have become distrustful. You are questioning Martin and his motives with this story, as well, I suppose, as my own. And of course, why should you not? You have come all this way, and—I too must remember, this is all quite a surprise for you. A mystery arranged by Martin, for you alone to solve. So dramatic! But, my dear Emit, I can promise you, our Martin was a tortured man. A broken man. He suffered greatly for all he had done. In my opinion, far more than he deserved. And he was dying—did you know this? Liver cancer. He was in terrible pain. That he was still alive when he found me is beyond belief. But he had this story he needed to tell. And all that he has done—" she gestures to the house "—giving me these gifts, and offering you this truth, was to make peace with his demons. So please, I ask again. Will you try to listen without judgment?"

"I'll do my best."

"Which is all any of us can hope for." She smiles warmly and picks up her tea and drinks. I realize I haven't touched mine, so I do the same.

"And so we return," Francesca says, setting down her cup. "To that night. Martin has built his room, Operation Midnight Climax—do you know this reference?"

"I do."

"Good. He has built his replica of a CIA recording room in the penthouse suite of a building the Chadwicks are renovating. When the night arrives, Martin takes position in his secret room. He is nervous. He is a police officer. He believes in justice. And yet he sits in a dark and dangerous space, waiting not to stop a crime, but to record one being committed—and a terrible crime at that. Because he is anxious, he has come early—far too early—and so must wait a long while. In time, Joe and Crystal enter. Martin begins recording. Joe is pawing the girl, asking her what she wants. Does she want him to be her daddy? Say it. He undresses her. She undresses him. The girl is barely of age and Martin is repulsed. And when Joe Chadwick has her kneel on the floor and take him into her mouth, Martin can stand no more. He bursts out of his hiding space. Both Joe and Crystal are surprised. Crystal picks up a lamp and throws it at Martin—remember, she is not the victim Martin believes her to be. She is accustomed to trading her body to survive, and Faith has instructed her. As Martin fends off her attack, Joe reaches for a pistol and aims it at Martin, who lunges and pins Joe to the wall. Joe has the pistol in his hand, his finger on the trigger, yet Martin has Joe's wrist. It is now a contest of who is stronger. In both body and will. Martin is winning, and he pushes the arm of Joe inward. He still has Joe against the wall. Against all resistance by Joe, Martin guides the hand which holds the gun so that it is under Joe's chin, and before Joe can let go, Martin tugs at the finger of Joe Chadwick, firing a bullet through the man's chin and out the back of his head. A bloody mess, everywhere. The girl makes to run, but Martin turns the gun on her. She stops, then she opens her arms and displays her naked body for him. Is this what he wants? To have her all to himself? He whips her on the side of the head with the gun and she falls to the floor.

"It is then that Faith Chadwick bursts in. 'What have you done?' she screams. 'You fool! You were only supposed to record him! Not kill him!' She immediately takes charge. She invents a plan. And because Martin is in shock, he goes along. Crystal too obeys. Faith tells them each what to do, what to say. And the rest, you know."

"Meaning, the story that Martin told Ronnie? Which was that Martin was next door, not in the recording room, and that when he heard a shot, he burst into the suite to find that Crystal had killed Joe?"

"Yes. Which was the story invented by Faith. She was the one next door, without Martin knowing. Seeing that Martin will not survive interrogation, and fearing that her role in having engineered the scene would—" she points to my book which sits on the floor "—*come to light*, as it is said, she has to save herself."

"But why would Crystal go along with it?" I ask.

"I suppose she thought no one would believe otherwise. If you are fourteen and a known drug addict and prostitute, in a situation where a police officer and the wife of the man you were naked in a room with say you are the killer, no matter how streetwise you are, how much trust will you have that anyone will believe you?"

"Fair enough."

"So the three agree," Francesca says. "The story will be that Crystal Lake shot Joe. Faith tells Martin to call his former partner, Ronnie Gilbert, because Ronnie knew of Martin's plan to build the spy room, and by involving him before the police he will no longer be in a position to hurt them. They invent a version of the story for Ronnie, then allow him to invent the rest. Which—if you will pardon me from breaking script, in my opinion, confirms that Faith Chadwick was truly an evil genius. Beyond trapping innocent people—including children—with her crimes, she engineered situations where her victims were forced to commit new crimes to save themselves. She did this with Martin, Ronnie, Crystal, and, I believe, Kai, and countless others to be sure. It was her way. This is why I call her an evil genius. She did not have to invent every story. She did not have to orchestrate every plan or pull every trigger. She only had to create situations where she could trap those who were perfectly suited to do the work for her. Such as Martin. 'We need a way to catch Joe!' she tells him. 'To save the children!' And Martin remembers a CIA plot he had studied at the academy. Then Ronnie. 'We need to explain why Martin—your friend and fellow policeman—is in this room with my dead husband!' And Ronnie invents a story that only he, another policeman, can invent. She has done more than involve them in her terrible deeds. She has made it so they feel they have no choice other than to commit terrible deeds of their own. As I say, evil genius."

Once more my hand is to my chin as I'm thinking. "Don't worry," I say. "I'm not second-guessing your story. I'm just comparing this to the versions I know. It's been a long time, though."

"Is good," Francesca says. "Let your mind work." Then she stands and picks up the tray with our barely touched tea cups. "I think maybe it is time for intermission. The risotto smells ready." And she walks into the kitchen.

As she's fixing us a meal, I consider how what I just heard aligns with what I remember. I'll have to sit down and map it all out to be sure. But so far, pretty much everything seems to check—which is not to say I believe it. Only that it doesn't contradict. And possibly a bit too conveniently so.

43

JUST LISTEN

"How wonderful it must be to be an artist," Francesca says, returning with the tray, this time loaded with two wide bowls of risotto. "I can only imagine what images must constantly be dancing in your mind."

"Hold on," I say before she can set the tray down. "Let me—" and I turn the wine crate flat. "It's not very high, but at least it will be stable."

"Sounds like the life of a very boring man," Francesca says, and she starts laughing.

She sets the tray down, then leaves through the doorway we'd entered. Several minutes pass, then she returns with a bottle of white wine. She pulls the cork and delivers me a very full glass. She pours herself a glass, then sets the bottle on the floor beside the tea kettle that still rests upon the pot holder.

Francesca does not drink her wine, but sets the glass on the floor. "I wish to stay clear for the remainder of the story," she says. "Though after, I will gladly drink with you until dawn."

The risotto is as delicious as it smells. And the wine pairs perfectly. Which I tell her.

"Grazie mille," she says. "I lived many years in Milan. I would be ashamed to poorly pair a grape with a meal." She takes only a bite of her risotto before setting her plate down beside her wine. "If you do not mind," she says, "I would like to continue."

"Please."

"The time following the death of Joe Chadwick is difficult for Martin," Francesca says. "He wrestles with what he has done. He built the room, killed a man, and allowed a young woman to take the blame for his actions. Kris Tao—Crystal Lake—was sentenced to two years in a juvenile correctional facility. However, she is released after only three months, at the pleading of Faith Chadwick. And for this, Kris is forever indebted. It is an old trick. Kris was Taiwanese. Her parents did not want her. They abused her, but they did not love her. Faith, however, put her in harm's way, then saved her. She completed the cycle, indebting Kris to her. Once back at The Nest, Kris becomes a different person. Good. Helpful. And because Faith continues only to encourage and praise her, in time Kris even becomes happy. I believe Faith did this as much for Martin as she did for Kris—if not more—for him to see how Kris was thriving, so that he would begin to feel better about what he had done. Does she do this out of kindness, or out of manipulation and self-protection? And before you answer, I want you to also consider whether both might exist simultaneously. Again, this is why I believe Faith to be brilliant. And over these past few days, while waiting for you to arrive at my door, I have wondered, did Faith even know herself the nature of her behavior? If her machinations—a word I very much enjoy—to manipulate others also helped people, did she even see them as crimes? But—" she laughs "—once more, I have gone off script. You see, this is why Martin wished me to practice. And so where was I—yes. Kris. She has returned to The Nest, feeling the loving embrace of Faith. And Martin, witnessing the transformation of the girl, grows to believe he has ultimately aided in saving her. The death of Joe then takes on new meaning for him. As sacrifice. And he chooses to see greater purpose in both the killing of the man and having allowed the girl to take the blame for his crime. In this, Faith has succeeded in brainwashing him, so that he now believes as she does, that to do bad is to do good. He returns to working with The Nest, and in time, as he sees Kris grow into a productive young woman, and the lives of other young people in The Nest prosper, his spirit too returns, and he is able to bury his guilt and shame—though never leave it behind entirely.

"Then one day, years later, Ronnie Gilbert appears. His former partner tells him a story of Midnight Climax rooms, of blackmail, and persistent abuse by Faith. And more. Recordings. Evidence. Martin is shocked. Confronted with these facts, he finally accepts how Faith Chadwick had used him, and had been continuing to use him—though never directly. After his murder of Joe, Faith was always careful not to push Martin too far. Only for small tasks, such as keeping an eye on an artist who she thought might have discovered one of the homes she used for hiding abused children. For these he was an easy tool to manipulate. Then Martin and Ronnie hear of a fire at your house. Your daughter Larissa has come with a laptop of evidence, and she and Ronnie rush to go to you. Martin says he will follow, but instead he goes to The Nest. He needs to see for himself. He searches the vault and does not find any of this evidence your daughter told him he will find. So he goes to the home of Faith to confront her."

"Okay," I say. "One minute——" I set my plate on the tray and pick up my wine glass and take a quick swig "——I need to ask. All the things you say Martin didn't know, such as Faith's deal with Crystal to seduce Joe, how could he later know them in order to tell you to tell me? Did he force a confession out of Faith at gunpoint before he killed her?"

"No," Francesca says. "Crystal told him. Before she did."

"Before——wait——"

"Yes," Francesca says. "Crystal killed Faith Chadwick. And Kai Sjugard."

*　　*　　*

"But, how——" now I'm completely spun around. "I thought Crystal was with Ronnie and Larissa?"

"Please," Francesca says, holding up a hand. "I will explain."

I nod for her to continue, then pick up my plate of food to keep myself from interrupting.

"Instead of following Ronnie and Larissa to the fire, Martin went to The Nest, then to the Chadwick home. He parks around the corner, not wanting to be seen. Though he leaves his weapon in his car. He has not gone there to kill, or even as a policeman. He wants only the truth. Still, after what had happened with Joe, he does not trust himself. He goes to the rear of the house, intending to slip inside, and finds that someone has already broken a window on the back door. Now he returns to his car and retrieves his weapon. He creeps into the house and hears voices. He makes his way to the master bedroom to find Crystal Lake holding a gun on Faith and Kai. Kai is admitting to her that he had set the fire, and between having learned of Faith's ongoing abuse of the girls at The Nest, and believing Kai has killed her lover——your daughter——she intends to murder both Faith and Kai.

"She sees Martin and begins to swing the gun wildly between the three. Martin sets down his gun and says he will not try to stop her. But not to waste her life.

"But Crystal is heartbroken. She has just learned that the surrogate mother she had never had, the woman she believed was her one true family, is nothing more than another liar and abuser——and the puppet master having ordered the murder of the girl she loved. Martin tries to convince her that there is no punishment in death, that if she truly wishes for them to pay, to let them stand trial and live out their days in shame and prison. This is when Crystal tells Martin what he does not know. About how Faith had arranged for her to seduce Joe, and how they both tricked him. Martin was already devastated. This only adds to his horror. In one evening he has learned that not only has Faith committed heinous crimes using a method he had devised for her, but that all the good he thought he had done by killing Joe was also a lie."

Francesca shakes her head. "Can you imagine the scene? These two poor souls, their lives having been ruined by this horrible woman. Both so broken. Everything they believed was true—" she mimes an explosion with her hands "—destroyed. Crystal is pointing the gun at these terrible people, her hand is shaking. And this is when Martin says no, to let him do it. He picks up his gun, and now the two stand side by side, weapons pointed at Faith and Kai.

"'What are you doing?' Crystal asks him. 'I let you take credit for my killing,' Martin says. 'I will not let you throw your life away for another.' And this is when Martin reveals a secret of his own. That the night of killing Joe, there had been a recording after all. A tape which shows Martin attacking, then murdering, Joe Chadwick. A recording which Faith has been holding over him, quietly, in case he ever slipped out of line. 'So you see,' Martin tells Crystal, 'I am going down for murder no matter what happens. There is no reason you should as well.' Kris looks to him to see if he is lying, and Martin looks to her to show he is telling the truth, and in that moment of distraction, Kai leaps from the bed for a bedside drawer. But before he can reach the weapon inside, Crystal begins firing, and she keeps firing, until the gun is empty and both Faith and Kai are dead."

* * *

"Fuck," I say.

Francesca picks up her wine glass and laughs. "Fuck, indeed."

"So . . . ?"

"Yes," Francesca says, quickly taking a drink of wine and holding up her finger. "Yes, I know what you are about to say. Ronnie and Larissa, where are they? The story you were told is that after leaving you at the fire, they found Crystal at The Nest, not twenty minutes later. And from there they went to a cabin in the wilderness."

"Exactly," I say. "But how could you know that?"

"Do you remember the report by neighbors of Faith hearing gunfire?"

"I do. They called the police, and Martin sweet-talked them away."

"Yes. And across the street, watching from their car, was Ronnie Gilbert and Larissa Huxley."

Again Francesca sips some wine, and I'm thinking this story must be coming to a close if she's drinking. So I down my glass and lean forward for the bottle. She refills mine, then tops off her own.

"How long had they been there?" I ask.

Francesca shakes her head. "I do not know. But they are there and they watch as Martin sends away the police, and before he returns to the house they step out of the car and greet him. At first Martin thinks his plan is foiled. Then he realizes Larissa is alive—of course she is. He had been with her at the station when the fire call came in. But in the confusion upstairs he had not realized the mistake Crystal had made. He brings the pair inside, and there, in front of two dead bodies, Crystal and Larissa reunite.

"Martin knows then what he must do. 'I am taking the blame,' he says. He is adamant. 'This is the only way.' He had failed to save Crystal all those years ago, then failed to save all the girls after her. Including Taylor, who he learns was killed by the fire Kai set. He is taking blame for all of them.

"Ronnie tells him he is a fool. That he has always been a fool. He is yelling, but not because he is angry. But because he is sad. This man who had been his friend, who had wanted only to do good in the world, had been used and manipulated just as so many others had. Martin says Ronnie is right. But it is too late. He tells them all to go.

"Larissa also says no. 'If you want your life to have meaning,' she tells him, 'if you want to be a martyr, then going to prison will do no one any good.' And she proposes a plan. She is an expert with computers. She will help Martin escape the country. She will help him get away and begin a new life. He can still take the blame. Only now as a fugitive, not as a prisoner. So that he can devote his life to doing the good he claims so desperately to have wanted to do."

"And is this what he did?"

She closes her eyes and tilts her head. "I think life is not so simple as that."

A few seconds pass as I let this sink in. I run it against what I think I know, and can find no immediate contradictions. But of course I wouldn't. Martin wouldn't have concocted such an elaborate plan to have me easily be able to poke holes in his story. Still, I find it hard to believe that both Ronnie and Larissa would have kept such a big secret—not to mention have helped Martin escape—though, if it is true, I feel a sting at the thought of their having possibly deceived me. But the feeling immediately gives way to the realization that, if there is any truth to this version of events, they would have of course lied, if for no other reason than to protect me. If they had done such an outrageous thing as help Martin escape, and their plan had gone wrong—which how could they be sure it wouldn't?—there was no reason to bring me down with them when I'd had nothing to do with it. But then, why not tell me later? After the smoke had cleared and they were safe? Ronnie had already confided in me his cover-up with Joe. I could clearly be trusted. Was it to spare my feelings for Larissa? So that, every time I looked at her, I wouldn't question her choice of ethics?

Francesca sits watching me as all this runs through my mind. When I realize how I've drifted off, I give an embarrassed laugh.

"You need to ask," she says.

"I do."

"Please."

"Do you believe this story Martin told you?"

"I do," she says softly. And I believe her—meaning I believe that she believes Martin. Whether I believe Martin is something I'm still trying to decide. And the best conclusion I can come up with is that I can't answer right now. This is something I'm going to have to sit with. For maybe a long time.

Francesca smiles, a kind and understanding smile, then she stands. "I am quite tired," she says. "If you will excuse me, I must get some rest. There is risotto, and plenty of wine. Help yourself to anything you wish. There is a room at the end of the hallway where you may sleep. There is a mattress, though only on the floor. However, it should be comfortable." She walks over to me, places her hand gently on my cheek. "It has been a pleasure to meet you, my dear Emit. Thank you for listening." Then, despite having said she would drink with me till dawn, Francesca walks quietly away.

I'm not at all tired. But I don't feel like writing. To write, I need to be clear, and I am anything but. I finish my bowl of cold risotto and polish off the bottle of wine. Then I carry my dishes, as well as Francesca's uneaten food and undrunk wine, to the kitchen and place them in the sink. Beyond the window, Bern is quiet and dark. Over the course of Francesca's recital, afternoon had turned to evening to night. I take Francesca's glass and return to my seat.

I realize that while Francesca covered the days of Martin and The Nest, I still have many questions. Such as: Where did Martin go after fleeing San Francisco? What did he do to survive? How did she and Martin meet? And whatever became of Crystal? Pretty much the entirety of the last twenty years. Which has me looking forward to what I hope is coffee with Francesca in the morning. So I down what's left of her wine and decide I should try to sleep.

* * *

I pad off down the hallway, find the bathroom, then the bedroom, which is only that, a room with a bed. Nothing more. I undress and lie down.

Wide awake, I replay the story I've been told. It's just credible enough for me to consider that it may be true, though I'm far from convinced that Martin isn't using me. As to whether Francesca is complicit, I'm unsure. As it stands, Martin's obituary will read: "Disgraced ex-police inspector suspected of multiple homicides dead by suicide after twenty years on the run." But with this story, in the hands of someone who he was surely banking on writing a book, he will be redeemed. Not fully, of course. But instead of being remembered as having killed his girlfriend and her young lover in a jealous rage, he'll be at least considered as an unsung hero. A saint for our times. A martyr whose big heart was so pure it couldn't help but be tarnished by the depthless filth of the world. Which is more than a little bump up in credibility.

And with that, weariness falls over me like a shroud. As I drift off, I hear the soft creak of steps on the wooden floor, then the sound of my door opening. The room is pitch-black, and a moment later I feel the soft touch of a hand sliding over my chest, up to my cheek, and the warmth of bare flesh as Francesca slips into bed with me.

44

INTERLUDE

"Tell him it's the guy with at least one illegitimate child, more than a few possible misdemeanors under his belt, and a hell of a lot more prostitutes in his life than he'd ever thought possible."

Silence hangs on the other end of the line, then the woman says, "Please hold," and I'm transferred to what, after a few seconds, I realize is an orchestral rendition of Black Sabbath's *Paranoid.*

I'm in Zürich, with Francesca. After spending the night together in Bern, I woke to find she had gone shopping, set a table, and prepared breakfast. Where the evening before we'd had all of a wine crate to eat at, there was now a small dining table with cloth, fresh flowers, and two metal chairs. "Is nothing," she said. "Only the table from the garden." But she had obviously made an effort, including going out for fresh croissant, smoked fish, and coffee. I'd hoped to talk with her about Martin's post-San Francisco years, then assumed I would leave. That was a week ago. And now we're in Zürich.

After a minute of listening to elevator-Ozzy, Adam picks up. "You can't say stuff like that anymore," he says. "San Francisco has bent over so far backwards trying to protect everyone's personal freedoms that no one's free to say anything anymore. How's living in a basement in Holland?"

"Well, Martin Zorn came to see me then shot himself the next day."

"I always said you had an effect on people."

I give Adam the overview of what happened, including the story Francesca told me.

"Shit, brother—and you believe her?"

"I believe that she believes. But it's been almost a week and I'm still not sure what to think. I will say it's an intriguing version of events. But he also had twenty years to perfect it."

"And to ensure no one is around to corroborate—or contradict."

"True. But if I'm honest, that's also why I never got around to writing it. Ronnie and I formed a bond, then went on to have more than a few adventures together. I liked the guy, and never wanted to cast aspersions on his career. After Randall was acquitted for his murder, though, the injustice brought back everything with Chadwick, and I realized now was the time."

"I do wish we had more than Francesca to quote—what about the girl, Crystal?"

"No idea. I did a web search but came up with so little nothing that it makes me curious. I intend to ask Francesca about her again."

"Which leaves only one other person. And I'm guessing she's not going to be very forthcoming?" He was talking about Larissa.

"You know her deal. She withdrew from the world years ago. She wouldn't even talk to me after Julia disappeared, when I was at my lowest of lows. I don't see how asking her to confirm that she helped cover up two murders will inspire her to leave whatever off-the-grid island-compound she's living as a recluse on."

"Think she'd sue? Any way to write the story without her?"

"Possibly to the first, and no to the second. I was thinking I'd change her name."

"Probably for the best. Keep her the enigmatic genius. Are there any links out there connecting the two of you? Anything to prove you're related, or connecting her to the scandal? Basically, anything for readers to deduce that she's the character, whatever you name her?"

"Not that I'm aware of. And if there were, I'm certain she would have scrubbed them from the Internet by now."

"Then we might be fine. I'll run it by the lawyers to be sure. And let me—" I hear him typing on a keyboard. While he does, I refill my wine and have a drink. Zürich is nine hours ahead of San Francisco, so while it's three in the afternoon for him, it's midnight for me. Francesca is asleep in the next room, and I'm drinking alone. After a minute, Adam says, "Looks like there was one documentary, *Dead in The Nest*, but that was well over a decade ago. But nothing recent. And no books, so . . . Yeah. Damn. Seems to me like you've got the market cornered on this one."

"So you're game?"

"Definitely. And true crime is all the rage these days—though you'll have to compete with all the damn podcasts and streaming series. But half of those don't even offer a possible suspect let alone present new evidence, so you'll already be a leg up there. And who knows. Play your cards right and maybe you'll get a Netflix deal out of it. Then you'll finally be able to cast Brian in something you've written."

"Yeah," I said. "But knowing Brian, he'll insist on playing Martin."

* * *

That first morning in Bern I asked Francesca to tell me how she and Martin had met. To which she smiled sadly and said, "Yes. Of course I will tell you. I assumed you would want to know. Have you ever visited Bern before?" I said I hadn't. "It is quite beautiful. Small compared to Zürich, Geneva too, but much more charming. Walk into town with me today. Would you do me that kindness?"

I didn't see how I could refuse. She was being more than hospitable. And I don't mean the sex. Though there was that too. Anyway, it was a pleasure to be away from Amsterdam. I'd already grown to feel claustrophobic, but not until leaving did I realize how much so. There was my basement apartment, sure, but it was more than that. It was the confining maze of canals and narrow streets. The ant trails. The gloom. Regardless of how I'd come to be in Bern, I was more than happy to have a reason to stay.

That first day together, Francesca and I just walked and took in the sights. We had coffee on the Münsterplattform, the park beside the Münster church with benches and tables overlooking the river valley, then we ate dinner down along the water. Every step of the way, Francesca insisted on paying. Again and again I tried to contribute at least my share, and each time she adamantly refused. She knew I had questions, but she wasn't ready to answer them. And I didn't push her. Which was easy, seeing how delightful a conversationalist she was. She had a playful yet sharp sense of humor too. I don't think I'd laughed as much my entire time in Amsterdam as I had that first day we spent together. When, after dinner, as we strolled along the quiet cobblestone streets, I managed to surprise her with an ice cream cone, she narrowed her eyes and shook a finger at me. "Determined, I see." But still I couldn't get her to tell me anything about how she'd met Martin.

* * *

The next morning, over another delightful breakfast, Francesca said she wanted to show me the countryside. I admit, I was enchanted by her. She was kind and generous, but she was also mysterious. Yes, there were the stories I wanted her to tell me, but there was something else too. With her, I felt as

Chalet, Lake Neuchâtel, Switzerland

if I was somewhere. And that was a sensation I hadn't felt in a long time. So I went with her to the countryside.

By train we traveled just over an hour to a region called Friborg, where, in the city of Estavayer-le-Lac, we boarded another, smaller train to Lake Neuchâtel. From the station I could see a medieval castle upon a hilltop, but the cab we caught took us in the opposite direction, along the lake and into the woods to a secluded chalet. The cab driver spoke only French, not Swiss-German, and not a word of English. I was glad Francesca was fluent, because I am not.

The air was thick and humid, as evenings often are in wetlands. Mosquitos buzzed our ears as the cab backed out of the narrow dirt driveway and onto the gravel road. Francesca just stood in the overgrown grass, staring at the chalet, smiling, like a child on Christmas morning.

She produced a set of keys and tried each until one opened the door. Inside was a cozy cabin that felt like a cross between a rustic ski lodge and a kids' summer camp. The way she moved around the small space, I knew it was her first time there.

"Another gift from Martin?" I asked.

She moved her head to say yes, but offered nothing more.

*   *   *

The walk to town was well over half an hour, and it was late afternoon as we climbed the hill to the village. Winding cobblestone streets delivered us to a vista point overlooking the lake and valley. We had an early dinner beside the castle and drank way more wine than we should have for two people who had to stumble half an hour home through woods in the dark to a chalet neither had ever been to before. But somehow we made it. Arm in arm and laughing.

Three more days we spent at the chalet. We slept late, cooked big meals, took walks, and drank copiously. I occasionally thought of the book I still intended to write, though I was no longer driven to work. I hadn't given up on it, nor was I procrastinating. Instinctually I knew this was an interlude. A moment between moments. One that, if I didn't appreciate fully, I would regret. And so I surrendered to the flow. I also let go of pushing Francesca for information. She too was in an interlude—we were in it together. And she would tell me in her time.

On day five the weather shifted, outside, as well as in. The temperature dropped easily ten degrees, and a chilly wind accompanied a light rain. Francesca's mood fell too. All morning she sat quietly staring out the irregularly shaped windows toward the nothingness of trees. After lunch, as I was washing dishes, she said, "I think now it is time to go to Zürich." To which I said sounded fine. Whatever journey we were on, I was a passenger. And so that evening we packed our things and boarded a train.

*   *   *

After disembarking at Hauptbahnhof, Zürich's main train station, Francesca guided us out and onto the street with the ease of one who has lived in a place for many years. And in short time we found ourselves at a small, two-story building for which she once more had a key. Entering, I knew immediately this was a place not like the others. The building in Bern had looked as if it had been completely renovated and was waiting for occupants to move in. The chalet, too, while simple and rustic, had also looked as if it had been emptied for its new owners to make their own. But this small building in Zürich was someone's home. There was furniture, maps on the walls, books on the shelves, and a closet full of clothes. I turned on a lamp with a thin red scarf draped over the shade to reveal a grocery list on the fridge, loose change in a dish, and a blanket on the couch—bunched up as if someone had just slid out from underneath. This place hadn't just been lived in, it was *being* lived in. But judging by the drooping leaves on all the plants, I guessed no one had been here for at least a few weeks. The mail on the desk was all addressed to the same name, Nathan Cohen, who I didn't know, and yet felt certain I did. This had been the home of the outlaw Martin Zorn.

Francesca moved around like a kitten in a new room. Wide-eyed, but not with any of the joy she'd shown at the chalet. She obviously hadn't been here before, and I was sensing this was the end of the line for Martin's gifts—at least in regard to buildings. With the way she'd continuously insisted on paying for everything, from train tickets to meals to generously tipping everyone who served us in even the smallest way, I was certain he had also left her money. And I was about to learn why.

45

TRANSFERENCE

"I met Nathan Cohen," Francesca says, "the man you know as Martin Zorn, here in Zürich."

After arriving last night, she'd said little more than she was tired, then she went to sleep. Which is when I opened a bottle of wine and called Adam. In the same way I'd known in Bern that an interlude had begun, I knew the interlude was over. And it felt like loss. Yes, I would be returning to the book—and my life—which was why, more than wanting to talk to my publisher, I wanted to talk to my friend. After which I finished the bottle and passed out on the couch. This morning I woke to find Francesca not in the bed. I searched the house and eventually found her on the roof, at a wooden table, under a mesh canopy. It's a nice rooftop deck with astroturf and potted plants, but she said she didn't want to stay in the house, so we went to a café. It's early June, and the morning is warm, already pushing hot. We are at a table in a side garden in the shade.

"If he lived in that house," Francesca says, "I did not know it. Not once did I visit Nathan in his home." She takes a deep breath and looks overwhelmed. Then she offers me a smile. "I wish to say, when you and I first met, you suggested I tell the story from the beginning. Maybe one day I can do that for you. Who knows, maybe one day I too will write my own book." She sips her cappuccino, but only as something to do. "You should know, in Amsterdam, I worked as a prostitute."

"I know. You went by the name Tulip."

She cocks her head and smiles curiously. And so I tell her the story of Danielle and Kitty.

"Oh my," she says, shaking her head with wonder. "Such a coincidence! You know I was to talk to Danielle for her art project?"

"She mentioned that you were on her list of women to profile."

"Wow. How amazing life can be—to learn we were already only one separation away!" Her mood had been solemn, but this coincidence has brightened her. Then the heaviness of what's to follow returns. "Please know," she says, looking at me in earnest, "Martin did not encourage me to seduce you. It is important to me that you understand this."

"I'm not worried about it," I said. Though, in the beginning, I had been. That first morning in Bern, "conflicted" was the best word to describe my emotions. But by evening, the conflict had passed. I'd sensed the interlude, and had already given myself over to it.

"Sex and intimacy," Francesca says. "From the outside they may look the same. But in practice they are very different."

"Of course."

She sighs softly. "I have been debating with myself of how much I might tell you," Francesca says. "The story of Nathan—your Martin—yes, absolutely I believe you must know. But I mean of myself." She pauses and I let her decide. "I think the fates, however, have chosen for me. I had been considering telling my story to your protege Danielle. In her absence, I will tell you."

I grin. "You know she's going to give me hell when she learns I got your story before she did?"

Francesca only smiles sadly in response; her humor is not up to strength today.

"I told you of Kris Tao—Crystal Lake's—childhood," Francesca says. "Of her having Taiwanese parents who did not want her. Do you remember?" Seeing me nod, she continues. "When Nathan told me of this, I understood. Like Kris, my father did not want girls. Kris was born in America, so all her father could do was detest, ignore, and rape her. However, I was born in China. When I was eight years old my father sold me to a man who came around every season to collect unwanted children. A broker, who then sold me to a man in Dubai. He would treat me as a princess, then lock me in a room for days with no food. Without warning he would turn from kind to cruel. And because I could not predict his moods, I grew to want nothing more than to please him. For one year I lived like this, until I was traded to a man in Milan. I was part of a stable of girls to be used at the whims of a group of powerful men. But unlike my captor in Dubai, I was treated very well. It was there in Italy that I was educated. Taught to speak Italian and English and trained in the art of conversation. When I was sixteen, I was then sold to a syndicate in Russia. I was a very short time in Moscow, then brought here, to Zürich, where I worked for many years. This is where I met Nathan Cohen—the man you know as Martin Zorn."

"What year was this?"

"Twenty-fourteen."

"So only five years ago. Do you know what he was doing before then?"

"I do now, yes. But only because I have recently learned. Until he found me in Amsterdam two weeks ago, I believed Nathan Cohen was little more than an American bodyguard working for the syndicate who owned my contract."

"You mean the Russians who purchased you from Italy?"

She nods and drinks her cappuccino.

"So you're saying Martin Zorn worked for a Russian crime syndicate?"

"Yes. He was a guard at the private club where I worked for many years."

"Do you not find that strange? That the man who was willing to kill three people to save young women would then go to work for a child-trafficking ring?"

"To be fair, my employer did not deal in children."

"I thought you said you were sixteen when you were sold to the Russian syndicate?"

"Precisely," she says, very matter-of-fact. And I decide not to push the subject.

"Okay," I say. "But even still, this was a criminal organization that dealt in trading human beings. How do you think he lived with himself?"

"Yes," Francesca says, "I see your confusion. I can explain."

I had yet to touch my espresso. Now I down the small, bitter shot, eager to hear how Martin Zorn went from crusader to muscle for Russian pimps.

"When I met Nathan Cohen, your Martin Zorn, I was a hostess in a private club. Nathan was a bodyguard working the door. The first night he saw me, he told me he wanted to save me."

"You see, now *that* isn't a surprise. And did you want to be saved?"

Francesca laughed. "I wanted to be free. Which I thought was the same thing."

"And did you believe him?"

"Men say all sorts of things. But Nathan felt different—not that I believed him, only that I felt he was sincere. He told me he wanted to buy my contract—which many men had also told me. Though of course none ever did. But even if what Nathan said had been true, he had no money. He was a nobody. A bouncer at a club."

"And so . . . You were friends? Lovers? Were you two married?"

"Married?!" She reacts as if she's never heard anything so crazy. "Oh, my, no." Then it comes to her. A huge smile blooms on her face. "Wait—you are talking about the ring—I cannot believe it worked!"

"So then I'm right?" I say. "It was a ruse? Martin's wearing a wedding ring when he came to see me?"

Francesca is still blown away. "I must say, I thought it silly—not only the ring, but those ridiculous clothes! 'No, no,' Nathan said. 'Emit will like this character.' And he was right! Is this why you came to Bern?"

"Yeah," I say. "I mean, there was the postcard, obviously, and the thought that you might be Crystal. But there was also the mystery of who Martin Zorn might have been married to."

She shakes her head in disbelief. "Well, then, I owe our friend an apology. I told him he was mad to be putting on such a show, thinking you would pick up such small clues. But he was right! And you—congratulations! You are a detective!"

I laugh. Mostly at imagining how Ronnie might react to me being called a detective. "And you're sure there's no other Mrs. Zorn out there? One you might not know about?"

"I do not believe so. Nathan asked me to help him find a cheap ring for the performance with you. And if there had been a Mrs. Zorn, would he have not left all his wealth to her?"

"Right, of course. And so did you and Martin—Nathan—ever have any sort of romantic relationship?"

"We were never physical, Nathan and me. But there was most certainly something special between us. He was very gentle. He would often take the money he earned from our employer and give it right back in order to take me out to museums and dinners. He often told me of the life he wanted to make for me, one free of being a servant. Still, I did not take him seriously. You might be surprised what men will pay a woman for. Sex is often incidental."

"Why do you think he chose you?"

"You know why."

"Because you reminded him of Crystal."

"Yes. I believe it is called transference."

"What ever happened to Crystal, by the way? Do you know?"

Francesca shakes her head. "As I said, until two weeks ago I knew nothing of the man Martin Zorn, and little of Nathan Cohen. On our dates, he was a listener. It is a type, you know." She finishes her cappuccino.

"Was it Nathan who brought you to Amsterdam?"

"No. The move was my fortieth birthday gift from my employer——" she laughs bitterly "——which is a joke. At thirty, I had already been considered old. I was demoted to being a second-tier girl, my client list became older, fatter, and less refined, and I was given a smaller room to live, without a window. At thirty-five I was made a hostess and received even smaller rewards. In normal life, we are supposed to gain more as we grow older; better home, nicer things. But when you are a possession whose worth is defined by the age of your body, these rules do not apply. At forty I was considered used up. I was told my debt was paid, though I must continue to pay interest——and would need to pay for the rest of my life. Making it so that I would be owned forever.

"I was transferred to Amsterdam, though once there I was allowed to have my own life. I tried to find normal work, normal friends, but I had never had a normal life or been a normal person, so I came to accept that such a thing was not possible for me. I admit, I gave up. Amsterdam is extremely beautiful. But I found life there to be quite depressing."

I laugh. She looks at me. "Nothing," I say. "I just happened to have the same experience in Amsterdam——with depression, I mean. Not with—— sorry. Of course it's not even close to the same experience as you. Shit. I just mean——sorry. Please, continue."

Francesca is entertained by my embarrassment, which is fine with me.

"Yes," she says, "well, ironically, it was only when I was free that I lost hope. All my life I was considered property, with very little personal free-doms. But within that prison I found my own strength. My dreams of one day being free kept me strong, always believing my real life was waiting for me. But then, when released, I found life to be not so different. I did not fit in, and there was no secret pleasure waiting. I had become disillusioned, and, as I said, fell into despair.

"Even so, I have always been a positive person, and did my best to find happiness in the life I had. I joined a community garden and grew vegetables. I found I was good with tomatoes. I would give them as gifts to everyone, including my clients. I would keep a basket in my window and offer each man a tomato as he left——they were always very confused!" She laughs, and I remember Kitty telling me about Tulip and her tomatoes.

"And in short time," Francesca says, "I accepted that this was to be my life, and I began to find peace. Then, one day, earlier this year——I remem-ber it was April because we were approaching Easter——I learned that my employer had been assassinated. His entire network dissolved. I waited for a visit from a representative of the new boss. These organizations, they are all connected, like roots to a giant tree—no, not even a tree. A field of grass, whose root systems are all one. But no one came. I saved my interest payments, but no one came to collect. Then Nathan Cohen appeared. Two years I had not seen this man who had sworn one day he would save me. I assumed he had come for the interest dues. But no. He had come to take me away. 'You are free,' he said."

"You mean because the boss was dead?"

"Yes. But much more."

An employee making the rounds stops at our table. As he gathers our empty cups he asks, "Kann ich dir sonst noch etwas mitbringen?"

"Would you like anything more?" Francesca asks me. But before I can answer, she bolts upright, very excited, as if she just remembered she'd won a prize. She asks the server a question I don't understand, and when he nods, she claps her hands and bounces up and down. She places an order in which all I caught was the word cappuccino, then the server hurries off.

"I almost forgot!" she says to me. And when I ask what, she says, "No. It is to be a surprise."

"There have been no shortage of those," I say. Then, getting back to the story, I ask, "So, to be clear, are you saying Martin killed your boss? To finally set you free?"

"No, no," Francesca says, shaking her head. "Is more complicated than that. Only . . ." She looks nervously around.

"What?" I say, also looking. "Are you afraid of retribution?"

She nods emphatically. "Absolutely. I had nothing to do with the killing, but I have most certainly reaped the rewards. These homes you have visited? They were Nathan's gifts to me. Along with a great deal of money with which to live." She pauses. It's not me she's worried about telling, it's the telling itself, to anyone. And I suppose, yes, to me specifically, because of what I might do with the story. "These were Nathan's payment," Francesca says. "For selling information. This is the first story Nathan told to me, in Amsterdam, and why I agreed to meet with you and honor his dying request." She pauses again, takes a breath, and looks me in the eye. "Yes, Nathan Cohen worked for a human-trafficking syndicate. But only because he was dismantling the organization from the inside—as an agent for Interpol."

* * *

The server comes and slides a plate onto the table with an inch-thick slice of toasted banana bread. Then he sets two forks and two perfect foamy cappuccinos in front of us.

"Danke," Francesca says excitedly as the man walks away.

"You'd think at this point I could no longer be surprised," I say. "But you're right—you're telling me Martin Zorn was working with the International Police? How is that even possible? Though I suppose it's not any less probable than him working for Russian gangsters."

"Yes," Francesca says, cutting off a corner of the banana bread with her fork. "Our dear friend was quite complicated." She slides the bite into her mouth and closes her eyes with a look of pleasure seemingly too immense for a piece of banana bread—and I like banana bread.

"Okay," I say, as I cut my own bite. "I'm starting to get turned around here. I really think you need to start at the beginning—or somewhere close."

"Of course," Francesca says. "You are a novelist. Your mind is finely tuned to how a story—"

"Oh my word," I say, not meaning to cut her off but being unable to control myself, having just tasted the banana bread. "This is amazing!"

Francesca smiles. "I know! I cannot believe I almost forgot! This is why I brought us to this café. I think it may be the one thing I truly miss about Zürich."

"Wow," I say, taking another bite and once more being blown away. "I feel kind of guilty enjoying this so much when we're talking about human trafficking and murder."

"Life is most certainly complex."

And for a moment we both forget about Nathan slash Martin, death, and child sex-workers, and savor the delicious bread with our cappuccinos. Then, as easily as we fell out of the conversation, Francesca jumps back in.

"When, two weeks ago," she says, "Nathan came to me in Amsterdam, he looked terrible. He said he had terminal cancer. I had not seen him in two years, and he explained how in that time he had worked with Interpol to give over our employer's entire network."

"But you said your boss was assassinated?"

"Yes. Because Nathan made it appear as if our employer was the one who was working for Interpol. So as the network began to be dismantled by the authorities, the organization turned on itself and was destroyed from the inside. But, as you requested, I must try to start from the beginning." She takes another bite of banana bread and once more reacts with ecstasy.

"Nineteen ninety-nine," Francesca says, completing her euphoric bite with a sip of cappuccino. "Martin Zorn kills Faith Chadwick and Kai Sjugard. Larissa Huxley and Ronnie Gilbert aid his escape to Mexico. They also arrange for a local robbery gang to clean out Faith's home, and in a matter of hours they have transformed the murder scene into a burglary.

"Once in Mexico, Martin suffers great despair. On this subject he dwelled for some time, but I will spare you the retelling and say only that, in those early days, many times he comes close to ending his own life. But at each moment he remembers the bargain he has made. In trade for his freedom, he is to devote his life to service.

"He begins at a small mission in a remote region, giving his time to the church, helping the elderly and poor. He volunteers with groups providing food for the needy, and in time meets people who are working to stop the trafficking of young children. He has nothing. No money, no possessions, but he works tirelessly, and over the years comes to organize and lead several chapters of what grows to be a major force against the prostitution of children.

"As you might imagine, he makes quite a few enemies. Drug cartels who use children as mules make several assassination attempts on his life. His car is rigged with explosives. Each time he survives, his reputation only grows. He becomes known as El Resbaladizo—*The Slippery One*—and posters with his face begin to appear around the municipalities.

"Through his work, he hears of new alliances between Russian syndicates and Mexican cartels, trading weapons for cocaine to sell in Europe. Martin learns that these syndicates are also connected to human trafficking, supplying western Europe with children from Africa and Asia, and who are now moving into Latin America.

"In 2012 Martin is diagnosed with liver cancer and given two years to live. Already every day his life is in danger, so he only presses on further with his mission. It is not long after this when he is kidnapped. Betrayed, he believes, for the reward. A sack over his head, his wrists bound, he is driven to a remote location. Only, when the sack is removed, he finds neither the cartels nor the Russians, but the Swiss branch of Interpol. 'You are Martin Zorn,' a man says to him. 'Ex-police officer wanted in the United States for two murders. You are also El Resbaladizo, wanted by Latin drug cartels. And we are here to offer you a deal.'"

I've been eating banana bread and drinking cappuccino and listening to Francesca's story as if I were sitting in a movie theater shoving popcorn into my mouth absorbed in the latest thriller. The story is so outrageous that I forget it's Martin Zorn we're talking about and wonder at what point I fell so under Francesca's spell that she realized she could feed me whatever wild tale she's dreamed up, believing I'd swallow it. And so I tell her just that.

"I think it must be the banana bread," she says. "It is quite intoxicating."

"It is. I can only imagine what it would be like with a good Tawny port."

She puts a hand on her heart and makes dreamy eyes, swooning at the thought.

"Okay," I say, about to take what I know is a bite more than my share of half the banana bread, only to stop myself, at which Francesca laughs and says, "We can always order more!" and I give in and take the bite I was probably going to take anyway. "Okay," I say again. "I need to ask, was Martin Zorn really known as El Resbaladizo?"

"Why? Is this some famous name I am unaware of?"

"No. I just mean, if you'd said he was called Zorro, then yeah, I would have called bullshit in a heartbeat. But even so, how many people get Mexican nicknames from drug cartels?"

Francesca shrugs. "How many people are famous rock stars, authors, and artists who work with private investigators and ex-policemen wanted for murder?"

"Touché."

"You are welcome."

"And so . . ."

"And so," Francesca says, rolling out her arm as if presenting a new car. "Thank you for allowing me to continue. However, this story is close to ending. Interpol makes Martin an offer, a deal to fulfill a role which only he can play. To the Russians he will offer to trade information about a large cartel operation which the Swiss have learned about, in exchange for a position in their organization. The Russians know he is a wanted man in Mexico and Central America, and so the Swiss are banking on—"

"Wait, but don't the Russians also know that Martin is a fervent activist against human trafficking? Why would they help him? Especially when they can turn him over to the cartels and curry favor?"

"Because the Swiss have unique information for Martin to offer them. Proof the cartels are attempting to double-cross the Russians, by cutting them out and creating their own pathways into Europe. There is a major shipment about to move, one which Interpol cannot act on for fear that it will expose their insider operatives. But by passing the information to the

Russians, they stop the shipment and turn the two burgeoning partners against each other. The alliance is already fragile, and by using Martin, the Swiss can exploit the rift, stop the shipment, and plant Martin inside the European operation. For the Russians' part, if they believe Martin is desperate to save his life, they will think they have him helpless—which is the best way to bait a Russian. They are savages for weakness."

"And so Martin agrees?"

"He agrees. Because he too wants to take down the syndicate. The child-trafficking trade in Latin America is enormous, but the Russian-Asian network is the head of the beast. And what does he have to lose? He has already been given a medical death sentence. If he refuses, Interpol will hand him over to the United States for prosecution—or worse, to the drug cartels, who will string him up in the town square as a warning to all who think they can work against them."

"And this is what year again?"

"Twenty-fourteen."

"So, you're saying after Martin left San Francisco, he lived for fifteen years in Mexico doing charitable work—more, being a hunted advocate?"

"Yes. And now he is headed to Zürich. Once more as a member of the police."

"So the plan worked?" I say.

"Yes, the plan worked. Martin trades information of the cartel's betrayal to the Russians, and in exchange they bring him in as a low-level employee to their organization. They know his human-rights leanings, and so they force him to give up the networks he has spent years cultivating in Mexico. This is Martin's deepest regret—more than Joe or Faith Chadwick, who now are distant memories, but of the numerous lives he knows he is endangering. But he must focus on the larger prize, and he needs to prove to the syndicate that he is loyal. He gives them the bare minimum, but still many lives are lost. Many of the networks and safehouses which he had helped to construct are compromised."

"And so the Russians put him to work as a doorman at a private club, which is where he falls for you?"

"Yes."

"I have to say, I'm surprised the Russians didn't just kill him, or turn around and sell him back to the cartels."

Francesca nods. "True, Russians can be vicious. But they are also opportunistic. Nathan is now one more human they can own."

"Fair enough. Also, what name was Martin going by in Mexico, do you know? Other than El Resbaladizo? Was it Nathan Cohen at that time?"

"Good question. I do not know. But can you imagine this sudden change of life for him? From underground outlaw activist in Mexico, to insider agent acting as a low-level enforcer in Zürich?"

"And, he's dying of cancer. Because this is what? Two years after he'd been given a two-year prognosis?"

"Which I think is the only thing keeping him sane. Believing he has little time keeps him focused."

"And so . . ."

"And so Martin does what Interpol has tasked him to do. From the door of a club he works his way into the Russian syndicate, earning favor and promotion, and feeding the Swiss intelligence community information along the way. He is—fittingly—a cancer within their network, destroying cells and turning them against themselves. Until, eventually, enough tentacles are severed that the head of the beast dies."

"One of those tentacles being your employer?"

"Yes."

"And all the while, Martin—Nathan—is taking you out to museums, telling you he's going to save you?"

"As I have said, the last two years of these operations I was in Amsterdam, so not present. But yes, for the three years before, Nathan Cohen and I saw each other regularly. And in that time I watched him rise through the ranks. Quite impressively, I must say."

"And the Russians never figured out that he was an ex-cop wanted for murder?"

"I cannot say for certain, but I would think at some point they must have learned. Maybe even during the time of the deal in Mexico. In fact, I think this must be true. Such information would have only helped Martin, earning him the Russians' respect, proving to them that he was in fact an outlaw."

I nodded. "Maybe that's why they didn't kill him—they knew he had nowhere to go."

"Yes, I think this must be so. This would explain too why they let him rise in their organization. Of course, as I said, all of this was a surprise to me. Seeing Nathan in Amsterdam, I was shocked by his appearance—and most certainly by his story. He had deteriorated greatly in the two years since I had last seen him. The cancer having finally won. And I will confess, like you, I at first did not believe him. Here was this man who had plied me with fantastic promises, then appeared at my door looking as a beggar, claiming he was responsible for destroying the criminal network which had possessed me all of my life. And yet——" she opens her hands "——you have seen all he has given me."

"And where did he procure all these gifts?"

"The Swiss government paid him. But he also took many liberties with syndicate funds, a move which, upon discovering, caused the Swiss to turn on him. Bureaucracies are worse than crime syndicates——one person makes a promise, another breaks it, and no one is accountable. At least in a syndicate, there is order. Responsibility, and consequence. A deal was being made with the Americans to return Nathan——Martin Zorn——to the United States to stand trial. The day he came to see me, he had successfully moved all his money so that it would be untraceable. He had little time. To get me as much as he could, he had to place it in various investments. One being properties. Including this home in Zürich, which he purchased from himself. Everything is now in my name, and, if I am to believe him, free and clear from the reaches of Interpol."

"So, then . . . The timing of the trial? Was that a coincidence?"

"What do you mean?"

"In the death of Ronnie Gilbert. You know that Ronnie is dead, right?"

"Yes, of course. He died in Australia. I remember reading this in your book, *Come to Light*. Ronnie had been working for you, investigating the disappearance of your wife. But please, remind me the details of the trial, because I do not recall."

"Right," I say. "Because the trial wasn't in the book. Only Ronnie's death. The gist is, two years ago Ronnie Gilbert was investigating a Bay Area tech mogul named Randall Fenton. He'd tracked him to a compound in Queensland, Australia. Ronnie and I were in regular touch, but then suddenly he went silent. Two weeks later, his half-digested torso was found in the stomach of a seventeen-foot crocodile. The presumption was that Randall had discovered that Ronnie was on to him, killed him, and fed him to the local wildlife." Francesca is nodding along, already knowing all I've said. But then I get to what she doesn't know. "Randall was charged with Ronnie's murder, and earlier this year there was a trial where I gave testimony. Then, less than a week after the verdict acquitting Randall in the murder of Ronnie, Martin stepped into my shop."

"I see. And you thought Martin visiting you was because he too had heard the verdict in this trial?"

"It's what he told me. That he'd come to commiserate over the death of our old pal, and the injustice which had been done by his killer going free."

Francesca continues to nod as she puts the pieces together.

"But from the story I'm hearing," I say, "I'm now thinking the timing was just a coincidence. It had to be, right? While the trial made for a perfect excuse for Martin to see me, it was just a stroke of luck that the verdict came when it did, since, really, he would have come to see me on that day whether there had been a verdict or not. Right?"

"I think this must be true," Francesca says. "Given the situation. He was in a very precarious place. He was dying. Our employer had been killed, the international police had turned on him, and he had bartered as much time as he could before he was to be extradited to America."

"So that he could set you up with a new life?"

"I believe so, yes."

"Then he shot himself so he wouldn't die in prison?"

"Or a painful death from cancer. But not before coaching me on the story to tell you—and paying you one last visit."

"I suppose I should be flattered."

"Maybe." She puts her hand on mine and flashes big eyes. "Though I think you were the only author he knew." Then she laughs.

* * *

I have more questions—how could I not? But we both need a break. So after our banana bread we go for a walk, Francesca saying she wants to show me Zürich. She takes me to the river where we swim. Then to Old Town where we walk old-world Switzerland along with thousands of other tourists. We pass a lovely day together, and at dusk enjoy dinner by candlelight. And in the morning, she is gone.

I'm unsurprised. Even expected it. She'd done what she'd been tasked to do—and more. And now, for the first time in her life, she is free.

46

THAT ONE KITCHEN DRAWER

If you've ever moved, then you know, no matter how methodically you pack, there's always that one drawer of stuff you never know what to do with. You tell yourself you're going to organize it, but in the end you just dump the entire contents into a box and promise yourself you'll deal with it properly when you get to wherever you're going next. But it's a lie. The mess either gets dumped into a new drawer as is, or is left in the box, which gets shoved to the back of a closet, unopened and forgotten—most likely next to a similar box from the previous house that just got shuttled from one closet to the next. Stories can be the same way. At the end, no matter how tidy a tale you've told, there's at least a few small dangling plot points that readers feel haven't been adequately addressed.

I'm saying this because this chapter, is that drawer.

I'm still in Zürich, and have been for almost three weeks, which makes over a month now in Switzerland. Francesca has not returned. I haven't heard from her, and I haven't tried to contact her. Which is fine. Who am I to interfere with her freedom?

I hadn't intended on staying this long. But I've been on a roll with writing, and frankly, I don't want to go back to Amsterdam. I look online and see the weather getting nicer by the day. But still, the idea of returning feels like squeezing myself into a very small seat on a very crowded bus for an interminably long ride.

Admittedly, it's weird to be in Martin Zorn's former home. I know that technically the house is now Francesca's, but still. Every day that I get up and write the story of Martin's last days in San Francisco, sitting in his chair, at his table, on his roof deck, I can't help but feel as if maybe I'm desecrating something.

As for Francesca, I assume she's happy for me to stay here. I have the feeling she delivered me to do just what I'm doing. I also got more than a feeling that she didn't like being back in Zürich. For which I can hardly blame her. She'd lived way too many years here as a possession. If one cold and lonely winter in Amsterdam has me shuddering at the thought of returning, I can't even begin to imagine the feelings Zürich must stir in her. That she'd been able to enjoy even one day in this city is a credit to her strength. Though I did see her look over her shoulder more than a few times.

That said, in short time I will also leave. Just as soon as I finish putting the final touches on this draft, then send it to Adam. I can't ignore my life forever. And in that regard, I've made a decision: I'll stay in Amsterdam for the summer, enjoy the long, warm days along the canals, and see if I can make a few art sales to drunk or stoned tourists, then once I smell the first hint of winter blowing in, I'll pack up and move back to San Francisco. It's time. While I'll have lived only one year in the Venice of the North, it's been seven years since I've lived in the City by the Bay. After Julia disappeared I ran away to Southeast Asia, and from there I've been bouncing around like a pinball. I want to say I'd never meant to be away for so long, but, truth is, I never had a plan. I was just going from one thing to the next, trying to find some peace. Even the decision to leave Amsterdam wasn't so much a decision as it was a realization. One that hit me several days after Francesca left, when Danielle called.

"Just making sure you're not dead," she said.

"Nope, still not floating in the canal."

"You ever coming back?" She'd tried to play it off as sarcasm, but she couldn't cover up what I daresay was genuine concern.

"Maybe not," I said. I'd meant it as a joke, but as I heard myself say the words, they felt true.

"Whatever," she said, with an icy chill. "Semester is over. And I can't promise to maintain regular hours for your endless flow of customers." And suddenly I felt bad. Because only then did I realize how insensitive I'd been. Last Danielle knew, a strange man had come into town and taken a local prostitute to who knew where, killed himself, then sent me a posthumous message which I ran off chasing for what I said would be a day or two, and after a week hadn't even thought to let her know I wasn't also dead. And that's when it occurred to me that maybe Danielle hadn't been the only one who'd been closed off and hiding beneath a shield of sarcasm. Which is when I knew for certain that I would be leaving Amsterdam, and that the only part of my time there I would miss would be Danielle.

26th Street, San Francisco — Patron asked to be unnamed

"Do whatever hours work for you," I told her. "And feel free to use my studio and computer as much as you need. Make yourself at home, and I'll let you know when I'm heading back."

She was quiet for a moment, and in the silence I sensed anger. It was as if she and I had been living in a state of holding our collective breaths, and finally we were ready to let them out. Only too long had passed, and all the things we should have said were no longer an option. She hadn't asked if I'd found Tulip, and I was glad. Francesca had intentionally left Amsterdam without telling anyone, and I was sure she preferred never to be found again. Which meant that Kitty, Danielle, and anyone else who'd been left wondering, they were just going to have to stay wondering. It was sad, the distance between Danielle and me, but it at least spared me having to lie.

"Cool," Danielle said. Then she hung up. It would be the last time we spoke.

A couple of days later she sent me a text: *Read your damn email!* On average I checked my email every two to three days, but since I'd been in Switzerland I hadn't checked it at all. I logged in, and amidst the hundreds of announcements that proved every form of human communication eventually devolves into a barrage of advertisements you never signed up for, I saw an email from Danielle. It read that she had completed her research in Amsterdam and was moving to Majorca. If I didn't return before she left, she would slip her keys through the mail slot. I understood then why she'd written and not called. Because when I phoned her, I got an automated recording saying the number was no longer in service. Her text to me must have been the last thing she did before removing the SIM card. I was starting to feel uncomfortable about being the last person people communicated with before significantly changing their lives.

*   *   *

Back to the story drawer. I know this is only a draft, but I also know Adam. He will find every dangling plot point and note it as if he were a third-grade math teacher chastising me for forgetting to carry the one—and yes, I know that's a mixed metaphor. Call it an homage to Ronnie. Just as I know that pointing out the holes in the story is Adam's job as editor. But I want to beat him to it. So I'm making my own list. Here goes:

Crystal. I searched for Kris Tao along with every possible name combination of Kris, Tao, Crystal, Tally, and Lake, and found nothing of relevance. I assumed this had been Larissa, having scrubbed her former lover from the web. I still daydream about running into Tally one day.

I also wondered if the reason she and Larissa had split was because Tally had in fact killed Faith and Kai. If so, it would make sense that neither of the two young women could have stayed with the other following such an event. Larissa, in her devotion to nonconforming ethics, might have been able to forgive Tally—might have even helped her start a new life, as she'd supposedly done for Martin—but Tally surely would have had to move on in order to forget the past and rebuild her life. Which I believe would have been equally true even if Tally hadn't done the killing. Learning the truth about Faith was a devastating enough blow to her version of reality. Whether she'd responded with a gun or not, leaving everything behind would have been the only way for her to move on. Or who knows, maybe Tally and Larissa were just two young people who had a fleeting love affair. Theirs certainly would not have been the first.

Ross Alley, Chinatown, San Francisco — Patron asked to be unnamed

What next? My commissions. While my studio had been untouched by the fire, it had been ravaged by water damage. Firefighters had literally chopped a hole in the ceiling with axes. I managed to recover all of my drawings from my flat files, though most were stained with what can only be described as smoke-water. Many of my patrons told me to keep the advance they'd paid, saying we could figure out the artwork later, and several wrote me checks for "future art"—a term that I adored and would later make use of—though was less about purchasing art than their way of supporting me in a difficult time. I was a bit overwhelmed, actually, at how supportive my patrons and fans ended up being. It never occurred to me that so many people would step forward to offer support. One fan even gave me a place to live, so that when the three months of insurance lapsed at the City Mews, I got to live rent-free in a two-story house on Twin Peaks.

I got back to work as quickly as I could. My throat took longer to heal than it took me to get back to drawing. I was able to have my smoke-filled brushes retrieved from my condemned building and set up a temporary studio in the City Mews. Larissa bought me a new digital camera and computer to replace the ones she'd already bought me—which I hadn't asked her to do but greatly appreciated—and in no time I was cranking out drawings. Which was exactly what I needed. Getting back to work was my way of creating structure and putting solid ground under my feet. It wasn't the first time—and it surely wouldn't be the last—that I would use my work as a cornerstone on which to rebuild my life, and I was grateful to have it. I began with the Stinson drawing. I still had days booked at Jerry Garcia's former beach house, and I took advantage of every one. Aside from enjoying the fresh ocean air in my damaged lungs, I was able to get the drawing done in time for Steven to give to his wife. A slew of new commissions came in too. Fun stuff, like Ross Alley in Chinatown, home of the Golden Gate Fortune Cookie Factory; the palm trees in Precita Park; and, "anything from Duboce Triangle," which were the kinds of drawings I loved to make. I got to stroll the lovely neighborhoods of San Francisco until a composition called to me. Never had I been so pleased to be the drawing monkey Larissa had deemed me to be.

The only commission to go awry was, appropriately, not even a true commission. It was the drawing for the local community group raising funds to restore the Conservatory of Flowers. I'd done everything I could to make the dilapidated structure look glorious, making a full-color drawing and even going so far as buying a dozen dahlias and setting up a still life to infuse the

Telephone Building, San Francisco — Commissioned by Ben Mori

Filoli Gardens, Woodside, CA — Patron unknown. Unfortunately, due to either the fire, bad record-keeping, or my faulty memory, I am unable to say who commissioned this drawing or why.

drawing with life. But the organizers of the private auction hated it. "Too pretty," they said. Apparently they'd wanted a drawing of how the building looked in its devastated form. "You're a master of cracks and imperfections," I was told. "We wanted a drawing capturing all of those details, to remind donors of the wretched state they helped save the Conservatory from."

It was a befitting irony, seeing that I would have loved to have drawn the building that way. And despite them arguing with me that they'd conveyed this desire clearly, I was certain I would have remembered such a strange request. They asked me if I could change it, and I literally laughed in their faces. I told them never mind, I would keep the drawing. At least then I'd be able to make some money from it. To which they said, "No, no. We've put you through all this trouble," and begrudgingly said they'd take it. By that point I was just annoyed and said no. If they wanted the piece, then they had to give me half of what it brought in at auction. They were offended but I didn't care. Ultimately we agreed I'd get a third of the sale, but of course, in the end—even after the drawing fetched double what I would have charged to make it—I told them to keep my third, as my contribution to restoring the historic greenhouse. I didn't even get a thank-you. Funny how the ones who want you to work for free think they can treat you the worst and make the most demands.

Next in the drawer is the Miata, which was destroyed in the fire. Another irony not lost on me, considering that for six months I'd been parking on the street and had pulled my little yellow ride into the garage only hours before Kai lit a match. That poor car. It had gotten the shit beaten out of it, then had its gas drained to set the blaze—which I was told by the fire department. The insurance company gave me a whopping thousand bucks in compensation. Less than I'd paid to get it out of impound.

Oh, and of course there's Brian. I wouldn't want to forget my dear twin brother. If you could see me right now, you'd see I'm shaking my head. Freaking Brian. Eventually he did call me back. After twenty minutes of him boasting about his newfound celebrity in China, he was even less impressed by the idea that he might be a father—or about my house having been set on fire—than he was about the Mill Valley cop he'd pissed off. "My guess is she's probably not the only one," was all he had to say about potentially having a daughter. Which Larissa found hilarious. And made me think I might actually be the uncle.

On that topic, while in those days the ability to determine which of identical twins had fathered a child was out of reach, the technology is now as easy as ordering pet food online. But in order for a test like that to be run, someone would have to get close enough to Larissa to get her DNA. Which she's made even more impossible than the test was all those years ago. As I've already noted, Larissa isn't talking to me—and not just to me. As anyone who has heard of Larissa Huxley knows, she's probably the most famous recluse since Howard Hughes. Making not just sorting out fatherhood, but getting her to corroborate or refute Martin's story, impossible. Which is an irony befitting our time: one of the most influential architects of the digital information age refuses to speak to anyone. If ever there was a cautionary tale, Larissa's seems to be it. How she came to be that way is a story for another book—and one I would most definitely get sued for writing. Though it is a story I would like to someday tell. I suppose we'll just have to see how this one goes. For now it's just going to have to remain in the drawer of dangling plots.

And while we're on the subject of information, here's a little bit of trivia for you: The house Faith Chadwick lived in is called the Whittier Mansion, which has an even more sordid history than having been the residence of an uncredited blackmailer, pimp, and all around schemer. In the 1940s, the thirty room sandstone was purchased by the Nazi government as a consulate. The consul, Fritz Wiedemann, had been one of Hitler's closest friends— right up until the führer discovered Wiedemann was having an affair with the Hungarian princess he'd been infatuated with, which was when Adolf shipped his old buddy Fritz off to San Francisco. According to *Chronicle* columnist Herb Caen, Wiedemann had been known around town as a playboy, until the u.s. government could no longer ignore the atrocities of the war in Europe, and sent him back to the Nazis as they joined the fight. So yeah. You could say that the building has had more than its share of shady residents.

Oh, and I almost forgot—Betty. I should have thought of her sooner— then and now. Poor thing, she had to learn about the fire by coming upon the scene. Five-forty-five in the morning, sun not even up, arriving as she did every day to open the shop only to find a scorched building. She ran home and called Adam at the office, except he hadn't gone to work that morning—opting to see me instead—so he didn't get her message until the afternoon, which meant that for half the day she was left worrying I might be in the hospital or dead. When Adam finally did get her message, he phoned her back and calmed her down, then rang me at the hotel. Ocampo had just left, having told me about the killing of Faith and Kai. I could barely think let alone talk, but I was able to listen as Adam told me that Betty was going

Whittier Mansion, San Francisco

to take the unexpected time off to fly back to Honduras and care for her sister. The next day, at Thanksgiving dinner, Larissa asked me how I was going to help Betty now that she was out of a paycheck, and when I replied that she was leaving, Larissa offered to buy her plane ticket. "It's the least I can do," she said. "After having tricked her into letting me into your place."

Which reminds me of one more story: The evening after Larissa and I hiked the Battery to Bluffs trail, when I began the drawing of Marshall Beach, she and I ordered dim sum and watched an episode of *Glory Days*, Brian's new show. Larissa had been able to get the episode onto her laptop, by way of what she called a P2P network, something she said had just been released to the online community, and to which she'd contributed a great deal of code. At the time I had no idea what she was talking about, but now of course I understand that it had been one of the first major global file-sharing networks. As for the show, Brian played a debonair American industrialist courting a wealthy widow. Everyone spoke Mandarin, except for Brian, who spoke English with a Texas twang and had all his dialogue subtitled in

Noe Valley, San Francisco — Commissioned by Angela Windin. She gave me keys to her unit, then left for the day. She had a very large and rambunctious puppy who I played with and gave a few treats from the jar on the counter. That night I got a call asking what I'd done to her dog. Apparently she'd returned home to find her place destroyed and the pup having thrown up all over her bed. She loved the drawing, though.

Chinese. So while we watched the entire episode, he was the only person we could understand. Afterward, Larissa said, "I'm not sure I should have watched that. Even though I know he's acting, that character is how I'll forever think of him." Which was a painful reminder of why Brian had gone to China in the first place, having been typecast by pretty much all of America. Still, it was fun to see him on TV again.

*　*　*

I'm sure there's still a slew of random items in this story drawer—the literary equivalent of loose rubber bands, user manuals for long-discarded electronics, and leftover hex nuts for an Ikea shelf that apparently doesn't need them seeing that it's still standing—but there's one subject that warrants more than being tossed into the catch-all box of leftovers: Martin Zorn, aka Nathan Cohen, aka El Resbaladizo. Interestingly, try googling El Resbaladizo, then going to images. There's a kids' book about fishing, and a lot of "slippery when wet" road signs, but far down in the list you'll see a wanted poster with a sketchy rendering of a man's face. It looks a bit fake—though so do a lot of the other wanted posters I found—and the portrait is a bit vague. But I can tell you, had I been on vacation in Mexico and seen that poster, I would have paused and said, "That could be Martin Zorn." And so I'm choosing to believe that this is one part of the story that Martin couldn't have fabricated—or, rather, that he could have, but the foresight and effort it would have taken would have been beyond meticulous, and I just don't think Martin was that hellbent on convincing me. A postcard with a return address as a clue, even a wedding ring to spur my curiosity, those I can see, but to have a portrait drawn and poster dummied up, then planted on a website dedicated to cartel memorabilia seems a bit much. Though of course I can't really know. He was known to have taken a page out of a CIA handbook in the past. And surely something like this would fall under the category of creating deep cover.

Also, I did some poking around on the Internet and believe I found Martin and Francesca's former employer: Stepan Ivanov. A nasty character, to be sure. He'd been gunned down outside a restaurant in Bangkok in April of this year, shortly before Easter, as Francesca had said. Three men with automatic rifles put thirty-two bullets into his body, his security detail curiously nowhere around. There was a long and thorough article about a significant number of arrests made by Interpol and the dismantling of what was considered one of the largest crime syndicates operating between Europe and Asia.

But no mention of Martin Zorn or Nathan Cohen. Which of course was to be expected. Though there was nothing in it to refute Martin's participation, either, which is equally unsurprising. Meaning that he—or Francesca—could have easily done the same research I had and reverse-engineered a story to fit facts that already existed. It would have been a lot easier than faking a Mexican wanted poster.

As for the rest of Francesca's narrative, I've made a decision: Regarding Martin's version of what supposedly happened in San Francisco, I will concede, it is possible. But so are theories about aliens building the pyramids. Which is the problem with not having witnessed events yourself. But it doesn't matter. Because what I've decided is, parsing out who actually killed Faith Chadwick and Kai Sjugard—or even Joe Chadwick—is irrelevant. What is relevant is to set the record straight about Faith. To tell the world who the woman truly was.

That said, I'm not sure I can get away with not offering my opinion—from readers, critics, or, more important, Adam. So, if forced to answer whether I believe the story Francesca told, I will say no. No matter how convincing Martin's tale, there is no alternative version to this story. When I think back to after the shootings, Larissa and Ronnie may have been tight-lipped about what had happened, but they were always that way. And while I was a bit of a mess—still recovering from having almost choked to death and failing to save Taylor—I don't remember having any sense that they were keeping secrets from me—certainly not one as big as having covered up two murders and helped a wanted man flee the country. But again, I don't know, nor do I think it matters.

My first night in Bern, lying in bed before Francesca slipped in beside me, I'd questioned Martin's motives for luring me to Switzerland. I'd assumed it was to rewrite his epitaph, to change his reputation from murderer to martyr. A proposal which I rejected. But if Martin had in fact been the crusader El Resbaladizo, a man who provoked drug cartels to kill him for his advocacy of children, then went on to become an embedded operative for Interpol who helped take down an international crime syndicate, then I'm of a different mind. His history should be rewritten. If he's to go down for the mistakes he made, he deserves to also be credited for all the good he did. Or at least have the possibility put out in the world. I mean, if tabloids can promote the existence of an incestuous sex colony called Zorntown, then why can't I suggest that Martin Zorn truly did dedicate his life to making the world a better place?

Duboce Triangle, San Francisco — Patron asked to be unnamed. After almost forty years, her mother, who had abandoned her when she was a toddler, got in touch out of the blue to say she had stage-four lung cancer. My client agonized for a week before deciding to come. "Not for her. But for me." They walked from the hospital and sat here, and, in the last days of the woman's life, said goodbye.

And it's for this reason that I think Martin's intent of luring me to Bern and coaching Francesca wasn't to make me question the truthfulness of my friends, or even to redeem his name, but to prompt me to finally do what we all should have done years ago, which is to go public about Faith Chadwick and the Operation Midnight Climax rooms. What I'm saying is, I think even Martin didn't care whether I believed him. Maybe the only point of the story he had Francesca recite was to get me to crack open the vault of secrets I'd been keeping locked in my mind. Maybe he didn't care whether I told his version of events, but wanted to make sure I told mine. Though it's also possible that I'm giving him too much credit. Which, considering how I'd felt about him for the twenty years before he stepped into my shop, is in itself an accomplishment.

And what of Francesca? If Martin's story was only a ruse to spur me into loosening my tongue, was she in on the plan to convince me? Or was she also misled? Doing only as she'd claimed, fulfilling the request of a dying man who gave her a new life? As I told Adam, I believe that she believes. But even that might be too simple an answer. Francesca has seen into the black hole of human nature far deeper than I probably ever will, or ever hope to. I think all she cares about is the quality of her life in the moment. She never knew Martin Zorn. She only knew Nathan Cohen, and even him not really. She didn't know the cop who went wrong, only the criminal who went right. A man who, in the end, was, as he promised her he would be, her hero. Her savior. He helped slay her evil overlord, set her up with property and riches, then rode off into the sunset. He gave her a fairy tale. Which, for himself, is all he ever wanted: To save the girl.

Which is why I've taken the effort to include his version of events in a book that was supposed to honor the legendary private detective, and my friend, Ronnie J. Gilbert. Yes, the acquittal in the trial of Ronnie's death had prompted me to start writing, but I have to wonder: Would I have truly been able to tell this story without Martin's return? Difficult to say. What I can say is, he did return, and I am finally telling all I know of Faith Chadwick. And—as an added bonus to me—I'm now able to do something even the renowned Ronnie Gilbert never could, which is offer some insight into the mystery of what became of Martin Zorn. And that is no small part of the plot to leave dangling.

Precita Park, San Francisco — Patron asked to be unnamed

Potrero Hill, San Francisco — Commissioned by Terry Proctor. Gift for his daughter and son-in-law

(Preceding page) Legion of Honor, San Francisco

Powell Street with Saint Peter and Paul, San Francisco — Patron's name withheld. The request had been for "Anything from North Beach." And while not unhappy with the drawing, they were confused by the composition, unable to picture the block. I told them I'd drawn the image from life, and even offered the cross streets, Powell between Green and Union. Still, a day later there was a message on my answering machine, "I can't find it." I didn't return the call.

A WOMAN WALKS INTO A SHOP

47

FURTHER ADVENTURES

Today is Thursday, December 12, 2019. Almost exactly twenty years after the murders, fire, and death of Taylor. Finally, this story is officially going to print. It also happens to be my fifty-eighth birthday. A subject about which I have little to say, other than I remember being a boy and hearing my grandmother—who was hardly older than I am now but looked to me as ancient as time itself—say she still felt like a little girl, and me thinking that she'd gone senile, or whatever word my young brain had for the condition of losing one's mind to old age. Probably "batshit crazy," which was a favorite phrase around my house. Well, Gram, I can now say I understand. Because when it comes to feeling the years, I too am as crazy as guano.

I suspect the puzzle-loving Ronnie Gilbert also felt the same. Born on September 3, 1957, he was four months shy of turning sixty when half his body was discovered inside a seventeen-foot crocodile known as Tasmania; a scant older than I am now, but as vibrant as they come. His actual cause of death was never determined. As Ronnie might have said, there was just enough of him to write a parking ticket, but not enough to tow to impound.

It's been six months since I was in Zürich. I stayed in the former home of Nathan Cohen aka Martin Zorn aka El Resbaladizo just long enough to finish this draft and send it off to Adam, then I returned to Amsterdam, where my hopes of enjoying a summer of long, warm days and free-flowing tourist Euros were dashed upon the rocks of three very large and unhappy Russian gangsters bursting into my shop, inquiring about a man named Nathan Cohen and a prostitute named Min Zhao—who I guessed was Tulip aka Francesca Molinari. I managed to extricate myself, but not until after several long and harrowing days, after which I promptly gave up on Amsterdam, paid a

447

company to pack up my studio, forfeited my deposit for having broken my lease, and boarded the first plane back to San Francisco.

For much of the entire eleven-hour flight back to the u.s. I worked on my laptop outlining my not-so-little run-in with the Russian mafia, thinking I would include the experience here as an epilogue. But by the time the plane touched down at SFO I knew it was an unnecessary addition—though plenty enough of a story that I might have a follow-up book if I wanted to write it.

"Why don't we just hold our horses on a sequel and focus on getting this puppy in the can," Adam said when he picked me up from the airport.

"You're starting to sound like Ronnie with your mixed metaphors," I told him.

"I liked that guy," Adam said. "And these days, the popular term is *malaphor*. Though it hasn't made it into the official style guides yet."

And so my last adventure in Amsterdam will have to wait. However, I do need to share one very important revelation from that escapade, which is that Martin Zorn was indeed the character Francesca conveyed—at least in regard to his years after leaving San Francisco. If my Russian friends are

to be believed—and I have no reason to doubt them—I can now confirm that the wanted poster for El Resbaladizo is real, as is Martin's having infiltrated and crippled—as well as having ripped off—a very large and powerful criminal network. How I came to be so sure of this information is, again, a story for another time.

And I want to say it was almost worth the ordeal. Confirmation of Martin's post-Nest-affair life gives me a great deal more respect for the man than I had previously granted him, and pleases me even more that I'm able to contribute the tale of El Resbaladizo to the mix of Zorn-lore. As to the credibility of his deathbed version of who killed the Chadwicks and Kai, it changes nothing. Others may feel differently, but I still choose to believe that, despite Martin having been an outlaw crusader, his attempt at revisionism was nothing more than to provoke me to write.

And I'm glad it did. Because the question I posed earlier about whether I would have been able to adequately write this story without Martin's return is no longer undecided for me. I undoubtedly would not have. And for that, I find myself grateful. Because of Martin, you now you have the fullest story I am able to tell—and not just of Faith and The Nest, but of how I met the witty, hard-boiled, and malaphoric character who was the private detective Ronnie J. Gilbert. He was my friend and I miss him, his death having come far too soon. I've got many more stories to tell about my puzzling pal, and

I've already decided to write a few of them down. Which must be a pretty not-so-terrible idea, seeing that while Adam had hedged on a book about my Russian gangster episode in Amsterdam, he quickly jumped on a follow-up book of Ronnie stories—though he flat-out refused the title, *The Further Adventures of Ronnie J*, which I proposed only to see him wince. And so, to borrow the last line from one of the twentieth century's most famous series: Ronnie Gilbert Will Return.

* * *

Until then, from the drawer of my own career, one last scene:

San Francisco, January 2000; less than two months after the murders, the fire, and all the mayhem told in this book.

I was living in my temporary home at the City Mews. It was a comfortable enough place, nicely furnished, with room for a makeshift studio, but I found myself constantly wanting to leave. I also kept making up reasons why I didn't want to replace my car, and bought a bicycle instead. Late at night, when I was unable to sleep—which was often, and unusual for me—I would force myself to work on commission drawings, but the rest of the time I would ride my bike to random spots around the city and draw in my sketchbook.

Always in the wind, and sometimes in the rain, I would pick a neighborhood and ride until I found a café. I'd order a coffee and maybe a snack, then camp out for hours drawing people. I worked in a dozen different sketchbooks, on all kinds of papers, with pens, pencils, markers, brushes, inks—whatever I'd decided to put in my bag that day. It wasn't for an exhibition, a book, or a commission. The life I had been living was gone. Reduced to literal ashes. And so I was doing what I always did—and still do—when things went awry: I threw myself into work.

Because the truth was, I wasn't okay. And not just because of Taylor dying or even losing my home. Yes, I was still processing all the terrible events that had happened. But it wasn't only death and destruction that had me unsettled. My life before the Nest Murders had been fine, but not great. I'd been neither happy nor unhappy. Which was the real reason I think I'd remodeled the flat, even why I'd let myself go into debt. Something in me knew I needed a change, but didn't know what, or how to make it. All through my twenties,

and even into my thirties, I'd been quick to toss aside anyone and anything for the novelty of something new. It was why my marriage had lasted barely three years, and why a map of my career looked like the wanderings of a drunken goat through a minefield. But this had been different. I knew that change for the sake of change wasn't going to solve what was ailing me. Which left me feeling only that much more stuck.

In a perverse way, the fire simplified things. With all the distractions gone, I was left with only myself to deal with. Which was why I got a bicycle instead of a car, and why I worked in sketchbooks. I wanted to live as simply as possible; wanted my world to be as compact as I could make it. If I wanted to go somewhere, I had to use my body to get there. And if I wanted to work, I would have everything I needed slung over my shoulder. It was my way of regaining order. Lives had ended, my home and business had been destroyed, all of which had been beyond my control. My simple little life, though, of riding around and drawing, that was all mine. No one cared if I did it, and no one cared if I didn't. Some might have seen it as cold and meaningless, but for me it was like being alone on the open sea, nothing visible but the horizon. An all-encompassing, almost crushing, freedom.

One day I was at a café on Bernal Hill, Progressive Grounds, when a woman approached my table and asked if I ever did portraits.

"It's been a long time," I said. And when I looked up, I realized I recognized her. I didn't remember her name, but I knew very well who she was. She'd commissioned me to draw a house where, as an eighteen-year-old on her own for the first time, she'd taken refuge with a poet who'd hid her from the Mormon Church and helped her start a new life. It had been the Excelsior commission that had led to, well, everything.

"What?" she said.

I was smiling and shaking my head. "Nothing," I said.

"I'm Beth. I commissioned you to draw—"

"I remember." Though I was glad she'd told me her name. "Naples Street. How did the chapbook to honor the memory of your poet friend turn out?"

"Good, I think. I've been meaning to get you a copy."

"I'd love to see it. And now you'd like a portrait?"

"Maybe," she said. Suggestion in her voice.

"Why not," I said, ignoring it. "Have a seat. I'm rusty so can't promise anything. So how about this: if you like it, you can buy it, and if not, then you will have helped me practice. What do you think?"

"Sounds good."

"I've got a book with me if you want something to read," I said as she sat down. "Might help you to relax and forget that someone's staring at you, or at least help pass the time."

She said she had a magazine, then pulled a copy of the *New Yorker* from her purse.

Even though I was primarily working in sketchbooks, that day I happened to also have my watercolor block on me. I took it out, crossed my legs, and laid the rigid-backed block of paper on my lap. But before I began drawing, I did as I always did. I looked. I studied her high cheekbones, and the hint of freckles beneath her eyes. I observed the kink of her hair and its off-center part, the broadness of her shoulders, and the sharpness of her collarbone.

She glanced up, met my eyes, and smiled shyly from my gaze. Then she opened her magazine and looked back down. That was one big difference from drawing cityscapes. When you looked at buildings, they didn't look back. Which I decided was no longer a good thing.

I uncapped my pen and began drawing.

ACKNOWLEDGMENTS

A WORD FROM THE AUTHOR

The Commissions is the third of the Emit books, though what I consider to be the first in the "Emit Hopper Mystery Series." With the first two books, I thought each would be the last. *Close Enough for the Angels* was supposed to be a one-off, and I was surprised when, in the final edit, the idea for a second book hit me. I was equally surprised when the same thing happened at the end of writing *Come to Light*. That book wrapped up Julia's arc and the disappearances in Lone Pine, and I saw the two books as companions, completing the original story. But it was in the final draft of *Come to Light* that I created the character Ronnie Gilbert, and while he had barely a walk-on part—and was killed—his personality stuck with me and sparked new possibilities. I considered writing books solely with Ronnie, but felt I could contribute more to the detective genre by keeping Emit as a foil—a "Watson" to Ronnie's Holmes (or a lesser known, but one of my favorites, Archie Goodwin to his Nero Wolfe). Also, I understood Emit, and saw Ronnie as part of his world rather than the inverse. I immediately set to mapping out a detailed overview of Emit's life, and found I had a plethora of opportunities to tell more stories. Only then did I begin thinking of Emit as a series.

One direction I felt bound to explore was that of the classic rock and roll lovechild. A first version of Larissa's story was released online in 2020 as the novella *Iterations*, which featured Ocampo as a subplot. I'd also been writing more straightforward detective stories with Ronnie, and during the pandemic I combined the two to make the novel you hold here.

Having Emit take on commissions as a major plotline is a nod to my own professional life. Which is why I want to acknowledge all the patrons who have supported me in the making of not just this book, but all my books. As Emit describes in his brief account of art history, commissions have long been the lifeblood of career artists, and that has certainly been true in my case. Invitations to draw have taken me all over the world and introduced me to countless people I would have never otherwise met. Which is why I would like to sincerely thank all of my patrons. More than having provided me with the means to continue drawing and writing, your interest, trust, and generosity have continually broadened my experience as a person, as well as given me the chance to give back. As I have Emit say, the ability to make something that is personally meaningful to someone is a unique opportunity few other professions offer. And for this I am grateful. To every person who has ever commissioned me, I extend my deepest thanks and gratitude, though for this book I will name only those whose drawings appear in this story: Reto Auer and Stéphanie Dreyfuss, Tom DeCaigny, Kelly Gillease, Kelty Green, Eileen Hassi, Brian and Kelley Johnson, Christopher Kim, Mike and Kaitlyn Krieger, Aleta Lee and the San Francisco Arts Commission, Robert Lieber and the National Parks Conservancy, Woody LaBounty, Zachary Lara and Sonya Yu, Noé Lutz and Amanda Brosius Lutz, Rena Macapagal and Colin Sebestyen, Angela Nguyen-Dinh, Terry Proctor, Korri Rolla, Jim Rowe, James Schalkwyk, Peter Sullivan and Erin Carew, and Shaun Supanich and Alexandra (Cricket) Berube-Moritis.

While the majority of drawings featured in this book were in fact private commissions, some originated as other projects. The vista drawing of Mount Davidson is a section of a forty-foot permanent glass installation I made for the San Francisco International Airport, and Joshua Tree was a mural for Google Ventures. The Warming Hut was a commercial project for the National Parks Conservancy, the "fog" drawing for a Ritual Coffee label, and the view of the Golden Gate Bridge from Fort Point for a limited-edition beer label for Anchor Steam Brewery. I chose not to cite these in the captions since the majority of attributions are fictional. However, I do cite a few real-life patrons, and some of their stories are even true—or at least partially—though I'll leave it a mystery as to which, and how much.

As for the remaining non-commission pieces, a few ran in my series *All Over Coffee*, which I produced for the San Francisco *Chronicle* from 2004-2015, and collected into three books and one novella. Several other drawings ran in the series *Spirits of The Bay*, which the writer Gary Kamiya and I produce monthly for the *Nob Hill Gazette* and the San Francisco *Examiner*, and, in 2020, made into a best-selling book with Bloomsbury, *Spirits of San Francisco*. I would like to thank Gary for both our ongoing collaboration and his friendship. Gary is an excellent writer and font of San Francisco history—as well as a great guy—and several of the histories I cite in this story I learned from him. The Film Exchange in particular was a delightful find, and the history of the Presidio as recited by the character on the Lyon Street Steps—who

I want to make clear is *not* Gary—is very close to the piece as Gary wrote it for the March 2021 installment of *Spirits*. With Gary's permission, I used several lines of his almost-verbatim text as a way to give the bow-tied character an air of authority. So while Gary didn't work directly on this book with me, our collaboration during my time of writing was a positive influence, for which I am grateful.

Regarding history, I also did a fair amount of my own research, more than with past Emit novels. This was due to having set the story so firmly in not just a place, but also a time. Having lived in San Francisco for almost thirty years, I'd experienced firsthand the first dot-com bubble of the late nineties, and wanted to root Larissa's character in that era. While I was able to pull a great deal from my memory, I didn't want to rely solely on my own perspective, so, aside from the customary internet research, I interviewed other longtime Bay Area residents for their recollections of the time. I also interviewed insiders regarding the mayoral runoff election, procedures of the San Francisco Police Department, practices of private detectives, and history of youth social services. For those who shared their expertise, thank you, Jen Burke Anderson, Mark Alvarez, Leanna Dawydiak, Maria Finn, Mike Florio, John Hessen, Jeffrey Long, PJ Johnston, Ruth Keady, Julie Kramer, Skot Kuiper, Laurenn McCubbin, Michael Meadows, and Candace Moray.

I would also like to specifically thank Peter Field, a San Francisco historian who graciously shared with me his vast knowledge of the Tenderloin. I'd gone to Peter to better understand the evolution of youth centers in the neighborhood, and it was through him that I learned of The Switchboard. I had not previously heard of the room-sharing network, though, once aware, was able to find a few online articles. To the best of my knowledge, all that I cited about this all-but-forgotten community service is true, and I'm pleased to be able to put it into print.

As for specific events, the runoff mayoral race between Willie Brown and Tom Ammiano was very much a real event, and one high on the minds of San Franciscans in November 1999, which was why I chose to set the story in those weeks between the general and runoff elections. Any suggestions of wrongdoing, however, or criticisms of those real-world characters, is nothing more than a reflection of rumor and public opinion of the time, which is well documented, and used here solely for dramatic purposes.

The Mission Bay project was also real, as were the public protests over its attempts to build on protected wetlands. However, any suggestions of illegal activities committed by developers, UCSF, the mayor's office, or any entity involved in this project, are purely fictional. I assert no wrongdoings or malicious actions on any of these real-world entities. Several of my doctors work out of the Mission Bay campus, and I'm grateful that they, and it, are there.

Additionally, the Conservatory of Flowers is also real, and did in fact sustain significant damage after a windstorm ripped through Golden Gate Park in December 1995. For several years the historic greenhouse sat in ruin as the community worked to raise funds, and not until 2000 did restoration get under way. The commission, however, was fictional. I have never been affiliated with the Conservatory, nor was I hired by any group attempting to raise funds for its repair. The choice to use the site in this story was twofold: First, historical timing. As with the election, I wanted a backdrop of real-life 1999 San Francisco to give the story authenticity. Second, I wanted one of Emit's commissions to go awry in a more interesting way than a patron simply disliking what he drew. And rather than attribute the bad behavior to an individual, this approach allowed me to pin the fussiness on an anonymous committee—which I think many can agree is an entity worthy of being thrown under the bus. I adore the Conservatory of Flowers, and extend my gratitude for letting me appropriate that era of its disrepair for this story.

I would also like to extend my gratitude to the Legion of Honor. The museum is truly one of San Francisco's treasures, and I'm happy to now be among the ranks of storytellers who have set a portion of their tale on its grounds, as well as in its galleries. I would also like to thank Melinda Lee and SLAC National Accelerator Laboratory for inviting me behind the scenes and allowing me to draw. And also, yes, the Jerry Garcia house is real.

As for the era, while I did my best to stay accurate, especially in regard to technology and events, I did take a few liberties. To start, the a cappella men's choir Conspiracy of Beards was formed in 2003, several years after this story takes place. They are a such a delight, though, that I wanted them to appear. I also compressed the timing of some cultural occurrences. Fancy donuts I remember coming onto the Mission scene around 2006, and I believe avocado toast emerged a few years after that. So, for those of you who lived in the epicenter of hip as I did, please forgive my playing fast and loose with the timeline of overpriced boutique offerings.

Another is the art exhibit mentioned in chapter 9, of photographs of men's penises. I did attend this show in the early 2000s, however, it wasn't at Adobe Books. Adobe did have many great underground art exhibits, but unfortunately I can't remember the actual venue where I saw these photographs, nor was I able to find the name of the artist. This is unfortunate as

I would like to include the citation. If anyone knows, and wishes to tell me, I'd be happy to amend subsequent editions to credit the gallery and artist.

And lastly, Operation Midnight Climax. Best to my knowledge, every detail as told by Ronnie is true. In the 1960s, chemist and spymaster Sidney Gottlieb, along with Narcotics agent George Hunter White, paid prostitutes to dose men with LSD and have sex as White watched from behind a one-way mirror in an easy chair. All for the purposes of determining whether a combination of sex and LSD could be used to coerce men into revealing secrets or committing crimes. When I first learned of this outrageous chapter of American history, I knew I had to write a story around it. Thank you, CIA, for proving that truth is stranger than fiction.

Two unforeseen events occurred as this book was about to go into production. The first, my publisher, West Margin Press, was sold. We'd made two books together—*Come to Light*, the second Emit Hopper book, and *You Know Exactly*, the third and final collection of All Over Coffee—and were set to put *The Commissions* into production when West Margin was acquired by Turner Publishing, and suddenly all momentum halted. It was sad to learn that the team I had worked with for five years was no longer there, and worrisome that I would have to jump in with an entirely new team, whom I had never met.

Then on November 6, 2022, the second—and more horrific—event occurred. I was driving home from my studio on a Sunday evening when an out-of-control driver going twice the speed limit hit me head-on in my lane. I was rushed unconscious to the trauma ward where I underwent emergency surgery for life-threatening injuries to several of my internal organs. I also suffered a brain bleed, a bruised carotid artery, a shattered heel bone, and an "impressive" list of other injuries, to quote one of my trauma surgeons. I was lucky to be alive. The recovery has been the most painful and difficult experience of my life, and continues to be, seeing that, as I write this, it has been over five months since the accident, and I am only now beginning to walk.

Any talk of books was of course out the window. In time, though, Turner and I were able to connect, and, with respect to my condition, we were able to push the deadline up until the last moment to get this book into production. I am very grateful. That I am able to compose this addendum to the acknowledgements—despite writing from bed—is a promise of the recovery which waits for me down the line. My hope is, on the day this book hits the shelves, I will be able to stroll into a bookstore to sign copies. We will see. I am optimistic.

Editorially I would like to thank the West Margin team who got this book off the ground: Jennifer Newens, Olivia Ngai, Rachel Metzger, Alice Wertheimer, and Angie Zbornik. And from Turner, who welcomed me into their fold and were willing to step up and run in order to deliver this across the finish line, I wish to thank Todd Bottorff, Amanda Chiu, Phillip J. Gaskill, Claire Ong, and Ryan Smernoff.

From my team I would like to thank Alvaro Villanueva for his design, Grace Chiu, Rhett Dunlap, and Scott Murphy for their reader's eyes and feedback, and JP Jespersen of Scale Up Art for photographing my large drawings. I would especially like to thank my parents, Paul and Linda Madonna, whose careful reading and keen editorial insights were vital in the shaping and refining of this story. Beyond their attention to this book, they have been integral in my lifelong development as an artist and author, having passed on to me their passion for stories, as well as their dedication to hard work.

And lastly, as with all creations, there are always others who contributed in ways unseen in the final product, but were invaluable along the way. For those not mentioned elsewhere, I would like to thank Jason Berkman for being the kitchen master, Guillaume Cohen for getting me to pick up the guitar again, MJ Bogatin for his ongoing legal expertise, Sebastien and Magali Dupuis for their continuous offers to put me up wherever in the world they happen to reside, my wife, Joen Madonna, for her all-around continued support of my creative pursuits, Kate Patterson for rallying public support after my accident, and Allison Davis, Aaron Proctor, Angela Melo, Romalyn Schmaltz, and Sabine Vermeer for their generosity.

I would also like to thank all the surgeons and nurses who saved my life and helped care for me. And I would like to thank my fans and readers for supporting not just my work, but also my recovery.

I may have dreamed up this story, written it down, and made all of the drawings, but it wouldn't be the book it is without the help of everyone noted here. Thank you.

—— Paul Madonna, San Francisco, April 2023

WEST MARGIN PRESS
AN IMPRINT OF TURNER PUBLISHING COMPANY
Nashville, Tennessee
www.turnerpublishing.com

WEST
MARGIN
PRESS

The Commissions: An Emit Hopper Mystery

Copyright © 2023 by Paul Madonna. All rights reserved.

This book or any part thereof may not be reproduced or transmitted in any
form or by any means, electronic or mechanical, including photocopying,
recording, or by any information storage and retrieval system, without
permission in writing from the publisher.

This is a work of fiction. All the characters and events portrayed in this
book are either products of the author's imagination or are used fictitiously.

Story and art by Paul Madonna
Cover by Paul Madonna and Alvaro Villanueva
Book design by Alvaro Villanueva

Library of Congress Cataloging-in-Publication Data
Names: Madonna, Paul, 1972- author.
Title: The Commissions / by Paul Madonna.
Description: Nashville, Tennessee : Turner Publishing Company, [2023]
Identifiers: LCCN 2023010228 (print) | LCCN 2023010229 (ebook) | ISBN
    9781513139289 (hardcover) | ISBN 9781513141411 (paperback) | ISBN
    9781513139296 (epub)
Subjects: LCGFT: Detective and mystery fiction. | Novels.
Classification: LCC PS3613.A28496 C66 2023 (print) | LCC PS3613.A28496
    (ebook) | DDC 813/.6--dc23/eng/20230404
LC record available at https://lccn.loc.gov/2023010228
LC ebook record available at https://lccn.loc.gov/2023010229

Printed in Canada

BIO

Paul Madonna is an award-winning artist and best-selling author whose unique blend of drawing and storytelling has been heralded as an "all new art form." His series All Over Coffee ran in the San Francisco *Chronicle* for twelve years (2004–2015), and his book *Everything is its own reward* won the 2012 NCBR Recognition Award for best book. Paul's work ranges from novels to cartoons to large-scale public murals and can be found internationally in print as well as in galleries and museums. Paul was a founding editor for therumpus.net, has taught drawing at the University of San Francisco, and frequently lectures on creative practice. He holds a BFA from Carnegie Mellon University and was the first (ever!) Art Intern at *MAD* magazine. Paul resides in San Francisco and does in fact take commissions, traveling the world to draw and write.

OTHER BOOKS BY PAUL MADONNA
All Over Coffee
Everything is its own reward
On to the Next Dream
You Know Exactly

EMIT HOPPER SERIES
Close Enough for the Angels
Come to Light

COLLABORATIONS
A Writer's San Francisco, with Eric Maisel
Spirits of San Francisco, with Gary Kamiya

CPSIA information can be obtained
at www.ICGtesting.com
Printed in the USA
LVHW071906240623
750448LV00002B/88